Saline District Library

3 4604 91075 1576

Large Print Fiction Sim
Simon, Rachel, 1959-
The story of beautiful girl

WITHDRAWN

P9-CRD-439

GRAND CENTRAL
PUBLISHING

LARGE
PRINT

Also by Rachel Simon

The House on Teacher's Lane
Riding the Bus with My Sister
The Writer's Survival Guide
The Magic Touch
Little Nightmares, Little Dreams

THE
STORY OF
BEAUTIFUL
GIRL

RACHEL SIMON

SALINE DISTRICT LIBRARY
555 N. Maple Road
Saline, MI 48176

MAY — — 2011

GC

GRAND CENTRAL
PUBLISHING

LARGE PRINT

This book is a work of fiction. Names, characters, places, and incidents are the product of the author's imagination or are used fictitiously. Any resemblance to actual events, locales, or persons, living or dead, is coincidental.

Copyright © 2011 by Rachel Simon

All rights reserved. Except as permitted under the U.S. Copyright Act of 1976, no part of this publication may be reproduced, distributed, or transmitted in any form or by any means, or stored in a database or retrieval system, without the prior written permission of the publisher.

Grand Central Publishing
Hachette Book Group
237 Park Avenue
New York, NY 10017
www.HachetteBookGroup.com

Printed in the United States of America

First Edition: May 2011

10 9 8 7 6 5 4 3 2 1

Grand Central Publishing is a division of Hachette Book Group, Inc.

The Grand Central Publishing name and logo is a trademark of Hachette Book Group, Inc.

Library of Congress Cataloging-in-Publication Data

Simon, Rachel, 1959–

The story of beautiful girl / Rachel Simon.—1st ed.

p. cm.

Summary: "A novel about a woman who can't speak, a man who is deaf, and a widow who finds herself suddenly caring for a newborn baby"—Provided by publisher.

ISBN 978-0-446-57446-4 (reg. ed.)
ISBN 978-1-4555-0009-3 (large print ed.)

1. People with disabilities—Fiction. I. Title.

PS3569.I4845S76 2011

813'.54—dc22

2010030910

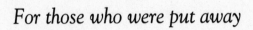

For those who were put away

Telling our stories is holy work.

—The Reverend Nancy Lane, Ph.D.

PART I

HIDING

THE WIDOW

1968

At the end of the night that would change everything, the widow stood on her porch and watched as the young woman was marched down her front drive and shoved into the sedan. The girl did not fight back, bound and tied as she was, nor did she cry out into the chill autumn rain, so surely the doctor and his attendants thought they had won. They did not know, as the car doors slammed shut, the engine came on, and the driver steered them down the muddy hill toward the road, that the widow and the girl in the backseat had just defied them right under their noses. The widow waited until the taillights reached the bottom of the drive, then turned and entered her house. And as she stood at the foot of the staircase, hoping they'd show mercy to the young woman and worrying about the whereabouts of the runaway man, the widow heard the sound the doctor hadn't been seeking. It was the sound that would always connect her to the girl and forever make her remember the man. It was the sweet, deep breaths of a hidden person. A sleeping stranger. A baby.

That November day had seemed as ordinary as any in the widow's seventy years. The mail carrier had delivered letters, birds had flown south across her fields, and storm clouds had wheeled across the Pennsylvania sky. The farm animals were fed; the dishes were used and washed; new letters were placed in the roadside mailbox. Dusk fell. The widow lit the logs in the fireplace and settled into her reading chair. Then, perhaps thirty pages later, the clouds cracked open, releasing a deluge that made such a din that she peered over her tortoiseshell glasses toward the living room window. To her surprise, the rain cascaded so heavily, the glass looked opaque. After half a century on this farm, she'd seen no sights like this before; she would mention it in her letters tomorrow. Drawing the lamp closer, she lowered her eyes to her book.

For many hours, she shut out the din and concentrated on the page—a biography of Dr. Martin Luther King Jr., gone just a few months from this life—but then became aware of a knocking on her door. She turned. Soon after their wedding day, when her husband was building onto the original one-room house to make room for a wife, she realized he'd never remarked on the view, with its sweeping fields, dense woods, and distant mountains, all watched over by the colorful vault of the sky. He lived here simply because the farm had been in his family and was thirty rolling miles, an hour's drive, and a county line away from the closest town, Well's Bottom, where she was a school-teacher. As she'd watched the walls go up, she noticed how few windows he'd included, and how small each was, and understood she'd have to be satisfied with meager portions of the landscape. The front door, for instance, was all wood and no glass, with only a single window set in the wall to its left. But tonight's storm obscured even that limited view. So the widow crossed the living room and turned the knob on the door.

She thought, at first, that there were two of them. A man and a woman. From under the roof of the porch, the man, a Negro, looked at her with startled eyes, as if unaware that the door upon which he'd been knocking had just pulled back. The woman beside him did not look up. Her skin was pale, and she was biting her lip. Her face was bone-bare, with shadows in every rise and dip. Was the woman as lean as she seemed? It was impossible to tell; she was covered in a gray blanket. No, several blankets. Wool, like bedding issued in the war, draped into layers of hoods and capes. The man's arm lay protectively around the woman's shoulders.

The widow turned back to the man. He too wore coverings, but they were not the same as the woman's. USED CARS, read one. OPEN TILL NINE, read another. The widow recognized them as large signs from businesses in Well's Bottom. Water was pouring off them, as it was from the sodden wool; her porch was now a puddle.

Dread squeezed the widow's chest. Five years into retirement, she was long past the time when she knew all the faces in Well's Bottom, and she did not know these. She should slam the door, call the police. Her husband's rifle was upstairs; was she agile enough to bound up to their bedroom? But the man's startled look was now melting toward desperation, and she knew they were running from something. The widow's breath came out heavily. She wished she were not alone. Yet they were alone, too, and cold and frightened.

"Who are you?" the widow asked.

The woman slowly lifted her eyes. The widow caught the movement, but no sooner had she tilted her gaze up—the widow was slight, five feet one, and the woman before her was tall, though not as tall as the man—than the woman jerked her head back down.

Unlike the woman, the man had not acknowledged the widow's voice. But he had noticed his companion's quick gesture and retreat, and in response he gently rubbed her shoulder. It was a touch of tenderness, and even in the dim light that reached the porch from her reading lamp, the widow knew it was a look of caring. Yet she did not know that, in a trance of seeing what she'd forgotten she'd once felt herself, her face, too, revealed so much she was not saying.

The man looked back at the widow. A pleading came into his eyes, and he lifted his free hand. The widow flinched, thinking he was preparing to strike her. Instead he opened his fingers and flicked them toward the inside of the house, like a flipbook of a bird flying.

That's when the widow realized the man could not hear.

"Oh," she said, breath expelling her ignorance. "Please come in."

She stepped aside. The man moved his hands in front of the woman. The woman nodded and clasped one of his hands, and they stepped over the threshold.

"You must be—are you?—please," the widow mumbled, until, as she closed the door, her thin, schoolteacher voice finally settled on the proper statement: "Let's get you out of those wet things." Immediately she thought herself foolish; the man could not hear, the woman was focused on the lamp, and anyway, their backs were to her. As one they crept across the living room, their makeshift raincoats dripping, but the widow couldn't bring herself to say anything. They appeared too relieved to be inside, mindful only of the closeness between them.

The man walked with muscular legs protruding from the oversize signs. His was evidently a body accustomed to labor, though why his legs were bare in November, the widow could not imagine. As for the woman, the blankets hung too low for a glimpse of anything aside from shoes—shoes that seemed too large. The woman's gait was uneven, her posture a slouch. Yellow curls wisped out from the woolen hood, and the widow thought, *She is like a child.*

The fire had gone low, and now the widow drew open the fireplace screen and added a log. Behind her she heard the woman grunt. She turned. The woman was gazing at the fire, and as the widow watched, the woman's face filled with curiosity. The man tightened his arm around her shoulder.

There were only two chairs by the fire: her reading chair, with muslin covers over the worn armrests, and the wooden chair where her husband had read his sporting magazines and westerns. The sofa sat farther back. *I should offer that*, she thought. Before she could, they lowered themselves to the chairs.

The widow stepped back and took them in. Her

husband had lost the hearing in one ear before he'd passed away; otherwise she'd never known a person who couldn't hear. And she'd never known someone quite like this woman. *I should be scared*, she told herself. But she thought of the passage in Matthew, which she'd not been in church to hear for years: "I was a stranger and you invited me in."

She moved toward the kitchen and glanced back as she crossed the dining room. They were still huddled together. The man's hands were aloft, gesturing his words. The woman was grunting again, the sound easing like an assent.

Give them privacy, the widow told herself. Everyone needs privacy; most children could not add 13 + 29 if you stood behind their shoulders. Privacy could go too far, though; look at her husband, his heart encircled by silence. Look at her now. Except for monthly trips to the market, she was alone three hundred sixty-four days a year, one degree short of a full circle of privacy. Though there was that one degree, Christmas Day, when the students of hers who'd blown like seeds across the country returned with children and grandchildren to visit relatives in Well's Bottom, then stopped in at the widow's open house. Her privacy was so complete, it was almost zero. *But almost zero*, her student John-Michael once said, *is totally different from zero*.

The widow let herself into the kitchen and put on the kettle. Yet even as she pulled down the flour, sugar, and oats she'd need for cookies, she asked herself larger questions. *Who are they? Why are they out in this storm?* The thought returned the pounding rain to her awareness. The river between the counties was sure to flood. She couldn't hear her spoon in the batter.

In clear weather she could hear a great deal from her house. The songs of birds. The distant gurgle of the river. The rare vehicle out on Old Creamery Road, half a mile down the slope of her drive. Even the mail carrier's truck, his AM radio wafting up her fields. But the best sound came when the mail carrier idled at her curb and flipped the mailbox flag from up, where she'd placed it the evening before as she'd secured newly composed correspondence to her students in the box, to horizontal, once the carrier ferried her greetings away. She hadn't always heard that mailbox flag. Then Landon, the student who'd loved making dioramas and had grown up to be an artist, fashioned a little metal lighthouse that, one Christmas, he gave her as a gift, then attached to the mailbox with a brass hinge. It wasn't just any lighthouse. When it was laid flat, the sign of no outgoing letters, its windows were dark, though when it was vertical, its windows lit up—and revealed the top of the lighthouse to be the head of a man. Her lighthouse man, she thought of it. How she loved hearing its brass hinge squeak.

She slid the cookie dough into the oven. Then she inched open the door and peered out.

The woman was facing into the flames. The man was rising from his chair and peeling off the wet signs. The widow expected him to drop each to the floor. Instead he folded them like large sheets and set them before the fireplace. Uncovered, he was revealed to be wearing only an undershirt and loose shorts. Either he'd recently lost weight or the clothes were not his.

What are they running from? Should I ask? Or should I just give comfort?

She stepped back inside the kitchen.

The refrigerator was well supplied. She had milked the cows this morning and baked bread. She'd picked apples from her trees only last week and made apple butter. All this she put on a plain serving tray. She did not need to be fancy. She'd never built up finery after her husband died, though a few of her students had given her gifts to that end: a four-piece tea set, a silver tray. She needn't put any of that out now. But as the kettle sounded and the bell on the timer dinged, she changed her mind.

Silver tray full of cookies, bread, fruit, and cheese, she pushed open the kitchen door.

In the living room, the man was seated and

the woman was shucking off the woolen blankets into a heap beside the chair. The widow was momentarily annoyed—she'd thought the man would handle the woman's wet garments properly. Then the woman, with one blanket still on, ceased moving and began making soft sounds. This time, though, the sounds were not grunts; the tone was lighter and higher than before.

The widow set the tray on the dining room table and stepped into the living room. She rounded the chairs and approached the wet cloths, wondering where she could dry them. The sounds continued. The widow turned, her back to the fire, and looked at the strangers.

Tucked deep into the folds of the woman's last blanket was a tiny baby.

The woman—the new mother, the widow suddenly understood—held the child, her arms shrouded by the blanket. The man was leaning toward the child. In his hands was a piece of damp cloth—the muslin cloth that had covered the hole on the armrest. He was using it to wipe the blood from the infant's face. The baby was making the whimpering sounds that the widow had mistaken for the woman.

The man's touch was gentle. He had removed a pitcher of water from the dining room table, and now he dipped the muslin inside, wetting it again. Then he pushed back the blanket and cleaned the kicking body. It was a girl, the widow saw. She saw too that the baby's skin was white. The man was moving with the caution of a father, but he was not this child's father. Somehow he and this woman had come together, and maybe he had even delivered the baby. Yet he had done it out of a different sense of duty from the one stirred by the sharing of genes.

"Oh, my goodness," the widow said.

The young mother looked up. "No!" she cried. "No, no, no, no!"

The man turned his face toward the mother, then followed her gaze to the widow. He stared at her hard, though his eyes wore no fear. They wore only a new form of plea.

"It's okay," the widow said, knowing it wasn't okay at all, whatever *it* was. There was a baby. A couple on the run. And they were *different*. They were *not right*.

She should call the police. She should run out of here and drive herself to safety. But her mind was accelerating even past those thoughts, so far past them that it hit a curve and turned back toward itself and then hurtled backward in time.

She scooped up the wet blankets and burst out the front door onto the porch.

As she stood staring out into the rain, holding the drenched blankets, she thought of him, her only child, the son who'd never grown as big as a name. She saw the doctor striding into her hospital room, her husband, Earl, in the chair beside her. Earl had drawn himself up as the doctor took a deep breath. "God knows what's best with children like these," the doctor said. "He takes the ones who are defective." She had said, "What do you mean, defective?" The doctor had replied, "It's gone now. You can forget this ever happened." Her husband's face became pleats, and he twirled down into the chair. When the moon rose that night, they got in the car in their new silence. He insisted they give the gravestone no name.

But this baby, inside her house, was alive.

She threw the blankets over the railing to dry and went back in.

The living room was empty. So was the kitchen. She called out, "Where are you?" They had to be inside; she hadn't heard the back door open. She went into the basement and checked around the washer, the root cellar, the sump pump. Back on the first floor, she opened the closet under the stairs. Then she mounted the stairs to the second floor.

The bathroom door remained open, as she'd left it, the towels untouched. She turned the knob for the bedroom door. The spread lay tidy on the bed. The two closets—hers on the left, Earl's on the right—were not occupied, and the rifle had not been moved. The other bedroom, her study, where she kept her books and writing desk and Christmas ornaments, looked the same.

No, it didn't.

She turned on the lamp. Her desk blotter—the map of America that had once hung in her classroom—was askew.

She looked to the ceiling. They must have found the panel above her desk that led to the attic, where she stored thirty years of student papers and long-forgotten mending. The man and woman must have found the tucked-away space where she rarely ventured, climbed in, and closed the panel.

These were people accustomed to hiding.

She stepped on her chair to her desk. For years now, she'd felt the strain of arthritis. She still managed her farm chores, though even with few animals left, and even with letting all but a small garden go to seed, they took longer than ever. Yet this was not a time to concern herself with aches; she tugged the rope for the folding ladder, opening it until its legs touched the floor beside the desk. She set her hand on the rungs and climbed up.

It took time to adjust her eyes to the pale light in the tiny attic. Then she saw them on their knees, leaning over the basket of mending, and in the basket she could hear the baby.

She watched them cast their caring looks into the basket, the woman leaning with obvious exhaustion against the man, her arm around his waist, his around her shoulder. As they showered their love upon the child, the widow was struck by how these two people—one Negro, one white—clearly shared hopes and feelings for this child, and for each other. Their color did not seem of the slightest consequence to them, nor did the woman's childlike manner or the man's deafness; and so, although she had never seen a couple such as this, she decided it was of no consequence to her, either. She simply stood in the shadows, admiring their unbridled caring.

Then, grasping what she needed to do, she stepped back down the ladder.

In her bedroom, she opened her husband's closet. She had long thought she should give her husband's clothes away. But she'd grown used to the way a turn of a knob and the sight of a shirt could fill her inside, as his memory, untainted by the pain of vanished parenthood, ushered her back to the early days of their marriage, when he hadn't stifled his tenderness, nor she her affection. Now she pulled out a shirt and laid it on the bed. At its hem she placed trousers. She unhooked a jacket, too. She remembered him wearing it when he first drove her to this farm, she newly arrived from Altoona for a job at the schoolhouse. He had looked so smart in that jacket.

She opened her own closet. The woman too

needed clothes; her misshapen attire was thread-bare and as worn as an overread book. The widow set out a white dress, left over from the days of church. She found white slippers, a shawl, and un-derthings. Remembering the aftermath of birth, she unearthed a long-forgotten pad in the bath-room.

Then she heard them emerge from the attic, shutting the ladder. She stepped into the hall—and they were finally fully visible. The man was maybe twenty years older than the young mother, who was a natural beauty. Her hair was ropy and unkempt, but her bones were delicate, not bone-bare, as the widow had first thought; the woman's features were almost elegant.

The widow urged them into the bedroom.

"Yours," she said, and by the woman's astonished look, the widow knew her word had been under-stood. The woman gestured to the man. The two moved forward, and with no indication they had any right to be alone, they stripped the clothes right off their backs.

The widow went downstairs. She stoked the fire and set the dining room table. They would sit, proper guests in proper clothes, and eat a decent meal, whoever they might be.

Later, so many miles from here, she would won-der how she could not have known. Yet maybe no one could have known. Her farmhouse was two hours away—two counties over. How could she blame herself for what she had never seen?

She heard them leave the bedroom, and by the time she'd reached the foot of the stairs, the man and young mother were descending the steps toward her. Newly dressed, hands clasped together, they were both breathtaking. The jacket brought out the man's handsomeness. He looked fit as a farmer on Sundays, turned out and proud. He had helped himself to one of her husband's hats, too, the brown woolen cap she'd loved so much. It looked so good on him. The dress and shawl brought out the mother's loveliness. Both their faces were radiant.

The widow touched her chest as they came toward her. "Don't you look like a dream."

Thwunk, thwunk.

The young mother froze, one step from the bottom of the stairs, and held back the man.

The widow whirled around. *Thwunk.* It was a pounding on her front door.

She gasped. Even above the rain, the sound overtook the room. She looked back to the couple. Their faces wore terror.

"No, no, no, no!" the woman said.

The man said nothing. He must have felt the force through the floor.

All this happened in an instant, so quickly that the widow had only enough time to turn back before headlights came on and shone through the front window.

"Police," said a voice on the porch, sounding more weary than menacing.

The widow glanced back at the couple again. They looked as if they wanted to run but hadn't the slightest idea where to go. She whipped back toward the front door.

"What do you want?" asked the widow, making her voice louder than the rain.

"If you'll just open the door."

"I would appreciate knowing why you're here." She extended her arm behind her, gesturing for them to stay where they were.

"Martha Zimmer?"

"That is correct."

"Are you all right, Mrs. Zimmer?"

"Why wouldn't I be?"

"Please just open the door."

"I would like an explanation."

"Don't make this difficult. We've been out here for hours, and we just want to finish our job and get home."

"I believe the Constitution would support me in saying that I have a right to know why you're shining a light through my door."

"There are two people missing, Mrs. Zimmer, and we're concerned for their safety."

"*Their* safety?"

"Yes."

"Perhaps I misunderstood. I thought you were concerned for *my* safety."

"Look, we don't want to break down this door. If you'll just open up—"

"And from where are those at risk to themselves *and* to me missing?"

"A school."

"I taught at every school in Well's Bottom except the high school. Since when does the high school send out police rather than truant officers—and at this hour of the night?"

There was a pause. She could hear shuffling. Through the window beside the staircase, she saw silhouettes rounding the porch toward the back door.

"I've asked a question," she said. "What school?"

"The State School, Mrs. Zimmer."

The words hit like a hard wind. She knew. She'd known all along. She could see it now, the name printed in block letters on the wool blankets draped on her porch railing, illuminated by the headlights: the Pennsylvania State School for the Incurable and Feebleminded.

She whirled around. The couple no longer stood on the steps. But before she could search, the front door flew open, and she heard the back door do the same. And into the house came policemen— two she'd seen in Well's Bottom, four she'd never set eyes on—and also a tall beanpole of a man she'd never seen before, who wore white like a hospital orderly. He must have been an attendant from the State School, the place behind the high walls, the place for the defectives, the place her husband would never drive by after their baby— after their *defective* son—had been born and died.

And the flurry was all around her. They were swarming her house, no question about privacy, no response as she circled the floor behind them, saying, "Please, be civilized!" They were going through the closet under the stairs, the living room, dining room. When they poured into the basement, she returned to the door and looked outside. With the headlights beaming, she could see halfway down her sloped field, though she made out no runaways. Just three police cars and a sedan from which a man was emerging. He wore a trim mustache and expensive raincoat, his gray hair parted in the middle. He opened his umbrella and came up the drive.

"Got the girl," she heard a voice say from the kitchen.

"Where's the boy?" another voice called out.

"Not on the first floor."

"Try the second."

The footsteps spread out behind her as the man in the raincoat reached her front door.

"I'm Dr. Collins," he said. His voice was low

and quiet, just what she would expect of a doctor. "You have my apologies for this disruption in your evening." He extended his hand.

She shook it, hearing feet moving through the second floor, closets opening. She felt motion behind her and turned. The young mother was being marched out of the kitchen and into the living room. Her handler was the skinny attendant, a bald, goateed man with wire glasses. The young mother's face was as downcast and fearful as it had been on her arrival.

"What is all this about?" Martha said, releasing the doctor's hand.

"Nothing to cause you any concern," the doctor said, "now that we've found them."

"Did they do something wrong?"

"They know the rules. Unapproved departures disrupt the order in our facility."

Martha turned toward the woman. The attendant was reaching into the pocket of his white uniform, producing something that looked like a straitjacket with extra-long sleeves.

"What is that?" Martha said.

Dr. Collins said, "Camisoles are for their own good."

The attendant was now threading the woman's arms into the sleeves of the camisole, crossing the sleeves over her chest, and drawing the long cuffs behind her back.

The young mother glanced at Martha, a rage in her eyes. But she was not resisting the camisole, even as the attendant tugged the sleeves tight behind her and buckled them together.

Martha winced. The attendant, noticing her reaction, said, "You got to do this. They don't learn anything; they don't understand anything. This is the only way to get them in line."

"But it must hurt."

"They don't feel pain. They're not—Look, if she knew right from wrong, she wouldn't have stolen these clothes from you."

"I *gave* her the clothes."

Dr. Collins said, "A kind though unnecessary generosity."

"I'd be glad to let her keep them."

"So," the attendant said, walking around the young woman so his face was in hers. "What did she say to you when you gave her this dress?"

The young mother lowered her head.

Martha knew the young mother had only a single word in her vocabulary. She tightened her lips, as she often had with Earl.

"He's not up here," she heard, and then the police were clattering toward the first floor.

She looked to the ceiling—the ceiling where she no longer heard footsteps. *The attic!* she thought. *They missed the attic! And they never said they were looking for a baby!*

"Maybe you officers should search outside," Dr. Collins said. "After all, he got her here on foot. He's not afraid of the natural world. Go check the outbuildings."

They hurried outside. The doctor stepped into the doorway and watched.

Martha turned back and looked for the captive mother. She found her in the dining room with the attendant. She wanted to do...something. But what? A hundred thoughts landed inside her, then scattered, until only one remained. She asked the woman, "What's your name?"

The young mother met her eyes, then blinked back down.

"She's an idiot," the attendant said. "A low grade. Her only word is 'no.' It's as far as her little brain goes."

"That's enough, Clarence," Dr. Collins said without entering the dining room.

"I'm just telling the truth," Clarence said. "The lady asked, so she should know."

Martha moved closer to the young mother. "What's your name?"

The woman flinched but didn't look.

"Doc, can't I bring her to the car now?"

"She's Lynnie," the doctor answered, again not leaving the doorway.

"Lynnie," Martha said, and at that Lynnie lifted her lids and looked. Yes, her eyes displayed the dullness Martha thought all retarded children wore. Why hadn't she noticed that? Because Lynnie was so beautiful, and her eyes contained so much emotion.

Martha said, "And the man? What's his name?"

Clarence expelled a laugh. "He's got no name. He's Number Forty-two."

Martha moved so she could look to the doctor for explanation, but he'd stepped onto the porch and was talking with one of the officers, who was pointing down the drive.

Martha turned back to Lynnie, and their eyes met. Martha thought she saw a different emotion, one that she hadn't seen before and could not identify.

Perhaps it was from noticing this that Clarence picked up the thread. "She heard you," he taunted, moving until he was beside Lynnie, facing Martha. "She's just got no sense of manners. When someone gives you clothes, what do you say?" He pushed Lynnie toward Martha.

Lynnie angled her gaze away from Martha. Martha thought at first that she was being shy or meek. But something told her there was more in this movement than words could say. She followed Lynnie's eyes. They were directed at the tiny window on the far living room wall, the one Martha had tried to look through at the very start of the storm.

The window was open. And the figure of a man—Number Forty-two—was tearing across the east field, arms bent at right angles, legs fast and powerful. He dove into the woods.

Martha turned back to Lynnie. This time her emotion was clear. It was one Martha had felt herself but had never worn on her face. Defiance.

"You're not listening," Clarence said to Lynnie. He shoved her toward Martha. "Thank the lady. Do your most cultivated grunt."

Lynnie was now so close that Martha could feel her breath, but this time Lynnie didn't turn her gaze toward the window. She leaned in so her lips pressed against Martha's ear.

Martha could feel Lynnie's breath warming her neck. She braced herself for the one word Lynnie knew, the one Martha had already heard. The one that meant defiance.

"Hide," came Lynnie's whisper.

Martha pulled back and looked at Lynnie. The face showed nothing.

Martha leaned in once more. "Hide," Lynnie said again, and added, "Her."

"What'd she tell you?" Clarence said. "Was she a good girl?"

Lynnie held herself still. Then she turned her face toward Martha's.

Martha looked into her eyes. They were *not* dull. They were green and pretty and, yes, *different*. But they knew how to hold back tears and were doing so right now.

Dr. Collins said, "We'll be going."

"They got him?" Clarence asked.

"Not yet, but he won't get anywhere tonight. It's too dark, the river's flooded, and he's got to be exhausted. They'll pick up his trail tomorrow."

"It'll be Forty-two's lucky day," Clarence said.

He tugged Lynnie away. Martha felt the breath leave her cheek, and she stood without moving, her eyes locked onto Lynnie's as the young mother was pulled across the room and turned toward the door. For a second Martha wondered if she had truly heard those words, yet they rang so loudly inside her, she knew she was not mistaken. Finally Martha pulled herself together and hurried to the doorway. The door still sat wide open, and she looked outside. Dr. Collins was getting into his sedan. The police cars were turning around. In the still-falling rain, Lynnie was being marched down the porch steps without an umbrella.

Martha shifted her gaze to the staircase inside her house and looked up to her second floor. Then she turned back toward the doorway. "Lynnie," she called out, and on the bottom porch step, the fragile figure, arms bound across her chest, white dress already soaking in the rain, paused and looked back.

Remember everything, Martha told herself. The

green eyes. The curly golden hair. The way she tilts her head to one side.

Then Martha stepped onto her porch and said, with more certainty than she had ever known before, "Lynnie, I will."

The School

LYNNIE

1968

$\mathcal{T}$urning from the old lady's voice, Lynnie walked down the flooded driveway of the farmhouse, ankles sloshing through water, Clarence at her heels. Her body still ached from the birth. But this water felt purer than the water she waded through when the lavatory clogged and awful liquids puddled on the floor. Finally, after so many years of such horrible things, she had something of her own: one pulse from which she'd found strength, another pulse to which she'd given life. Then Clarence shoved her, and it all came back. Everything had been taken away. After three days of freedom, she had nothing, not even the choice of where to put her feet.

Her arms were bound, Clarence was keeping her in line, and soon she would be punished at the School. *The School.* That's what they'd called it in front of the old lady. The residents who could talk referred to it more honestly, saying "this Dump" or "Sing Sing." For a long time, in Lynnie's mind, where word-shapes drifted about, sometimes finding form, sometimes not, she'd thought of it as simply the bad place. Then, when she learned Buddy's sign for the School—*Buddy*, she said to herself, mind-speaking her name for him with exhilaration—she thought it was perfect: a trap that snaps closed on an animal. And knowing her feet were being marched back to that trap, Lynnie had a sick sensation and felt like she wanted to bite someone. But she would not bite. It would make matters worse.

The back doors of the sedan were already open. In the driver's seat sat Mr. Edgar, the heavy man who worked for Dr. Collins. Usually Lynnie saw him only from the window of the laundry building as she piled clothes into the rolling bins. He'd be walking to the administrative cottage, where Lynnie's friend Doreen, who delivered the mail, said everyone spoke "a lot of high words." Now, coming close to the sedan, Lynnie could see Mr. Edgar's hair. Slicked with Brylcreem, it held the ruts from the comb, the way fields held plow marks in the mud. Beside him sat Dr. Collins. He was bent over Lynnie's chart, fountain pen in one hand, cigarette in the other. Lynnie took all this in, though she did not know the words "Brylcreem" or "chart" or "fountain pen." She did know the words "Dr. Collins," but the residents were expected to call him "Uncle Luke" instead. Lynnie, though, didn't call him anything—soon after she'd come to the bad place, she'd stopped speaking. Uncle Luke had never noticed. To him, she was just one of three thousand residents, and he was, as Doreen said when he waltzed down the paths, giving tours to well-dressed people, "the kind of person who couldn't walk by a lavatory faucet if it was clean enough to show his own face."

Uncle Luke wasn't even noticing her now, as she passed his window—he was concentrating on adding notes to her chart. She stuck her tongue out at him, though before he even glanced her way, Clarence clamped his hand on her shoulder. "There you go," he said, his tone polite for Uncle Luke's benefit. Then he pushed Lynnie into the back and slammed the door.

She tried to see through the windshield to the farmhouse. The headlights went only so far, and all she could make out was a rectangle of light from the doorway and the silhouette of the lady who'd said she'd do what Lynnie had asked. Lynnie had worked so hard to speak those words— *Hide her*—and her heart had lifted at the old lady's answer. But Lynnie could not see the tiny window in the attic, much less the edge of the woods.

Clarence slid through the other door, and Lynnie pushed up against her window. She had to get out. She had to find Buddy. Yet there was no way out, and all she could do was gulp air. This was not good—if they knew you were afraid, they'd be rougher. She tried to think about Kate, the attendant with the red hair and sweet temper. Instead her mind fixed on Smokes, the attendant with the dogs, and her gulps just got faster. So she resorted to an old habit. When she was little and her body felt floppy, she liked how rolling her head made colors flow like ribbons. After she got what the doctor called muscle tone, she still rolled her head, only with her eyes closed, because she'd discovered that when she stopped a head circle, her mind landed in another place and time. It was like washing machines: After the spin, you find lost socks. So as the sedan headed down the sloping drive, she rolled her head until she landed outside of now.

"You don't own anything in this dump," Lynnie's first friend, Tonette, was whispering, "except what's right inside. So keep it there." In the hospital cottage on Lynnie's intake evening, Tonette pointed to her head. She was tall, brown, and skinny, with hair like springs in a pen, and she handed Lynnie a bowl of Jell-O. "I'm telling you so you start on the good foot." Taking the Jell-O, Lynnie didn't follow the reasoning: "Things'll be easier if you keep to yourself." It wasn't until what happened to Tonette a little later that Lynnie decided to stay quiet.

Clarence shimmied toward Lynnie. "Looks like she lost weight on her adventure," he said. Uncle Luke and Edgar paid no attention. "I'm just telling you," Clarence added, his voice louder so they'd hear, "for those files." Lynnie didn't always understand other people's actions, much less motives, though she did grasp that Clarence had no genuine desire to help them. He just wanted them to praise him to his sidekick, the attendant everyone called Smokes.

Lynnie almost swung her feet up to shove him off but controlled herself, knowing he'd lash her ankles together. Instead, she looked out the window. If Buddy was among the trees, she wouldn't have to fight Clarence—Buddy would just run up to the car, haul the door open, and save her. The sedan reached the turn onto the country road, and suddenly a sight rose out of the dark. It was the small lighthouse man she'd seen earlier tonight, when they'd come around the bend of this road, searching desperately for a place to rest. She'd touched Buddy's arm. It was so much like the one from long ago, with her sister, and that had been a safe place. She'd once drawn it for Buddy: a tall, strong place by the sea. She wanted to explain to Buddy earlier tonight that the lighthouse man was how she knew they'd be protected. But the baby was in her arms.

Clarence, following her gaze, looked at the lighthouse man, too. Then he turned forward, threw his arm across the seat, and touched her shoulder. The feel of him brought back so much she did not want to see: the bucket, the growling dogs, the taste of cloth. She shrank away; he just moved his arm closer. As the sedan drove past woods and other houses, she wondered, Was Buddy in that yard? Behind that tree? How long would it be before they ran away again? Before she held the baby in her arms?

How Lynnie wanted to batter Clarence with her feet, to bite and writhe and shriek. Yet she couldn't. When Buddy came to break her out, she *had* to be in her usual cottage, which she wouldn't if they tossed her in solitary. So she pressed her feet to the floor and clenched her teeth. Then she looked out the windshield onto the long country road, hoping Buddy would appear before they crossed the river.

She woke when the sedan was slowing down. It was still night, and beside them was the high stone wall of the School. She'd missed the bridge over the river. She'd missed whatever glimpse she might have had of Buddy. Her chest hollowed with disappointment. Above the stone wall, she could see the rain had stopped, but with the clouds too thick to allow the sight of even one star, her throat went acid with sorrow. Over the summer, Buddy had taught her that stars wheeled slowly across the sky throughout the night. Now, without any stars to be seen, she had no way to gauge how close they were to morning.

Then the tower clock came into view, rising on the hill. The clock was all a person could see from the road, the wall sealing off everything except the gate. But the sight did Lynnie no good; she couldn't read clocks. Still, as Mr. Edgar hummed to the radio, Clarence drew on his pipe, and Uncle Luke snored, she stared at the clock. It glowed yellow as a moon, and with the rain on its face, it seemed to be crying.

Only twice before had she taken in this view. Three nights ago, when she and Buddy had run off, she'd looked back. There it was, the clock that lit all the cottage windows. Buddy pulled at her arm and made his sign for run. With his hand in hers and her trust in him, they ran.

But there was another time, before Buddy, Kate, Doreen—even Tonette. Lynnie was little then, the small self she still hid inside, like a tiny bowl hidden inside a larger one. She lowered her eyes now and looked inside to that smaller self, to the time before she first saw this view, to the time when she had no idea about stone walls.

In that time, she knew the world of her kitchen, where she played inside the bottom cupboard with her sister. They'd open the wooden doors, pull themselves into the kingdom of pots, and put cake pans on their heads for hats. Her sister knew many words. She knew how to move them up and down, too, into a song. Lynnie would take her sister's arm and grunt into her wrist, feeling vibrations. One song was their favorite: *A-tisket, a-tasket. A green and yellow basket. I wrote a letter to my love. And on the way I dropped it.*

Lynnie didn't know about dining cottages then. She knew about dining rooms, and the underside of the table, where she and her sister kept Betsy Wetsy dolls and looked at Mommy's and Daddy's shoes when they were sitting with serious voices, saying things like "accepting this tragedy" and "her hopeless future" and "we've done nothing to deserve a retarded child," while her sister played jacks and Lynnie picked at the knot in Daddy's oxfords. Her sister would ask if Lynnie knew what was cooking and then name the smells: "potato latkes"…"hot chocolate." Lynnie loved smells. She loved putting her face in wool coats under the beds. To this day, she could still smell the sweet scent of her sister's chewing gum. She could even remember placing her cheek on Mommy's perfumed chest when she hoisted Lynnie from under the table, saying, "I just can't do that."

Although so many years had passed since then—years of bedrooms with forty beds, all with

iron frames—Lynnie could still remember her bedroom. It had two pink headboards, one for her
bed, one for her sister's—"Nah-nah," the first word
Lynnie could say ("Finally," Mommy said, hands
clasped in joy when Hannah called her into the
bedroom, her face glowing)—and windows with
curtains. Lynnie remembered a bathroom, too, but
for a long time she sat on the changing table instead, as Daddy said, "Five already and still in
diapers and making sounds like a baby." "Please
don't keep bringing it up," Mommy said, removing
the pins from her mouth.

Lynnie could conjure up the living room, too.
It had a carpet and fish tank and books. Books
were not as fun as fish. Nah-nah would sit on the
couch and read while Lynnie pulled herself along
the floor on her arms to watch fish with their
shiny colors. "She still doesn't crawl?" Aunt This
One said from behind. "She's already six." Aunt
That One said, "It's been obvious for years that Dr.
Feschbach was right." Mommy said, "She'll crawl.
She'll walk." "She'll never go to school," Aunt
This One said. Aunt That One said, "And think
of the shame"—here she whispered—"that her sister will feel, once she can understand."

Mommy cried. And other people's crying did
something to Lynnie. It came at her like a storm
and burst inside and thundered until she had to
push it out of her chest, so she'd flip on her back

and kick and scream. It always worked, because soon the crying would stop. Sometimes Nah-nah would come to her side, saying, "She doesn't understand." Only Lynnie *did* understand. The way to get rid of crying was to kick sadness back into the air.

And Lynnie could still see a restaurant. She could walk by then, and they went inside and sat at a booth, and her parents asked what she wanted. "Burger!" she squealed, one of the biggest words she knew by then, and people stared. They stared again when the food didn't all make it into her mouth and dribbled like finger paint down her face. The waitress came over with extra napkins. The waitress did not stare. The waitress did not look. Daddy said, "I wish you'd listen to reason," Mommy got ready to cry, and Nah-nah suddenly said, "Let's hold hands to the car," and they went to sing Elvis in the backseat.

Then there was that place called a synagogue, with stained glass and a huge room they walked past to reach a rabbi at a desk, where Mommy sat holding Lynnie on her lap against her big, hard belly, saying, "Everyone's got their opinion. You know where my husband stands. So I turned to books. Dale Evans said the only place for her retarded daughter was at home. She said the girl was an angel. But Lynnie's, well, embarrassing." She swallowed hard. "Pearl Buck had a retarded daughter, too, and she said they're happier among their own kind. But Lynnie's my little baby!" The rabbi folded his hands and said, "I think you'll regret sending her off. It would feel as if you exiled her into the wilderness." "Thank you, thank you," Mommy said, and started to sob, and then Lynnie's chest was hurting so much, she threw herself to the floor, bucking and wailing, and then Mommy was saying she was sorry and hauling Lynnie away.

And she could bring to mind a playground. Nah-nah in her Brownie uniform ran off to jump rope with friends, and Lynnie stayed in the sandbox, drawing with a stick—circles rolling into circles like a Slinky—until a boy came and stomped all over her design, and then she was on top of him, slapping away. Right away, Mommy was running, pushing the stroller with the twins, flying into the sandbox, pulling Lynnie off the boy, yelling at Hannah on the way home for not watching her sister. "Admit it," Daddy said that night as Lynnie sat at the top of the stairs and Nah-nah, beside her, hummed their favorite song, taking Lynnie's arm and, for the first time, pressing *her* lips to Lynnie's wrist. But Lynnie still heard Daddy. "She's almost eight. If we don't place her now, this is what every day will be like. For the rest of all of our lives."

Then she was sitting a long time in the car. She was in the back, flipping the ashtray lid on the door up and down, up and down, when Nah-nah suddenly said, "Is that Lynnie's school?"

Lynnie looked up and saw the tower. It rose behind a stone wall, taller than the temple, and Lynnie felt proud. She was going to school, and her school was so big.

The car turned at an opening in the wall and pulled up to a gate.

"It looks like it should have a moat," Nah-nah said under her breath.

Daddy heard. "Remember our talk last night," he said.

Mommy said, "Act your age, Hannah."

Nah-nah turned to Lynnie, and in her eyes Lynnie saw a look she'd never seen on her sister before. Much later, after Lynnie took a dictionary of words and understandings into her mind, she remembered this moment and knew how to identify this look. In other faces before this first view of the stone walls, she'd seen pity, or fear, or ridicule, or contempt. In Nah-nah's face she'd seen only playfulness and affection. At this moment she saw guilt.

Then a guard was opening the gate, and they were driving up the hill toward a cluster of buildings. Her parents pointed, describing what they knew from the brochure and Uncle Luke's letters: Those were the cottages where the residents lived, each for a different classification.

"They call them cottages?" Nah-nah said. "Each one's bigger than *my* school."

"This is an impressive place," Daddy said. "It covers twelve hundred acres."

There were even larger buildings in the center of the property—"That must be the laundry, gymnasium, classrooms, hospital," Daddy said. "They're self-sufficient here," he added, glancing in the rearview mirror to see Hannah. "They even grow their own food."

Lynnie looked. Beyond all the buildings were fields with crops growing, pastures with cows, chicken coops, all of it tended to by men in denim overalls and gray T-shirts—"working boys," Daddy said they were called. Beyond where they could see, Daddy said, was a power plant that serviced the school. Near the power plant was a baseball diamond, and beyond that were huts for the staff, whose salaries included room and board. Far beyond the huts, on the other side of a rise, was something Daddy did not know about, so he did not point it out. Only later did Lynnie learn about the cemetery, on the day she resolved to stop speaking.

All this was connected by walking paths, and beneath the paths were underground passages that were there, Mommy said, "to keep you warm during the winter." Except for two men in white uniforms, one with three snarling dogs, no one was on the paths. "I think they keep everyone busy," Mommy said.

"With school?" Nah-nah said.

"Sure," Mommy said, though she didn't sound sure.

"And training," Daddy added. "They teach them to make rugs and how to repair shoes. Good skills for when people get older."

As they made their way to the parking lot, they did see someone else: a woman in white pushing a boy in a wheelchair. "Oh, these grown-ups must be attendants," Mommy said.

"Attendants?" Nah-nah said. "I thought this was a school."

"It's a different kind of school," Daddy said, his voice curt. "I told you that."

Nah-nah looked again at her with guilt, and that was when Lynnie began to get scared.

"And you, Lynnie, stop with the ashtray," Daddy said.

"It's only another minute," Mommy said, and her mouth seemed full of water.

Their car continued up the hill. Lynnie looked one more time to the tower and tried to make sense of the hands. They were standing up straight, pressed tight together. Like the covers of a book that no one wanted to read.

Clarence yanked Lynnie out of the sedan. She

stood, wobbly from the trip, and as Uncle Luke talked to him about "you being adequately compensated for extending your shift," she looked to the cloudy sky. Although she still couldn't see stars, she remembered how, for the longest time, stars had been nothing more to her than twinkling dots. Then Buddy pointed to the sky on some nighttime landscapes she'd drawn, crushed one of his sugar cubes over the paper, pushed the powder into patterns, and used his signs to teach her the names of the constellations: Cup, Feather. By tomorrow night, the clouds would have lifted. They'd look at the stars together as they ran away again.

With Clarence at her side and Uncle Luke in the lead, they mounted the marble steps for the building with the tower. It stood out from other cottages, with its oak door, brass handrail, plush hedges, and windows that had no bars. Lynnie, waiting while Uncle Luke removed his keys, shivered inside the old lady's dress. As much as she hated being bound into the camisole, she was glad for it now, as it shielded her from the wind. She also realized, when Uncle Luke opened the heavy door, that she needed a bathroom and had never used the one in here.

Still in pain from the birth, she wasn't sure she could hold it in. Yet she could not bear the thought of revealing her need to go, so she squeezed the tops of her thighs. Beneath her dress she felt the pad the old lady had given her, a reminder of what all her time with Buddy had showed her: She could do much more than she'd ever believed.

Although Lynnie hadn't been in this office since her first day, it looked the same: the desk for the secretary, Maude; the Persian rug; the Windsor chairs; the grandfather clock; and, off to the side, the wooden door to Uncle Luke's office. It smelled the same, too: leather, tobacco, books. Lynnie inhaled, enjoying the scents, as Uncle Luke retrieved a cigarette from a silver holder, then looked at Clarence, waiting until he got the hint. His jaw set, Clarence lit the cigarette with his lighter. Then Uncle Luke turned his back on them both and lifted the phone. Lynnie heard a ring across the grounds, and with a pleasant skip in her throat, she realized it was nearby—maybe even A-3, Lynnie's cottage. If so, maybe Kate might be there, and Lynnie would be safe.

Kate, like most staff, put in overtime. There was too much to do, with one attendant to every forty residents. Maybe that was why some staff had a mean streak toward residents and one another, though fortunately some staff didn't. The best ones even brought in snacks from home, showed photos of their children, ignored the nasty nicknames— "Left-Hook Larry," "Mr. Magoo," "Poopy-pants," or the one made up for Lynnie, "No-No." They might even try to develop a resident's skill.

That's what Kate had done. Five years into Lynnie's stay—five years after Lynnie's intake IQ test classified her as an upper division imbecile and they stuck her in a cottage with other low grades—Kate noticed that Lynnie wasn't just pushing the mop around when she did the janitorial work that was part of her treatment. She was making designs on the tile with the mop, the suds sparkling like iridescent crescents in the light. Kate told a psychologist, who ordered a new IQ test, and then Lynnie was promoted to the moron cottage. That's where she met Doreen, a short, blond girl with Chinese-looking eyes, whose iron-framed bed was twelve inches from her own. A little while later, when Kate bent the rules and brought crayons to the dayroom, she observed that Lynnie drew horses—proud blue horses with flowing green manes. "That's so good, sweet pea," Kate said, and arranged for Lynnie to come to her office in the staff cottage. Kate told everyone it was so Lynnie could help out, but really it was so Lynnie could sit at Kate's desk and draw. Kate kept pads and colored pencils in her file cabinet. When Lynnie arrived, Kate would lock the door and unlock the cabinet, and when Lynnie left, Kate would place Lynnie's art in the drawer and turn the key in the lock.

Down the hill, the ringing phone was picked up. "We're here," Uncle Luke said. "Come get her."

He set down the phone. Then he opened the door to his office, passing a seated Clarence without a glance, and closed his door.

Clarence's lips got thin. If Lynnie hadn't heard that Clarence's friend Smokes was Uncle Luke's brother, she wouldn't have figured it out. Uncle Luke never let anyone see him favoring his brother and Clarence over anyone else. Yet everyone knew he did, because Smokes and Clarence got away with everything. They were the only ones with dogs. They were the only ones who smelled like alcohol. They were the only ones who—

Lynnie turned to the window. She had something better to think about: Buddy holding the baby high and laughing; Lynnie feeling new warmth when she held the baby in her arms.

The door opened. She spun around.

Kate!

Lynnie let out a joyful sound but held herself back from running for a hug.

Kate looked at Lynnie with a sad smile. When Kate first arrived, after losing her husband to another woman, she'd been curvy, with nice makeup and dresses with full, colorful skirts. Over time she'd gained weight, lost the makeup, and taken up smoking. She still embroidered her attendant's coat, though she wore gray or brown skirts now and a necklace with a gold cross. She'd also grown weary, and inside her eyes, Lynnie was sure she could see Kate's smaller self.

"Do a careful intake," Uncle Luke was saying. "We have no idea what he did to her."

Kate said, "Forty-two is such a gentleman. He wouldn't do anything."

"If he was so trustworthy," Uncle Luke responded, "he wouldn't have pulled this stunt."

Kate said nothing as Uncle Luke then went on, instructing her on what to do with Lynnie. Lynnie turned and saw Clarence's gaze on her. She closed her eyes and sucked in her lips.

Then Lynnie felt a hand on her arm, and she and Kate were moving forward. From behind, she heard, "It seems worth time and a half to me, Doctor." The door opened and she was outside.

The clouds had cleared, and constellations gazed down upon them. Lynnie looked up, and the names came back. Over there was Pony. Down near the horizon was Cup. And right above was the one she loved most, Feather.

Lynnie reached for Kate's hand, and they walked. Past the classrooms that never got used, the gym with rusty hoops and a moldy ceiling. They crossed to the next path. The boys' colony was down the hill on the left, the girls' on the right. Sometimes she heard high brow boys at night, beating one another, doing vulgar things. Tonight was as quiet as the moon.

Finally Kate squeezed her hand extra hard. "I was so worried about you," she said.

Lynnie looked into Kate's face. Lynnie longed to tell her, *The baby was coming, and we snuck away, and it hurt, but it felt so good.* She longed to tell about the love she felt for her baby, holding her aloft from the floor of the abandoned bomb shelter where she'd given birth. She longed to tell about the kiss with Buddy in the old lady's bedroom, the kind of long kiss they'd shared only in the cornfield when the stalks were high enough to hide them. She longed to tell about the walk down the lady's staircase, the police, Buddy running into the woods.

But except for those times with Buddy in the cornfields, her mouth had fallen into such disuse, she'd mostly forgotten how to speak. She spoke with drawings—though she wasn't near any pencils. If only she could speak as well with her hands as Buddy. But only she understood his hands, and even she wasn't perfect at that.

"Just tell me if you're okay," Kate said.

Lynnie nodded.

"Thank goodness. I was just sick with worry."

They reached the hospital cottage. Kate mounted the first step. "I asked if you could sleep here tonight, so you'd have one night where I could stay with you, and only you."

Lynnie pulled her back down the step.

"What's wrong?"

She pointed to A-3.

"You really want to go back tonight?"

It's where he'll look for me, she wanted to say, only she could not. Instead, she nodded.

"All right," Kate said. "I'll get in trouble, but better me than you."

They continued on. Past the first cottage with the girls, A-1. Then A-2. Finally, A-3. All along, Lynnie thought of how much harder it would be a second time. They'd planned their escape for the busiest hour, when the staff was herding everyone into bed. She'd slipped out the door, knowing she wouldn't be missed till later. They'd even packed pillows in her bed—Doreen had helped earlier in the day, saying, *Packed you in there like a mummy.* Now they'd be watching.

Lynnie and Kate climbed the three steps to the door of the cottage. Of course Kate had to tug at the rusted knob. At last it gave way, and they stepped inside.

The smell, the smell. The first time Lynnie took it in, she'd tried to run off, and the attendant had caught her, and she'd bit him. It was a smell that got inside your nose and under your eyes and beneath your teeth. A smell so hard to breathe through that some attendants smoked just to taste something else. It made Lynnie sleep with the blanket over her face.

Kate, if only you knew how good the night smelled when I found the right place. I couldn't sign to Buddy with the baby in my hands, so I made a sound of happiness and set my lips on Buddy's, and he made his voice move up and down until we met at the same sound, and then we held that note, the baby between us, our bodies humming together.

They crossed the short lobby. Suzette, the other night attendant, was leaning back at the desk, a book open across her eyes, her mouth open beneath it. Suzette didn't break up fights fast enough, though from what Lynnie could tell, the girls didn't fight as much as the boys. The only trouble was if the boys made it to the girls' side of the school. It had happened only once. Suzette wasn't there that night, and Kate wasn't, either, and— *Oh, do not remember.*

They entered the dayroom. The benches and plastic chairs were empty. The floor was dirty, waiting for working girls to wax it during breakfast. Even the TV was off. Lynnie remembered how much worse things were before the TV. They'd sit in the room with nothing to do except crack jokes and make up games— or make fun of one another and try to steal the few items someone had gotten from her family. Residents claimed their seats and held them for years.

Kate whispered as they moved in the direction of Lynnie's sleeping room, "You're going to get punished somehow, but I'll try to get you off light."

At the end of the dayroom, they turned toward the lavatory. Good.

They passed the sinks. The toilets. There were ten, all lined up behind what looked like separate metal doors, only inside there were no dividers, so one attendant could watch ten residents do their business all at once. Lynnie reached for them, but Kate didn't notice. She was saying, "Let's get you bathed. I'll tell them you were cooperative, and maybe they'll be less severe."

Kate stopped at the edge of the bathtubs and, moving behind Lynnie, began unbuckling the camisole. "I can stay and watch you here tonight. But I have to go home in the morning."

The camisole came off. Kate tossed it to the side.

"Where did you get such nice clothes? Your hair rolls down this dress like Rapunzel."

Lynnie grunted with gladness.

"I'm sorry you won't be able to wear this." She began working the top button loose.

That first night so many years ago, the receiving nurse had said Lynnie could keep her clothes for special occasions, which turned out to mean whenever Uncle Luke showed officials around, bragging about how wisely the public's money was being spent. Lynnie didn't know that when the School first opened in 1905, residents wore uniforms for visits, the boys resembling military cadets, the girls domestic workers. Now they wore clothes from home, which were inevitably nice because they were kept in lockers for which the residents had no keys. Even so, sometimes clothes vanished. "No one has anything of his own here," Tonette told her that first night. "Not even a toothbrush." She was right. Every morning the lavatory had a line as they all waited to use the one toothbrush.

Lynnie felt the dress drop to her ankles. "Honestly," Kate said, "I wish you'd gotten away." She unhooked the old lady's bra, noting it with admiration; it was the first bra Lynnie had ever worn. The state recently approved funds to fix a hole in the barn roof though once again rejected the request for brassieres. It was Buddy who'd fastened this one onto her.

What will Kate do when she finds out? Lynnie hadn't had to work too hard at hiding her growing belly, with the oversize clothes, the mushy food, the sweating she did in the laundry. She'd hid nothing else from Kate all these years. *Will she be angry? Will she tell?*

Kate reached up and hooked her thumbs around the panties and pulled them down.

Lynnie stood naked in the chill room, so much she'd not said revealed.

"Dear God," Kate croaked. She came to Lynnie's front and took her into her arms.

* * *

That night, Lynnie lay in her bed next to Doreen, looking across the rows to see Kate pacing back and forth, smoking. She knew Kate would watch over her tonight, which left her free to sleep and dream and wake. It would be the same fitful night as any other—but on this night, she would not be afraid.

In her first dream, she hears sounds from the boys' side. They start nice and then get frightening, with one word rising above all the shouts and groans. She plucks that one word—no—and practices speaking it in bed, and soon that word is her own.

The dream turns like a page in her drawing pad, and now she is in a dream where that one word is all she has. The door opens and she backs away and the bucket falls. "No, no, no, no!"

She woke with a start. *Where—what—* Oh, yes, it all washed back inside her. As if she needed proof, there was Kate, on a chair in the doorway, staring at her cigarette.

Back into dreams. Lynnie is in the laundry, and a dryer breaks down, so she wheels a bin of clothes outside. There she stands before the clothesline, inhaling grass and trees, freshly plowed fields. A spring breeze lifts her shirt, reminding her that something is happening inside her body, something that came into her on a night she could not "No" away but is starting to understand. As she pins laundry to the line, she hears a motor puttering and, above that sound, hands clapping. She looks around. A tractor is drawing near, and on its seat is a colored man in a straw hat. She has seen him doing handyman chores, bringing corn to the kitchen. Once she saw him digging a grave. Now he is sitting high, smiling, tapping the seat beside him.

Girls and boys are not allowed near each other at the School, at least not when anyone is watching. She looks around. No one is watching.

The man makes signs with his hands. She understands he means, *Come up here*. She sets her bowl of clothespins on the ground. He reaches down and hoists her up. She sits beside him, and he fishes in his pocket and pulls out one white feather, two, three. He collects them into a bouquet and hands them to her. She wonders how his wrist would feel against her lips.

She woke. Kate was standing again. This time Suzette was nearby.

"But are you going to put it on her chart?" Suzette was whispering.

"Of course I will. She had a *baby*."

"I wouldn't."

"A *baby*. And it's somewhere out there. And someone in here is responsible."

"That's my point. You want to stir things up like that?"

Kate said nothing.

"You know what they'll do to you?"

"What about *her?*"

"They get over it. It happens to them all the time."

"To the point of *pregnancy?*"

Suzette said, "You know there's that doctor in Harrisburg who gets rid of it."

"No one caught this one. It got to full term, from what I can tell."

"I bet it was Forty-two's."

"It wasn't."

"How do you know? It's not like he was sterilized. I'll tell you, those places with the sterilization programs had the right idea. It saved a lot of worry. Too bad no one has them anymore."

"I know when they began spending time together, and the math says it wasn't him."

"Well, what does it matter."

"What does it matter? Someone in here did it, that's what. And then—my God, those two delivered a baby by themselves."

"What I mean is, what does it matter who the father is. So it's not Forty-two; it's another resident. So what. You know what will happen if they find that baby."

"I know." Kate's voice was very sad.

"So why report it? Besides, what if word gets out that a resident *escaped* and *had a baby?* They'd have

Collins's head and everyone else's. Where would we work then? What kind of jobs are there around here for folks that never finished high school? Or whose ex doesn't pay child support like yours? The whole town'll go down the tubes. You want that on your head?"

"I'm not talking economics. I'm talking morality. We can't leave a baby out there."

"Just forget about it."

"Have you lost your mind?"

Then Lynnie was down again, dreaming of escape. She is running across the fields of the School with Buddy. Here is the ladder by the back wall; here is the ladder on the other side; here is the satchel he packed, waiting below. She turns back one last time.

Then, ahead: woods and valleys and fields. Into a town. Into a backyard. Buddy lifts the door to a hidden cellar. There is a cot and generator and lamp and tin cans and canteens. Buddy understands them all. That's why they rely on him. They call him a deaf-mute, a low grade, but they just can't understand his hands. He shakes open a blanket. *Lie down*, his hands say.

And through the memory dream of the birth, she heard Kate, alone again in the sleeping room: "Mother Mary, please give me a sign. Tell me what to do."

* * *

Lynnie woke with the shock of the sun. She could hear residents rising from bed.

Buddy had not rescued her during the night. The baby must still be with the old lady.

"You're back!" she heard, and turned her head. Doreen was sitting up.

Lynnie made to roll onto her side, but something was wrong. She couldn't turn.

"They tied you up!" Doreen said, suddenly noticing.

Lynnie looked: Leather restraints were buckling her wrists and ankles to the bed frame. She fought against them, tacking back and forth, grunting with anguish, but they held.

"Guess they're afraid of you running off again," Doreen said.

Lynnie twisted her head toward the doorway, her throat tight with anger. Kate was no longer there. Suzette's shift was over, too. And Lynnie could hear feet approaching—though not the floppy shoes of working girls coming to strip beds or the soft shoes of attendants on the day shift. They were the thuds of two pairs of boots and the scrabble of many sets of paws.

She knew who it was. She closed her eyes.

Paths Less Traveled

MARTHA

1968

*M*artha sat before the tiny attic window, waiting to see the dawn. She had always felt a shivery pleasure at this time of day, after the egg collecting, before she fried Earl's breakfast and drove to school in their Buick. Even after their child had died, when their home had stilled, she would look out the kitchen window to see Earl striding over the fields from his early chores, woolen cap on his head, his solid frame silhouetted against the lightening sky, and she would feel such a gratitude for the constancy of sunrise that her longing for all she'd lost would soften. Now, handling the chores alone, she sometimes felt so stirred as she returned to the house at this hour that she'd fancy herself heading to the second floor, opening one of the undersized windows, climbing outside, pulling herself to the roof, and spending the morning sitting at its peak, gazing up at the sky. But although she'd applauded audacity in her students, rashness was not her way. Last night, however, having sat in the dark attic, protecting the baby in the basket, dwelling upon the magnitude of a task that had arrived without warning, instruction, or duration, she could think of no better place to fix her eyes than the sky. Perhaps just gazing into its limitless depths and knowing that no matter how dark the night, the revolution of the earth always brought day, she'd find a way to answer the question of how she was to hide this infant.

Martha and the baby couldn't remain in the attic. It was stuffy and dim and wouldn't prevent a baby's cries from carrying down to the road. Besides, children gained nothing from seclusion. Martha remembered teachers who'd tried to silence class clowns and incorrigible brainy students by sentencing them to the cloakroom, though to her mind, banishment lessened everyone. The exile could not learn from others, and the class was deprived of inquisitiveness and wit. So by the first colors of dawn, Martha had already come to this much: This baby must be hidden from the authorities, but if she remained with Martha beyond this day—or, goodness knows, this week—she must be out in the world, able to see and be seen by the sky.

There were more pressing matters, which had come to Martha moments after the sedan disappeared at the bottom of the hill and she closed her front door: *I am alone in a house with a baby*— and an icebox with only cow's milk, shelves unfamiliar with diapers, an attic with no trace of baby clothes. Her stomach quaked. *I have no idea what I'm doing.* She'd assisted Earl with newborn animals and held her students' infants and toddlers, but the basics of feeding and changing and dressing a child were daunting. *What if I cannot rise to the occasion? Why did they come to my house? How could I have let motherhood pass me by? Why did I allow Earl's sorrow to deprive me of something so essential?*

Stop, she'd told herself. *Self-pity is a worse adversary than ignorance.* Right now she did not need those answers. She just needed necessities.

So last night, returning to the resourcefulness so familiar to a farmer's wife, she'd taken a deep breath and gathered herself together. In the kitchen, she remembered the student who'd come from Boston last Christmas with her husband and three children and left behind baby formula, which Martha had saved to return this year. She found it in the cupboard and read the instructions. They cautioned the need to boil the bottles before adding milk. She picked around her cupboards and was just at the point of resorting to a mason jar when she remembered a few small bottles Earl had used for a motherless calf. She filled them, leaving most in the icebox, as the instructions said, and bringing one to the second floor. There, in the linen closet, she found washcloths to use for diapers, towels she wet for a sponge bath. These improvisations allowed her to make it through the night in the attic, clumsily feeding and changing the baby.

Now, as peach light eased toward gold and the baby slept on in the basket, Martha pressed herself close to the window. Earl had made this one particularly small, but by angling herself just so, she could make out the first glow of sun above the eastern treetops, gilding the woods where the man had disappeared. He had seemed so protective, so tender. Martha remembered one of the most confusing moments last night: the officer insisting that Lynnie and Number Forty-two had to be taken into custody for their safety, then contradicting himself, saying *Martha's* safety was at risk. Which was it?

A ray of sun struck the window. She'd never been in the attic at this hour, so she'd never seen the way the rising sun lit the brick-shaped glass. Nor had she seen the crack in the lower corner, its diagonal cut a prism. She laid her fingers on the crack. The glass yielded immediately, as if it had been waiting for freedom, and fresh air swept the stuffiness from the room. And just that tiny piece of sky, in the form of an autumn breeze, and just that view of her field, still watery from the storm, brought her clarity; and she arrived at her first step for the day.

It wasn't that much of a step, Martha thought as she let herself down the ladder, slid a suitcase from under her bed, and popped the latches. Unlike the way Earl had looked far ahead with his seed purchases and crop rotations, it hardly rose to the level of a plan. Earl had felt planning was the vanquisher of chaos, though Martha had never shared this certainty; they'd planned their baby's nursery yet failed to subjugate the cruelest chaos imaginable. So she'd limited her planning to next week's classes or, since retirement, the open house at Christmas. Looking out into this new day, however, had reminded her that the School would resume its search, and since she could not allow them to hear the baby cry, Martha and the baby had to leave.

Her mind fastened to the moment, she laid clothing in the suitcase. One cotton dress, one cardigan, one nightgown, one set of undergarments: enough to take them through tomorrow. Perhaps that would not be sufficient, so she added enough to last a second day.

She brought the suitcase into her study. She'd left the ladder from the attic open but did not retrieve the baby just yet; there was still more packing ahead.

She pulled boxes of Christmas decorations from a shelf. There, as she'd expected, was the collection of doll-sized Santas and elves and angels that a heavyset, rosy-cheeked student, Eva Hansberry, had given her over the years. A quiet girl, Eva ran a corner store in Well's Bottom, along with her husband, Don, and their teenage son. The store had been in Don's family for decades, a cramped place that sold canned goods and detergent and cough syrup and sodas; and every year, after Eva received their shipment of holiday knickknacks, she gave one to Martha. Martha did not like these sentimental figures; she'd saved them only because they came from Eva, who dressed them in felt-and-brocade outfits she sewed herself. Last night, as Martha wondered what she could possibly put on a newborn, she remembered these tiny clothes.

Though now that they were in her hands, she hesitated. What kind of an adult would emerge from a baby dressed this way? Fanciful? Religious? Mawkish? Martha projected a slide carriage of images, all of them contrary to herself, only to interrupt her musing. Nothing that happened so early in a baby's life would determine personality, and there was no guarantee that anyone who cared for this baby today would do so tomorrow. Martha packed these clothes.

That done, she asked herself where to go. She

needed a location where she could assess the next day or two. Also important were more formula, diapers, and authentic clothes—and advice on caring for a newborn. Then it came to her: Eva. Perhaps the store was inadequate for an overnight stay, but supplies and maternal knowledge could be found there. It opened at eight a.m., an hour from now, which coincided nicely with the time it would take to drive that far.

She removed her address book from her desk. There was a pay phone at the service station between the farmhouse and Well's Bottom. It was on Old Creamery Road, just beyond the two-lane bridge that crossed the river. Calling from there, where she'd arrive a half hour from now, would be more considerate than calling this early. She flipped open the address book and lifted her pen. Then her telephone rang.

Martha's phone did not ring except on December 24, when students called to ascertain whether her open house would proceed the next day, and she was always stunned out of her chair when that first call came. Now she felt more than startled. The School authorities, and perhaps the police, must already be on their way to search for Number Forty-two.

Or—they had learned about the baby.

What had seemed to be a hastily constructed plan suddenly revealed itself to have been absurdly slow. Why hadn't she departed last night? Why had she wasted time packing?

How soon could she and the baby vanish now?

She threw the address book into her suitcase and clicked the latches shut.

In the attic, the baby was still asleep. Martha lifted the basket gently. The baby didn't stir. The phone completed its fourth ring. Holding the basket close, she returned to her study.

Seventh ring.

She held the basket with one arm around the rim, and with the other she lifted the suitcase. Then her desk blotter caught her eye. This map was her most prized possession, as precious as a family portrait; her students had moved to thirty-nine states so far, and each of their homes was marked with a dot. She worked it free and hastened downstairs.

The phone rang for the twelfth time, then stopped.

She seized bottles of formula from the icebox, a jacket from its hook. The phone began again as she got into her Buick, set the basket on the floor in the front, threw the map into the back. She turned on the engine and pulled around to the front field.

The driveway to the road was flooded.

"Darn." The word brought her palm to her lips. It was the worst profanity she ever thought, and she never uttered it. But the word, now out in the air, did not make her feel as coarse as she'd imagined. She set her hands on the steering wheel and steered away from the gravel drive and onto the field itself. Mud flew, her tires found traction, and she began to descend. It was a thrill, moving over the field without a proper surface. Even more thrilling was the last sound she heard as she reached a break in the trees near the bottom. It was the twelfth ring—the second round of efforts to reach her—and then silence.

She emerged from the trees and turned the car onto Old Creamery Road.

On her left stood the lighthouse man, waiting for the mail carrier. Would she tell her students about this event at Christmas? Would she write them letters about it later this week? The baby began to moan; Martha could not think about the future. She rounded the car past fallen branches and headed east.

After a few miles, during which Martha saw no one on the road, the child quieted. Yet Martha herself could not calm down. She was heading toward a student she hoped would provide assistance, though she had always refrained from turning to her students for support. There was, after all, a natural law to the universe. Parents watched over their children. Wives yielded to their husbands. Teachers guided their students. Yet a mother had just entrusted Martha with her child. Martha had already done what her husband would never do. Would it truly be a violation if she turned to a student this one time?

This much she knew: She had begun to change last night. She had climbed to the attic, and sat beside the baby, and thought, *I am all you have now.* And she'd felt an opening in her chest where she hadn't known anything was closed. She had reached down into the bed of mending, and when her hands touched the baby's flesh, she remembered that she'd never touched her son. She'd lifted the girl slowly. The baby was light, her tiny eyes closed. Martha held the baby to her chest and felt the little heart beating into hers. It was a heart she'd waited decades to hear; and she thought, *What kind of life awaits you? Will you be reunited with your mother soon? Or will you never know who she is? Will I be a part of your life? Or can I only fulfill her dream for you if I say good-bye?* The openness in her chest pulled her toward the baby, allowing their heartbeats to fall into step. Martha's heart was bigger, but the baby's heart beat louder.

Now, hoping to hear something about the desperate flight of the School escapees, Martha turned on the radio. The news was on, though it was talking about last night's storm, saying many roads were closed. She'd barely been noticing the road, and she refocused. She was just about to pass the one intersection that provided an alternate route, Scheier Pike, a twisting, hilly, two-lane highway. But Scheier Pike went north through the mountains for twenty miles before the next bridge. So Martha stayed on Old Creamery Road, the straight shot to Well's Bottom.

Soon the woods that had hugged the shoulder for the first many miles thinned to pastures and orchards, and Martha saw that low-lying areas were indeed flooded. The sports came on, and then more news. Martha listened until the reporter returned to talking about the storm. How could they say nothing about two people who had disappeared? She turned off the radio.

Ahead was the entrance to a camp for Boy Scouts that was closed for the season. It was the last landmark before the river, and just after she passed it and the road began its long slope down, Martha finally saw another car. It was moving slowly, and she saw through its back window that it was following other cars. As the road tilted toward the river, their speed dropped. Then they all came to a halt.

She waited. The man in front of her stepped onto the road, looking ahead.

She lowered her window. "Can you see what's happening?"

"I think the bridge got washed out."

She should have considered this. But the bridge had never been closed before.

"Darn," she said again, this time without her hand to her lips.

She opened her door, hoping to see this novel sight. People ahead were already walking forward. She was around the final bend from the bridge, so the walk would not be far—yet what if she happened upon a police officer? She closed the door and rolled up her window. Her watch said ten after eight.

They could wait this out, she thought. There was already a truck behind her, so waiting was the most cooperative option. Then she heard a whimper, and as she looked into the basket, the baby opened her mouth and began to cry.

The panic of last night returned, though for new reasons. What did this cry mean? Was the baby hungry or in need of a diaper? Was she simply unsettled by the cessation of the car's motion? The baby's volume rose. Then Martha remembered she wasn't quite the Martha she'd been yesterday. She knew how to angle a bottle. She knew she could find first steps.

She told herself, *Just do what you need to do—as any mother would.*

She made a U-turn and drove away from the river.

This time she felt only anxiety and doubt. She

had nothing to provide guidance besides a shriek-
ing baby, the contents of the car, and the road
before her.

She moved forward, her thoughts scrambling.
Then she saw the entrance to the closed camp.
She could turn off the road, that's what she could
do. Quiet the baby here.

The chain closing off the dirt road into camp
was on the ground, so she drove over it. She had
not been down here for years, though nothing had
changed, and soon she entered a campsite with fir
trees and wooden bunks. They hugged the western
bank of the river, where there were swimming and
fishing areas and, farther down, a low-head dam.

She stopped the car in the muddy parking lot
and could see the river across the campsite. The
water was brown and rushing fast and had swelled
far up the banks.

Martha reached into the basket and took the
crying baby in her arms. The girl's face was red and
her cries pitiful. At least Martha now had a better
sense of how to translate this particular sound; the
makeshift diaper was not wet.

With the baby in one arm, Martha opened the
back door, maneuvered the suitcase, and removed
a bottle of formula. She sat down in the car and,
with the experience of last night instructing her,
figured out how to hold the baby; the cries, however, persisted, and the baby would not open her

mouth to receive the nipple. After a few moments of terror, Martha did the only thing she could think of. Baby in her arms, bottle in one hand, Martha stood and walked slowly.

The effect was swift. By the first patch of bunks, the baby had hushed. By the second, she'd begun taking the bottle.

Martha decided not to turn back until the child was finished. Besides, it felt good to be under the sky, even if it was obscured by trees. It felt good to take in fresh air. The scent of sap and fir and wet soil, the sound of the baby sucking, helped Martha's heart beat more evenly.

Soon she came near a swimming dock. Built out from higher ground, it remained barely above the water. Perhaps as she enjoyed this respite from her worries, she might take a step onto it to see the swirling water below. The baby swallowed, making noises of contentment, and as Martha neared the dock, something atop a post at the far end caught her eye. She tested the planks with her feet and moved out over the water. As she and the baby neared, she saw that it was a hat. No, a cap, just like the one her husband used to wear.

Just like the one she'd given to Number Forty-two.

She stopped. She could see it clearly. The brown wool. The moth-eaten hole.

She looked behind her. The bunks responded

with silence. She almost called out, then remembered he couldn't hear.

She went to the edge of the dock and retrieved the cap with her free hand. She held it up to her face. It smelled like Earl, and she closed her eyes and felt him beside her on the bed, felt herself longing to reach over and rest her hands on his chest and look into his eyes with such love that he would see through his haze of sadness and find her again, right in front of him. Then he would touch her face, and forgive the universe its chaos, and forgive her their broken child.

She opened her eyes. *Where was the man?*

Maybe he'd slept on one of the shores or climbed one of the trees to avoid the water. She scanned the river. The streaming water was the color of earth. She saw nothing but far more water than the banks ahead could hold, rushing toward the net that marked the swimming boundaries of the camp, then onto the edge of the low-head dam. She hadn't noticed the roar from the dam but heard it now. Surely Old Creamery Bridge would be closed all day. Everyone on this side of the river would have to remain here.

She turned and looked upstream. The view was similar, though a huge branch was in the water, racing toward the campsite. The currents were so swift, the branch passed beneath the dock within seconds, then sped on. *It will get caught in the net,* she thought. When it didn't, she realized the net had torn. She watched the branch tumble over the edge of the dam.

She fingered the hat, looking to both shores for traces of the man. Still feeding the baby, she left the dock and picked her way down the western bank. She saw nothing except debris streaming along in the river: past the final float for swimmers, past the torn net, past the signs that read, NO BOATING BEYOND THIS POINT. She walked until she reached the vertical face of the dam. As she'd expected, in the churning water beneath, the branch and debris bobbed on the surface, got sucked under, then returned to the surface, over and over, stuck in the cycling water. Then something captured her gaze. Rising to the surface was a piece of dark clothing. Her husband's jacket—which she'd given the man. It went under, and her husband's shirt rose.

She went cold. Number Forty-two must have come to the dock in the rain, hoping to swim across the river to make his way back to Lynnie. He must have taken off the cap and set it on the dock. He must have dived into the water in the night. But he'd been swept downstream and over the dam. The backwash had caught him and sucked his clothes from his body.

The net had been put up because canoeists had been lost. Some had never been found.

* * *

Martha's heart pounded as she drove the only way she could: west on Old Creamery Road. It was impossible—the man could not have drowned. She had only just met him. She had watched him look at this baby with a care that could conquer all the trouble he and Lynnie must have endured to reach the farm. Yet his strength had been no match for the current and the spinning water.

She touched the cap, which lay on the seat beside her, in that way touching both Earl and the man. Then she raised her hand to her lips and breathed in the scent of the two men who were no more.

Thank goodness the baby was asleep again. Thank goodness she might never know what happened to this man. Yet Number Forty-two had helped this baby escape into the world; and could there be a tale more worthy of remembrance? Maybe Martha should write it down when they reached wherever they were going tonight. Maybe she should place this sad story inside the hat and make every effort to ensure that whatever happened, both remained with the baby.

Martha turned the radio back on. Surely she would hear about a body found in the river. Though the authorities would probably keep it quiet until they knew the man's identity—and since he'd be wearing nothing except her husband's trousers, if even that, they would not be able to identify him. He would just be a man who, if found at all, would be buried as John Doe.

Martha kept looking at the baby, then pulling her gaze back to the road. Everything was going wrong. Lynnie had been apprehended. Number Forty-two had drowned. Martha herself was driving in the opposite direction from Well's Bottom. It was already nine o'clock.

She should return to the farm.

She had a barn, a springhouse. She could hide the baby in one of them. She was heading that way anyhow, unless she took Scheier Pike—which would only deposit her at the distant bridge. What if that was out, too?

She could not think. She could barely see. She felt like an egg dropped from up high, shattered into pieces that skittered to faraway corners.

The intersection was near. She thought of Robert Frost, coming upon two roads diverging in the woods. One wanted wear, and although he longed to take the other, he took the one less traveled by, and that made all the difference.

She was not a poet. She was not an adventurer. She was not even a mother. She was only someone who had given her word to a request she had not understood. For the first time, she wondered: What would happen if the baby was found?

But how could Martha take that chance?

There it was, up ahead: two small signs. One

pointed the way home, west on Old Creamery Road. The other pointed north, Scheier Pike, the way she never needed to go. How she ached to return to her house, with everything she knew, with walls so unbroken by windows that they'd protect her—though not the baby. And now, fingering the brim of the hat, she felt more obliged than ever to do as Lynnie had asked.

She took the road north.

The Well's Bottom of 1968 bore a remarkable resemblance to the Well's Bottom of 1918, when Martha and Earl drove off from the church where they'd just wed to his farm out in the country. Mom-and-pop stores reigned, the local theater bore a grand chandelier, Independence Day was celebrated on the town green, freight trains carried coal and steel, and the number of births approximated the number of deaths. A few differences did distinguish 1968. There was talk of a new bypass that would siphon trucks away from Main Street. A Chinese family had opened a restaurant. A few people owned color consoles, with wavy green television pictures. But the riots of Detroit and Newark and Los Angeles, and the marches in Washington, were distant news. Change was not screaming in Well's Bottom. Change was barely a whisper.

Yet when Martha reached town, she imagined

she heard that whisper. She pulled into the most inconspicuous place she could find, an old stable in one of the many alleys that paralleled the main streets. It was noon, and except for two stops for feeding and changing, the child's eyes had been closed. Though as Martha lifted the basket, she felt her own vision open, as she took in what she'd always seen and suddenly found different.

Arm encircling the basket, Martha passed two children as she hurried the block to Eva's back door. Dressed in yellow raincoats and galoshes, they were laughing at a puppy jumping through puddles, and for the first time in her life, Martha was struck by the ease with which they played right out in the open. Martha looked up to the silver blue sky. Somewhere under that sky was Lynnie, somewhere else the body of the man. Martha had seen none like them playing in puddles. She had never noticed that before.

The back door said, HANSBERRY PHARMACY— DELIVERIES. Martha stepped onto the wooden stoop and pressed the bell. She could hear voices on the other side of the door. It felt like the first day of school, as she stood outside her classroom and heard, at the far end of the schoolhouse, children enter the building. Though today there would be no "Good morning, class," or even "Welcome to fifth grade." She felt as bereft of vocabulary as Lynnie was.

The door opened.

Eva was pushing her brown hair back toward her ponytail as she took in the figure at the door. Her round face was as flushed as ever, and for a moment it seemed she was so caught up in her responsibilities, she could not make sense of the face into which she was gazing. Then she caught herself. "Mrs. Zimmer?" she asked.

Martha opened her mouth, but nothing emerged.

"What are you...," Eva began, and then asked, "Is everything all right?"

No, Martha wanted to say. There was so much that was not all right—so much about which she knew too little—so much *she should have known*—that she just stood, her mouth a stone.

In the silence between them, Eva's expression darkened with worry. Now her gaze went down, apparently trying to determine the problem that brought her old teacher to the store—a scraped elbow? cut finger? Her gaze lit on the basket. Her eyes widened.

She looked up at her old teacher. "Please," Eva said. "Come in."

Eva offered Martha a seat at a Formica table in the stockroom, where Eva's teenage son, Oliver, often did homework, and where a compact kitchen allowed her to serve dinner without going to the apartment upstairs. She put on a kettle, and Martha, forcing words out, told her about the night before. Eva's eyes were kind, and when she heard a customer enter the store and disappeared through the swinging door, Martha remembered why Eva had been the confidante of many girls in eighth grade: She had a gentle way about her and listened without judgment.

Martha heard the bells on the front door, and then Eva returned. "I put up the CLOSED sign," she said, and, sensing Martha's needs, took the baby from her hands. Looking into the tiny face, she explained that Don was delivering a prescription to an elderly couple across town and would return momentarily; did Martha need to hide the baby from him?

"He can know," Martha said.

"Then may I bathe her?" Eva asked, and Martha, for the first time since the knock on her door last night, started to cry.

Eva did not press for Martha's grander plan, as she found a bathing basin, placed it in the sink, and filled it with water. She did not ask Martha for a next step as she tenderly washed the last remnants of the birth. She simply described what she was doing and invited Martha's hands into the water, and the tears receded as the baby grew clean.

Then, after producing diapers, flannel infant clothes, and formula, Eva rocked the baby in her arms. "I don't know what I'd have done in your shoes, Mrs. Zimmer."

Martha wanted to say she was just doing what seemed right. But the back door opened then, and Don came in. Tall, bearded Don, with his blondish red hair. He gave Eva a confused look, and she asked him to sit, and as Martha listened to Eva tell Don what happened the night before, Martha thought, *I am not alone in this*. Only then, as relief spread, did she realize how tense she'd been.

"Actually," Don said, leaning forward, "I've had some experience with the School."

Martha started.

"You might remember that I attended seminary. Well"—he shook his head—"right after I finished, I worked at the School as a chaplain."

"I had no idea."

"I held services, but the staff rarely brought anyone, so after a while I just went to the cottages to talk to the residents. That was eye-opening…and troubling. Finally, I just couldn't do it anymore. I told Eva I'd rather take over the store."

"It wasn't an easy decision for us," Eva said. "But it was the right decision."

"So here's an educated guess about why Lynnie wants you to hide her baby. Sometimes the state takes kids away from parents who are doing a bad job raising them, and the kids get placed in the School. They're treated just like any other resident—which, I'm afraid, is miserably. Lynnie was probably worried about that happening to her child."

Martha said, "Lynnie would have been there to keep an eye out for her."

"I doubt it. Babies are isolated from the adults. She might never have seen her again."

Never see her baby again, Martha thought. A long silence passed. Martha held the baby close to her chest, cradling her head the way Eva had showed her. She felt the body, so light in her arms, so warm against her sweater. She felt the breath against her chest.

Finally Martha said, "I'm too old to care for a child. Should I go to the School and try to get Lynnie out?"

Eva and Don looked at each other and then down at the table. "They'd never release her to you," Don said. He looked back up. "You're not re-lated to her, you're not an official. You don't have any connection to her."

Martha said, "But I obviously can't leave the baby in the care of anyone around here. Whatever will I do?"

For endless minutes, no one spoke. Then Eva stood up and walked across the kitchen, her arms folded over her chest. Looking out the window, she said, "Do you remember what you used to teach us in arts and crafts? You'd say, 'Follow your inclination. It will take you to thoughts you'd never known you'd had.'"

Martha remembered saying that, year after year, to her classes. It was the opposite of planning. It was the path less traveled.

"I never forgot that," Eva said, turning around. "Not that it helped me with tests." She smiled. "But when I was sitting in front of a pile of construction paper and glitter, it reassured me that I'd be able to do something beautiful with it."

Martha smiled, pressing her cheek to the baby's soft stomach, inhaling the sweet scent. It was so like milk and honey. So beautiful.

She looked up. "I just wish I knew my first step."

Eva glanced at her husband and back at Martha. "We can help you with that," she said.

They set out at dusk. Don was driving the first car—Martha's Buick. Martha and the baby were next, in the used Dodge that Don had purchased that afternoon. The car dealer had lost his signs in the storm, and along with the road closings, he'd thought he might not get business for days. So he was glad to strike a deal with Don, especially once he found out the car was for a young family fifty miles off. Taking up the rear of the caravan was Eva, in the Hansberrys' Ford wagon, with teenage Oliver. He'd agreed to help out at Martha's farm until she returned.

"When will that be?" Oliver had asked, putting on a coat over his football jersey.

"Soon," Don said.

"A while," Eva said.

"I have no idea," Martha said.

And then they all laughed.

While Don was buying the used car, Eva copied down the listings in Martha's address book. She also gave Martha a crash course in child care. Then she dashed off to the florist; they'd decided they needed four flowers.

The sun was down by the time their chain of cars had reached the borough limits; the moon was high by the time they reached Old Creamery Bridge, which had reopened late in the day. After they crossed the bridge, they turned into the campsite.

The river still overran its banks. With Oliver holding a flashlight, they went out to the dock, where Don, putting to use his clerical training for the first time in years, led them in the Twenty-third Psalm, paying respects to a man whose body might never be found.

Martha felt the baby's heart again beside hers as they all said, "Though I walk through the valley of the shadow of death, I will fear no evil, for Thou art with me." She understood that for Eva and Don, these words mattered. Yet she could not help but wonder how there could be a God if people treated this man as they had, and Lynnie was forced to live in a place like the School—and this child could be doomed to a life of desolation.

As the prayer settled over the night, Eva produced the four chrysanthemums, and Don, Oliver, Martha, and Eva each tossed one into the water.

They embraced by the cars, then drove out of the camp in single file. Martha felt oddly different and knew it was the whisper of change again: She was not the person she'd thought herself to be only last night.

She clicked on her turn signal, and at the intersection she turned north. The others continued straight ahead, palms lifted, waving good-bye and good luck.

The Hand Speaker

NUMBER FORTY-TWO

1968

*N*umber Forty-two did not know that prayers were uttered on his behalf that November night, when Martha and the baby stood on the dock with the Hansberrys and sanctified his death with a psalm and flowers. But this was not because he couldn't hear.

It was because of the night before, when he'd embarked on a trail now followed by the chrysanthemums that had just been cast into the water and begun voyaging downstream, twirling like the ladies' hats he and his big brother Blue had once watched from a pecan tree at a church revival. Ahead of the flowers, the dam waited to catch them in its spin, just like it had caught Number Forty-two, as Martha had surmised. But she couldn't know that he'd once seen what dams could do, when Blue took him fishing and they

saw a raccoon bobbing beneath one, unable to escape. Nor could she know that last night, as the
water plunged him down the concrete wall of the
dam and he was sucked into a spin, his blood went
electric with panic—and purpose. With how fully
Beautiful Girl had opened his heart and how perfect Little One had felt in his arms and how fran-
tically he needed to return to them both. He went
into a frenzy of kicks and elbows, but he was already spinning a second time, the coat leaving his
body, the shirt buttons popping, the sleeves drawing away from him like a departing spirit. Chest
screaming in a plea for breath, he looped a third
time, thinking of all he'd survived to get so close
to freedom, raging at the cruelty of going down
like this. And then he seized hold of the raccoon
memory: He and Blue had made a guess at what
men would do in similar straits, and he followed
the guess. He tucked his chin, drew his knees to
his chest, hugged himself—and the water shot him
forward like a man from a cannon. He flew along
the bed of the river, arms at his sides, legs behind
him, heart lifting, until he finally broke the surface—in the same spot where the three remaining
flowers now rose from the depths.

He heaved his arms up to swim to the shore.
The currents, though, drove relentlessly ahead,
herding him on. Past the split-rail fence that
marked the edge of the Boy Scout camp. Below

Old Creamery Bridge. The river widened and the miles tallied up swiftly, along with barns and trailers. Businesses began appearing—a lumberyard, factories, mills, where a wheel scooped up two of the mums. And then, just as the river opened wide, he spied, in the rushing water beside him, the refuge of a floating door.

Forty-two hoisted himself onto the wood. Winded, weakened, unable to stop the charge forward, he held on, beneath bridges, past flood walls, into the nighttime glow of a city. *Again*, he said to himself, his thoughts coming in the southern drawl he'd spoken before the fever. *I can't believe it. Running again.*

He jumped his mind to better places. Little One sleeping in the old lady's basket. Beautiful Girl shaking her head no to the first many houses, pressing on until the one that felt right. That first tractor ride, when Forty-two spoke to Beautiful Girl with his signs, and she slowly lifted her hands and tried to copy his. For so many years at the Snare, he'd just been ignored or smirked at or bossed around. The only others who'd signed to him—an official he saw once, and a man stuck there like him—made nonsense signs, and when he showed them how to do it right, their eyes went blank. But that day on the tractor, Beautiful Girl watched his every gesture, her brow deep in concentration, until her smile opened wide with respect.

But—and the sadness of it flickered in his gut—Beautiful Girl did not know his name.

In the place he called the Snare of Stone Walls, he'd been a John Doe. More specifically, he was the forty-second John Doe caught in the system. He didn't know this. He did know how to count, because his mama had taught him: There were two rooms in their shack, four directions to the wind, seven brothers and sisters, ten silver circles to one green rectangle, twelve houses in the dale where they'd lived. After he got stuck in the Snare, he kept count of the times the circus came and got all the way up to twenty-three. After the last planting season, he counted forty-two breaths to get from the tractor shed to Chubby Redhead's office, where Beautiful Girl would be waiting. So forty-two was his favorite number. But he'd never thought it might be his name. He'd never read his chart. He'd never read anything. He'd never set foot in a school.

Only he knew his real name.

It was a name his mama made up after the birthing lady left: Homan. Mama was thinking of homing pigeons, hoping the name would send a message to his daddy to come back from the other woman's house. Her wordplay did no good, and by his teething time, Mama had to move them in with Gramps and Mama's baby brother, Bludell—whom everyone called Blue. After the fever, when

Homan's brothers and sisters kept their distance, thinking they could catch deafness, Blue made up a sign for Homan's name, and whenever Homan met someone new he'd use it, saying it with his voice at the same time. *HO mun*. They just laughed, shaking their heads as if he were simple-minded. Soon, like Beautiful Girl, Homan became two people: the one inside that was the truth, and the one outside that almost everyone believed him to be.

The lone chrysanthemum rode on downriver. Ahead lay a concrete slipway, and above it was a warehouse with smashed windows. It was the kind of site that attracts rule breakers: underage beer guzzlers, soldiers shipping off to war with finally relenting girlfriends, hippies. And one desperate, banged-up man who'd washed up from a door, as night had begun draining into day.

Homan wanted to run as soon as he came to. But he was lying on his side, and when he opened his eyes, he saw the silhouettes of a man and woman standing over him and felt a hard tapping against his legs. It was the man, he realized, poking him with his foot, as if checking to see that Homan was alive. With the morning sun rising behind them, Homan couldn't see their faces. Now, though, he knew the way east, and east was the way to Beautiful Girl.

It seemed a good idea to take stock of his surroundings before he made a move, which meant
giving the once-over to this couple. Blue had
taught him this rule when Homan could still hear:
Always know the jabber who sharing your ring.

The shape of their hair and features told him
they were white. The woman was thin and wore
her hair curled at the shoulders like a lady he saw
on television. When she stepped closer, Homan
could make out her clothes: a short fur coat, a
tiny red-and-white polka-dot dress with a red sash,
white boots to her knees. The man circled him, as
if Homan were a skunk that might spray, and when
he moved into the sunlight, Homan could see his
cheeks were a foamy white—shaving cream, Homan recognized. *What this joker doing outside with
shaving cream on? People out in the world going crazy?*
The man, in a leather coat with jeans, was stout as
a pig going to market.

The woman bent beside Homan. She was pretty
but couldn't hold a candle to Beautiful Girl—who
must have been back in the Snare already, waiting
for him to return. He propped himself up on an
elbow as the woman looked to the man with the
shaving cream, her mouth moving. Homan had
barely understood Mama's and Blue's lips, so no way
was he following anyone else. His leg was hurting,
too, and he wanted to look down to see why. But
just as he was about to, the woman—*Polka-Dot*—

reached forward to touch Homan's leg, and that made the man—*Pudding-Cheek*—narrow his eyes with a sneer. Dot turned up toward him, and he nodded at her like he meant the opposite of a nod, and with each nod Dot shrank into herself.

Then Pudding was walking away, waving his arm behind like he was pushing a door shut. Dot kept touching Homan's hurting leg, and he could see she was younger than Beautiful Girl. With a face that looked scared for herself and sorry for him, she opened her mouth to speak.

He shook his head hard and pointed to his ears.

Everyone froze for a moment. Five whole breaths passed.

Then Pudding stormed back and got going with the Yell Face, and Dot started in on the Baby Talk Face—the faces most hearing folks put on when they caught on about Homan's deafness. He hoped they'd give up fast. *Don't let them make you feel like some no-account flea,* the McClintocks used to sign, *just 'cause you ain't hearing. They talk at you and think they a growed-up crow talking to a baby crow. But they really a crow talking to a lion.*

Dot and Pudding went on, now to each other, and Homan sat up. To the left stood the warehouse, before him stretched a parking lot, and beyond it were weathered picnic tables. One had things piled on top—they looked like cans of soup and shaving cream. Farther out were dumped washers. The lot had only one rusty car, its back-seat heaped high with clothes.

He recognized what everything was, though he hadn't grown up around warehouses, washers, or slipways. He'd grown up around cotton fields, tin bathing tubs, wooden stoves. He'd grown up going to the woods with Blue and learning to track deer, or looking into the paved streets of the Fork, where the white folks' houses began. The last colored house before the Fork was where the McClintock boys lived and ran an auto repair shop. Like him, they did not hear. He'd goof around with them in front of their garage, watching the talk of their hands. He and Blue would bring them fish they'd caught in the creek.

Blue had once explained that creek water went up into clouds and came down as rain. Much later, when Homan saw Beautiful Girl's drawing of a tall tower overlooking the sea, he was amazed by the huge, aqua water, so different from the creek, so filled with white foam and pointy waves. Beautiful Girl, seeing him marvel, drew another picture, of a person crying. She pointed to the tears, then back to the picture of the sea. Homan understood: Crying came from the sea and went back to the sea. He folded the first picture into his pocket and hid it in the barn, under the hay.

Dot and Pudding still disputing, Homan knew it was time to make a run for it. The river was flowing south, he could see. He just had to make his way north along the shore all the way to the dock, then go east. He had no idea how far he'd come and might have to do a fair amount of swimming upstream and trespassing, but he'd taken harder journeys before.

He rose to his feet—and his leg buckled like a car hood falling closed.

The couple whirled around. He looked down. His pants had torn, and the leg beneath had a bloody streak. With a blast of fear, Homan realized that with one hurt leg, he'd have to limp the many miles between him and Beautiful Girl, and right now he couldn't even stand.

But look: Dot was making a pleading face at Pudding, and Pudding was shaking his head. Then Dot combed her fingers through Pudding's fuzzy gray hair, untied the knot of her red sash, and used it to wipe shaving cream off Pudding's lips. His eyes softened. Then they draped Homan's arms over their shoulders and walked him to a picnic table.

They ain't no threat, Homan told himself. *Just bide your time till you can leave.*

While Dot went back to the car, Pudding took a seat at the picnic table with the cans of shaving cream and soup. He picked up a slice of steel that had been lying flat and flipped it end over end—a knife. Pudding peered at Homan out of the corner of his eye to make sure he got a look. Then Pudding stuck the knife straight into the wood so it jutted up into the air.

Dot returned from the car, holding some things in her arms, with a worried look on her face, like the boys who cringed around the guards. She set her things on Homan's table: a paper sack, brown glass bottle, and white box with a red cross on it. Then she took a sandwich from the sack, opened the top of the bottle, and handed both to Homan. He hesitated. But she made a smile at him through her worry, and the sandwich did taste good. The drink did not—it was bubbly and had a bitter smell like the one the guard with the dogs had every day. Yet Homan was too thirsty to stop.

The girl knelt beside him and used a cloth to wet down the gash.

All this time, Pudding was spooning up soup from a can. When he finished, he pulled the knife from the wood. That was their sign, Homan guessed, because Dot set down her cloth then, hurried over, and sat on his lap, legs on either side of his hips. She took the knife from Pudding, drew the edge against the shaving cream, and wiped it on the bench between strokes.

Homan finished the sandwich, watching. The world must have changed a lot in twenty-three years. Womenfolk were shaving men's faces—right out in the light of day.

When Dot finished, Pudding stabbed the knife

back into the table. Then she gave him a huge kiss, and he pulled her too close. Homan looked away. He wished he felt good enough to jump in the river. He wished he knew where he was or could understand maps. The one map he'd seen, at the McClintocks', looked like nothing more than a sketch of a deer leaping.

He was suddenly so tired. He set his head on the table, tasting the bitter drink in his mouth, and the taste made his tongue feel fat. So when Dot came over from the newly shaven Pudding and made a lay-your-head-on-a-pillow gesture and indicated the car, he let them move him across the lot. For a long time to come, when he looked back on this bend in the river of his life, he couldn't believe he'd downed that brew without a second thought or given in so quickly to the drowsiness.

The car stank of mold and potato chips. He remembered how Beautiful Girl loved to breathe in scents, but only if they were pleasing, like pinecones and lilacs and the air before a rain. Once he picked the sweetest-smelling white flower from the magnolia tree near the administrative office, hid it until they saw each other again, then set it behind her beautiful ear.

Dot pushed clothes to the floor, then tossed Homan a sleeping bag and pillow.

Just lay here a short while, he told himself as the couple walked toward the warehouse, Pudding re-

moving his jacket, Dot her fur coat. When the
sun progressed and the couple was still gone, he
thought about the way Beautiful Girl's hair
smelled with that flower and how he'd buried his
face in the scent. By the time the car pulled away,
sleep had taken him over.

He dreamed of running.

He was little, running fast across the yard to the
tree with the tire swing. His uncle Blue caught up
to him and they jumped on the swing together.
Homan tickled Blue's stomach, and their laughing
swung them high into the sky. Blue was eleven
years older and told Homan he should think of
him as his big brother. And Blue was the best big
brother a boy could ever have.

The next running Homan dreamed of was sad.
He was six and saw Blue running away from him,
out of their shack. It was muggy and raining. Blue
must have run to the road where the women were
coming home from the houses they cleaned, because he ran back with Mama. She crumpled next
to Homan with fearful eyes. Then the washcloth
was on Homan's head, and he was on Blue's mule,
Ethel, and they were all running. His body hurt
so bad. Mama bolted into the hospital, came back
out, pointed to the next town over, with the hospital that let colored folk in. By the time the mule
got there, the rain was done and the moon high.

But Homan couldn't make out the bugs or Mama's voice. He pulled Blue close, saying, "What's going on? I can't hear nothing!" Including, he suddenly realized, himself.

He got laughed at a lot after that, and it made him so mad that he kicked the crap out of trees in the yard. Then one day, Blue pulled him along and ran to the McClintocks'. He'd never paid them much mind before, and that day he learned the boys were deaf—and spoke with motion, using signs their daddy taught them before they moved here. Every day after, he and Blue rode Ethel the mule to the McClintocks', and Homan learned a language of pointing and jabbing and fist closing and finger flicking, frowning and shrugging and waving and saluting, brow raising and eye narrowing and lip pursing and head tilting. His anger ran off, and happiness moved in.

When the revival came to town, they all headed to the church. They climbed the pecan tree outside the windows and peered in, touching their hands to the glass. And Homan, feeling the congregation's voices resonate, thought that now that his eyes could hear and his hands could speak, he didn't miss using his ears. Then Fattie McClintock signed, *What you think God is?* Homan asked, *He like the seasons, right? Like the way you ask seasons to end a drought or cold snap and sooner or later they do?* Fattie said, *Yeah. That's what God is.*

Then. That afternoon.

Homan was fifteen, Blue twenty-six. They were at the McClintocks', shooting the breeze around the car they were working on. Ethel was chewing lunch in her feedbag. The boys were eating molasses cake. Wayne Sullivan drove past in his big new car—then drove past again, slower. His daddy was Mr. Landis, the white man who owned the shoe store and lived with his wife in the house in the Fork that Mama cleaned. Wayne's mama was Mr. Landis's other lady, Velma Sullivan, who had such a fair complexion, you'd never know she was colored. Mr. Landis kept her and Wayne in their own house at the edge of the Fork. Now Wayne was passing the McClintocks' shop a third time. His friends were with him, and he flicked his lights on and off until he caught the McClintocks' attention. Then he popped his eyes wide and waggled his tongue. His friends scratched under their arms, opening and closing their mouths like animals.

Mighty fine behavior for a rich boy, Tallest McClintock signed.

Fattie explained, *He just mad his girl brought us her car yesterday.*

Then he especial mad at him, added Buck-Toothed McClintock, pointing to Blue, *owing to he gave her a ride home on that mule while her car was setting here.*

Homan felt the old tree-kicking anger come

back. He told himself to ignore Wayne and might have succeeded if Blue hadn't shouted something out. Homan could only guess what it was, but the look on Blue's face said it was a name for nasty folks. Like maybe "Swine-butt."

Then Wayne braked the car, and before Homan knew it, the whole pack was taking baseball bats from the back and climbing out and slamming those bats on the car the boys were working on. Right on the windshield! The headlights! The boys, trying to stop them, got pushed to the ground. Blue grew so mad that he body-slammed Wayne, bringing him down, too. The McClin-tocks, rising to their feet, laughed—*That'll teach him to get above himself*, they signed. Wayne scowled at Blue as he got up, slung the bat over his shoulder, and dusted himself off. He turned to go. He fixed his eyes on his car. But just before he reached it, he turned back, right in front of the feeding mule. Then he lifted that bat and smashed Ethel in the head.

With a scream Homan could see, Blue ran after the car. But it was going too fast.

That night: Blue crying in their bed, Homan shaking with rage.

He would always remember how, the next morning, when he and Blue went down to Wayne's house, the honeysuckle was in bloom. They had no weapon. They had no plan.

The shiny new car was sitting out in front of Wayne's house.

Homan, full of anger, darted to the car, opened the front door, and slid behind the wheel.

Blue gave him a *What you doing?* look through the windshield.

Homan smiled as if to say, *You'll see.* Blue pounded on the hood. But Homan just went ahead and did what the McClintocks taught him to do. The car moved forward. He pressed his foot to the pedal, picked up speed, and jumped out. The driverless car drove up from the curb, across the lawn, and into the living room wall.

He felt the ground shake. Blue's eyes went wide with delight—and then horror. The front door was opening, Miss Velma was coming out in her robe, and Wayne was behind her.

Blue made one of the only signs he knew. *Run.*

Homan ran out of eyeshot of their house, feeling Blue at his feet. He ran to the end of the block. He knew Blue was lagging behind. He wanted him to run faster, faster—*like me!*

He whipped around to make sure Blue was there.

Blue was three houses back—lying on the ground. Not moving. A red hole in his chest. Wayne was nowhere near. It was Mr. Landis who was there, standing above. It looked as if he'd spent the night with Miss Velma and brought his shotgun. And was now turning the barrel from Blue, looking to the end of the street, seeing right into Homan's eyes, raising his gun—

Homan ran.

He tore down the next block. He leapt one fence, two, five, yard to yard to yard. He ripped into groves of trees, through a lake, across tobacco farms, over streams. He ran as though his feet were on fire. Blue was gone. They would be after Homan. Mama would lose her job. Mama could never take him back. He had nothing left but running.

He ran all day and all night. And the next day and night. He ran through towns and then across states whose names he didn't know. He ran in rain and heat and snow. He ran long after he gave this time in his life a name. *The Running*. He ran and ran until they caught him in Well's Bottom, a place where no one believed that hands could ever speak.

He felt the car come to a stop. It was night now, but Homan wore no watch and did not know how to tell time. He tried to angle his head to see the stars. The sky was thick with haze.

He felt the door open. There was Pudding, indicating with his thumb that Homan should get out.

His leg still hurt, though he could stand. The day had grown cold, so as he looked around, he wrapped the sleeping bag over his shoulders. Brick buildings were pressed tight together, lining streets without trees. Stores were gated closed. A train bridge crossed overhead a few blocks off. It was a city, he understood. Why had they stopped here? And why was Dot sitting on the hood, fingering the ends of her hair, while Pudding was reaching into the trunk, pulling something out? Another fur coat, Homan saw as the trunk closed. Rabbit fur. He remembered finding a rabbit outside the barn once and holding it up so Beautiful Girl could stroke it. This made her smile.

Pudding was acting so strange, patting the coat like someone was already in it and he was checking the fit. Then he handed the coat to Homan.

It felt good, with a lining that was smooth against his skin and the softest fur on the outside. He'd never worn a fur coat, and he felt fancy and lucky, even though it was too small for the buttons to reach the holes. He held the front together.

Then Pudding made a gesture toward something at the end of the street.

It was a fenced-in lot, with gray-and-orange trucks parked in neat rows and a small building in the center. The fence was chain link with barbed wire on top.

He looked at Pudding with a question on his face. Pudding just waved his hand, egging Homan forward. Homan shot a glance at Dot, who was still on the hood, gazing nowhere. Maybe they were saying he was free to leave, and he almost laughed with relief. But Dot had been nice to him, so he clapped his hands to signal a good-bye.

Pudding threw his arms in the air. His nostrils grew wide, his eyebrows fierce, and he began speaking. Dot lowered her head, answering into her lap. Then she jumped off the hood and walked toward Homan.

He couldn't understand what was happening. Pudding was jabbing his finger at her, and she was turning to Homan, making eating gestures, pointing at the building. He didn't want to laugh anymore. He wanted to run. Then he thought of Pudding's knife. If Homan didn't do what she wanted, what would happen to her?

She took Homan's arm and he allowed her to step them forward, toward the truck lot. Soon she picked up their pace, looking over her shoulder to see Pudding. Then she turned back and rubbed her belly, as if showing Homan how good the food inside the fence would be.

At the gate, she reached up and turned a dial on a padlock. It sprang open. She walked inside the gate with Homan. The lot was not well lit, and he could smell no food. He felt her hand leave his arm and turned. She was running outside the gate, then locking it behind her.

He lunged at the fence. But as much as he shook it, he could not get out.

Pudding was leaning against the car, pointing to the building. Homan looked at Dot. She cut her gaze away from him, then wiped her cheeks. She turned and walked away.

He could not believe, so soon after breaking out of the Snare, that he was in a lot with nothing except parked trucks and one lonely building. No food. Not even any lights.

Then he saw a short man standing behind the glass door of the building. The man wore a vest and small glasses, and he opened the door and urged Homan to come in. If Homan did, he might have trouble. But what was he going to do out here? And the guy was more of a shrimp than the littlest guard at the Snare. If Homan could outwit the water below the dam, he could pin a pipsqueak like that to the floor. And maybe get something to eat, too.

He went inside, entering a room with a counter and cash register. Without turning on a light, the man gestured toward a doorway, then a flight of stairs. Homan went first, glad there was a window in the staircase letting light from a streetlamp in. He glanced out the window as he passed. Between the trucks and the fence were weeds. In one spot there was just dirt.

Upstairs was a room with a couch and table. A plate with a hot dog sat on the table.

He stepped toward it. The man grabbed him by

the arm and pulled him back, looking annoyed. Homan made a pleading motion. The man said something, and Homan shrugged. Finally, the man curled his fingertips in like spider legs. Homan realized he meant, *Give me.*

Give him what? Homan was the one expecting something.

The man snatched at Homan's new coat.

Homan backed up. The man narrowed his eyes. Homan backed up more.

The man lunged, grabbing again at Homan's coat, sliding his hands beneath. Homan felt the lining give and the man pull back. In his hands was a small package.

Homan understood: The coat was like an envelope. The man just wanted what was inside.

Then the man thrust a real envelope at Homan and shoved him toward the stairs. He tore down them as fast as he could, dashing through the office and into the lot.

Dot was waiting outside the chain-link fence. He ran toward her, grinning, waving the envelope in his hands, ready to get going to Beautiful Girl at last.

But now Dot was running away, and a flashing light caught his eye. He looked around. Three police cars were peeling down the street toward the lot.

He ran. Freeing his arms, shoving the envelope

into the jacket lining, he ran. Not toward the gate, where police were jumping out of cars. He ran to the rear of the lot, where he pulled himself to the top step of the biggest truck. He turned to look. Police were fanning over the lot. He could not let them send him to jail in Edgeville. Or send him back to the Snare. He could not let them arrest him for whatever was making Dot and Pudding drive off right now.

The truck door was unlocked. It took nothing to turn on the engine. It took nothing to press the gas and steer for the chain-link fence. It wasn't even hard to jump out the other side and watch the truck pass right through.

The police tore after the truck. He tore the other way, around the side of the building. He ran to the dirt by the fence and fell to his knees and dug wildly.

Then he was in the hole. For a second he thought of Beautiful Girl, pushing the baby out. He scrabbled forward, thrust himself through, grabbed the ground on the other side.

And he was out. Tearing down the streets, breath hard in his chest, skin sweaty.

Ahead he saw a freight train passing on the bridge, just like so many he'd seen in the Running. He could do it, even though he was no longer fifteen.

Up the train bridge he scrambled. *You can't let*

no one break you, Blue used to say when someone did them wrong. *If you don't let no one break you, you win.* One last heave and he was over the train. One last jump and he slammed down onto a box-car. He pressed his body to the roof.

The train picked up speed until it was shooting through the city, high above the streets. He didn't know where he was leaving. He didn't know where he was going. He just knew he had to get back, and he had to do it soon.

Inside Cinderella's Coach

MARTHA

1968

M artha heard a locomotive in the distance be-fore she opened her eyes. The sound was soothing, so much like the breathing near her ear. The breathing, after all, must be Earl's; and how con-tent she felt being close to him again. Slowly, though, she remembered that Earl had not slept beside her for years, and her farmhouse was nowhere near a train. Then unfamiliar scents be-came apparent: a rustic cabin smell, floral soap, furniture polish. She turned over, groping across the sheets for Earl, tasting a candylike tartness. She kept no candy in her pantry—but then she re-called thumbing up two sourballs from a bowl at a hotel registration desk. Her arm arrived at the far edge of the sheets; the bed was empty. Yet some-one was breathing. And suddenly she saw it again: the suitcase, the drive to Well's Bottom, the journey north on Scheier Pike, the sign in front of her student Henry's hotel, the bell on the registration desk.

The baby.

She sat up. Sunlight cast tree shadows on the window shades. The baby lay in the bassinet Eva Hansberry had given her and that Martha had set up when they'd reached the hotel last night at three a.m. As she'd assembled the bassinet at the foot of the bed, she'd thought about how she had never been up so late, much less while changing a baby. She'd inhaled the woody scent of a fireplace in the lobby two corridors away and listened to rustlings of the mountains outside. She'd peeked behind the shades, but night was too dark in this corner of New York State to see anything. Then, with the baby finally sleeping, Martha put on her nightie and turned back the quilt. Sleep came so swiftly that when the baby's cries woke her later, she discovered she'd failed to draw the quilt over her body. The bedside clock said ten after five. She'd hurried to the baby, worried she'd failed with her, too, and was relieved the cries were only for a bottle. At the next feeding, six fifty, darkness was lifting and the scent of coffee and eggs was drifting in from the dining room; in no condition to make an appearance, she'd slept yet again. Now, although the sun was strong, she was no more ready to face the world.

Saddened by the resurrection, then loss, of Earl, Martha glanced at the bedside clock. *Nine fifteen!* How was that possible? Martha had never enjoyed late risings; she agreed with Earl that "sleeping in" was synonymous with indolence. The hotel clock simply had to be in error. She glanced at her wrist. Incredibly, her watch matched the time on the clock.

She moved to the foot of the bed and knelt beside the bassinet. Earl was gone—but the baby was already familiar. Martha cupped the little head and stroked the thin coating of hair. The baby's face seemed more intricate each time Martha looked, much as books revealed new depths on each rereading. Now, in morning light muted by shades, the baby's cheeks seemed more active, the lips in constant motion. Martha moved in closer. The tiny body invited infinite rereadings as well; for the first time, Martha noticed the baby place her fist to her lips, then suck as if her fist were a bottle. Martha recalled Eva saying the baby would need to feed every few hours; and slowly it occurred to her that she was not seeing overlooked eloquence in an oft-studied novel, but a simple request for a bottle. How about that. Babies asked to eat even in their sleep.

Laughing at her own lofty thoughts, Martha opened the cooler Eva had packed with bottles and that Martha had, after check-in, filled with ice, leaving out one bottle after each feeding so it would be warm enough by the baby's next meal. She retrieved a full bottle from the basin counter, worked her arms under the baby, and sat on the bed.

While she slid the nipple between the pink lips and the baby sucked, Martha considered how, for all the depths she kept finding in this face, there was already much she could recite verbatim. The skin was pale; the face heart-shaped; the eyes set close together. The nose was turned up and slightly large, with a pronounced indentation beneath the nostrils. The lips rose like the crest of a wave; the chin was tiny as the tip of a triangle; the whorls in the ears were sinuous as streams. Martha had to talk herself through each step—patting the baby's back until she burped, changing the diaper, setting the used diaper in the bin Eva had provided, putting on another. She was pleased she'd needed no instructions in contemplating a baby's face.

Holding the child on her shoulder, patting so she would fall back asleep, Martha opened the shades. Rays of light threaded between hemlocks and white pines, and she could make out a sliver of porcelain blue sky. She stood looking, telling herself she needed to decide what to do with the baby. The options seemed as foggy as her recollection of the registration desk. How long could she stay in this room? Should she give the baby to someone better suited to being a mother? As the child breathed back to sleep, Martha wrestled with the unanswerable. Then she returned her to the bassinet and, with relief, turned her attention to this face yet again. It was such a pleasure to gaze upon, and as she studied the fine details, she remembered a belief she'd held as a teacher. There were two kinds of students who liked the library: those who devoured one book after another and those who savored the same book repeatedly. Some teachers saw the former readers as intrepid, the latter tentative, while Martha had held the view that old comforts, by encouraging patience, prompted discoveries. Now, though, Martha understood those rereaders differently. Aware that she was about to behave uncharacteristically by climbing back under the quilt in midmorning, she realized it was not the rereading that led to fresh insights. It was the *rereader*—because when a person is changing inside, there are inevitably new things to see.

A knock, not the baby, woke Martha the next morning.

She drew herself up. The knock paused. She looked at the bassinet, which was bathed in dawn light. The baby was still sleeping. *What an easy child*, Martha thought, then laughed at herself for presuming she knew what she was talking about. The knock started up again.

Through the door came a man's voice: "Mrs. Zimmer?"

"I'll be right there," she whispered.

She put on her slippers and crossed the room, then realized she wore the same nightie she'd worn the day before and was hardly ready for visitors. Embarrassed, she pulled the door ajar and allowed only her head to be seen.

Henry stood in the corridor. She still thought of him as her student, but he was not ten anymore. Henry was a man, barrel-chested and dark-haired. Even after the adventures she'd read about in his letters and heard firsthand last Christmas, when he and his wife told her they were purchasing a fixer-upper of a resort in New York State, Henry still resembled the energetic student he'd been. He stood before Martha, theatrically bearing a tray on his palm, grinning.

"Room service," Henry announced in a spirited tone. "Compliments of the house."

Martha smiled, though she made no move to open the door farther. She dearly wanted to; the scent of bacon, eggs, and toast, rising from a silver lid covering a plate, reminded her that she hadn't eaten since she'd pocketed the sourballs when she'd checked in. She was, however, not accustomed to being seen in nightwear. "How very nice of you, Henry. But it's not necessary."

"Au contraire," Henry said. "Your favorite

teacher shows up in the middle of the night, your kids get all enthused about plying her for info about Papa as a kid, she doesn't show up for meals, she's got her grandniece's kid with her, she doesn't crack the door for a day and a half—tell me you wouldn't worry she's starving to death."

How could Martha have crossed anyone's mind when she hadn't crossed her own? "You're right. I suppose I lost track of time."

"I kept saying to Graciela, Let's see how she's doing, bring her a meal, blah, blah, Graciela kept saying let you be, I kept saying we gotta do something—"

"I'm sorry to have caused any concern at all."

"Concern? This is the tastiest dish on the breakfast menu. Of course, you don't have to stay all cooped up, you know. My kids are right down the hall"—he indicated with his head, and Martha heard giggling—"and what they wouldn't give to sit next to you in the dining room."

"I'm hardly dressed for that."

"Come as you are. You could get anything off the menu, and Gracie would put your order in before all the others. Not that there's competition. We've still got a ways to go to build up our clientele." He made an endearing shrug. "We've got all kinds of attractions. My kids. The paint job I'm doing in the game room. My kids. The washing machine by the pool. I happen to be a liberated husband, and I know diapers pile up fast."

As if it wasn't embarrassing enough to be caught in her nightie, here she hadn't even considered laundering diapers. Certain the room must smell, she could say nothing.

"Graciela asked me to tell you she'd be just as happy helping you out as doing her work around here. Painting's not really her bag, you could say. So if you just want to stay put, give me those diapers, she'll take care of them, and we'll leave you alone. We know you have to get to your sister's soon, but until you need to leave, we could practice our hospitality."

Martha was wordless again, though for a different reason. She'd almost missed the earlier reference to "grandniece," but now she remembered. Two nights ago, when she'd pulled up to the sprawling hotel, she'd been so tired, so eager to settle the baby in, that when Graciela, her brown, waist-length hair askew, her dark eyes bleary, had answered the bell Martha tapped in the lobby, she'd made up a story on the spot, bristling at how readily a person could lie. She'd said her grandniece was having the kinds of problems young people were having these days—allowing vagueness to suggest discretion—and while her grandniece was receiving care, she was transporting the baby to her sister. Henry and Graciela didn't know that Martha had no sister. They knew only that her husband had died and she herself had no children.

From Graciela's reaction—interest in the baby, assistance in them reaching room 119, no interrogations—Martha knew her dishonesty had sufficed.

"I appreciate the help with diapers. As for eating, what you have here will do just fine."

"Whatever you say, Mrs. Zimmer."

"I'll set the soiled diapers out later. Would you mind leaving the tray at the door?"

"We've come prepared to provide luxury dining in your room." He gestured with his foot, and a young boy missing two front teeth pushed a cloth-covered cart next to his father.

Martha felt her face fall into the familiar teacher's smile, the one that shaped her cheeks every September, when new students settled at their desks and turned their eyes forward. It was an easy smile that felt like the opening of a door and inspired those on the other side to walk in.

"And who's this?" Martha said.

"Ricardo," the boy said, half-shy, half-assertive.

"Aren't you helpful, Ricardo," she said.

He giggled. "I'm good with the little paintbrush, too."

"I'm good with the roller!" a girl called from someplace just out of sight in the corridor.

"Wait your turn, Rose," Henry said, his voice indulgent.

"I'd like to give you more to do, Ricardo," Martha said, "but it would be just fine if you left the cart and the tray out here. I'll bring them in myself."

"Are you coming to dinner later?" Ricardo asked.

Henry said, "She doesn't know yet, Ricky."

He looked as if he wanted to say more. Then he caught himself and muttered to Ricardo and his unseen siblings about the customer always being right. Father and son set down the food and walked away from the door, toward a gaggle of suddenly talkative kids.

Martha had no idea she was so hungry until she wheeled the table in. The meal was pure home cooking—scrambled eggs, fresh bread, jam, bacon, and unusual and delicious pastries that Graciela must have learned to make growing up in Peru. Martha savored every bite.

Then she moved to the bassinet. This impulse to look endlessly at the baby made Martha feel sheepish, yet she couldn't resist sitting on the floor and touching the apple-round, irresistibly soft cheeks. The baby started, then relaxed, and Martha noticed how her hands had been held as fists all this time. *The ability to make a fist is apparently instinctive*, she decided, thinking about the ways they had been put to use throughout history. She touched the tiny fist, wishing she could keep this baby from ever knowing about war—and then the baby opened her hand and grabbed Martha's pinky. Martha giggled; the baby was holding *her*. Astounding. *A person comes into the world with a fist—and a grasp,* she thought. *Yes, we are built to fight one another, but also to embrace. How cleverly we are created.*

Then Martha remembered Earl's gaze averting when they passed a church. *Created,* she thought again. She herself had given little thought to how we are created or whether she wanted to resume attending church.

Yet there was so much to read on this perfect face, whose every feature had come from nowhere. No; every feature had come from a mother—who'd escaped a place so cruel, she wanted to hide her baby. This baby had also come from a father—who was not the numbered man. Was the father another resident? Maybe one with only the faintest understanding of what had happened between him and Lynnie? Maybe one who'd loved her, even if she'd not loved him? Though maybe she hadn't even liked him. Maybe she'd been—

No, Martha could not let herself think that.

She quickly slid into other, perhaps even harder, questions. If the perfection of this baby's face might be construed as proof of the divine, what did the imperfection of a handicapped body or mind prove? Did it argue against the existence of a larger power, as Earl felt after they'd buried their son? Or that, if there was such a supreme being, he could err?

The baby relaxed her grip, and Martha pulled her hand free.

Martha paced the room, running her hand through her hair. It would be unwise to drop into a spiritual abyss. She had too much to think about and barely enough energy to run a bath. Hoping to divert her thoughts in the way to which she was accustomed, she opened the desk drawer and found stationery and a pen. She flipped through her address book, searching for someone to whom she could write a letter. Yet the correspondents who'd welcome theological questions would be stymied by her immediate concerns, and vice versa. Besides, she was hardly prepared to reveal her predicament. She laid down the address book, listening to the whistle of the wind, the baby breathing. She set the stationery before her. She picked up the pen. And as the ink made its first mark, she found herself writing a letter to someone with whom she'd never corresponded before. Using the fine penmanship that had led years of students into script, Martha wrote, "In case I am not around to tell you, here is how you began in the world."

"Mrs. Zimmer?"

"Oh," Martha said, startled, her hand to her chest.

She turned to the door, pages of writing beneath her hands. The room was dark again.

"I hate disturbing you"—this time it was Graciela, her voice softer than Henry's and laced with her Spanish accent—"but you need a visit."

Martha drew the door open.

Graciela stood in slacks and a turtleneck, holding a tray. "We worried when you didn't come for dinner. I made you a nice meal. I brought fresh diapers, too."

Did Martha detect a slight note of annoyance in Graciela's voice? She did, after all, have several children to look after and a hotel to run. Of course she'd be annoyed that Martha wasn't following the house schedule. How rude of her. "I'm so sorry to have put you out."

"We were just worried about you."

Fortunately, the baby began crying. "If you'll excuse me," Martha said, turning toward the room. "Would you mind putting—"

She felt the door give as Graciela came inside. "Please. I know what you are feeling. No one should do this alone." She marched over to the bassinet and said, peeking in, "*Hola*, little one." Then she set the new tray on the dining cart. "I will care for her while you eat."

"I can't—"

"You can." Graciela moved over to the baby and picked her up.

Martha was mortified, standing there in her nightgown. Her hair must be filthy. The room must look like a fright.

Graciela went into the bathroom to change the wet diaper. Relieved to have someone take charge and in no state to resist, Martha sat down for her dinner.

"Let us take a walk today," Graciela said one morning.

For six days now, she'd been stopping by when she and the five children vacuumed the corridor in which Martha and the baby were staying. Graciela would retrieve dirty diapers and deliver new bottles of formula. Henry, busy with building projects, had come by three times a day with trays of food. Martha had not asked for these services, yet she was grateful; left to her own devices, she fell into a hole of too many questions, too much sleeping, and a trance of bassinet gazing. At one week old, the baby already held her in her gaze.

"A *walk?*" Martha asked. "It's almost December, and we're in the mountains."

"We can stroll inside the resort."

"I enjoy being in the room."

"We will take the baby. You need to get blood moving in your veins."

She gestured beside her in the hallway. Graciela had come with a baby carriage.

Martha's earlier relief at being cared for bloomed all the more in her chest. She put on one of her two dresses and combed her hair. Then she set the baby inside the carriage.

"The resort is a zigzag," Graciela said, turning the carriage to the right as they stepped outside Martha's room. Worn carpet lay on the floor, and flimsy paneling covered the walls. "It was falling down when we bought it." She laughed. "It still is."

But as Graciela pushed the carriage ahead, the corridor seemed a wondrous place. Martha felt as if she'd been in the room her whole life.

"Down at the one end, where you came in, is the lobby. The fireplace is the oldest thing about the resort. We're thinking of having marshmallow roasts on Friday nights. It is one of the ideas Henry has to draw people here." Graciela pushed her luxurious hair behind her ears. "The dining area, he is going to paint that. We will have a game room, too. Henry has a lot of ideas to make our resort popular."

They zigged into a new corridor. These were separate buildings that had been connected.

"Out that way"—Graciela waved her arm—"is a beautiful lake. It is why we picked this place." She went on, her voice lower. "When Henry first brought up the idea of leaving our life in Brooklyn, I have to admit, we quarreled for months. He told me we could find a place where the children could run free, I could set up my potter's wheel, our son Alfonzo could practice his drums without bothering neighbors. Then we came to see this hotel." She made a little laugh, as if recalling that first trip, and said, her voice brighter, "And when we walked around and he saw so many possibilities, and then he showed me the lake, well, he just won me over."

Martha looked at Graciela with surprised admiration. This marriage was not the conspiracy of somber coexistence Martha had lived. Graciela and Henry were quite different, yes, and did not always agree, yet they helped each other along until they came to share the same dreams.

They passed into a corridor with peeling paint, and as Graciela talked about the amount of effort that lay ahead of them and how she simply had the faith that it would all work out, Martha wondered how she would respond if Graciela pressed her about the duration of her stay. A week was already longer than her lie would have required. How much more time could she and the baby remain here?

Back at the door to room 119, Graciela said, "The kitchen is that way. You can make your own meals, though it would be such a pleasure to have you join us. And *you*," she said into the carriage.

Martha fit her key in the door. "You and Henry are being very considerate."

"It is good to be able to help someone out. But," Graciela said, "I have a question."

Martha felt her grip tighten on the knob.

Graciela reached into her skirt pocket and withdrew an envelope. Martha made out that it was addressed to the hotel and had a postmark from Well's Bottom. She also recognized the handwriting though could not place it. *Oh, no*, she thought, even though it was improbable that the School could have found her.

Graciela said, "One of your other students wrote us."

Right. Martha had forgotten. She'd felt so desperate about the new baby, she had completely forgotten the plan. Now it came back. It had been Eva's idea to write letters to Martha's students. Not all of them, of course. Just the few with whom she was closest, the ones who were, or had become, deeply appreciative of their time in her classes. The handful who seemed most likely to offer assistance—which included Henry. This letter helped explain why Graciela and Henry had been so generous for so many days.

"When did you receive this?" Martha asked.

"Right after you arrived."

And they hadn't said anything.

"It is lonely out here in the sticks," Graciela

said, her voice taking on a wistful tone. "We have been here a year and you are one of our only guests. I'd love for you to stay as long as you'd like."

"I'm very...Thank you." Martha reached for the carriage, then thought to add, "What else did Eva say?"

"She said we should not ask questions."

Eva was as trustworthy as Martha could have asked for. She'd picked wisely.

"You said you had a question," Martha said. She lifted the baby and muttered, "She's such a good baby," hoping this would stave off whatever it was that Graciela had to say.

"You have been here a week," Graciela said, "and we still do not know. What is her name?"

By the end of the second week, Martha and the baby were venturing out for walks on their own. By the end of the third week, they were spending their days in the hotel lobby, warming themselves by the fire, the children taking turns holding the baby. At the end of the fourth week, Graciela suggested Martha take the baby to a doctor friend of theirs. "She needs her first examination."

Graciela drove. The day was windy, with snow across the mountains and valleys, creeks turning sapphire in the cold. Martha wanted to hold up the child and say, *Look at the world! It's yours!* Instead, she thought, for the first time in all these weeks, about the letter she herself had received from Eva. It read, "Oliver came across tire tracks running right up to the woods, so we know a search party has been looking for the missing man. But the tracks did not go to the house, which must mean they're still not aware of the baby." Eva didn't ask how long Oliver would need to keep working, so in Martha's reply she'd sent Eva a check for twice the amount they'd discussed, prolonging a discussion of time while worrying that the postmark could lead to her being found.

The white-haired doctor worked in his house. Telling him she was the grandmother, Martha placed the child on a baby-sized table and was pleased to see that even though her easy child (*her* easy child) was unaccustomed to doctors, she had no trouble looking him in the face and cooing when he touched her skin.

The doctor made pleasant conversation, mostly through the child. "You're looking so healthy," he said. "So well cared for." Finally, near the end of the exam, he said, "And does your grandmother need a birth certificate?"

Martha looked out the window to the snow. "Yes."

The doctor said, "I'm going to need two things to write this up. The first is the truth."

Martha looked at him.

"I know from Henry that you're a trustworthy person, and therefore this child must be in your possession for a good reason. You can tell me. My career is a story of secrets."

She took a breath and told him; and when she finished, the doctor fed an official form into his Smith Corona and typed, "Father: Unknown. Mother: Unknown. Address: Unknown."

Then he looked up. "The other thing I'll need is her name."

Martha shook her head. "I don't know."

That dusk, Martha stared out at the trees. Presenting herself as a grandmother already seemed as if she were betraying Lynnie. How could she go so far as to give the baby a name?

It was terribly unfair. Here Martha was, getting her pinky grasped, her heartbeat matched, and her face watched as if it were the face of the sky. She was dressing and bathing and feeding this baby. She was relishing the pleasure of pushing her in a carriage. Lynnie was getting no more than a bitter memory.

A wind bowed the tops of the trees in the night sky, and the thought came to her: *The best way to hide something is not to conceal it from sight, but to give it a convincing disguise.* Coming to care about the baby made them look as if they belonged together. Becoming her grandmother and naming the baby were ways to belong together. This was not betrayal; it was an act of conscience. Loving this child was the right thing to do.

On Christmas Day, when Martha's students arrived at her farmhouse only to find a note on the door saying, "Martha went visiting this year, check back in 1969," Henry came into the lobby of his New York hotel and told his children, and Martha and the baby, that he wanted to celebrate the holiday in a particularly festive way. When the children asked how, he said he'd show them that evening. "It's Papa's plan for attracting guests," Graciela said, glancing to him with a knowing smile. "It works in Central Park, so maybe it will work here. But we all have to dress warmly."

As the sun was setting, Martha dressed the baby and herself in layers, then joined Graciela and the children while they roasted marshmallows in the fireplace. Martha still had no name for the baby. Yet when she looked at Graciela and the children, and saw so much trust and affection in their faces, she knew she and the baby shared those same feelings when they looked at each other, too.

Henry came in the front wearing a top hat and Victorian coat. "Ladies and gents," he said in a British accent, "your adventure awaits." He bowed and doffed his hat.

Everyone hurried outside, and there, standing

on the circular driveway before the hotel, was a horse-drawn coach. It was twice as high as they, with a handsome, curved shape—"like Cinderella's coach!" Rose, the oldest daughter, exclaimed—and the horses' harnesses jingled with bells. His idea, Henry explained with excitement, his breath showing in the night air, was for him to take young couples in this coach down to the lake and back. It would be a romantic place for a man to pop the question and honeymooners to sip champagne. And tonight, his family—and Martha and the baby—would get the first ride.

The coachman held the door open. Martha, with the baby tucked under her coat, stepped aboard. She sat on the seat facing the front. The others piled in, and Henry pulled a sheepskin blanket across their laps. "This'll keep you toasty," he said, and closed the door.

Henry and Ricardo climbed onto the driver's seat in the front. "Giddy-up," they said, shaking the reins. The bells jangled into the night.

The ride was slow and beautiful. Graciela and the children pointed out their sledding hill, the ice-skating pond, the place where Papa planned to build a gazebo. She talked about how Papa had won her over right along this path, when he talked of buying this very carriage. "Sometimes you think you know what you want," she said, hugging her children, "until you see how much more you can have." Martha watched the silhouettes of the trees. Lining the ridge of the mountains, they nodded at her in the wind.

She felt the child snuggle inside her coat and drew her arms close, hugging them both. When she looked up, they'd arrived at the lake. This was the point, Henry had explained, where the man would propose. "Graciela," Martha asked, "what's the lake called?"

"We named it after Tía Julia," Rose said.

"Yes," Graciela added. "But we used the 'j' sound. So it is Lake Julia."

"Lake Julia," Martha said. "That's good."

"That's *good?*" The children giggled.

She opened her coat. The child looked up at her with the hugest smile Martha had ever seen. The sheepskin blanket meant nothing. The smile warmed her in a way she had never felt. This was the love that had been taken from her so long ago, returned to her arms at last.

"Welcome to your first Christmas," she said. Storms could come, she knew. Winds and rain and hail. Right now, though, the baby's smile seemed sure to last forever.

"May we always be this happy," Graciela said.

"May *we* always be this happy," Martha repeated, touching the baby's face. And then she added, "Julia."

Turning Pages

LYNNIE

1968

$\mathcal{F}$inally, on Christmas Day, they sent Lynnie back.

She was not expecting to go back. For all she knew, her punishment—"the debt No-No has to pay to society," Clarence told her with a look of false sympathy—was going to last forever. After all, for five weeks she had lived and worked in Q-1, the "behavior ward." Q-1 was the cottage for residents who couldn't care for themselves or were viewed as uncooperative. Some were even kept in cribs through the day unless a working girl like Lynnie wheeled them to the dayroom TV. Clarence and his second-shift pal, Smokes, had come in early after Lynnie was captured just to escort her to Q-1. They were the ones who'd put on the restraints—"so you won't run off again," Smokes said as he'd unbuckled the leather ties, eyes blank behind his thick glasses, mouth chewing his toothpick. Lynnie knew the restraints were there to put her in her place, but that didn't stop her from squirming and howling and chomping her jaw at their hands.

The humiliation hadn't stopped with the leather ties. When Clarence and Smokes had walked her into Q-1, Smokes told her, "You'll be sleeping in a crib now, 'cause you're a big baby." Then he looked at Clarence, who laughed. After they left, Janice showed Lynnie her crib and Bull locked her few possessions away. They gave her a dry scrubber—a mop with a concrete block for a mop head, which she was to cover with a cloth to wax already waxed floors. She wanted to hurl it back at them. Yet she forced herself to do as they wished, positioned so she could always look up to a window. She'd think, *Buddy's under that same sky, and he's coming back.* She'd envision him appearing in the glass, saying with his hands that they'd escape again. She'd see them running through the underground walkways, emerging at the wall, and hurrying back to the old lady, who'd show them where she'd hidden the baby.

The first few days, as the milk in Lynnie's breasts dried up and her arms ached to hold the baby, the jubilation induced by this private movie overrode her resentment of the punishment. By the end of the first week, she began to worry. What if something had happened to Buddy? What if he'd made his way back and didn't know she'd been moved to Q-1? What if he'd gotten lost in the tunnels as he tried to find his way to her—or someone had found him and assumed he knew what had happened in the closet?

The good thing was, Q-1 residents were fun. Gina roared with laughter when the Benson & Hedges commercials came on where smokers had accidents that chopped their cigarettes in two. Tammy rocked back and forth beside the linen cabinet so when Bull unlocked it, she could run off with a towel she'd unravel and make into a twirly toy, entertaining herself. Marion did imitations of every irritating staff person from Uncle Luke down, sometimes right behind their backs. Though Lynnie hated how staff didn't pay the Q-1 residents enough attention, letting Tammy bang her head against the wall till it got bloody or Gina lie in her own waste all day. And Lynnie hated that her work was so much like the staff's that Marion sometimes mocked her, too.

But the best benefit of being in Q-1 was how far it was from Clarence and Smokes. For five weeks, as Lynnie shot looks out the window, ready for Buddy to appear, she would also glance toward the boys' colony. There Clarence and Smokes, officially second-shifters but really, since they lived on the grounds, all-the-timers, prowled around the boys' cottages day and night. The boys' colony was only three buildings away from A-3, while Q-1 was far down the hill, with Janice and Bull during the days, Ruthanne at night. All three were large, like most attendants in the lower-grade cottages. They weren't mean-spirited, even if they were neglect-ful.

So when Lynnie woke to Janice and Bull, she didn't need to be on guard, though she hardly enjoyed a happy waking. How different that was from A-3, where before she'd even opened her eyes, Doreen would be talking away, describing the make-believe finery they'd put on when they got up. Then, while they were dressing in their usual dour clothes, pretending to be movie stars, they'd look over to see Kate coming to supervise the morning shift—her face appearing in the sleeping area, her white smock brightened by embroidery, her red hair high.

Unhappy wakings were the point, Lynnie re-minded herself every morning. She'd run off, and since that was the worst violation short of vio-lence, the goal was to deprive her of the little that brought her gladness: Doreen, the laundry, visits to Kate. Whenever she thought about this, Lyn-nie felt her teeth clench, but she was grateful they were unaware of her even larger losses. They could have surmised, if they'd noticed that with every day, Lynnie was moving more sluggishly and the defiance that had led her over the wall had given way to resignation.

Now, Christmas morning, dry scrubbing the sleeping room, Lynnie looked up and saw a smudge of red moving down the hallway.

Lynnie's hands ceased pushing the dry scrubber. Could it possibly be Kate? Kate had been here only once all these weeks. She might have been a supervisor, though she was still subject to the rules. Unlike Smokes and Clarence, who could jaunt about wherever they pleased, even with dogs—the benefit of Smokes being Uncle Luke's brother— Kate had her assigned cottages and that was it. Even wandering around to find, as she once did, an old loom, on which she tried to teach residents to weave, was against the rules. But every so often, Kate broke the rules.

And it *was* Kate! In the doorway of the sleeping room!

Lynnie held herself quiet, as Kate stood a long minute, her face a picture of pain. Lynnie almost made Buddy's sign for *Come here*. She felt her voice moaning.

Finally Kate cleared her face back to the way it always looked. She cleared her throat, too. "Hi, sweet pea," she said, her voice raspier than usual. "I'm taking you back to A-3."

Lynnie threw down the dry scrubber and ran along the rows of cribs, squealing, arms open. Kate had already opened her arms, too, and Lynnie threw herself into Kate's hug.

How lovely. Kate had her Kate smell—cigarettes and gardenia soap and a skin-scent found nowhere besides Kate—and her cheeks were soft, her breasts big and comforting. Lynnie knew she smelled of all the nasty smells in this cottage. Kate held her anyway.

If Kate can come back, Lynnie thought, feeling the pulse in Kate's neck, *Buddy can, too.*

They pulled apart. In the center of Kate's eyes, Lynnie saw Kate's smaller self, and it felt smaller than ever. Lynnie moved her vision to take in Kate's whole face. She was smiling, though the smile was framed by sadness. Lynnie could feel herself smiling the same way.

"Let's get you packed up, all right?" Kate said, indicating a cardboard box she'd left at the door. "I'm supposed to get you back before lunch."

Lynnie was leaving! Right away! She gave her head a quick roll, not to escape the now, but to find Buddy in her memory so he could share this moment. She found him after one turn: He was walking her through the cornfields, and they were laughing at how the corn hid them from everyone else, and then he spun around and took her in his arms and kissed her. She fell into the kiss, and everything in the whole world dropped away. It lasted a lifetime, and when they pulled back, a red feather drifted down from the sky and came to land between their chests. She looked at him, and he at her, and then something she could never have imagined occurred.

Lynnie followed Kate through the rows of cribs to her locker, and even though she felt lighter than she had in five weeks, she could not put a spring in her step. When they reached the bed and Kate said, "Do you want to just watch me pack?" Lynnie nodded.

Kate lowered the sides of Lynnie's crib, and as Lynnie sat down, Kate produced a chain of locker keys. *Someone is doing something for me*, she thought. But the happiness that gave her could not sweep away so much sadness.

The locker door was dented. Kate finally got it open, and Lynnie peered in.

Dumped inside were her treasures. Lynnie gasped, remembering, as Kate reverently set each on the bed. On top was the white dress from the old lady, still as delicate as spiderwebs. Beneath the dress were the balled-up clothes Lynnie had brought from home—a crinoline dress, a pair of pedal pushers, a sun suit, a blouse, a pair of Mary Janes, and a set of underwear, all of which she'd outgrown. After Kate removed the clothing, there was the photograph. Kate handed it to Lynnie. It was her family before the twins: Daddy and Nah-nah standing before the fish tank, Mommy crouching down, and Lynnie sitting on the floor, legs splayed before her in baby shoes, eyes half-closed, mouth half-open, Mommy's arm coming forward to hold Lynnie, who could not sit by herself. Lynnie pushed the photo away.

Then she saw, in the far corner of the locker, the pouch that held her crown jewels.

"Do you want to see if it's all still here?" Kate said, and Lynnie nodded. Kate untied the pouch and removed the precious objects one by one.

The plastic horse Nah-nah had given her the morning she'd left for this bad place, a magnificent blue horse with a green mane that held one leg high in the air. Lynnie often thought of it when she drew the horses in the fields, which were hard to draw because they kept moving. This one stayed as still as Nah-nah herself, who had never grown older in Lynnie's mind.

The shoestring Lynnie saved when Daddy once replaced the laces on his shoes. He was going to throw it away until Lynnie threw herself at it as he crossed the room to the trash can. He seemed irked, and then something softened in his eyes, and he bent down and placed it in her hand and closed her fingers over it. That was the face of his she liked to remember.

The lucky-charm bracelet Mommy had given Lynnie on one visit. At each visit Mommy cried worse, so Lynnie had to push harder to get the crying out. Finally Mommy came wearing sunglasses because her eyes were so puffy. She handed Lynnie the bracelet and said, "You can wear this when you're a big girl." After Mommy hurried away, her face pressed into her hands, Lynnie's attendant put the bracelet in her locker. She had never worn it. And eventually Lynnie realized Mommy wasn't coming back.

Oh, and look. *The feathers*. Each one from Buddy. There was the bouquet of white feathers from their first tractor ride. The plumes of brown, blue, or yellow, some with black lines or tan spots, that he gave her whenever he had to repair something in the laundry. Crests of orange he asked Doreen to deliver when her mail rounds took her to the barn or garage. The feathers he handed over with a bow when he came to Kate's office, which shimmered blue and green and purple. And her favorite: the red feather that had sailed down in the cornfield that day. Lynnie had hidden them all in her waistband, and then Kate had secreted them in her pouch.

There was one other thing in the pouch. A metal pencil sharpener Doreen had snuck away from Uncle Luke's secretary, Maude. Lynnie was hoping to use it if she ever had the good fortune to own her own pencils. Kate had raised an eyebrow when the sharpener appeared in Lynnie's hand. Then she'd said, "Serves them right," and stored it at the bottom of the pouch.

But as Kate returned these gems to the pouch, pencils were not what Lynnie wanted to add. There had been no time to take anything from the baby. Lynnie still carried so much with her: the feel of the baby's body against hers, the sleeping face that had yet to witness what Lynnie knew all too well, the knowledge that the baby was too helpless to fight. Lynnie did not own as much as a lock of the child's hair.

"I wish I could have gotten you out of here sooner," Kate said as she set the box on the bed and began moving each item inside, folding the clothes as she did. "But I'm lucky I got you this fast. I think they were aiming to leave you here until doomsday."

Lynnie did not know what "doomsday" meant, though she could not ask for clarification.

"I haven't reported anything," Kate continued. "I was worried they'd do something worse to you. And me." She paused. "You know, they do things to us if we speak up."

Lynnie did know. Years ago, she'd heard that an attendant had come to work one morning and noticed a resident pointing to his feet. They were bloodied and swollen, and even though the boy wouldn't say what happened, the attendant knew that someone who'd taken offense at something he'd done must have stomped on his feet. The culprit could have been anybody—there were no locks on the cottages, and on the second shift, no one kept tabs. The attendant told a supervisor. The next day, the attendant found feces in his coat, and that night his Ford was scratched with car keys. He quit on the spot and had to move as far as Elmira to find a job. The resident was put in casts. No one ever found out who'd crushed his feet.

Kate looked out to the room of cribs. "I remember when this was a nursery. So many little babies, sent to this place within a few weeks of being born. At least that's over." She paused. "Doreen came here as a little baby, right?"

Lynnie nodded. She'd heard that Doreen had famous parents—a glamorous actress and a renowned playwright—who brought her here at one week old. They never visited, so even Doreen didn't know if this was true. One day, after seeing the photo of Lynnie's family, Doreen got the courage to ask Maude if she had a family photo in her file. Maude told her the files were none of the residents' business. That's when Doreen started playing make-believe in the morning. Every shirt was a ballroom gown; every pair of pants, nylons. The nickname that attendants invented for her was "Siamese If You Please." Doreen preferred "Bridget Bardot."

An old attendant once told Lynnie about the nursery. The staff was so overworked, they went down the rows, changing one diaper after another whether the baby needed it or not. The same happened with feeding. The attendant compared it to factory work, only with better pay.

When Lynnie had thought of all the tragedies that could occur if anyone knew about her baby, the nursery had certainly come to mind. But there were worse things than being raised in Q-1.

"That's it," Kate said, folding the box flaps closed. "We can hit the road." She looked at her watch and added, her voice less serious, "Of course, I *am* ahead of schedule."

As with "doomsday," Lynnie didn't know what "ahead of schedule" meant. Both had to do with time, though to Lynnie, time was confusing. Aside from not reading clocks, she had no understanding of calendars, much less history. So except for what Buddy had showed her about the stars, and except for knowing the seasons, she could not see time. Time was something she viewed as belonging to other people. That's why they could tell it and she could not.

That was also why she did not question Kate's haste after she got Lynnie's file from Janice and hurried Lynnie toward the door. They were "ahead of schedule," which meant, it seemed, they had to leave quickly. Though Lynnie did wonder why Kate did not take the fast route—the main path—when they got outside. Instead, Kate got onto the ramp that sloped into the ground, leading to the tunnel. Sometimes residents were herded through the tunnel on snowy or rainy days to cross the grounds. It was also good for hiding, which was why she and Buddy would escape through here when he got back. But Kate didn't need to hide, and the day was warm for Christmas. Yet Kate held the tunnel door open, so Lynnie went in.

The underground corridors were made of concrete, lit by bare bulbs. Lynnie did not like the stretches of darkness, so after stepping from the ramp, she was glad to reach a bulb quickly. Bravery was needed here. Buddy had shown his bravery when they'd run through the tunnel, and it had won them freedom. Tonette had shown it too when she'd gone through the tunnel for a secret talk with the nurse. Except Tonette's bravery had won her nothing.

When Kate reached Lynnie at the bottom of the ramp, she said, "I keep asking myself something, Lynnie. You were gone three nights. I was worried sick the whole time. I knew you'd be safe with Number Forty-two, but the world has many things no one can control. Even really smart, capable people like him." Kate turned them down a corridor to the right. "I'm not supposed to talk to you about what happened. But that's why I brought you here. We're told you'll forget it all like that."

She snapped her fingers. "You haven't forgotten, have you?"

"No."

"I didn't think so." She paused. "Do you want to keep thinking about it?"

Lynnie nodded hard.

"I would like to think about it, too, if I knew what to think about, that is."

Lynnie could not understand what Kate was saying. This was one way staff was different from the residents: They talked in riddles. Sometimes they lied—though not a lie like not speaking. Their lies weren't about hiding who they were. They were about hiding what they knew.

Kate took a deep breath. She said, "I want to help you. Only I can't if I don't know what went on. I looked in your chart"—she indicated the folder from Q-1—"but those days were torn out. So, Lynnie, if we go to my office this afternoon, would you draw me what happened when you ran away?"

Lynnie thought of Tonette. She thought of how, after it all happened, they told Lynnie she could go to the cemetery to tell Tonette good-bye. Lynnie had gone with a few attendants, and they'd stood in the cemetery, watching a man dig Tonette's grave. Had Lynnie been able to read, she would have known the headstones around them had no names, only numbers, for the order in which people died, and that Tonette was the six hundred seventy-second person to die. But all Lynnie could understand, as working boys lowered Tonette into the ground and the blond, bearded pastor read a prayer and Lynnie couldn't stop crying, was that Tonette tried to speak up and now she was here. Remembering what she and Nah-nah had done when their grandfather died, Lynnie wiped her eyes, bent down, and set a pebble on the grave.

That's when she'd made up her mind to stop speaking.

They reached a doorway at the top of a ramp. "You can take your time deciding," Kate said. "I'll find you after lunch, okay?"

Throughout lunch, Lynnie thought about what Kate wanted. The dining room was loud, as always. There had been a time when silence was enforced, but the staff had gotten too sparse for that, and besides, everyone was excited about the movie tonight. Usually movies were shown once a week. Today was a holiday, so they'd get one extra.

The dining room was like usual in other ways, too. This pair of friends here, those three there. Lynnie sat with Doreen and Betty Lou, though she disliked Betty Lou, who had a hoarse voice and said rude things. Before Lynnie's escape, she'd decided she'd had enough of Betty Lou, but Lynnie had not taken any action. She couldn't risk having anyone think she was thinking.

Now, though, thinking was all she could do. Should she let Kate know what happened? Kate felt strongly that Lynnie should, and Lynnie had never deliberately disappointed her. Lynnie also had endless proof that Kate acted in her best interests: Kate had never tattled about Lynnie's drawings, or the treasure-laden pouch, or the secret hours in the office with Buddy. If Lynnie revealed the truth to anyone, it would be Kate.

But Lynnie remembered the last time she saw Tonette. One day, when Lynnie was leaving the dayroom for dinner, another resident had given her a push. The bloody nose sent her to the hospital cottage, where she got to see Tonette. After Lynnie's nose cleared up, Tonette came over and whispered, "See that nurse?" She pointed. Tonette said, "She just came over from the hospital in Scranton. She's not sick in the soul like Clarence and them. I'm gonna tell her what I've seen." This went against Tonette's own advice. "Why?" Lynnie asked—a word long since lost to her lips. Tonette said, "'Cause things happen here that shouldn't." She closed her eyes a moment, then opened them. "I know I'm taking a chance, but it's getting personal." Lynnie had no idea what she meant. Tonette said, "After dinner tonight, I'm telling them I gotta go back here to work. Then I'll sit her down and unburden myself." Lynnie said, "Be careful."

That night, Lynnie fell asleep thinking about Tonette going to the nurse and wondering if the next day things would be different. And they were: The staff looked tense at breakfast. She didn't hear anything more for two days, and then word spread. A resident named Wanda, who had a temper and who'd been throwing furniture around and beating anyone who got near, had been put in solitary. And when Tonette was caught talking to the nurse, she was put in solitary, too—in the same cell where Wanda was waiting to tear anything and anyone to pieces. The story made its way over the stone walls, and Uncle Luke told the papers it was an accident; the staff hadn't known Wanda was inside that same cell. Police came to investigate, but no staff would talk, and Tonette couldn't either. She was already in the cemetery.

Now, Lynnie looked across the dining hall. Kate was wiping food off Gina's face. Her touch was not rough, as with some of them, and she talked to Gina as she wiped. When Kate returned to feeding Gina, she looked up and caught Lynnie's eye. Then she smiled. Not a happy-sad smile. A Kate-in-the-morning smile. A smile that said, *I'm glad to see you.*

Lynnie said to herself, *It's only Kate.* Then she stopped thinking of Tonette. Yet she knew, as she spooned up her lunch, that beneath her reasons for not wanting to tell was something even worse. She had not let herself think it since she made up the story she told Buddy. And with Kate's smile across the room, she would not let herself think it now.

So Lynnie drew.

Kate kept busy at her desk. The radio was on low, with a man who sang, *And I think to myself, what a wonderful world*... Although Lynnie liked this song, today she barely heard it. She was too caught up in her blues and purples, which she used for the night sky, and too involved with her grays and whites, which she used for the wall. The ladder was brown. She and Buddy were black shapes, running away.

"That's what I thought," Kate said when Lynnie finished. She looked at the picture a long time. Then she said, "What happened next?" She pushed a blank paper in front of Lynnie.

Lynnie stared at the paper. She hadn't realized Kate wanted more. There *was* more, but when she'd drawn memories for Buddy, she'd used single drawings. She'd never drawn "What happened next?"

Kate waited. She turned off the radio to help Lynnie concentrate. Then she pulled a book off a shelf. Nah-nah had read books, and, like them, this one had pictures.

Kate sat beside Lynnie at the desk. "This book tells a story using drawings," she said, "and each one tells the next part of the story." She turned page after page. The book was about a yellow duck named Ping, who lived on a boat with his duck family. One day he got tricked into going onto a stranger's boat, where he got caged in an upside-down basket. He was upset, and it looked like he'd never escape. Then a little boy set him free, and Ping found his way home.

Lynnie had not understood years ago what she saw now: A book wasn't something you could open anywhere and then flip to anywhere else. You opened it at the front and went forward, and the pages went from one to the next, each adding to the last, and the story grew more exciting with each page. It was like the way corn grew from the seed that got planted in spring to the tall rows you hid inside in the fall. A story grew.

Understanding something that had never been clear before, Lynnie drew. She drew the bomb shelter. She drew the baby being born. She drew them stealing the signs in the rain. She drew them running over Old Creamery Bridge. She drew them making their way along a road with many trees. She drew them stopping on the road with the mailbox with the lighthouse man. She drew the old lady letting them in.

"And then?" Kate said. "What happened next?"

Lynnie drew one more picture. The old lady was standing in her doorway. The baby—seen through the attic window—was sleeping in her basket. Number Forty-two was running into the woods. The sedan was driving away.

Kate held up the last drawing and looked at it closely.

Then she turned to Lynnie. "You left the baby there because you wanted to protect it."

Lynnie nodded.

"Why? You didn't know that woman at all."

Lynnie sorted through the drawings. She pulled out the one with the lighthouse man.

Kate looked at her. "I don't get it."

Lynnie wanted to tell Kate about the sea. About that time when she and Nah-nah were on a beach, far away from Mommy and Daddy and the party they were attending, where Daddy had said to Nah-nah, "It's such a nice day, Hannah. Why don't you take Lynnie for a walk." She wanted to tell Kate about the storm coming up suddenly when they were far down the beach. About them running to the big tall tower and finding a door and climbing round and round and round. And coming into the top. And going over to the window. And looking out to the storm. And Nah-nah saying, "It can't get to us now. We're way up here, and you're safe with me."

Lynnie had drawn that tower once for Buddy,

perching it beside the sea. He'd stared at the water a long time, puzzling over what it was. She drew him another picture of a person crying and pointed back to the sea. He folded up the first drawing and put it in his pocket.

But Lynnie could not tell any of these memories to Kate.

Kate said, "Well, I don't understand, but do you want me to report any of this?"

Lynnie shook her head no.

"I wish you'd say yes, Lynnie."

Lynnie shook her head harder.

"Oh, Lynnie." Kate made a sigh and looked out the window. "Why *not*?"

Lynnie looked down at her pencils and rolled them between her hands.

Kate said, "All right. I think I can guess why, and if I'm correct, then I'll understand. I won't like it, but I'll understand."

Lynnie looked up.

Kate said, "Did you think the baby might go through what happened to the other babies here? The ones in the nursery?"

Lynnie looked at her a long time. Then she felt something happen inside. It had happened once before, right here in this office, when Buddy had rocked his arms as if he were rocking a baby in a cradle, then asked with his face, *What happened?* She'd paused a minute, then done exactly what she knew she'd do if Kate ever asked her the same question. Lynnie had pointed out the window to the boys' cottage, the one that overran A-3 that night months before.

Who? Buddy asked with his hands.

Then she'd drawn boys swarming the cottage in the dark, the light too dim for her to see.

Buddy had shaken the bars on the staff office windows, enraged. The next day he'd begun plotting their escape.

Should she do it again? Once a page has been turned, can it be turned back? No. She was the new Lynnie. She knew how a lie felt.

Kate said again, "That's why you left the baby with her, right?"

Lynnie cut her eyes away and nodded.

But she'd had to lie, Lynnie thought when Kate brought her to the common cottage, where they showed the movies. The sun was setting, and Lynnie could see Clarence and Smokes and the dogs as the lights came on outside. Usually during a movie she sat far from the window, but she'd arrived late. She tried to concentrate on the movie, about a singing lady who could fly by holding an umbrella. Doreen sat across the room and kicked her feet back and forth. Betty Lou called out that it was stupid. But Lynnie kept turning to the window. It was hard not to, with it so dark in here and Smokes and Clarence standing under a lamp, Clarence puffing on his pipe, Smokes wrapping a dog chain around his wrist. Then she realized Smokes was making a dog jump at Clarence. Clarence was backing off, looking scared. Smokes was laughing. "Sissy," she heard him taunt. "Sisssssseeee." Clarence froze, then stepped closer to the dog, which bared its teeth—and he whacked the dog in the head. The dog shrank back, whimpering. Clarence wiped his hands, showing his job was done. Smokes tipped an invisible hat in approval.

She'd had to lie. She could not open an umbrella and let it carry her away.

Soon it was routine. Listening to Doreen until she fell asleep, then looking to the tower clock in the window and thinking of Buddy coming and carrying her to the ladder. He would have to carry her, because as every day passed, she felt herself growing numb. Her legs did not want to move, her arms had trouble in the laundry, and she knew it was from the wanting. She remembered the same numbness after the first visit from Mommy, when Nah-nah wasn't along and Mommy said she wouldn't be coming, and that Uncle Luke said everyone would do better this way. Lynnie remembered more numbness later, when she caught on that Mommy was never returning. Ever since, Lynnie had wondered which was worse: the sudden good-bye you know is a good-bye or the long good-bye you have to guess. Now, after a sudden good-bye from the baby, she was beginning to worry, as the snows thickened and the stars sparkled with the clarity of deep winter, that Buddy was going to be a long good-bye that she would have to guess.

Kate did something called praying, and Lynnie knew it was to ask for favors. Kate had once tried to explain Jesus Christ and Mary. Then Lynnie remembered hearing about God, who didn't have a name. He had a tune, and her mother sang it when she lit candles every winter and they all ate chocolate coins in gold foil and Lynnie got a funny top to spin. But Kate did not sing this tune, and Lynnie did not know God's name. So that meant she could not pray.

Instead Lynnie thought about the pictures that came after the pages she already knew. She imagined drawings of the baby on the farm with the old lady. The baby would be sitting up, standing, someday even running. She tried to see the color of the baby's eyes or hair. Would they be hers? Or would they—No. The child *had* to look like her. The child *had* to be happy. The child *had* to make friends who would hum with her, ride blue-and-green horses, play with Betsy Wetsys.

She played this picture game with Buddy, too. Though she could only see him driving the tractor, fixing machines, handing her feathers. The pages would not draw themselves for him.

So Lynnie worried when Doreen came to her one day in Kate's office. Lynnie had just finished drawing—though not the future she could not see. She was drawing the past she *could* see. Feathers of all colors, curling in the air like smoke.

Kate was locking the pictures in the drawer when Doreen came in, wearing her mail delivery sack across her shoulder, and said, "Someone's looking for Lynnie."

Kate immediately shut the door. "What are you talking about?"

Doreen explained she'd just been in the main office. A heavyset woman with brown hair in a ponytail had shown up and told Maude she wanted to visit with Lynnie. "Maude asked if she was your family, and she said no. Maude said that was against the rules, and she left."

"Lynnie," Kate said, "do you know why this woman would want to see you?"

Lynnie shook her head, but she knew it had something to do with her escape.

Kate thanked Doreen, and when she left the room, Kate opened the file cabinet. She paged through the pictures. Nothing like this woman was in them.

She sat down and folded her hands on the desk. She said, "I know you don't want me to tell anyone, and I said I wouldn't. But Lynnie, I'm terribly worried about the baby. You have a baby out there in the world. Your baby. This woman might know something about your baby."

Lynnie looked at Kate. Maybe this woman knew the old lady. Maybe Lynnie could find out about the baby. Maybe Lynnie could even learn the color of the baby's hair.

"And I'm asking you, I'm begging. Let me find out why she wants to talk to you."

Lynnie thought a long time. Even if she couldn't be with the baby, she could know about the baby. She could draw the pages she would never see.

No. She could not.

She looked away.

Kate set her fingers on Lynnie's hand until Lynnie met her eyes. "I know you're mourning the loss," Kate said. "But I have to ask you something. Please be honest with me, and I'll honor your wishes." She took a deep breath. "Do you want me to go find your baby?"

Lynnie had not considered this.

"Just say I can do it," Kate went on. "I'll go find that old lady's house and make sure the baby's all right. I'll tell you everything you want to know— and I'll never tell another soul."

It would be so wonderful. Lynnie could draw the missing pages. She could know she'd saved the baby. She could know she'd saved *her daughter*.

Except. If they found out, the pages would not look like what Lynnie envisioned at all. They would look like Tonette after Wanda finished with her. They would look like the animal after the dogs got through with it. They would look like what Lynnie saw in his eyes that night.

Lynnie stared down at the lighthouse. With the old lady, the baby would be safe. She looked back up into Kate's eyes. Then she turned another page, a page she so longed not to turn.

"No," she said.

The Big Drawing

HOMAN

1969

F inally, after five months: a hut where he might rest.

Homan couldn't believe his luck. A hut was jutting out from the bottom of a rock cliff. Standing in knee-high grass, freezing in a wind so strong that it made young trees bow, he stared at it in the dusky light. One story high, with two windows and a chimney, the hut was startling in this place without people and buildings. For months he'd been sleeping outside, huddling under a blanket he'd snatched from a clothesline, wishing the buttons on the rabbit-fur jacket didn't fall so far short of their holes. If only he were narrower in the chest. If only he hadn't lost Roof Giver's shirt and jacket in the river, when getting to Beautiful Girl was as simple as going east. But his chest was broad, those clothes were gone, and the train had taken him west.

He'd had his first taste of luck after the initial forty nights, when he found a bag of old clothes in some woods. After that, though he still spent his days far from houses and shops and cars, looking over his shoulder for police and scrounging up anything to keep the hunger away, at least his teeth weren't chattering, except at night. When the cold got too wicked, he'd venture into towns, staking out empty garages, houses with tucked-away places underneath porches. He hated sunrise, when his predicament would jolt him awake. Yet he loved sunrise, too, because that was when he'd see them, right there in his mind. Beautiful Girl standing in the cornfield, hair blowing in the breeze. Little One in a crib, able to reach up now and touch his face. Just before he'd jump up to start running again, he would lift his hands. *Good morning, beautiful girls,* he'd sign. *I'll be back soon as I'm able.*

Now he set his blanket-sack on the ground, along with all it contained—his lost-and-found wardrobe, berries, a fishing rod and spear he'd made for catching meals, a tent, pocketknife, and canteen left at a campsite—and made his way through the high grass.

When he came up to the hut's door, he pressed his palms flat against the wood, hoping that if anyone was inside, he'd feel vibrations. The door did not tremble beneath his hands, so he looked from one window to the other. There was no motion inside, just the reflection of the stars coming out like a crushed cube of sugar. He waited a moment, gathering courage. Then he reached for the knob and cautiously pushed the door open.

With the moon as his light, Homan could see a few feet inside. There was an overturned chair and a table with a broken leg, a stone fireplace built into a wall. On the mantel was the glint of tinfoil from a pack of cigarettes and a book of matches. Maybe the smoker was just waiting to jump him. But the hut had the musty odor of a home long forgotten. Holding the door with his foot, he grabbed those matches and got one lit.

The room grew clear. The walls were lined with dusty shelves. The floor was bare, with weeds tufting up from the boards. And the far wall wasn't the rock of the cliff. It looked like it went *inside* the rock. He saw a lantern on a peg and lit it. The fourth wall was a cave.

Holding up the lantern, he spun around to be sure he was alone. No one. He turned back to the cave. It was empty, except for a bed made of branches. No blankets, no pillows, no grizzled old man giving him the evil eye. If only he'd found a place like this when the baby was coming instead of a cellar in a backyard. Then they would never have gotten chased out. Then they would never have gone for miles in the rain—or spent all these months without each other.

Lantern high, he ran to retrieve his blanket-sack.

Only when he closed the door and jammed the chair beneath the knob did he realize his luck was better than he'd thought: On the shelves were tins of fish and packets of beef jerky. He ate until he could eat no more, then lay down on his clothes, hiding in the cave behind rocks, in case anybody did break in. Relaxing for the first time in too long, he fell into a heavy sleep.

After bolting from the truck lot and the swarming police, Homan hadn't planned on being alone for so long, only to end up finding refuge in a cave.

Instead, as he'd grabbed on to the rushing freight car, he'd felt pumped with hope that he'd get back fast to the Snare. All he had to do was keep fear at bay until they pulled into a train yard, then hop a boxcar back to the city he'd just left and find his way to the river. It wouldn't be simple, but he could do it. He *had* to do it. So that night, stomach down to the metal, air currents ballooning the rabbit jacket and his pants, he'd pushed away fear by thinking of her. Beautiful Girl sneaking into the barn one afternoon, where she laughed as he taught her to milk cows. Beautiful Girl in Chubby Redhead's office, where she wedged the radio in his pocket so he could feel the vibrations and they moved their feet in a slow dance. Beautiful Girl holding him in the cornfield, on what he would name the Day of the Red Feather.

Eventually, still gripping the train, Homan turned his head. He couldn't tell how long he'd lain here, but the stars were the stars just before morning, and the landscape was countryside.

He realized he was on the run again. Yet he felt nothing like the rage that had overtaken him long ago, at the end of the last Running, when the gates of the Snare had clamped closed. Furious with the police, the judge, and, yeah, himself—*You caught for speaking your name! You ain't never mouth-speaking again!*—he'd then spent months fighting and throwing things. He didn't belong there! He wasn't no dimwit! His tantrums only got him put in the building with the most violent boys and a nurse feeding him a syrup that made his thinking muddy. Desperate for something, anything, better, he remembered how Blue had fought meanness in the world. *I don't let nothin' break me,* he used to say. *Not folk who think they better'n me. I got things to do, and being your big brother the highest one, and nothin' gonna stop me from that.* Even through his mind-haze, Homan understood: Blue found his place in the world by giving himself to another. It galled Homan to consider doing that with droolers and head bangers. But he had to get his mind back.

So one day he saw that Shortie, who slugged anyone passing by, didn't get to punching until his favorite guard left every night. Just before the shift change, Homan started rolling a ball to Shortie. It took a while for Shortie to care, but then the ball got his mind off his guard and the slugging happened less. Soon Homan started wondering who else needed giving. He took over diapering Man-Like-a-Tree. He figured how to get Whirly Top to dinner: Go up next to him, spin round and round like Whirly Top until Whirly Top stepped out of his whirly circle. One day Homan helped Big-Bellied Handyman set a window straight. Soon he started getting privileges.

Giving, he found, made him proud. And pride made him bolder with doing what he had a knack for—unclogging pipes, oiling hinges, driving the tractor. And doing a good job made him get more privileges. Finally he was almost as free as a Stuck-for-Life could get. Until, that is, Beautiful Girl grew into a woman and he wanted to be even freer.

Dawn rose through the hut's window, and, as always, Homan reached toward the dream selves. Beautiful Girl was combing her fingers through her hair, her face up to the sky, smiling, as blossoms showered down from a tree. Little One, growing up fast, was crawling under the tree, pulling up clover. Even though Homan was far from sure about what had happened, he told himself Little One was in the safe hands of Roof Giver. Yet when he saw Beautiful Girl in the mornings, he pictured Little One with her, and then made his good-morning greeting to them both. Today, he remembered he didn't have to jump up and run. In a hut with a locked door, he could lounge about as late as he pleased.

He'd long fancied the idea of staying in bed, starting when he was still in Edgeville and leaving boyhood behind. He'd wake thinking about a lady being in bed with him, and the saddle part of him would be all afire. He'd want to take care of business, and on the rare mornings when his brothers and sisters and Mama had gone off and Blue was out with Ethel, he would. Forget that luxury in the Running. Then he'd wake with his eyes darting and heart thumping and have to just get up and go. How he'd come to envy all the folks who could lock their doors. He'd see them through their windows, putting their arms around their women, kissing their lips, their neck, unbuttoning shirts, lowering the shade. Things were even worse at the Snare. If the guards caught a boy doing things to himself, they'd whack his fingers with a belt.

But no lady caught his eye for a long time. Even Beautiful Girl didn't have that effect on him at the start. When he first saw her, she was young and he was digging a grave, and what made him pay notice wasn't her long blond hair and wide, open face. It was how she cried as the coffin went into the ground. After that, he began noticing her across the dining room, walking the grounds: She never got pushy or hotheaded, she had a friend and visited a redheaded guard. She didn't smile much—and when she did it was sunshine. Only when she grew tall and took on the curves and walk of a woman did he realize she was as beautiful outside as she was within. Then, in the mornings, he thought of her. But once he knew there was a baby in her, and that she suffered when the boys did what they did, he decided to wait until after they were free.

This morning, in the cave, he had a locked door. So he finally let himself stop waiting.

The morning after escaping Pudding and Dot, he woke hugging the railcar as the train rocked to a stop. Sunlight warmed his back. He stretched his arm beside him, pointed his fingers down, and looked. The shadows were short, which meant it was close to noon and hiding would be harder. Yet he had to find a train going back. He propped himself up on his elbow.

He was in a train yard. To the left was a building where men in uniforms milled about. To the right were railcars, then grass and hills. If he could steer clear of the men, he'd be okay.

With none of the men looking his way, he sat up. His body was stiff and tired, he needed to relieve himself, and when he stretched out, his leg still hurt. He was hungry, too, having not eaten since before the truck lot. Then he remembered the envelope the man had pushed into his jacket. He shouldn't take the time to look inside except it was thick as a sandwich, and maybe that's what it was. He rolled to his side so he couldn't be seen and pulled the envelope out of his pocket.

Inside were tissues tied with twine. He undid the knot, and disappointment hit like the smell of rotten egg. It was just a fat stack of green rectangles. Money. He remembered customers paying the McClintocks with money, but he'd never used it. He flipped through the stack and saw each rectangle had a picture of a man. Some were bearded, some clean-shaven; some were stout, some thin. Maybe ten silver circles didn't equal all of these. What equaled what? How many of these did you need for a new engine, a car wash, a hamburger?

He stuffed the money back in the envelope and pushed it deep into his jacket.

Then he sat up again and looked down the train cars stretching behind him. He didn't see a ladder to climb down. He turned left, searching the roof's edge for something to grab on to. Nothing. He turned right. There, at roof level, were the polished shoes of a man.

Homan did not lift his eyes. He knew the man must have climbed to the roof, maybe after yelling up. Homan whirled to his other side and saw, down the side of the train, other men climbing up. Homan whipped back and looked. The man had a leather stick in his hands.

Run!

Off he went across the top of the train. In cowboy movies at the Snare, he'd found this thrilling. But doing it? His stomach was tight, his limbs lit by lightning. He might fall between the cars! They could have a shotgun! He forced himself not to look back. He hurdled over one train car, two, three—then pitched himself off. The ground came up fast, and he fell hard. New pain shooting up his calf, old pain stinging his knee, he flew down the line of trains. He knew he was fast, he was happy he was fast, and he wished to high heavens he didn't have to be.

But now he could finally head back, he told her dream face that morning, before he left the hut with his spear to catch lunch. His legs had long needed to heal, his bones to thaw, his belly to fill—and now they could. *Just hang on till I rest*, he assured her. *Won't be long now.*

Though as he made wider and wider arcs from the hut, searching for game, he wondered how he'd find his way back. Blue had taught him to hunt. Tramps in the Running had taught him to jump trains. Homan had taught himself how to steal farmers' chickens. But how would he get from an unknown here to a far-off there? Trains weren't safe now, and for buses he had to know money. He'd seen Ride Thumbers on TV, though how would he tell a driver anything? And what was the name of the town where the Snare was found? What was the name of the Snare?

But wait. A rabbit stood a few feet off. Unlike the last two, it wasn't watching him, so if he was quick, he'd get his lunch. He tightened his hand around his spear. The rabbit caught on as the spear flew forward, but it hit its mark before the creature could run.

Pleased, he retrieved his meal. What was he doing, worrying about how to get back? Not for one minute since he'd been parted from Beautiful Girl and Little One had he let himself cry. He'd made mistakes, that couldn't be disputed, and he'd stumbled so far from the train yard that he might as well be in Edgeville. Yet he'd got clothes. Shelter. Food.

He built a fire. Maybe he couldn't imagine how he'd find his way back once he got rested, but as he held the rabbit over the flames, he thought about how he'd just found lunch at exactly the right moment. The hut had appeared just when he'd needed it, too, and the train, and the loose dirt in the truck lot. Maybe the thirty-eight years he'd been on this earth hadn't been a long stagger from one calamity to the next, the way he'd always supposed. Maybe there was more to it. Because hadn't his doglegged journey also taken him to the McClintocks, and Shortie, and—he watched her now, the steam from the laundry all around them, her hands following his, speaking his sign for her name—Beautiful Girl?

Over the next many days, as he kept nursing himself back to vigor, he thought that maybe when you're making your way forward into your life, it just *looks* higgledy-piggledy, the way, if you were a fly walking across one of Beautiful Girl's drawings, all you'd be able to see was green, then blue, then yellow. Only if you got in the air before the swat came down would you see the colors belonged to a big drawing, with the green for this part of the picture, the blue and yellow for others, every color being just where it was meant to be. Could that be what life was?

Part of him rolled his eyes for thinking something so dumb-assed. Because why, if he was supposed to get the fever and start the Running and get caught in the leghold of the Snare, would catastrophes just keep on coming? But part of him gave pause. What if the moments, good and bad, had to be there? What if there *was* a big drawing? Did that mean there was a Big Artist?

A week passed. His body began to fill out. Another week passed. His bruises receded.

By the third week, he wasn't feeling sure about this new wondering. He was, though, feeling so sure of himself that one afternoon, he decided that tomorrow he would get on the road again and somehow start making his way back toward Beautiful Girl. This meant it was time to do two things. One was to take care of some hiding, so he took off his boots, got out the pocketknife and money, and slit secret pockets into every spot in the boots that gave under the blade. Then he slid the money around his feet. Now he could ditch the rabbit coat.

That task done, he needed to go farther than he'd gone before and survey the possibilities for setting out. He'd come to the hut from the south and run into a wide river when he'd gone east. So that afternoon he walked north, until he finally came to a rocky ridge.

Below was a broad, tan building and, beyond it, lawns and streets and houses. He crouched down and peered through bushes. To one side of the building was a parking lot with yellow buses; to the other, a field ringed by stands filled with people. As he watched, young men in matching tops and bottoms ran out of the building, followed by another group in other matching clothes. The first group fanned over the field, which was when he realized he was sitting above a baseball diamond. At the Snare, the guards played baseball, and once Homan got privileges, he joined in. But he'd never had a front-row seat to a real game.

As the first batter went up to home plate, Homan remembered playing the game himself, his bat belting the ball into the air, his legs taking him base to base. He wished he could be down on that field right now. The pitcher threw the ball, and Homan decided that even if he couldn't be there, he could play as if he were—and imagine Beautiful Girl watching. So he stood and hurled a make-believe ball into the air. Then he swung his arms, mimicking the batter, and when the ball flew past the bases, he held his arms wide like the outfielder, jiggling his legs back and forth until he smacked his fist into his palm as the ball hit the player's glove. The crowd burst into applause, and Homan, along with the dream Beautiful Girl, slapped his palms together, too. For the next many innings, he struck batters out and stole bases. Then, in the middle of a play, he spotted something outside the field. Past streets and shops and houses was a tall cement bridge that spanned a river. He clapped right then and there at the sight. How clear his way would be tomorrow. How perfect that his wandering had led him here. *See?* he signed to Beautiful Girl. *Said I'd get back, and this how.*

That night, already dressed for his leavetaking

tomorrow, he lay down in the cave on his makeshift bed, smiling into the dark. He didn't only feel closer to believing there really was a Big Artist—he *hoped* there was. Because then, no matter how many hardships he had to face on his journey back, they'd be a lot easier to bear.

But when he woke, it was still night. At first he thought it was the excitement of leaving that got him up early.

He passed his gaze over his sack, ready to go. He wiggled his toes, feeling the money in the boots. Then, wanting to see the stars, he turned his gaze toward the windows.

Glass exploded into the room. He rolled behind the farthest rock in the cave, his breath hard. Then they were climbing through. Had they hollered first? They were coming fast, shining a flashlight, finding him, yanking him to his feet. He was strong again, so he could fight, shoving one across the hut, flinging his arm back to get another. *Why this gotta happen tonight?* he wondered just before one of them grabbed his arms and pinned them behind. *Because there ain't no big picture, you stupid lunk.* The light hurt his eyes so much that he felt blind. *Sorry, Beautiful Girl. Look like I'm in a second Running.* Then their fists stormed down upon his body.

Accomplices

KATE

1969

*W*ith Lynnie's drawings on the seat beside her, Kate drove across Old Creamery Bridge. The drawings were her map. She'd removed them from the locked drawer, knowing Lynnie objected. But Kate had not gone into this line of work simply because she'd needed a job when her husband took up with another woman and she'd lacked the guts required of waitresses, the flexibility in her child-raising schedule for factory shifts, and the savings to cover cosmetology school; she'd come here because of a transformation of her own. Those first months after her husband left, she sobbed and slept and had vengeful thoughts. Then she woke one morning realizing she hadn't protected her three young children from her husband's temper, having been too caught up in her own pain. Searching for direction, she returned to church and committed herself to righting her wrongs by caring for others. That was when she applied to the School. Soon she became so attached to the residents that even in the midst of harshness and disillusionment, she believed this was the work she'd been meant to do. She knew some co-workers had other motivations and that although they enjoyed a smoke with her and shared cake on their birthdays, they thought Kate a troublemaker for treating the residents as she did. Kate, though, found her work an act of penance. She thought often of the Gospel of St. John, when Jesus says, "Love one another. As I have loved you, so you must love one another." She thought too of the Gospel of St. Matthew: "Whatever you did for one of the least of these brothers of mine, you did for me." She taught her children that every person— from the one-legged veteran who played organ at their church to the stuttering old man who ran the boiler room at the elementary school to her children themselves—deserved kindness. So how could Kate not try to learn what she could about the baby, even if Lynnie had asked her not to?

But Kate hardly felt virtuous as she continued along Old Creamery Road. She felt remorse, having allowed almost four months to lapse since Lynnie had illustrated her escape. For a while she'd told herself she'd take action as soon as she could get a break from so much overtime. Then yesterday, while driving home from a sixteen-hour shift, she'd admitted to herself that there were less noble reasons for her delay. Suzette was right: If Kate brought this story to light, she'd probably lose her job. So for months she'd lain in bed at night, looking at water stains on the ceiling, worrying about Melinda's braces, Jimmy's chances of getting into college, and not thinking about finding the baby.

Yesterday, though, the staff was abuzz with a rumor that Doreen's parents were opening a show on Broadway. It seemed implausible that two celebrities so frequently in the papers—one of the most photographed film stars in Hollywood and a prolific and revered playwright—could have a child never mentioned in the press, so Kate had long assumed the talk about Doreen's parents was only talk. But yesterday she felt pushed inside in ways she couldn't explain. This was something that happened to her from time to time and which she laughed off to the staff as intuition. The truth was she believed it was the hand of God. So she asked a friend in the file room to slip her a key, and last night, in the darkness after her second shift, she let herself in.

The cabinet with Doreen's folder was near a window. Kate pulled the chart and held it up to the light of the tower clock. Sure enough, there were the names in the rumors. Poor Doreen. Here she had a family that owned four houses, two Oscars, and a Pulitzer. All Doreen owned was a broken telephone that she'd found in the trash and hidden under her bed.

Kate thought, *I need to learn if Lynnie's daughter is all right. If she's not, then I will do for her what someone should have done for Doreen: make sure no harm comes to her.*

Now, as she lit her fifth cigarette since crossing Old Creamery Bridge, she saw a road sign ahead. In one mile she'd hit the turnoff for Scheier Pike, a road she'd forgotten about when she'd embarked on this drive. Should she stay straight on Old Creamery Road or make the turn?

She looked at the drawings beside her. The one with the bridge was followed by one with two figures—and the baby—running along a wooded road. But woods lay along the northern route as much as the western one. If only those pages hadn't been removed from Lynnie's file. If only Kate had the courage to confront Clarence. Not that Clarence would be forthcoming; he once laughed at Kate when he learned she'd been trying to teach a few of the more dexterous residents to use the weaving loom. "Like that'll fix them," he'd said. She'd wanted to say, *That's not why I'm doing it. It's so they can do something interesting with their days.* Instead, she'd said nothing, as she'd said nothing about this expedition. This time, though, her silence wasn't from fear of being thought foolish or naive. It was from fear of revealing Lynnie's secret.

Crushing out her cigarette, Kate took a guess and stayed on Old Creamery Road.

She shuffled the pages to the next picture. Apparently the old lady's house had a mailbox with a strange decoration. Kate slowed her car, looking. What would she do once she found where she was going? Since last night, she had prayed about what she would say to the old lady. The answer had come: Sounding official, she would say she worked at the School and had come not to take the child back, but to find out whether assistance was necessary. That way, the old lady wouldn't call Dr. Collins or the police. Though what if the old lady said she *did* need assistance? What if she handed the baby to Kate? The sudden presence of a baby in her house would surely set tongues wagging across Well's Bottom. Kate should have asked Father Geoff what to do. Maybe he knew of a home far from town where the child would be welcomed, or a discreet adoption agency. But Lynnie wanted the baby with the old lady for some reason and did not want the baby traceable to her. Moving the baby to some couple or agency would require Kate's involvement, and even if Father Geoff was careful, there would be a connection that could lead back to Lynnie. Maybe the baby was fine where she was. Kate hoped so.

She rounded a bend, and there it was: the mailbox with the decoration. A lighthouse. Right, she saw, checking it against the drawing. The lighthouse was down, no longer waiting for a mail delivery, but aside from making it vertical, Lynnie had captured it so well, even drawing in the face, that Kate said out loud, "You really are something, sweet pea."

She turned in at the driveway and proceeded up the gravel drive.

The site resembled the final drawing with great accuracy, too. Fields lay to either side of the drive. At the far end of the drive was a simple house with a porch and small windows.

Then, as Kate pulled up to the front of the house, she saw something that wasn't in Lynnie's drawings. Planted in the ground before the porch, a wooden sign said, FOR SALE.

Kate got out of her car. Though spring had arrived, the wind was blowing hard. She pulled her coat tight. Through the tiny window she saw furniture. She knocked, but the wind blew too hard for her to hear footsteps. So she kept knocking until she'd knocked enough.

She cupped her hands and lit a cigarette. She stepped off the porch.

There were the woods Number Forty-two had run into. She eyed them, knowing that wherever he was, he was long gone from here. She thought of how blank she felt when her husband first started staying late at the box factory. Blank, yet consumed with dread, realizing somehow that something other than work was keeping him out late. But she'd had months to get used to the idea of him being away from the house, until that one horrible night when the familiar force came up in her: It was time she *knew*. She'd left the kids with her neighbor and driven to the factory. The supervisor was surprised Kate's husband had talked about overtime—they hadn't done overtime for ages, he'd said—and with mounting clarity she'd driven down every road in Well's Bottom, faster and faster, searching for his car. Finally she'd seen it outside Jeanette Dory's apartment—and seen her husband walking a pregnant Jeanette down the steps.

That was beyond terrible. Yet looking at these woods, Kate thought of how much worse it must be for Lynnie, who had lost her first and only love—and baby—in one night.

Kate shook her head. Her breath came out in the air; snow had begun falling.

She rounded the house. She could see a barn and chicken coop and gear shed. She looked up to the second floor of the house. No lights were on anywhere.

You have no one but yourself to blame, she thought as she returned to her car. No, she could blame whomever altered the files. She could blame her bill collectors, Melinda's crooked teeth, her fear of Jimmy getting drafted. She could blame herself for acquiescing with Lynnie that the baby would have a better life—no matter what—if no one at the School found out.

She pulled back down the drive, praying. "Father," she said, "please care for that child, wherever she is. Come into her heart so she can find You in the times ahead."

The snow was falling more thickly. She threw on her wipers and radio and was glad she was unlikely to see cars on her way back to Well's Bottom. Then she thought of coming into her house, facing herself in the mirror—and facing Lynnie tomorrow. There would be no accusation in Lynnie's eyes, though Kate's conscience would always ache.

She reached the road. She hadn't yet turned on her headlights, but she did now, and that's how she made him out: a young man at the mailbox. His hands were inside, and he seemed to be removing mail. His Buick was pulled onto the shoulder, still running with its driver's door open. He looked into her headlights. A teenager, he wore a varsity jacket from Well's Bottom High.

She snapped off her radio, and then she heard his. This must be why he was now looking at her so startled: He hadn't heard her coming.

She rolled down her window.

"Can I talk to you?" she asked.

"You here to see the farm, ma'am?" His voice seemed to be manufacturing confidence.

She glanced to the drawings, then back. "I'm trying to find the lady who lives here."

The boy got a cool look on his face. "I'm the caretaker. I don't know anything except she wants to sell the farm."

"Do you know where she is?"

"I told you. I just take care of the grounds."

"You must know something."

"I swear. I really don't."

"Then where," she asked, pointing, "are you bringing that mail?"

He looked down to his hands. He looked back up.

Kate said, "I have no interest in causing trouble. I just want to know about..." She pursed her lips and fingered the cross on her necklace. "I just want to know if she's all right."

"All right enough to want to sell her farm."

Kate looked at the falling snow. She thought of what Lynnie wanted. But this was Kate's only chance. If she didn't speak up, she'd spend the rest of her life in the flames of guilt.

"No," Kate said. "I mean if *she's* all right."

The boy looked at her as if he didn't understand.

She let out a breath. "The baby."

* * *

Oliver led Kate to Hansberry Pharmacy, and for the next three hours, as an unexpected spring snow piled high outside the back door, Kate and Eva talked. They drank through two pots of tea as afternoon turned to dusk. By the time Kate rose, they had made a decision. They would not tell Lynnie what happened to the baby, and they would not ask Martha to bring the baby back. They would be messengers who reported only to each other, and only with two messages—whether the baby was thriving in her life, and whether Lynnie had changed her mind. If the baby was doing poorly, or Lynnie altered her position, they would break their vows of hiding; but otherwise, they would be doing the right thing. They took each other's hands, then fell into a hug. The snow was still falling when Kate stepped into the alley. She dabbed at her eyes, then squared her shoulders with resolve and hurried out into the night.

PART II

GOING

Samaritan Finder

HOMAN

1969

$\mathcal{T}$ he back of police cars was getting mighty familiar.

There it was, the odor that greeted Homan's every entry: cigarettes, leather, sweat, coffee. How Beautiful Girl would hate this mix of smells. This being morning—a crisp morning in a flat land of shrubs and grass—there were doughnut smells, too, making his belly clench with hunger. He punched himself on the thigh as he sat, furious. *Five times in police cars! Five times you not watchful or got hunger too bad for staying careful! Now here you go again.*

He folded his arms hard over his chest and stared at the chicken wire separating the back from the front, glimpsing his reflection in the rearview mirror. What a sight. Hair like an unsheared sheep, skin grimy, shirt mottled with food and dirt and worry, eyes wild. He shook his head in disgust. Maybe it was just as well Beautiful Girl was with him only in his mind.

He tried calming himself as the car rolled forward. He'd done what he could, same as the other times. He'd raised his hands and even tried what he'd promised himself he'd never do again once he got to the Snare—he'd dared using his voice. As best as he remembered, he'd said, "I'm deaf!" The police had looked at each other while he said it again and again till they got some understanding—and then didn't haul him off to a Snare or stick him behind bars or even ascertain if he was a wanted man. Hallelujah, he'd have thought, if he didn't know better.

He hadn't, the first time. He remembered how it began now, as the police car cruised down this main street, passing people going about business he'd never known—holding a sweetheart's hand where everyone could see, buying a paper, strolling into a grocer's. It was from watching everyday life that he'd been put in that first police car. He'd thought he was hidden as he'd watched the baseball game from the ridge. But someone must have caught sight of him playing along and gotten a nasty notion. Like Wayne Sullivan, only in a pickup.

Now, looking out the window, Homan wasn't surprised to see the car he was in heading toward the police station. His heart thumped harder. If only they did with him what the other officers had done, he'd be safe. He held his breath.

That first time, the boys who beat him in the cave brought him to the police station. When they pulled up, Homan had the presence of mind to peer over the rim of their pickup and see the boys talking with an officer. From the way one boy pointed to his face—bruised from Homan's punch—Homan figured he was accused of jumping the kid. *Ain't this world just upside down?* he imagined himself telling Beautiful Girl. The officer marched him into the station, and Homan wondered which was worse—his bruises from the fight, or his dread.

They sat him on a bench and men came over, doing Yell Faces. One handed him paper and a pencil. Another set a picture before him. From the squiggles Homan knew it was a map, only it looked like a mitten, not a leaping deer. A lady brought him a sandwich and soda, and he ate but skipped the drink, thinking of Dot and Pudding. All the time, the dread wouldn't quit. He still wore his boots, and in his boots was the money, and that gave him confidence. Somehow he'd tell this to Beautiful Girl in the flesh—and soon. Somehow. Finally, two men without uniforms took him to a car without a police light. They put him in the back and drove.

It was yet one more not-understanding in a long chain of not-understandings. Night fell but they kept driving. He couldn't see much except lakes and trees. They reached the edge of some city. Then they opened the door and hauled him out into the cold.

They stood before a place with lit windows, and then walked him inside. It smelled like the laundry building at the Snare, and he smiled, thinking of Beautiful Girl. It was warm, too, and machines were churning wash. When he turned to the men, he saw they'd gone outside. He ran after them only to see their car already pulling onto the road.

He was still free! But, watching their taillights disappear, he got the understanding. He'd been driven far, far away from their town, then tossed off like dirty laundry.

That's what happened again and again. He'd find new hiding places, get his hands on new clothes, and make it for weeks. Then someone would spot him, an unkempt deaf nuisance who looked crazy, and he'd get driven away again. Once they even put him on a bus, handing the driver a ticket. Beautiful Girl and Little One were counting on him. He still saw them in the morning in his mind—Beautiful Girl breathing on Chubby Redhead's tiny makeup mirror and drawing his face with her finger; Little One splashing suds in a tub bobbing with toys—but Somehow seemed remoter every day.

The cops were now passing the police station. He let out his breath. They continued right on out of town, into a brown land sliced up by fences. They just kept on driving. Cattle grazed in the distance. Machines on stilts that looked like birds pecked away at the ground.

After a long time, the car came to a stop in front of a lone ranch house, and a white man and woman came out. They had silver hair, starched clothes, and faces not too cozy with smiles. The man opened Homan's door. Homan felt scruffy and gamey beside the Silver Hairs, and he couldn't imagine why they were ushering him into their house. Later, he would recall this moment as launching one of the most perplexing chapters in his life so far. Now, though, he was just grateful to be entering a house, never thinking what he'd be asked to give them in return.

Immediately, he marveled at how well they treated him. For the first time he had a room of his own, with a desk and dresser and bed. The dresser was filled with nice trousers, white button-up shirts, dungarees, white undershirts, pajamas, socks, even drawers. The food was three squares a day, Silver Wife cooking it good and hot. They didn't use Yell Faces. They treated him as just one of their three guests. They asked only that he tend to the pigs in the back.

The Silvers required something of the two other guests, too. One had skin the color of clay, a black braid, and a stocky build. The other was scrawny, pimply, and blond. Their chores were to accompany Silver Husband when he drove to inspect the pecking machines out back, to sit watching TV preachers with both Silvers, and to spend their afternoons reading a book, the same one Homan found waiting inside a little brown suitcase on his bedspread when he arrived. It was a fat book with a leather cover and pages with golden edges, and it had pictures of an old man with a long beard holding a rod in the air while a river peeled back, a boat setting out in the rain stuffed to the brim with animals, a boy letting loose a slingshot. He guessed it was the Bible. The McClintock boys had told him stories from the Bible—the miracle of loaves and fishes, the Good Samaritan. Maybe these were other stories, but how could he know? He'd set the book in the suitcase and the suitcase under his bed. So in the afternoons, when everyone sat at the dining room table with the book, he went to the garage, which was filled with treasures like broken TVs, old vending machines, and bookcases in need of repair. It was egg-frying hot in the sty and garage, yet with the pigs, a toolbox, and the dream faces of his girls, he was fine.

He figured the two boys had been taken in like him, maybe at their own down-and-out time. But they could read and hear. When he was messing around in the garage, he'd look through the window and see the boys watching the preachers intently and talking to the Silvers, the book open before them. They even ran the praying at meals when everyone clasped hands. Homan kept wondering if the Silvers would expect him to join in, but they left him to his own devices. This arrangement, he thought, wasn't half-bad.

Just one thing gave him the willies. Sometimes when he'd come inside, he'd catch the Silvers making a look at each other. There was also talking at dinnertime, with eyes flickering in his direction. It seemed the price he was paying for this luxury life was letting himself be talked about. He could put up with that till he figured out how to leave.

Leaving was the problem. He wasn't in a place where he could hide behind buildings or jump freights. He was in a land with one long road and one lone house. Cars and trucks whizzed by now and then, but how could he grab a speeding vehicle? There was no traffic light or stop sign as far as he could see. He could just start walking out in the boiling sun, but the police had brought him here, and it seemed a fair bet they'd bring him back.

He considered stealing Silver Husband's car. He'd sit inside it in the garage, feeling the wheel. Even though it was different from the cars at the

McClintocks' and the Snare, it was no puzzle. And even with him not hearing other cars or being able to ask directions, he could easily get away. Except sooner or later things might go wrong. And if the police caught him for thieving, he'd end up serving time before holding Beautiful Girl again.

Then one morning, the Silvers piled him and the boys in the car and drove down the road a long, long way, to a crossroads with a diner, grocer's, service station, and wide field of nothing. A red light blinked above the spot where the roads came together. They pulled into the empty field. A crew of men was already there, and soon a cement truck pulled up with its barrel spinning and another with gray blocks. The crew gathered around Silver Husband, who held up a megaphone. Then they went to work building something, and Homan was expected to join in. He had no idea what they were building, but he saw, as they poured cement for a floor, that it was going to be so big it could easily hold the circuses that came to the Snare. The next day they went back, and the next. It became his job to build walls with the gray blocks. He also helped put on a roof, run wires for lights and pipes for a lavatory, and—this one got him—construct a stage. The mystery of this building and the comforts of the Silvers' home got him off track from getting away just now.

Then one day, after he and the crew set up rows

of chairs inside the building, it got clearer. Just before sunset, he and a few others were sent to the roof for more work, and there he saw, lying flat and waiting to be raised, a huge cross. As he was helping to lift the cross upright, then holding it in place while others secured it, he looked down at the flashing red light marking the meeting of the roads. At the service station across the way, two young men stood with packs at their feet, holding their thumbs out, and a truck driver at the pumps waved them over. They hoisted their packs and got into his front seat, and off they went down the road.

Right. Ride Thumbers. He'd seen them on TV. That was what he had to do.

Getting himself back to the crossroads wouldn't be hard, since they'd been coming every day. It was making a break for the service station that would be tricky—and getting a driver to take him without him needing to speak.

Someone turned on a spotlight. The cross lit up and he stepped out of the beam, looking down to the crew below. It was a nice sight, everyone applauding. Then he looked across the road to the trucks. *That our answer, Beautiful Girl*, he thought. What a nice sight it was, too.

The next day, for the first time, the Silvers, Braidy Boy, and Scrawny Boy got dressed in finery.

Silver Husband put on a suit, Silver Wife a dress with pearls and nylons, the boys pressed shirts and ties. Homan made to do the same, but they shook their heads no and indicated he was not joining them. He couldn't believe it. Finally he was ready and they were acting like his brothers and sisters, leaving him alone.

After the meal, he took refuge with the pigs. Out the window he watched everyone get into the car, carrying their little suitcases with the books, and as they rolled toward the road, he ran after them. But they drove off. He stood at the road, watching the bumper move toward the horizon. He went up to the house and kicked the siding. He went to the clothesline in the back and threw punches at the pants, shirts, sheets. It made him feel good, and not just for evening the score. With each punch he felt how all that church building had muscled him up really good.

He slammed back into the house. He could walk right out of here. He should! Though as he paced in the kitchen, looking out to the pecking cranes, he admitted to himself that he didn't want to be out in the elements again, dirty and frightened, desperate for a dusty hut. He needed to leave, but if he waited until they took him back to that blinking red light, he'd at least get to travel in a truck, maybe even with his new clothes and some food. He just had to find a sack to stuff with provisions. No, enough of sacks. He'd use the little suitcase that came with the book.

The suitcase was still under his bed. He loaded his arms with edibles scrounged from the pantry and headed through the living room. There he saw the TV on, with a preacher like always. What sense did it make leaving on a TV for a deaf man? He made to walk off—

Then something snagged his attention. This show didn't look like the usual show at all. This show was taking place in a huge room with crowds filling the chairs. He knew those chairs. He knew that room. Those were the walls he'd helped lay. The stage. And on the stage a preacher in a white suit stood before a microphone, making a Yell Face, raising his arms in the air. He was so worked up, his hair bounced on his forehead.

Homan sat on the couch. Preacher Bouncing Hair was moving across the stage, sweat rolling down his face. The stage sure looked impressive. Homan had been stubborn about sanding and painting, and he was glad. He imagined Beautiful Girl sitting beside him, looking at him with pride. He laced his hands behind his head and set his feet on the coffee table.

Then he noticed men pushing a ramp to the front of the stage. This was strange. Preacher Bouncing Hair didn't need a ramp, and anyway, he was already on the stage.

Next thing he knew, Preacher Bouncing Hair was making a Come Up wave toward a girl in the aisle. She was in a wheelchair, which a woman behind her was pushing. The crowd was turned to them, and the young girl and the woman had shining eyes.

Homan unlaced his hands and sat up, his elbows on his knees.

The woman—the girl's mother, it looked like—pushed the girl up the ramp and onto the stage, and Preacher Bouncing Hair set his hands on the girl's head. His mouth moved. The mother was weeping, the audience praying. The girl was looking into the preacher's eyes.

Then Preacher Bouncing Hair flung his arms back from the girl and made a huge Yell Face. And the girl stood up from the chair! Homan couldn't believe his eyes. The girl took a step toward the preacher. Her mother set her hand on her breast, folks were crying all over the room, and then— and then—the girl kicked her wheelchair away and skipped across the stage! The audience was beaming, crying, clapping, praying. The girl spun around like a dancer. Preacher Bouncing Hair was raising his arms. The crowd was on its feet.

Homan stared at the television. *No girl needing a wheelchair gonna suddenly jump up and become a ballerina! Maybe the Bible gots miracles like loaves and fishes, but this a trick. No matter what Preacher*

Bouncing Hair say or how hard he fling his arms, legs that don't move don't just fix themselves. Any more than eyes can just fix themselves, or brains, or—

And a chill came over him as he was filled with understanding.

The next morning, he woke to the dream face of Beautiful Girl, lying beside him in the hay of the barn, and Little One, crawling on top of them. Gazing at them, he was sure that his new plan was exactly right. So he felt prepared when Silver Wife handed him nice clothes to put on.

He went into his bedroom to put on the white button-up shirt and pressed pants and retrieved the little suitcase, now filled with utensils, canned food, and extra clothes. He left the book under the bed. He left the shoes they'd given him, too, and put on his own boots, newly shined. When he emerged with the suitcase and stood beside the boys, dressed up with their suitcases, too, the Silvers smiled, never noticing anything was up.

They all got into the car, and as they started down the long road, he saw a trouble he hadn't considered. Braidy Boy was sitting on his one side, Scrawny Boy his other—like guards. He tapped his feet and patted his hands against his thighs. They were all talking, he saw, and probably about him. Probably all that talk they'd been doing about him was a master plan to get him to this preacher.

He looked at his knees and shook his head. Well, he was going to get away, and that's all there was to it.

Then his eyes lit on his suitcase, lodged between his knees, and he felt a jolt of guilt. Here he was, so ready to return their hospitality with thieving and disappearing. They might be taking him on a fool's errand, yet they were just doing what they believed right, and that made them better by far than the good-for-nothings he'd run into through the years. They'd been decent, too, feeding him, giving him a clean bed, shooting no nasty looks. *Maybe you owes them,* he thought. *Maybe you should just walk in that church and do what they want.* Besides, what if they knew something he didn't— and the preacher *did* have the power to bring back his hearing?

Homan hadn't given thought to getting his hearing back since he'd met the McClintocks. Now he thought of them and him conversing, their hands carnivals of stories. He remembered, too, the day at the revival, when they all hoisted themselves up the tree and pressed themselves to the windows and then the singing and clapping and hollering and sermonizing danced through the pane and inside their skin. He hadn't missed hearing after that. Well, there were times when he'd longed to hear Beautiful Girl's voice, and surely he would want to hear Little One's first words. And there was no arguing he wouldn't be in such a mess now if strangers could understand his speech. But what if hearing made him forget how to listen with his eyes, and skin, and nose, and mouth? Or what if the hearing he got was bad, like a TV picture that wouldn't come in clear?

He saw the church now through the windshield. Toweling his palms off on his trousers, he hoped they'd pull into the front lot, which was just a hop, skip, and jump from the crossroads and the trucks now at the service station. Then they drove up, and he saw the front lot was for folks with canes and walkers and wheelchairs. The Silvers went into the back lot, which was awfully far from the service station. He'd have to let himself go in-side—and if he was quick thinking, he could find a place to stash his suitcase and then, when they weren't looking, make his break.

They entered the flow of people coming through the huge front doors, and as soon as they were inside, the Silvers and the boys got caught up shaking hands with others they seemed to know. He wanted to slip off, but someone always man-aged to be at his side. Finally, after what turned into endless hellos, it seemed he'd get his chance. His guards didn't head straight to the seats. They went to the lavatory and took him.

The bathroom had a line, which meant they'd need to be occupied with their business before he could escape. He took in the other churchgoers, wondering if they'd nab him if asked to. It was hard to tell. Most looked well-to-do like the Silvers and put-together like the boys. A few also had differences: An old man wore the dark glasses of the blind, a young man had crutches clamped to his wrists. Homan looked to his guards. In front of him, Braidy was staring into space. Scrawny had gone to the mirror to comb his hair. Homan was not being watched.

This was his chance, maybe his only one all day. He took a step—

And something brushed the back of his arm. He turned. Behind him was a teenage boy in a wheelchair. Above his navy pants, navy blazer, and untucked white T-shirt, he wore his black hair longer than anyone here and carried a light-hearted smartness in his long-lashed eyes. He was looking up at Homan and moving his lips, and as he swept his arm up, making the kind of motion hearing folk made while speaking, it was clear his condition affected his arms and hands. No way was Homan going to lose his chance for this kid. He gestured to his ears and shook his head no. The boy widened his eyes, then nodded, and Homan backed away. But the boy reached out again, his wrist a swim stroke in the air. Then he pulled up the bottom of the T-shirt and motioned, and Homan knew: The kid was in the bathroom to drain the bag that helped him do his business, and he couldn't drain it alone.

Homan shook his head. Not him. Not now. The boy made a hopeful face, and Homan held out his hand to emphasize: No. His chance wouldn't last long, he saw, shooting a look across the room—Braidy was letting himself into a stall, Scrawny examining a pimple. Homan was already shrugging an apology as his eyes settled back on this kid, but when he saw the hope melt into disappointment, he remembered. He was in the Running, going up to one person after another in a train station, trying to get someone to buy him a ticket. He tried talking, miming, pleading—and each one looked at him in fear or hurried by until he got so mad that he shoved one smirking peewee down and ran out the side door. How could he *not* help? It was just one kid and one time. And Braidy Boy was answering nature's call, and Scrawny Boy was buffing his shoe, and Homan could move fast—he'd sure emptied enough bags at the Snare. He set down his suitcase and made a hurried gesture toward a urinal. The boy pushed himself across the room and started pulling down his elastic waistband, and when he could do no more, Homan did what he'd done a thousand times: took out the tube, drained it, and arranged the boy's clothes back to their proper look. The boy peered up with gratitude. Probably Homan was the first Samaritan who'd known what to do.

The deed done, Homan whipped around—just in time to see Braidy step out of the stall and Scrawny turn back from the mirrors. His neck tightening, Homan spun back to the boy, who was, amazingly, gazing into the room with a wry smile. It made Homan look harder at this kid. The boy had a comic book sticking out from his blazer pocket. Freckles danced across his cheeks. He smelled like mint and chocolate.

Then he turned his face up toward Homan, nodded in the direction of the rest of the room, and quickly, so only Homan could see, rolled his eyes. Homan laughed the first laugh in he didn't know how long and rolled his eyes, too.

It felt so good meeting a kindred spirit that Homan almost didn't mind returning to the lobby with his guards, and as they escorted him into the room for the service, he cast his thoughts back to Shortie and Whirly Top. Walking down the aisle toward the Silvers, clutching his getaway suitcase in front of his chest, he remembered how much he'd come to enjoy having friends. The boy—Samaritan Finder, Homan named him—must have felt the same: He'd reached his hand toward Homan before they parted and pressed his fingers into Homan's for a shake.

The day went on and on.

Sandwiched between Scrawny and Braidy, his

suitcase stowed under his chair the same as they'd stowed theirs, Homan imagined the trucks he'd seen when they arrived were long gone. He tried to will more trucks in their place. He tried to will the boys to leave.

Then two muscular men in suits pushed the ramp along the floor to the center of the stage, and as they locked it in place, the boys stood and motioned for Homan to get to his feet. For a moment he debated remaining in his chair, but stubbornness would only create a scene. Besides, the odds of escaping were better if he was standing—even if he had to leave his suitcase behind. Only as they marched him, empty-handed, toward the aisle did he see so many folks already there, with crutches and wheelchairs and canes and companions of every age and girth. Having no belongings was the least of his worries. There was just so much blocking the way.

The boys exited the row into the long line waiting for the ramp. The other hopefuls parted with friendly nods, and he and the boys took their place only a few heads from the stage.

The man at the front of the line had draped his arm over a woman's shoulders and was pulling his leg—fully encased in a cast—up the ramp, and Homan knew he had only so much time to survey his surroundings. He turned to his left, then right, taking in endless rows of filled seats fanning out to the distant walls and side doors. Too bad he was so close to the front, he thought, turning around. As he'd expected, Scrawny was positioned right behind him, with the long line extending as far back as Homan could see. The room was as hard to cross as a river.

Then a motion right behind Scrawny caught his eye—a hand wave at waist level.

Samaritan Finder! Despite his sinking heart, Homan broke into a smile, and Samaritan Finder did the same. But there were hands on Sam's wheelchair, and when Homan lifted his eyes, he saw two dark-haired women behind Sam, gazing at the stage with expectation. Except for one being heavier than the other, they shared a family resemblance with Sam. Yet Sam was paying them no mind, and when Homan met his eyes again, Sam gestured toward the stage and shook his head.

Homan nodded in agreement. Then he turned and saw that the spotlight on the stage now shone on a blind man. He'd thrown off his glasses and was walking forward with a halting gait, a dead giveaway he couldn't see better than before. Why would a person put himself through this? Did he really believe he could see? Or did he just want to fake to please his companion?

A man with crutches picked his way up the ramp, with Homan next in line.

He gazed into the huge room, and though he

couldn't find them, he knew the Silvers were watching. He wished he hadn't stuffed their suitcase with stolen goods. He wished he could repay their hospitality with his cure. Yet he saw now that most people here wanted so hard to be fixed that they'd do anything, and he didn't want it that hard. Beautiful Girl hadn't asked for him to be fixed. Her face had lit up whenever she saw him— just the way he was. If she didn't care about fixing, and he wasn't sure he wanted fixing, forget faking. When his turn came—on the stage, in the spotlight, on TVs across this land—he'd be the biggest failure of this preacher's life.

The man unhinged both crutches and tossed them off. One landed on the stage, one down below, at the foot of the ramp.

Homan should have run off from the bathroom. Braidy and Scrawny would have given chase, maybe tackled him by the trucks, but that would have been a happier situation than becoming the fool of the day. Well, only the first. He'd have company when Sam failed, too.

He met Sam's eyes. Sam was looking hard at him, nostrils round with resentment. He flicked his gaze to Scrawny, who was consulting with the women behind Sam's chair. Next thing Homan knew, Braidy was yanking him aside, and the women were pushing Sam forward.

It all happened so fast, Homan didn't have time

to ask himself what was going on. He didn't need to—Sam was looking up at Homan as he passed, his jaw rigid, his eyes wet. Homan reached out his arm in sympathy, and they touched hands.

Then Sam and the women went up the ramp.

The spotlight shone down on the stage as Preacher Bouncing Hair placed his hands on Sam's head. Homan spun around, searching the crowd, hoping someone was seeing what he saw on Sam's face. But everyone was praying, and when he realized there was nothing he could do, he decided that even though he'd never prayed before, he was going to start now. He'd do it with his hands, just talk right out there in the open. So he did, making his signs hard and fast.

Please, Big Artist, he prayed. *If you even there, that is. Sam just a kid. Get him down from there and put me in his place. So what if I look like the biggest laughingstock in the world. I don't even care if Bouncing Hair for real and I get something I ain't sure I want.*

The preacher's hands flew off.

Sam sat there in his chair, staring at the preacher.

One breath. Two breaths. Five.

And then—

The stouter of the two women marched across the stage and stopped right before Sam. He glared, and though she tugged his arms, he didn't rise to his feet. With an anger in her eyes, she moved her mouth. He did, too, his expression defiant. She lunged, grabbing his shirt as he rolled back, and then he spun his chair so she'd lose her grip. Hands on her hips, she rounded the chair and stepped near—and he slid his arm to the floor, caught it in the cuff of the cast-off crutch, and held it before him like a battering ram. Shocked, she stepped away. The preacher looked confused. Sam turned and locked his eyes on Homan's.

And Homan suddenly knew what to do.

Shoving Braidy out of the way, Homan hurtled up the ramp, seized the chair, and rolled Sam down. Scrawny tried to grab Homan as they hit bottom, but Homan pushed him off, snatched up the other crutch, wedged it by the armrest, swerved Sam around the family behind him, and then they were off, charging down the aisle, passing others waiting in line, hurtling beyond the gapes of the audience, using their double-barreled crutches to make anyone who wanted to stop them jump aside. It was a thrill, dodging the crowd, making their way to the lobby, flying outside, racing toward the van Sam pointed to.

Homan didn't know why Sam was leaving or where he wanted to go. He just knew he'd found his way out and Sam had, too, because when they reached the van, Sam pushed a purse on his side toward Homan, and Homan reached in, and there was a key ring—with the van key.

You caught my prayer—and you did me even better! he thought, looking back at the church after he got Sam in the van and slid himself behind the wheel. He could see Scrawny and Braidy and Sam's womenfolk bursting out of the church and pointing toward the van. But Sam was already motioning for them to go *now*, even as the boys and the ladies came running. Homan hit the gas, and Sam opened his mouth with joy, and they shot out onto the road.

MARTHA

1969

ℒook, Ju-Ju," Martha said. "The ducklings have gotten so big!"

She gazed into the stroller and stroked the tawny curls. Julia, seeing the pond ahead, kicked her ten-month-old feet in excitement. "Remember when we first found this park? The ducklings hadn't even been born. Goodness. Can it possibly be September already?"

Julia couldn't reply, though it hardly mattered; Martha loved speaking to her. She was an unfussy child, smart and gorgeous; her face was heart-shaped and broad, eyes dark and lively, curls as merry as cursive writing. Julia wasn't always merry: Her expression was often serious, and she was less prone to laughter than many children. But whenever Martha spoke to her, Julia broke into a smile so sweet and trusting, Martha felt light in her chest. This was not, however, the only reason she talked a lot to Julia. It was because talking, along with their daily routine of park walking, block stacking, bubble blowing, and hand clapping, made them appear like any happy grandmother and granddaughter. Despite their still-unusual living arrangements, house-sitting for her student Landon in Maplewood, New Jersey, Martha felt sure that as long as they continued living in an inconspicuous—and, as had already proven necessary, elusive—manner, no one would suspect the truth.

At the edge of the duck pond, Martha sat on their regular bench. For the first time, she'd reached this park before Ivamae and Betty. She'd been so worried about what might happen later today, when Landon finally returned home from his summer house, that she'd driven here from Maplewood too quickly. She checked her watch. Only ten forty. Martha looked toward the edge of the park for her friends. *Her friends*. She smiled to herself. Her students had loved learning the history of words—how, if you traced the origin of "pajamas," you'd walk back in time and across the sea to India and Persia. Or how "hello" was invented by Alexander Graham Bell so people had something to say when answering a phone. "The language you use," she'd pointed out to them, "shows us history." And when she cast her gaze back to the

Martha of last September, there was no hint of the word "friends" in that land.

"Matilda!" she heard.

She spun around. Ivamae and Betty were coming toward her, pushing the strollers with the children they looked after. Martha waved.

"I knew you'd be here early," Ivamae said, her voice as deep as the gospel she sang on Sundays. The four-year-old she looked after, Audrey, jumped from the stroller and ran to Martha, calling, "Miss Matilda!" Betty followed, three-year-old Lawrence sucking his thumb.

"Of course," Betty said, her Irish youth still broguing her words. "She's nervous."

Martha hugged Audrey. "Did you bring your bread today?" the preschooler asked.

"I did."

"Can I have some for the ducks?"

"Yes." Martha reached into the bag hanging from Julia's stroller and removed a loaf of fresh bread. She said to her friends, "Well, it's a big day, but I'm hopeful it will work out."

"I'd be a mess," Betty said. "When husbands come back after working overseas all summer, they can get strange ideas in their heads."

Ivamae said, "I once had a husband tell his wife to stop working, and after that she didn't need me anymore and I had to find a new job."

Martha sucked in air so she wouldn't reveal that

Landon had no wife and would hardly make such a pronouncement. Yet she also knew that, as a successful artist accustomed to quiet, he might find the presence of an old woman and a baby to be intrusive. It was indeed possible they'd have to leave his house, and with it this park and these friends.

Ducks were now waddling near. Martha handed Audrey some bread, which she tore into pieces and threw at the ducks. "They like your bread, Miss Matilda," Audrey said. "Me too."

Betty, taking a seat on the bench, said, "My ex liked it when I baked."

"That's a man for you," Ivamae said, lowering herself as well. "He likes your baking, but that doesn't stop him from running around."

"I didn't want him home anymore anyway."

"It would have been a far better thing if you'd tossed his sorry behind out first. It's always best when you do your own deciding."

Martha longed to join in with details about her marriage, her living situation, her entire autobiography. But, afraid of misjudging their capacity for secrecy, she'd resigned herself to a guarded friendship, which often amounted to listening and murmuring sympathetically. This appeared to satisfy them; after all, she was an elderly woman looking after a child, the same as they, and they enjoyed her company.

Not that Ivamae and Betty thought Martha was

a nanny. The first day they'd met, in the spring, she'd offered the same lie she'd used with Henry and Graciela, then Landon. That day, as she'd just started finding her way around Maplewood, she'd come upon this park in nearby South Orange. When she walked Julia toward a bench, she saw two women her age, one dark, one fair, both with white hair and strollers. She'd talked to Julia as the women sat laughing on a bench and the children with them fed the ducks. Then, as she was pushing a sleeping Julia back toward the Dodge, she heard a deep voice say, "Beautiful child you got there." Martha looked over, and the Irish-looking woman said, "Good behavior run in the family?" Later Martha understood that was her cue for saying Julia was no relation and Martha was a nanny. But having been only recently initiated into the need for deceit, she reached for the same mistruth she'd already used. "She belongs to my grandniece"— and here she opted to embellish—"and, with her working in Manhattan, and her husband's business taking him overseas, she needed someone around." Betty said, "You feeling back in practice?" Martha brushed Julia's fine curls with her hand. "I didn't have any of my own. This is new to me." Ivamae tilted a bag of candy her way. "Come back tomorrow," Betty said as Martha reached in. "We'll coach you." She did, and their instructions picked up where Graciela's had left off. It was as if there were a secret language of mothers that no woman knew until she moved to that distant land.

Betty said, "We should be giving you more hope. Maybe nothing will change."

Martha said, "I'm just trusting they'll want me to stay."

The three friends brought out their lunches, and as they ate, Martha hoped Landon would indeed want her to stay. He'd hinted in his last call from Cape Cod that she needn't rush to leave, adding that he had several commissions and would spend most of his time in his metal-working studio. Martha worried he might come to feel differently once he became aware of the disruptions of a child.

The three friends finished their lunch and balled up their bags. Wouldn't it be nice if Julia could grow up with Lawrence and Audrey and Ivamae and Betty? Martha lifted her out of the stroller, held her close, and looked out to the pond. *What is the history of the word for "child"? What is the future of the word for "mine"?*

She felt so at home around here, Martha thought as she made the turn onto South Orange Avenue, Julia asleep in the back. And, this being a costly area, house-sitting was certainly ideal. Eventually they would have more money; Eva had written that she thought she'd find a buyer for the farm soon, and Martha could always teach again. Teaching, though, would have to wait until Julia was in kindergarten, and that was four years away. *Four years.* Martha tightened her grip on the steering wheel. She was seventy-one already, and every day, as Ivamae and Betty spoke of pains in their knees or their fear of broken hips, Martha had to acknowledge that she too would begin to slow down. It seemed as if she were in a race: Julia's freedom versus Martha's health. She remembered what Henry had said when he'd slammed the trunk of the Dodge and hurried to the driver's window to say good-bye last spring: *It's all going to work out, Mrs. Zimmer.* He'd been right, as the summer had shown, so she simply had to believe that the next few hours and next few months—and heaven help her, she did not wish to be greedy, but the next many years—would show her that, too.

She was well aware, however, that Henry had offered his optimism in haste as she'd left his hotel. She remembered that terrible moment now, as she drove down Wyoming Avenue toward Landon's. The first months of Julia's life, when they'd remained in the hotel, had been equal parts peace, play, and child-rearing practice. Martha was writing letters regularly, sometimes to the older Julia, sometimes to the handful of students to whom Eva had written when everything first happened—asking them to send their correspondence to Eva, who then mailed them to the hotel in a manila envelope. Henry needed extra hands, too, so some afternoons, when Julia was asleep, Martha sat at the front desk. By late spring, Martha had produced enough letters to Julia that Graciela gave her a keepsake box—a two-foot-square wooden box lined with felt and carved with flowers, animals, and plants. The top had hinges, and whenever Martha set a letter inside and the hinges squeaked with the joy of a baby bird being fed, Martha would think, *Even if they—whoever they might be—come to cart Julia away, she'll have my words to hold on to.*

Then came a Sunday in May—Mother's Day, of all ironies. She shouldn't think about it, she told herself, driving past the reserve where she often took Julia to feed deer. Yet it happened once so it could happen again; she couldn't let herself forget.

Martha, having helped the children bake a cake for Graciela, had returned with Julia to room 119 to rest up for dinner. She'd lain down in one of the dresses she'd brought from the farm and was half-asleep when she heard footsteps run up to her door, followed by insistent knocking. "Mrs. Zimmer?" It was Graciela.

The moment she opened up, Graciela flew into the room and shut the door. "There is a man in the lobby looking for you."

Martha took a step back. "Who?"

"He would say only that he is here on official business."

"*What?*"

"He would not tell me what he meant. He said he would only tell you."

"He didn't give you a hint?"

"He said...he said you had information on a missing person."

Martha forced her eyes to hold steady, so she would not turn and look at Julia.

"Did he...was he a policeman?"

"He was not in a uniform. But he said he was from a school."

"*A school?*"

"It makes no sense. A missing person, a school. You are retired."

"What did you tell him?"

"That you were out, and we would call him when you returned. He said he had come a very long way, and he would get a room and wait. We could not say we were full. The parking lot is empty."

"Is he in a room?"

"He is in the lobby. I wanted to make him leave, but Henry said we should tell you before we do anything."

Martha finally turned and looked. Julia, beautiful Ju-Ju, lay asleep in the bassinet. Martha sat on the corner of the bed and set her hand on Julia's chest. "Oh dear."

"He must be mistaken. You know nothing about a missing person."

Martha dropped her hand to her lap.

"Julia, she does belong to you. Yes?"

Martha nodded. She ran her fingers down Julia's little dress and held the tiny hands in hers. Finally she looked at Graciela. "We must leave," she said. "Will you help?"

That very hour, they left. Henry, asking no questions, just moved them out quickly through a back door while Graciela staffed the desk and the man in the lobby looked at his watch. Then, while Henry took over the desk, Graciela called Landon. Already in Cape Cod, he said Martha could have his house in Maplewood all summer.

It won't always be like this, she told herself as she slipped away down the service road. Yet having no idea how she'd been found, she committed herself to doing everything she could to stay hidden. She would adopt a false name with those who did not already know her. She would stop using return addresses when writing to Eva.

Now, as Martha pulled up to the house in Maplewood, Landon's Jaguar was already in front of the garage, which he'd converted into his metal-working studio. *Please say we can stay.* But they would leave if they had to.

Martha carried Julia through the back door. The

aroma of noodles and spicy sauce suffused the kitchen, and a jazz recording came from the living room. Julia made questioning sounds. They headed down the hall, past Landon's suitcases still waiting to go upstairs, past the table where Martha kept his mail. Some envelopes had fallen to the floor, and there they remained. Martha looked at the disarray. Could she live with someone so untidy?

They stepped into the living room. Landon, in black sweater and black jeans, was in a chair, one hand cradling a phone, one hand holding a letter. His eyes caught them as they stood in the archway, and he waved. "I need to go," Landon said into the phone. Martha could smell Landon's cologne across the room. She'd forgotten the cologne. She'd liked it the night he'd come back to this house to give her the key, but now it smelled out of place, in this home of warm milk and applesauce and grilled cheese sandwiches. Julia squirmed in Martha's arms, and Martha hurriedly carried her to the playpen in the dining room.

Martha was sitting on the floor, handing Julia's favorite doll over the bars, when she heard Landon hang up, then call out, "Mrs. Zimmer!"

She turned as he strode into the dining room. Then he caught a look at Julia. "She's so much bigger!" he said, looking down. *That's how I used to be*, Martha thought. Now she would bend to the child's level. Landon was not about to do that, so Martha rose.

"Mrs. Zimmer," he repeated, "it's been great having you house-sit this summer."

"It's been our pleasure."

"But, oh, look, look." He thrust a letter at her. "Did you notice this?"

"What is it?"

"It's from the Rosati Foundation. I got their Master of American Arts grant! Fifty thousand dollars for my contributions to the fine arts!"

"That's marvelous!"

"I am on cloud nine." He did a little pirouette. "There is a catch, though it won't mean anything to you. And that cute little baby."

"A catch?"

"I have to do a few demonstrations for the public so they can see what a metal sculptor actually does. But they'll just come right to my studio. You won't even know they're here."

"I'm sure we won't."

"Oh, and I do have to take on a few apprentices. It'll be short-term. It's not like you'll be tripping over strangers in the house."

She forced herself to smile.

"I know you've been wondering if you could stay, so I'll cut to the chase. Stay! Stay!"

She bent down again to the playpen. "Did you hear Uncle Landon? He's such a nice man."

"Oh," Landon said, "the pasta!"

She watched him run off to the kitchen, and only after he was out of sight did she return to Julia's eyes. "What are we going to do now?" she said.

That night, it took ages to get Julia to sleep, though Martha hardly minded. As fond as she was of Landon, this was not an acceptable situation, yet she could not imagine how to refuse his invitation. In the classroom, Martha had had no trouble finding words, but this facility had not persisted outside the schoolhouse doors. Even with Earl—*especially* with Earl—it was easier to sweep her assertions, opinions, and even preferences under his. It had never occurred to her to question whether she lacked the courage to state them or felt he mattered more than she; she'd simply become skilled in going along. Now she was in a new time of her life. Might the kinds of words come to her that had never come before?

Hoping an answer would present itself, she went downstairs and found Landon in the living room, drinking from a carafe of wine. He said, "There's tea for you in the kitchen."

After she had settled onto the love seat, teacup beside her, she busied herself with knitting while he told her the high points of his summer. She lost herself in his stories of life on Cape Cod until, just as she finished her tea, he turned the topic.

"What's it like, Mrs. Zimmer," he said, "suddenly having a baby to take care of?"

She looked at his plants. Julia loved the flowering ones.

"I mean, is it what you thought it might be like? If you ever thought of it, that is?"

She gazed at the yarn in her hands and began moving them methodically. "I'd been alone many years. When my husband was alive, I felt comforted by his presence. Just hearing him in another room was satisfying." She left out what had not been satisfying, though now, thinking of the pleasure she'd come to feel every day, she remembered the discontent she'd once harbored. "It's late," she said. "I'm sorry. I'm speaking gibberish."

"No. Please, go on. Except for one possibility that went kablooie, I don't know that I'll ever have anyone important in my life, let alone a kid. It's embarrassing to admit."

"Don't be embarrassed. I'm in your house. With a child."

"Then don't you be embarrassed, either."

She knit awhile. Finally she said, "I think I can say that having Julia around has returned the feeling of a presence to my life, though in a different way from the one I lost."

"What do you mean?"

She stopped knitting and closed her eyes. "Even down here in the living room, I feel as if I can hear her breathe through the ceiling. With my eyes shut, I can see her sleeping in the crib, her face so peaceful in the streetlight coming through the curtains. I feel she knows I'm here, too. And that is...very nice." She opened her eyes.

He poured another glass of wine. "You want?"

She shook her head. "My husband was a teetotaler."

"Excuse me. Isn't he, you know, dead?"

"A person gets set in her ways."

"I'll say. At seventy she takes up with her grand-niece's baby and leaves the only home she's known most of her life. That's set like concrete."

She allowed herself a small laugh.

"Come on, Mrs. Zimmer. Live a little." He snatched a glass off a shelf and hovered the carafe over it. "Just a thimbleful?"

"All right."

He poured a full glass. "Then you'll have more than enough."

She had not touched alcohol in fifty years, and it seemed ludicrous for her to do so in this situation. Though to her surprise, the wine was delicious. *Earl is not here.* She took a second sip. *Julia is here. Landon is here. And I am here. Whoever I am.*

She set down the empty glass, aware that she already felt askew. It was not a feeling she wished to have, but it softened the awkwardness of sitting here with a young man who had opened his house to her. She lifted her knitting. It took effort to move her hands.

"Can I ask you something?" Landon said. "You don't have to answer. She's not your great-grand-niece, is she?"

In spite of herself, Martha smiled into her knitting. Then, regaining control of her face, she looked up and said, "Tell me why you have two homes, Landon."

He ran his hand through his hair. "Some people are just restless. Remember how I always wanted to sharpen my pencils? I did that about ten times a day just to look outside."

"I do remember." She smiled more openly.

"When I started getting sales in galleries, I wanted to have a second place to retreat to. You know, my parents moved to New Jersey before I went to college, and this house was a little close to them, and I don't know about you, but I can't be myself around some people. Yet I didn't want to ditch this place, so I started going away for the summers, renting places up and down the coast. Then I visited a friend on the Cape, and decided to buy a home there."

Martha heard Julia make a sound in her sleep.

"Do you need to check on her?" Landon said, overly worried.

She shook her head. "That's the sound she makes when she's having a happy dream. I wondered at first how to tell if she was having a dream or a nightmare, but it's gotten easy."

"You really love her, don't you."

She nodded, head down, and felt her eyes fill.

Landon said, "I have an idea. My place on the Cape is just sitting there all winter. It's in one of those all-year-round towns, so it has heat. And privacy. You could stay there instead of here."

"That is so... That is very generous."

"Like I said when we talked in May, it's nice being able to do something for someone who meant so much in my life. Besides, something's happening to you, Mrs. Zimmer."

"I beg your pardon?"

"You look less...oh, I hate to say it, but I will. You look less lonely."

She peered up at him.

"In school, you were always cheerful. And also at those Christmas parties. Yet there'd be moments when you'd get another look, a sad look. Far away."

Had her struggle been so apparent? How could she hide Ju-Ju if she couldn't even hide herself?

"That's why I made that lighthouse man for you," he went on. "I wanted you to have company."

"Really? I didn't know that."

"But you don't have that look at all now. And you're wearing pants and blouses, not dresses all the time. And your hair is different. Not tied up."

She felt herself blush. "Sometimes, with Julia, combing and ironing aren't convenient."

"The point is, you look less sad. I think this is all—whatever it is—good for you."

She eyed him. "Even though you don't know whatever it is, Landon?"

He took one last sip. "Even though I don't know. And I don't need to know, either."

And so on a day in October, when the leaves were at the height of their color, Martha and Julia pulled into a driveway in the town of Harwich Port, on Cape Cod.

It had been hard to say good-bye to Ivamae and Betty, especially in a cloud of dishonesty: She told them her niece's family was moving and she'd been asked to accompany them. She would stay in touch, she promised; and could they give her pictures of themselves? Then she drove away, trembling with loss. How long could they keep living like this? Would she ever be able to have not just friends, but friends who would know her autobiography?

Landon's house was on a side street off the main road, Route 28, and set high above the water. Like its neighbors, the gray-shingled, two-story house was entered from the side and had a small side lawn, hydrangea bushes, cedar trees, window boxes, rosehips growing along the back fence—

and a view of a calm Nantucket Sound. Martha opened the car door and brought Julia out, almost intoxicated by the salty scent.

She jiggled Julia. "Look," she said. "Our next home."

She gazed around. None of the other houses had lights in their windows.

"Well," she said. "We do indeed have privacy. We just have to make sure that privacy doesn't become loneliness."

She peered down the street. One of the houses had a ladder reaching up to the second floor. A man was climbing down the ladder, a golden retriever waiting faithfully at the bottom.

"Ju-Ju," she said, "what do you say we do?"

Julia looked into Martha's face, then reached out her hands and tapped Martha's cheeks. One of their many habits, it always made Martha laugh, and that made Julia laugh, too.

It's always best when you do your own deciding, Ivamae had said.

"That's right," Martha said. "We can make new friends." She shut the car door and nuzzled Julia's face. Then they went to meet the man with the dog.

Ghost

HOMAN

1970

S am rapped on the dashboard with his stick and pointed to the roadside stop up ahead, but Homan had already seen them.

He'd gotten a lot of practice spotting Ride Thumbers in the months they'd been together. Having a third person around meant one more body in the van, throwing off any police on the prowl for a young white boy on the run with a colored man. A third person also meant one more set of hands to help Homan maneuver Sam into campgrounds or up steps too high for the portable ramp they kept in the van. And it meant one more companion to join their amusement. Though even when it was just them, life with Sam was constantly amusing. So much so, Homan thought as they'd entered this cloudless land of red-rock mountains, it sometimes even took a homing pigeon's mind off the problem of finding his way home.

These Ride Thumbers weren't like any they'd picked up before. For one, they were a pair, and two, they were girls. But maybe they'd be as much fun as the long-haired kid who'd invited them for an overnight stay in his family home or the gray-haired hiker who'd bought them beans from a roadside stand or the men of all ages and colors who'd escorted them to every manner of wonder: a desert of white sand, houses carved into cliffs, a humongous canyon of red, orange, and yellow plunging down to a river. What adventure might they have with these two?

Homan pulled the van over, and the girls grabbed their bags and ran toward them. They were far younger than him and a little older than Sam. The tall blonde wore a blue top and purple skirt. The short, dark-haired one had a cowgirl look, with a red vest over a white shirt and jeans.

Like everyone, they were surprised when they opened the side door. The front of the van had a driver's seat, though on the passenger side were tracks that kept Sam's wheelchair in place. The back of the van had no seats, just a lounge chair secured in place, egg-carton foam laid out flat, the portable ramp, and their clothes. Homan leaned over to unroll Sam's window. Homan didn't know what Sam was saying but figured it amounted to,

Welcome, ladies. My name Sam, and this my friend, he deaf and I don't know his name. Him and me do some things different from you. That chair help keep me from setting too long in this one, and you can make yourself at home in it, 'cause I like being co-pilot. Or set on the foam, it for when I sleep. Just get yourself situated and tell me where you off to. We ain't got nowhere to be, so we'll go wherever you please.

Homan watched over Sam's shoulders as the girls' faces got playful, which always happened when Sam talked to ladies. Sam had the kind of pleasure-loving manner and young-boy cuteness girls couldn't resist, with his thick black hair, knowing smile, and blue eyes never far from a twinkle. So it was no wonder the blonde was giggling when she tossed her bag in the van, bringing the scent of strawberries. Her friend came in after, a sack on her shoulder, beaded bracelets around one wrist. Strawberry threw herself into the lounge chair. Beaded Circles sat on the foam.

Homan waited to hit the gas while they talked, Sam no doubt asking how to get where these Thumbers were going. Strawberry found a pen and drew on her arm—maybe a map—then leaned forward and laid her arm on Sam's thighs. He ran his thumb over her inky skin, and when she sat back he made the gesture he and Homan had invented early on, one of the few he could easily do, holding his hands in the air and indicating by their distance apart how far they'd be going now. This drive would be short, though how short— till afternoon? tomorrow?—Homan couldn't tell. He wished Sam knew his signs. But Sam could barely bend his wrists, his elbows went only so far, and except for one thumb, his fingers were more for show than action. That's why he used his stick to point, and a mug with a handle to drink, and a leather sleeve that held eating utensils. Mostly they relied on their faces and sweeps of their hands, Homan keeping his disappointment inside. It was the price he had to pay to be with Sam. That, and the fear of police bearing down on them, this time for kidnapping. Homan had painted the white van brown, and Sam had chucked his navy suit. And if that wasn't enough and they got caught, then going to prison for stealing the Silvers' car would be a walk in the park by comparison.

Strawberry sat back then, grinning like a just-fed cat, and as Sam gestured to the road ahead, Homan felt the now-familiar burn in his gut. It could happen anytime—during a laugh with Sam, at a scenic overlook with a Thumber, while drinking orange pop—and suddenly Homan would wish Beautiful Girl were along, then remember why she wasn't. The anytimeness of it was hard, but mornings were worse. Beautiful Girl would be waiting for him, just like when he first got lost, only now she'd be on the far side of a window. Sometimes she'd be drawing and look to the glass. Sometimes she'd be lifting Little One from a high chair and gazing outside. He'd come near, signing, *Good morning, beautiful girls*, over and over. But they'd just keep searching out the window. *How in the blazes you ever finding your way back?* he'd ask himself when he'd open his eyes. Then he'd take in the grandness of the view, or the sight of his friend on the foam, and wonder: *Is it bad to want fun till you do?*

Homan bumped his knuckles against his stomach to push the burn down deep. Then he placed his hands on the wheel and drove.

That first day with Sam, so many months ago, as Homan had sped off from the church, Sam moving his forearms like a bandleader, both of them laughing, they went onto and off roads for the longest time, hoping to throw any pursuers off the scent. Finally, after a tangled-enough path and seeing no one in their rearview, Sam gestured for Homan to pull over, then open the glove compartment, get out his stick, and unfold a page. From its ropy design Homan knew it was a map, and the sight of it distressed him even more than the prospect of rotating red lights. He'd been lost so many times over, and maps were such a snaggle, and Sam couldn't tell him where they were, and

Homan had no idea how far he'd gone since he'd stood in Roof Giver's bedroom with Little One sleeping in the basket and placed a pretend wedding ring on Beautiful Girl's finger. He set his head on the steering wheel in despair.

A moment later, Sam tapped him with his stick. Homan looked over and saw Sam eyeing him with concern. Sam waited a few moments, then pointed to a paper bag on the floor.

Inside was a heap of candy bars in silver-and-blue wrappers. Sam directed Homan to get one, tear off the wrapper, and fit the candy between his thumb and index finger. As Sam chewed, he nodded for Homan to take one for himself. Homan hesitated. Except for what he'd found in garbage cans, he'd never eaten candy outside the Snare circuses. Sam nudged him on with a push of his chin. So Homan peeled off a wrapper and sank his teeth in, and for a moment the chocolate and peppermint swept his hopelessness away.

He pulled back onto the road, following Sam's pointing stick. He had no idea where Sam wanted to go, but without a clue about his own route, Homan just drove, making the most of being in charge of a vehicle. He found the turn signals. He figured out the cigarette lighter. He reached for the wipers and got a spray of water instead. A few miles later, Sam called Homan's attention to another bag, this one filled with bubble gum. Sam popped in a piece and blew a huge bubble. Homan tried but didn't know how, until Sam showed him. It took a few rounds, and soon they were blowing pink bubbles together.

Many miles later, Homan tried to teach Sam something, too. He set another candy bar on his lap. Then he pursed his fingers together like a beak, touched them to his mouth, made a chewing motion, and smacked his lips—his sign for candy. Sam looked curiously, so Homan did it again, pointing to the candy. Slowly, Sam's face awakened. Homan moved his hand in a way that suggested Sam might try it. But Sam could get only so far before he shook his head.

The highway deposited them onto a main street. They cruised for a few blocks until Sam pointed to a parking space and Homan pulled the van in. They were in front of a serious-looking building with stone steps. It wasn't a house—thank goodness. What was it?

Sam gestured toward the stone steps. Of course: He needed help getting inside, and Homan could give it, having gotten Man-Like-a-Tree up steps many times. Homan set up the portable ramp and wheeled Sam down. Then, with Sam turning himself backward, Homan hauled him up the steps and inside the big glass door.

They entered a large, cool room with a stone floor, high ceiling, and countertops at chest level.

Though Homan had never been in one before, he knew they were in a bank.

They crossed the floor to a counter where a lady looked at Homan, and Homan nodded down to Sam. She leaned over, and he talked up to her. Then Sam gestured for Homan to get something from the purse chained to his belt. That's where he kept the van key, and now Homan removed a wallet and slim book and gave the lady both. She handed back a paper Sam signed—the pen, like the candy, between thumb and forefinger— and gave him an envelope of money.

Things were getting interesting.

Their next stop was a five-and-dime. Aisles sprawled tall before them like corn in a field, only instead of vegetation, there were sheets and dishes and aprons and detergent and anything you could need, packaged and folded, price tags dangling. They moved through, Sam pointing with his stick, Homan placing goods in a cart: Sterno, canteens, a pot, plates, a camping knife, a flashlight, lighters, egg-carton foam for Sam, a sleeping bag for Homan, blankets, pillows. So today wasn't their final day together. Homan almost clapped his hands in applause.

Next was a used-clothing store. There they tried on shirts and jackets and shoes and pants, positioning themselves before a mirror, each commenting with his expression whether the selection flattered the wearer. Sam fancied leather jackets, T-shirts with long-haired guitarists, pajama bottoms with elastic waists. Homan, who'd never had his pick of clothes, couldn't make up his mind, so he let Sam decide: a green-and-red-checked suit with a yellow button-up shirt. They also saw a cooler and an old lounge chair, and Sam nodded to get them, too.

Last stop was a grocer's. Homan had seen stores like this only from curbs, and being in one put him in a daze. So Sam made the picks: bread and sliced meat and chips and pudding and pop and candy. Then Sam pointed to a rack of magazines. The ones he wanted were up high and had brown paper covering their fronts, and when Homan got them down, he peeked behind the paper. The covers all had pictures of busting-out-of-their-undies ladies. Homan gave Sam a look with one brow raised high. Sam made his face all angelic, and they laughed.

Then they drove a long time, the sky turning from day to night. Finally Sam gestured down a side road that wound away from the highway, until, far from the nearest house, they stopped and got out. It was chilly, and Homan built a fire and wrapped Sam in blankets. They ate, and it was delicious. Then afterward, an extraordinary thing happened. While they were savoring their dessert, Sam moved his hands up and down with a questioning look and pointed to the pudding. It was the first time Homan saw the gesture, but he knew Sam meant, *Show me your sign.* Astounded, he made the sign for pudding. Sam nodded, then made his question again: *gum, moon, fire.* Homan signed and signed and felt something uncurl inside him, like baby shoots rising from the soil.

He showed Sam tricks he'd worked out at the Snare. After taking the bottlecap from his pop, Homan made it disappear from one hand and appear in the other. He pulled the lace from one of his new shoes and tied a knot with one hand. Then Sam got his own idea—a fancy form of mischief. They took a clear plastic bag that a jacket had come in. They untwisted the wires from the price tags and threaded them through the bottom of the bag. Then they set the bottlecap in a cradle they made of the wires, poured in Sterno, and set it aflame. The plastic bag rose. As they laughed with amazement, it lifted higher and farther, glinting with stars, floating above the land. It was a happy ghost only they could see, an explorer who'd sail on forever.

Show me your sign, Sam asked once it was out of their sight.

Homan almost replied with *bag* or *sky.* Instead he pointed to Sam and signed a word that, for so very long, he hadn't let himself think. *Friend,* he signed. *My friend.*

* * *

Now, months after they'd launched the ghost, half a day after they'd picked up the girl Thumbers, Homan steered the van into hills toward what he realized was a house.

Night had fallen. In the outdoor lighting that greeted the four of them, Homan could see vehicles parked on the grass between the driveway and the front walk. The house was long with a flat roof, and all the windows were lit, with people visible in every one. It was not the first party he'd ended up at with Sam, but it was the largest and most remote. They'd driven into mountains to get here, winding past fir trees, looking up at birds with wide wings.

The girls were giggly and full of life, and as soon as he'd parked, Beaded Circles jumped out of the van. Strawberry followed, then twirled herself around like a dancer. She began running toward the house, then turned. By then, Homan was out, and Beaded Circles—who'd offered far more assistance than the other—was helping him with the ramp. Strawberry pranced back, speaking, as Homan guided Sam down the ramp. When Sam reached the ground, Strawberry curtsied. Then he set his palms on the knobs on his wheels and pushed down the walkway to the house. She came right along, doing a slow, gliding dance beside him.

Homan turned to Beaded Circles, who was

watching her friend and shaking her head. She looked up at him, her face friendly but not flirty, and tipped her head for them to follow.

The size of the crowd made entering the front door a chore. Homan and Beaded Circles shouldered their way into a room smelling of sweat, cigarettes, brew, cologne, and something like mildew. He could feel a thumping through his feet and knew music must be playing. Bodies in colorful clothes pressed close, dancing and conversing.

Being one of the tallest individuals in the room, Homan spotted Sam easily, with the crowd having parted so he could wheel through. Strawberry was moving alongside him, and Sam was talking to whomever turned his way, making his hand-tipping motion for wanting a drink. Homan moved through the crunch of food nibblers and brew drinkers, and whenever he looked back, Beaded Circles was following. He was in a group, he thought as the four of them wound through the crowd. He was in a group with a handsome young man and two lovely ladies, and he felt himself smiling. They reached a side room, where they lined up, waiting for amber liquid, Sam asking Homan with a motion of his hands to get his mug from the cloth bag on the back of his chair. Although Homan did not take a cup for himself, no one seemed to mind. They simply acted as if he belonged.

The house was surely owned by a rich man. It had rust-colored tile floors and animal hides tacked to the walls. Long, poufy sofas sprawled across the big room, which also had a color TV and a record player with huge boxes beside it— the sources, Homan discovered, of the thumping. The kitchen had green counters, a see-through table, and two iceboxes. The hallways led to three bathrooms, each showier than the last, and four bedrooms, one with a bed that wiggled like a flask of water. Homan imagined walking through this house with Beautiful Girl beside him, his arm around her shoulder, hers around his waist, both of them with wide eyes.

Then his little group went out to a back porch that overlooked an oval-shaped pool. Immediately, Strawberry ran down to the blue water. A few people were inside, their drinks on the diving board, their feet moving back and forth as they held on to floating toys. Strawberry turned to the porch and swept her arm toward them to come join her. Sam shook his head once, making a quick no, and for a change didn't have his ladies' man smile. Strawberry made a pout, but he did not give in. Nor would he meet Homan's eyes, and as he hastily rolled away, Homan wondered if diving into a pool was why Sam was in that chair.

He and Beaded Circles followed after Sam, along a terrace that hugged the rear and side of the house. Strawberry ran up, flipping her hair and giggling, and just as Sam got back his smile, they came to a patio with vines growing up a criss-cross fence. The vines gave off that mildewy smell Homan had noticed when they'd first come inside. The people on the patio saw Strawberry and waved, and then she and Sam went over.

Homan felt a touch on his arm. Beaded Circles was looking at him, discomfort in her eyes. She jerked her head toward the house.

Sam and Strawberry were talking to the others on the patio, and every face was full of pleasure.

Homan took a seat on a bench to Strawberry's right. Beaded Circles sat near him, on a wicker chair, looking uncomfortable. Sam was holding court, the other people listening, heads in their hands. He was telling a story. Maybe a story about diving into a pool.

Homan felt a tap on his arm.

Strawberry was offering him a cigarette. At the Snare, the big shot smoked cigarettes from a holder. The guard with the dogs chewed tobacco. The skinny guard smoked a pipe. Homan, disgusted to think of being anything like them, waved the cigarette away.

Then Strawberry did something he hadn't seen smokers do. She took the cigarette back, inhaled, and passed it to the person on her other side, who did the same. Homan understood, watching, that the cigarette, not the vines, was what gave the patio its odor. So it wasn't tobacco. But if it were mildew, it wouldn't be handed from person to person, everyone drawing in, even Sam, his fingers holding it the way he held candy and pens. Only Beaded Circles sent it along without raising it to her lips.

If Beautiful Girl were here, he wondered, would she want to stay on this patio with these smoking people? Or would she want to do what he'd seen other couples do as they'd moved along the terrace: go off together and sit in the distance, enjoying a party of two? He imagined them out on the grass, making his signs, laughing—and then the realization that he might never again have the opportunity to retreat into their private haven, where life, for all its bitterness, always tasted sweet, hit him as if for the first time, along with that burn in his gut.

He wanted to ice the burn away. He wanted to get up and run to the edge of the party, just beyond the light, and find her there, waiting for him. He wanted to take her hand and bring it to his lips, then point up to the stars, their fingers clasped together, as he had at the Snare. But he was inside the light at this party, and she was far, far away. And he was here with people who were not ignoring or mocking or deceiving him, but acting as if he were one of them. If he could not be here with her, he might as well try to belong.

When the cigarette returned, he took it.

Ummm. Warm and spicy and much nicer than he'd expected, it blew inside his mouth, down his throat, into his chest, through his belly, down his arms and legs, all the way to his fingers and toes. It felt as if his own breath were lifting him to a private place. It felt as if his own blood were vibrating him with new life.

Someone took the cigarette from his hands. He closed his eyes and felt as if he were the hot-air balloon, rising into the night. He was no longer a man who was trying to get home. He was a moment with the power of forever. He was a world that wanted no turning. He felt as glittery and vast as the stars.

He opened his eyes, and they were laughing. Not at him, but at how silly he must look, with so much pleasure on his face. And they were already handing him another. He sat back and inhaled, as deep as he could.

Mmmm, he thought, not letting the cigarette go. *Mmmm. The Tingling.*

Though the next morning, it was Sam who had changed.

Homan realized this when they dropped off Strawberry and Beaded Circles at another house, this one in a dusty town of small houses. A dog nosed open the screen door and came running across the dirt yard to greet them, and as it licked Strawberry's face, Homan wondered if they'd stay awhile. But after Sam made a distracted wave through the windshield and Homan and Beaded Circles shared a last look, Sam gestured for them to get moving.

Homan set his boot on the pedal and drove through the town to the highway. When he looked at Sam, the boy had his eyes fixed ahead. When he offered chocolate from the bag, Sam shook his head. When he saw Ride Thumbers ahead, Sam made a motion that said, *Keep going.*

By midday, they were doing something they hadn't done before. Sam, map on his lap, was directing Homan with purpose.

Over the next day and a half, Homan drove. At first they were on long roads with nothing except tan-and-brown desert, occasional small towns with trailers for houses, and cities where colored lights glowed like jewels. In days past they would have gone to see the sights. This time they drove on, even when they entered thick woods, wound through mountains of white rock speckled with black, and sped along on a road hugging a cliff, where they saw a lake so far below, it seemed like the bottom of the world. Except for breaking late at night in a campground, they stayed on their course. They *had* a course. If only Homan knew what it was.

But he did know, as soon as they'd left Strawberry and Beaded Circles behind, why Sam had
changed. The night before, at the party, after the
Tingling and some food, they'd all gone into the
room with the bed that wiggled to the touch.
Strawberry got on the bed, and Sam wanted to be
there, too, so Homan helped him from the chair.
Beaded Circles set a blanket on the floor, and then
she and Homan lay down, their bodies far apart.
Finally he was in a rich man's house, lying beside
a woman so close, he could smell night clinging to
her skin. He glanced to the bed. Strawberry was
on her side, Sam's arm was on her hip, and she
was moving her head as if they were kissing. He
turned back to Beaded Circles and felt a charge go
through him. Though he did nothing and Beaded
Circles did nothing, and he was relieved.

A little later he woke up, the way he always did
with Sam. Sam couldn't turn himself over, so Homan had gotten used to waking in the middle of
the night to roll his friend to the other side. With
Beaded Circles asleep, Homan sat up in the dark
and looked to the bed.

Sam was lying down. Strawberry was sitting at
the foot of the bed, her back to Sam, throwing her
arms in the air, and Homan could see her lips moving. Her face seemed angry or sad, and she kept
turning back to Sam, then away. Only when she
stood up did Homan realize she was in her under-

things. She grabbed her clothes and hurried out of the room.

Homan pulled himself up and crossed the room to the bed. Sam was on his side, turned away. *Good*, Homan thought; *at least he not on his back.* He walked around to see if his friend was awake. Yes, his eyes were open, but he was staring ahead, his cheeks glistening. He made a motion with his hands, only it wasn't a motion that was speaking to Homan; it was reaching for his own face. But his elbow didn't bend to do what he needed, so Homan did it for him. He sat on the edge of the bed, pressed his hand to his friend's cheek, and wiped away the tears.

He wondered where he and Sam were going now, on their long drive away from Strawberry and Beaded Circles. North, he understood, and then, as they left the road around the cliff and entered a long, flat marsh, west. He drove and drove, trying not to fetch forward in his mind with questions, or back to his waking this morning, when he went up to the dream window with Beautiful Girl. She was tickling a giggling Little One on her stomach, and they never looked up to the glass. Now he kept his own gaze straight so Sam could be alone with his thoughts, and Homan, though he didn't want to, could be alone with his. At some point Homan saw planes in the air, flying in formation. Later came houses, then towns, each larger than the last. He wished he could ask where they were going. He wished Sam could read all his signs. He wished he truly believed there was a Big Artist in the sky. Then it could tell him why Beautiful Girl hadn't turned to him, though he'd thumped and thumped on the dream window.

It was sunny when they reached the bridge to the hilly city.

It was a double-decker bridge, and they were on the top, and as he drove, he looked out to the sides. Sparkling water spread far and wide, with cargo ships leaving the port behind them and two islands to one side. Was this the sea Beautiful Girl had drawn for him in the picture he'd left in the barn? He looked at Sam, but he was doing what he'd been doing for almost two days: staring out his window, eyebrows tight, mouth in a frown. Homan turned back to the road, longing for Sam's spirits to lift. They passed through a tunnel, and when they came out the other side, he understood they were crossing the water to reach a city. No, it couldn't be the sea, not with a city so close by. And it was a city like none he'd ever seen, a city of hills and fog and brightly colored houses running up and down the crests like candy.

They left the bridge and headed onto crowded streets. Sam pointed right, and Homan drove. Past office buildings, then houses and apartments. Past people of all kinds on the sidewalks: white, brown, Chinese, children, middle-agers, old folks, ladies in short dresses, men in suits, soldiers in uniform. Then, in among the crowd, he saw Beautiful Girl. How was that possible? He slowed down, looking close. Sam gestured for him to keep on, but he had to see. There she was, moving along. He slowed the van and was just about to stop when he realized: This person was too short, her hair too dark—she didn't look like Beautiful Girl at all. He sped back up, freshly filled with sorrow. They rose up a hill so steep, at the very top he wondered if there could possibly be a bottom. Then they went down, passing right into mist. Homan glanced over at Sam, thinking, *You gotta come back to me. You all I got now.* Sam tapped his thumb against his armrest.

Then they pulled onto a street of houses that ran along a steep hill. The houses resembled the most eye-catching houses in Edgeville, the ones where the richest white people lived. Only these were even nicer and painted livelier colors—blue and purple and white. Some had small trees in small front yards. Each had a huge set of stairs rising up from the sidewalk.

Sam pointed to one house, and Homan stopped in front of it. He turned just in time to see Sam take a deep breath.

Homan took a breath, too. It would be a chore

getting up those steps. For starters, the ramp wouldn't sit straight with the sidewalk at such a tilt. Also, it didn't seem right that Homan should go through such a haul for someone who hadn't been meeting his eyes. But Homan knew how it felt to be swallowed by unhappiness, and how, when it did, you needed someone at your side. The way, after the fever, Blue had been at his. The way Homan wanted Sam to come back to him now.

So he figured out how to set the ramp to reach the sidewalk. Then he helped Sam out, locked the van, and heaved Sam's chair up from the back. One step. Two. Three.

They were going to have a devil of a time getting back down, he thought as they rose higher. The steps were making him sweat so hard, he hoped they'd stay there a long time, relaxing, sleeping on nice beds—and looking out at the view. From behind the chair, he could see it, as the land dropped down from where they were: a sheet of silvery water that seemed to have no end. Sailboats floated on the surface. Birds flew above. Was *this* the sea? He could not know unless he could taste it. But it was beautiful. He shook his head at himself for thinking the word. Then he closed his eyes and remembered her sitting in the office, drawing that picture. There it was: the tower to one side, the sea to the other. Yes. His word was right. *Beautiful*.

Finally: the last step.

Breathless, his skin sticky with sweat, Homan turned Sam around to the door. Sam had a grim look on his face, and Homan suddenly got a bad feeling.

Sam pointed to the lock, then to Homan's pocket, where he'd put the keys. Homan removed the key chain, and Sam indicated the one they needed.

The key fit easily, and he felt the bolt give way. He reached for the knob—but it was already turning. Someone inside knew they were there.

The door opened.

A tall man with glasses stood before them. He looked suspicious for a split second, as if he had no idea who'd be unlocking his door. Then his eyes took in Sam, and his face melted with relief. He opened his mouth, and inside the house Homan caught movement. Past the fancy-looking chairs, white rug, and paintings on the walls raced a woman, tears streaming down her cheeks. Both of them looked frightened and angry and delighted all at once—the same mix of moods he now saw on Sam's face. As the woman rushed to the doorway and threw her arms around Sam, Homan recognized her as one of the women who'd been with Sam at the church.

The man was now staring at Homan, and by the time the woman stopped hugging Sam, the man was looking at Sam and wearing a Yell Face. Sam seemed to be shouting something back, but the man kept on, and the woman started in, too. They were all going at once. They must have tagged him as the man who ran Sam off from the church. The woman was red-faced now, and the man was stepping outside, and even though Sam was doing his best to flail his arms and keep the man away, the man seized the back of the wheelchair, spun Sam around, and began heaving the chair over the threshold. Sam was facing Homan then, and he was also wearing a Yell Face, only it wasn't meant for Homan. It was a face of fury and resistance. The man pulled hard, and then Sam was in the house.

Sam spun himself around and confronted the man and the woman, gesturing to Homan, then himself. The man and woman didn't pay him any mind. The man was pulling the key from the front-door lock and shoving the key chain into his pocket. The woman was shaking her head no. Sam was pleading. Tears were everywhere.

Then the man dug into his pocket and pulled out his wallet. He took all the money he had into his hand and waved it for Sam to see. Sam shook his head no, but the man just stepped into the doorway, said something to Homan, and shoved the money into Homan's jacket pocket.

It all happened so fast.

The man was backing away now. Homan looked past him to Sam, trying to understand.

Sam's eyes were spilling over. But when his gaze met Homan's, he got a new look. One that was stronger than anger, more powerful than pleas. A look that said, *I'm sorry*.

Then the door closed in Homan's face.

He stood there a long time. He couldn't truly be standing there with his one friend gone.

Finally he stumbled down to the van, looking back at the house every few steps. The door stayed shut.

On the sidewalk he stared at the van. Everything he owned was locked inside. The new clothes. The sleeping bag. Food.

He went up to the van and punched it in the side, over and over. There was no way in. There was no hope for him. He howled out without knowing or caring if the police finally found him. He punched the van until his knuckles got bloody.

Then he ran. *Homing pigeon*, he thought with disgust, running up the hill onto a busy street. He ran without seeing traffic lights or cars. He crashed into a man walking a dog. He picked himself up and ran without caring. *You ain't no more than a ghost*.

And then, when he could bear it no more, he stopped right where he was, at the edge of a gas station, and lowered himself to the ground. He could not talk himself out of pain any longer. He had no one to be strong for. So finally, he cried. He cried with deep sobs, head bent to the ground, palms pressed to his eyes. He cried so hard that sorrow rushed out of his face. He cried until he felt like the sea.

Storytime

MARTHA

1973

"Look, Grammy! I found a Y!" Julia said, pointing to the sidewalk.

Martha glanced at her friend Pete, who was walking in front of them on a brisk Cape Cod morning in Harwich Port, his golden retriever at his side. Pete glanced back, giving Martha a curious look as if to say, *What's she talking about?* Martha smiled, then scanned the street before them, with its clapboard houses and tall elm trees. Sure enough, in a driveway not fifty feet away was the twig that had caught Julia's almost-five-year-old eye. "She likes looking for letters," Martha said. Although Pete was a grandfather in his seventies, his expression made clear that he didn't follow. Why should he? Except for bringing them dinner when they returned to Landon's summer house last week, Pete hadn't seen them since they'd left the Cape two and a half years ago. He didn't know that this past summer, when Martha was renting an apartment near Philadelphia from her student John-Michael, she had taught Julia the alphabet. Now, in mid-September, Julia saw letters everywhere.

"Can I have it for my collection?" Julia asked, looking up at Martha. The light brought out the blond in Julia's brown curls, which Martha thought the finest hair she'd ever seen. Julia preferred the straight hair she saw on TV, calling hers "frizzy." Martha said she could have both by wearing a hair band: The top would look straight, and a cascade of curls would remain. To this, like almost everything else, Julia agreed.

Martha said, "Let's take a look at it."

She let go of Julia's hand. Julia bounded ahead, her green dress, white suede jacket, and patent-leather Mary Janes making her more stylish than most people on the Cape, who preferred blue jeans and light jackets. Pete and Martha also dressed casually. Although retired, Pete wore the flannel shirts and tan pants that had served him well as a carpenter; and Martha wore what had become her usual ensemble: slacks, corduroy jacket, and tennis shoes.

Holding her prize aloft, Julia returned to Martha's side and clasped her hand again.

"It's not a very big Y," Martha said, looking at the twig.

"But it's a capital," Julia announced. "And capitals are so much better than little letters."

"They are?" Pete said. "Can I see it?" He examined the twig. "Well. It *is* better."

"Even Rodney knows it's better," Julia said, indicating Pete's dog. "Right, Rodney?"

"Ruff," Rodney said.

They all laughed. They'd met when Julia was eleven months old, on the first day Martha and Julia arrived on the Cape, when Pete had just finished repairing trim on his son's house, getting it ready for Gary's transfer to Denver. When Martha had gone over to meet him and his dog, Pete had smiled. For the next eight months, he was their welcoming committee. He'd grown up on the Cape, built houses for decades, and was a good source for shops, libraries, and doctors. Man and dog would stop by every week, Pete whistling as they got out of his Jeep. Martha told him how grateful they were that he checked in on them, with his wife in the nursing home and him visiting her every day. He'd say, "It's only neighborly, Matilda." Then last week, when she and Julia returned to the Cape, he'd added, "It's been a long time, and kids grow fast." He'd held her gaze, and then Martha had said, "It's so good to see an old friend." She didn't add that she was wearying of cultivating new friends only to move on. So when Martha told him today that they were going to the library for Storytime and he asked to come along, she was pleased.

"You know why letters come in capitals and littles?" Julia said. "Because little letters are baby letters. Capital letters are grown up. And they take care of the little letters. Like a family."

"Didn't you say capitals are better?" Pete said.

"Capitals *are* better. They can drive and turn apples into butter and bake bread and sew. They know everything! Baby letters only know this"—she brought her fingers to her eyes as if she were examining a pebble—"much." She slipped her hand back into Martha's.

How Martha treasured holding Julia's hand. Once as small as an acorn, it was now as big as a maple leaf. If only Martha could hold time as tightly as she could hold this little hand.

"What's that?" Julia asked. "That bird banging on the tree."

"It's called a woodpecker."

"I've heard of that. Woody Woodpecker." She laughed the cartoon character's laugh. "And what's that one, Pete? The red bird up there?"

"That's a cardinal."

"It's pretty."

Martha said, "It's also different from most other birds."

"Because it's red?"

"That's only part of why. Cardinals are also one of the only birds who—"

Martha stopped. If she said "mate for life," she might invite discussion of mommies and daddies, and it had been hard enough when Julia, a few months ago, asked if she had them. Martha, toweling Julia off after a bath, was caught unprepared. Slowly, trying to say as little as possible, Martha said that Julia's parents had passed away when Julia was little. "They loved you very much. That's why they asked me to...that's why they wanted someone to adopt you. They wanted someone who would take care of you forever, and who would love you as much as they did." Julia said, "So I'll never see my mommy and daddy?" Martha drew her into a hug, hoping no one who'd heard her made-up stories would try to fill in the gaps. "I'm here, Ju-Ju," she said.

So, watching the red bird fly to a branch and begin its lively song, Martha brought up the other rare trait that cardinals are known for. "Most of the time, man cardinals sing very complicated songs and lady cardinals don't sing at all. But sometimes when a man cardinal sings, if the lady he loves is nearby, she starts singing the same song at the same time. It makes it easy for them to find each other. And it makes for the prettiest sound you ever heard."

"You kidding?" Pete asked.

"No. It's called song matching."

The cardinal was singing, but no matching song was singing back.

"He's all alone," Julia finally said.

They rounded the corner to the front of the library. "Here we are, Ju-Ju."

"Look what I collected," Julia said, showing them the four twigs she'd acquired on their walk: Y, I, T, and V. "Do they spell anything?"

Pete said, "Not quite."

"I bet they spell a silly word," Julia said. "Like ooga-booga." She laughed. "Grammy, will you put them in your pocket so we can take them home?" She handed over the letters that spelled no word. Then she ran across the brick sidewalk toward the library door.

Martha looked over at Pete. "You don't have to come in with us," she said.

"I don't see Ann until three o'clock. This kind of thing is what retirement's for."

"Storytime?" Martha asked with a smile.

"And bakery after," he said. He nodded ahead. "Shall we?"

But how much longer would she have to maintain this charade?

She couldn't stop herself from asking the question, as she and Pete found adult chairs in the room with the children's books, Julia hunkered down in a children's seat, and normalcy resounded all around them: toddlers sucking thumbs, older children striving to look mature, mothers motioning to sons and daughters to behave, big brothers and sisters grabbing pictureless books in the corners of the room. The scene could only have been more normal if Martha belonged in it.

As they waited for the reader to get the children settled down, Martha wondered how many grown-ups here were harboring secrets. Until Julia entered her life, she would have thought few people engaged in deceit, but once she'd joined their ranks, she realized that without even knowing it, she had long been an honorary member. She'd just told her stories only to herself, tales that she was living a life rich in satisfaction. It wasn't that she hadn't felt something was amiss—she knew it every time she reached over to Earl in the bed and he turned away, or she looked out her small windows into the sky and thought of her son, lying namelessly in his grave. Yet her disappointment was so fathomless that it had never elevated itself to thought. Only when she met Henry and Graciela had it occurred to her that for decades she'd needed to cry. Did any of the people sitting here feel that lump in their throats, too?

The Storytime reader held up the first book for the day. Julia flashed a smile, then took on her serious expression, looking as if this book were the most important thing in the world. *She'll be a good student*, Martha thought. *I must do everything I can to get to see that.*

Without turning her head, Martha moved her gaze toward Pete. He sat with his thick, callused hands in his lap, wedding ring the only adornment. Here was a person who was living honestly. He'd showed her this when he came over last night with fresh clam chowder for their dinner. He'd played cards with Julia afterward and then, incredibly, washed the dishes while Martha read Julia her bedtime story. After Julia was asleep, Martha made him hot cocoa, and they sat and talked and looked out over the Sound as the moon rose into the night.

"Ann's Parkinson's worse," he finally said when Martha dared ask. "She can't talk. It breaks my heart, going to see her."

Martha sat quietly. With Earl, her silence had arisen from meekness. With her students and new friends, it was due to concealment. Though she'd also come to understand, in these last few years, that silence made space for other people's words, which was important for those who needed to be listened to. Pete was one of those people.

He sat adjusting the place mats. Then he said, "We used to do everything together. She ran the business during the day, I helped out at night, and after Gary was out of the house we went out on our boat. Now I go with Rodney. It's like when you replace an old oak door with one of those ugly hollow doors they make. You still have a door, but that's all you have."

She nodded.

He went on. "Everyone around here says I'm the most loyal husband they've ever seen. But— it's hard to say this, I hope you don't mind me saying it—I've gotten used to her not being there. I couldn't stand it for the longest time. Now I say, 'Well, Pete, what's for dinner?' You get used to new ways of living."

She wanted to say she wondered if she'd ever get used to living as "Matilda." She wanted to say Earl had spent years not telling her as much as Pete just did. She wanted to say *she* had never told *herself* that much—until she became a different Martha.

Does Pete feel a lump in his throat? she wondered as the Storytime reader led a hand-clap game. Not because he was lying to himself, but because he no longer had an oak door?

"What?" he said, noticing Martha looking at him.

"Oh. Nothing."

"You sure about that?"

"Well, I'm . . . just worried about Rodney."

He pointed toward the library windows. There was Rodney outside the glass, paws on the sill, staring into the room. "Man's best friend," he said with a smile. She let herself laugh.

A couple of young mothers turned around, and she realized her laugh had come just as the hand clapping stopped. It was as embarrassing as being caught passing notes in class.

She put her hand on her forehead, but underneath she glanced to Pete and saw him smiling gently at her. "Shh," he mouthed playfully.

As the salty air chilled and the leaves edged with gold, Pete became a regular fixture on their library outings. Martha looked forward so much to these mornings that several weeks passed before she realized she could now do something she'd been longing to do.

Since those first groggy hours in Henry's hotel, Martha had been asking herself questions she had not shared with others, much less felt equipped to answer. One day after Julia ran to the children's room of the library, Martha stopped Pete and asked if he would mind staying with Ju-Ju while she hunkered down with a book in the adult section. She was just going to browse, she added, trying to make her request sound casual, even spontaneous. She didn't want him to know she had several books waiting, some ordered from distant libraries, others non-circulating.

"'Long as we can still go to the bakery after," Pete told her.

That day, and for many weeks, as Julia and Pete sat in the children's room, Martha read.

Her readings took her through the history of institutions, from their origins as almshouses where people with disabilities were housed with other social rejects, like orphans and criminals, to the ghastly places they'd become: enormous facilities where thousands of individuals had nothing to do and where a chronic lack of funding meant decrepit buildings, minimal staff, weak medical care, filthy conditions, and abuse. She thought of Lynnie again, so beautiful in her white dress, so happy beside Number Forty-two. Then Martha imagined her now.

Something has *to change*, Martha would think at the end of every library session, when Julia and Pete would stand near the entrance to the adult section, waving to her. She would close the books and rise in a daze.

As the leaves shook free of the trees, Martha thought constantly about the horrors she had read about and how long they'd been going on. She could barely concentrate on her sewing, her cooking. Sometimes when Julia was watching television, she would look over, and seeing Martha holding her knitting without moving the needles, she would say, "What's the matter, Grammy?"

"I'm just lost in thought," Martha would say.

"Don't worry," Julia would say. "You can't get lost. I'm here."

Once, when Pete was able to sit for Julia, Martha drove far away, to one of these institutions. It was not easy to find, and even local gas station attendants weren't sure where it was. Finally she got there and sat for hours outside the brick entryway. It was so big, and there were so many Lynnies inside. And there were so many others just like it, all around the country.

At last she drove off, and as she made her way down rural roads, she spotted a chapel. It was so similar to the one that Earl made clear they would never enter again. She pulled over, and after telling herself she ought to move on, she walked to the door. It opened beneath her hands, and when she stepped inside, she peered at the blue and red light coming through the stained-glass windows and saw candles along the walls, illuminating the pews. She stood a minute as the door closed behind her, and when it clicked shut and no one appeared, she knew she was alone. She made her way to a pew and took a seat. In the silence and colored light, she thumbed through the hymnals and prayer books but could not find anything that seemed to address what she had on her mind. So she lowered her head to her hands and waited for prayerful words to come. For a long time she sat, and then what finally came was a question.

What can I, just one small person, do?

It was mid-November. Pete hadn't come around for a few weeks, and then one afternoon he called and asked if they'd like to take a ride on his motorboat. Julia had often said she wanted to go out on the water. Martha told him, "It would be our pleasure."

Pete wore a somber look when he arrived to pick them up. He said all the right things—"Nice looking outfit, Ju-Ju," noticing her pink dress and pop beads; "Haven't meant to be a stranger," he said to Martha. There was a heaviness to his voice and stubble on his face. By the end of the fifteen minutes it took to reach Oyster Pond, where Julia read, on the side of the boat, *"Two If By Sea,"* and he said, "Ann was a descendant of Paul Revere," Martha knew what had happened.

"I'm sorry," Martha said as they settled onto the boat.

"Sorry for what?" Julia said as she tied a life preserver around Rodney.

Pete looked at Martha, then looked away. "Thank you," he said softly.

They pulled into Oyster River and then passed through Stage Harbor and out into the Sound. "Wow!" Julia said, looking all around. "I love it out here!" She pointed to something floating in the water.

"That's a buoy," Pete said, anticipating her question.

She pointed out to the horizon. "And that's a really big sailboat."

Martha said, "Sailboats are something, aren't they?"

"And I know what these are." Julia was looking toward a long spit of land covered with shiny black beasts. "Seals."

Pete said, "That's right."

"It's like they're having a big party," Julia said as they rounded a long shore that Pete explained was an island. "And what's that?"

"A weather station."

Julia hugged Rodney to her and began giving him a tour of the sights, pointing out anything else she knew—birds, fish, other boats in the distance. After a few moments, Pete turned to Martha, and as Julia continued her private conversation with the dog, he said very softly, "What do you think happens?"

Martha looked at him. "What do you mean?"

"After we leave here. This earth." He returned to looking straight ahead, and she could see him swallow hard. "What do you think?"

"I don't know what I think."

"I don't either."

Then Martha, remembering something she'd come across in a book she'd once read, said to Pete, "But I like that story. The one about the difference between heaven and"—she looked at Julia—"the other place."

"Tell me," Pete said.

"A man asks God to show him the difference between the two places. God takes him to a large hall, where a party of skinny, miserable people are sitting around a table filled with every kind of food you can think of, and God says, 'This is'"—and Martha mouthed the word—"'hell.' The man notices all the people are wearing sleeves made of metal which don't bend at the elbow, so when they pick up food, they can't bring it to their mouths. Then God takes the man to another hall and says, 'This is heaven.' It's just like the first, with people wearing sleeves of metal, sitting around a table heaped high with food. These people, though, are laughing and smiling, and the man sees why. Each person who picks up a piece of food turns and feeds it to the person beside him."

Pete was quiet a minute. Then he said, "That's a nice story."

"It's just a story."

"But it helps. Like having you and Julia here. It helps."

Suddenly Julia called out, "Look at that!" She pointed toward a strip of land.

"Goodness," Martha said.

"What *is* that, Grammy?"

"Why, it's a lighthouse."

Pete said, "That's the Chatham Lighthouse."

"Why's it here, Pete?"

"Lighthouses are towers that send out lights over the water, so ships know where the land is. It keeps them from running aground."

Martha said, "Ju-Ju, I once owned a lighthouse."

"You did?"

"Not a big one. One that was tiny, like the size of"—she thought—"one of your twigs. Uncle Landon made it for me long ago. I put it on my mailbox."

"The mailbox at the end of our driveway?"

"A different mailbox. I was living somewhere else. I left the lighthouse behind when I moved away."

"Did it look like this, Grammy?"

"No. It had a unique look. The top of it, where the light was, had the face of a man."

Pete said, "Landon must have had some imagination."

"He does. He was always quite creative."

Julia asked, "Did he give it to you for your birthday?"

"No. For Christmas. He said he gave it to me because...I was lonely. He put it on my mailbox, and when the mail came every day, the carrier would move the lighthouse man from up to down. I'd listen all day for that squeak, and when it came I knew I'd have company."

"In letters?"

"Yes." Martha looked out at this lighthouse.

"That's funny," Julia said, laughing. "A lighthouse with the head of a man."

"It *was* funny. It would make me smile every day. That lighthouse man worked."

"How nice it must be," Pete said, "having students all over the country. And so many of them ready to do something kind for you."

"I'm very lucky," she said.

Then she turned to him and watched as he stared straight ahead, both hands on the wheel. And, as she would write in a letter to the future Julia, the answer she'd been seeking came; and there, on the water, she let herself feel the lump in her throat for the last time. Then she reached over and laid her hand on top of Pete's.

That night, Martha wrote a letter to one of her students, telling what she'd learned from the books and what she hoped he would do with the information.

The next morning, she and Julia walked to the mailbox at the edge of their driveway. As they passed over twigs, Julia read what she saw on the ground. Now that she could add the twigs up into words, she easily found the ones that spelled her name.

I might be just one small person, Martha thought. *But even the small can make a difference.*

"Do you want to put this in?" Martha asked at the box.

Julia took the envelope from her hands. "Who's it going to?"

"You tell me," Martha said.

Julia looked hard at the envelope, then said, "John-Michael!" Then she said, "That's my uncle who works on TV!"

"That's right," Martha said.

Martha opened the mail door, and Julia stood on tiptoes and slid her Grammy's letter in.

A Change as Big as a Book

LYNNIE

1973

L ynnie still could not tell time. But she knew, as she and Doreen walked down the path to Kate's office, that since the night she lost Buddy and the baby, she'd seen the leaves fall many times from the trees. She looked up now as a chilly wind shook the last of the leaves loose. The confetti of reds and browns made her ache, the same as it did every year. Doreen, though, did not notice the leaves or Lynnie's pained gaze. She was preoccupied with reporting the news, which consisted of anything she'd learned on her mail rounds earlier in the day. Today, she'd listened in the hall as two administrators discussed a new policy about TVs in the cottages: They were going to be encased in wire cages, so only staff could turn the channel. "They say it'll cut down the fights. Sure. You know what it really means. No more *Family*

Feud or *Green Acres* or *Sesame Street.* Just dumb old *Guiding Light.*" Then in the main office, she'd spotted new glasses on Uncle Luke's secretary, Maude. "And let me tell you, if you saw her on the street, you'd swear she's Jackie O." Doreen was like a radio broadcast, and Lynnie usually enjoyed listening. But Lynnie was having trouble concentrating today, and not only because of the spell of sadness cast by the dying leaves.

Lynnie was on her way to Kate's office, and every autumn, on the day when the last of the leaves whirled off the trees just as they were doing today, Kate gave Lynnie a new book. Then Lynnie would sit at Kate's desk, turning page after page while Kate read the story. Books amazed Lynnie. In a single book, a lonely elephant could come upon a speck of dust that contained an entire world—and fight powerful enemies to save it from destruction. A gentle bull could be forced into a bullring—but be so happy just smelling the flowers in ladies' hair that he gets sent home to his garden. Books had great, big change. At the School, the changes were small.

Take Albert, whom Lynnie could see in the parking lot up the hill right now, directing a car to a space, and who was the one deaf resident besides Buddy (*Buddy!* she thought, her stomach taking off like a bird launching). Albert loved uniforms so much, whenever a man in a uniform appeared in their weekly movies, he'd squeal with joy. Lynnie had never figured out why—his signs weren't like Buddy's, who hadn't understood him, either. But like Buddy, he'd gained the trust of higher-ups and was granted the privilege of choosing his own work, monitoring the parking lot. Someone gave him an old uniform, too, and in it he pointed staff to empty spaces and wiped parked cars with cloths. He seemed happier now, though Lynnie knew he still shared the one toothbrush in his cottage.

But as she watched Albert through the showering leaves, she noticed something unusual: The driver of the car he was directing was Dr. Hagenbuch, who'd quit a while back. People who left almost never returned. Not only that, he was accompanied by two men she'd never seen. She turned to Doreen, but her friend was going on about the sparkles on Maude's glasses. Lynnie looked toward the staff cottage. Maybe Kate would have an explanation.

Lynnie was not on her way to Kate's just to receive a book; the book was part of a festive occasion Kate called Lynnie Day, but which Lynnie didn't quite understand, not being aware that today was the anniversary of the night she'd lost everything. She just understood that when the leaves fell every year, her grief thickened, and then, when Kate invited her to the office for Lynnie Day and treated Lynnie to cake and a new book, the grief thinned. Now Lynnie had four books—and lately, Kate had practiced counting them with her, helping her work hard to pronounce each number: one, two, three, four. She wondered why Kate had stopped at four—Lynnie enjoyed watching *Sesame Street*, so she'd learned that numbers went all the way up to ten. Then this morning, when Kate saw Lynnie at breakfast, she came up and said, "Today's your next Lynnie Day! Are you ready to try saying 'five'?"

As Doreen and Lynnie rounded the last corner before Kate's office, they saw Smokes and Clarence and the dogs sauntering down to the boys' colony. Lynnie stopped moving for a moment, her breath caught in her throat. Though when Doreen kept on walking and chatting away, Lynnie reminded herself she shouldn't be scared. The staff cottages had been shut down, so Smokes and Clarence were no longer around at night, and as long as Lynnie stayed in the company of other people during the day shifts, she felt safe. She still felt her legs and arms stiffen when she saw them, and she still jerked awake at night, her mouth going dry, her breath a hard draw. But the sounds she woke to weren't what she heard over and over in her memory: men shouting and dogs barking, glass breaking and furniture crashing, shrieks echoing into the sleeping room and down the corridor where she'd run, the word *Here!* and the doorknob turning, *No no no no!* Now, when she woke in the middle of the night, she just heard snoring and sleep-talking, and instead of going tight with ter-ror, she'd think of those three days of freedom. She'd think of how, after they'd dressed in the old lady's clothes, Buddy made a circle of his pointer finger and thumb and slid the circle down one of Lynnie's fingers, as if giving her a ring. Then she did the same for him, and when he made a sign for her and a sign for himself, she knew he meant *wife, husband.* Sometimes, when she would wake in the night, she would make those signs to herself, and then she could fall back asleep.

"Here we are," Doreen said as they mounted the steps to the staff cottage.

Kate was standing outside her office door when they entered the building. "Hey, sweet pea," she said, opening her arms, and Lynnie came inside and felt the arms close and inhaled the gardenia scent of Kate.

The instant Kate led her into the office, Lynnie spotted the cake and wrapped book, both perched on the windowsill. Almost everything else was the same as ever—green metal desk, goosenecked lamp, typewriter, black glass ashtray, two gray chairs with crib-cage backs, file cabinets with Kate's plants, and radio on the windowsill. Though this summer, a framed photo of Kate's new boyfriend, Scott, appeared on the desk. Standing on a field chalked with white stripes, wearing a thick jacket with a picture of a lion, Scott was, Kate told her, a coach, which meant he helped high school boys play football better. That was around the time Kate started helping Lynnie try to speak.

Behind her, Kate turned the lock in her door. Then Kate continued what she always did when she invited Lynnie here to practice speaking: She snapped on the radio. Lynnie liked the top forty tunes, and now a bouncy song came on that she particularly enjoyed: *Tie a yellow ribbon round the old oak tree . . .*

Kate talked lower than the radio and loudly enough for Lynnie to hear. "It's your fifth Lynnie Day," she said with a big smile.

Lynnie tried to look pleased, though the ache she'd felt on her walk here remained.

"And I'm really happy to celebrate you today."

Lynnie pushed her lips up and felt a small smile appear on her face.

Kate held her gaze for a moment, smiling back. But it wasn't a mirror smile, where two people are lost in the same kind of smile together. It was a broken mirror smile, where the two smiles don't match, and each person is thinking something the other is not, so they're together and apart at the same time.

Then Kate said, "I can light the candles first, or we can hold off on the cake and begin our practice." She reached toward her ashtray, which was, as always, empty except for a book of matches. The ashtray used to be bursting with crushed cigarettes. After Kate met Scott there were fewer butts until one day there weren't any.

Kate lifted the matches. "Which should I do? Light the candles? Or practice?"

Lynnie knew what Kate wanted. Kate had told her, "You've been silent for so long that your brain and your mouth don't know how to work together anymore. But if you practice, even just a little every day, I think you'll be able to speak again." Lynnie could not bring herself to practice where others would know—speaking was so difficult, her mouth barely felt it belonged to her. The one exception was the laundry, where she would practice sometimes when all the washers and dryers were on, sloshing and thrumming, so Cheryl and Lourdes, loading laundry across the room, wouldn't know.

Still, she needed to feel more ready than she felt at the moment. So Lynnie pointed toward the matches.

The tiny flames came up one by one, and as they did, Kate counted: "One, two, three, four, five." She paused and added, "Do you want to try to say 'five'?"

Lynnie knew she'd make Kate happy if she tried.

And truth be told, cake was tasty, but it made her think about Buddy's sugar cubes. Practicing was a better way to take her mind off her sadness. So she shrugged and launched into the routine she'd learned would help get up her courage. She lowered her gaze and squeezed her fists together. Then she put one finger straight against her mouth, opened her lips, and pushed out her voice. "Uhhh," she said. It felt as weak as lint.

Kate, moving her lips and mouth slowly, over-enunciated. "Five."

"Uhhh-iiii," Lynnie said back.

"Close!" Kate said. "Very good."

"Uhhh-iiii," Lynnie repeated, this time louder.

"Good!" Kate said, turning up the radio. "You know what comes in fives, right?"

Lynnie held up her hand, spreading her fingers.

"That's right," Kate said.

Lynnie pointed to the number of plants on the windowsill.

"Good," Kate said. "And you know what Scott just taught me?" She drew her fingers together and motioned for Lynnie to do the same. "This is something the kids do when they score." She leaned forward and slapped her palm against Lynnie's.

What a funny thing to do! Lynnie laughed. Then she hit her palm back against Kate's. "Ennn!" she said.

"Again?" Kate clarified.

Lynnie nodded. "Ennn!"

They did it once more, and Lynnie felt so great, knowing she was speaking something close to a word. Practicing was difficult, but it was fun with the right person.

Still laughing, they lowered their hands. "I know," Kate said, "I jumped the gun on the practice. Let's have your cake."

She brought the vanilla-frosted confection down from the window and pushed it across the desk. The flowers were all the colors Lynnie liked—blues and greens and reds and oranges. She inhaled the scent of the frosting, the wax on the candles, the chocolate hidden inside.

Kate said, "To celebrate Lynnie!"

Lynnie blew, counting the numbers in her head as each flame went out.

Then she tore the wrapping paper. The book fell out of the paper and landed on the desk.

She sat down. The drawing of a house smiled at her from the cover.

"It's called *The Little House*," Kate said.

The house looked like the face of a child, with full cheeks and big eyes. Lynnie touched the cover with her fingers, and then Kate sat down across the desk and opened the book. Lynnie, feeling a smile take over her face, strained to say a word she used to say with Nah-nah, "Wow-wee," though the best she could manage was, "Eeee!"

"You're in a talky mood today," Kate said. "I think I better turn up the radio."

Lynnie kept her eyes on the cover as Kate went to the window and turned the knob. The song had changed, and now she heard: *You are the sunshine of my life. That's why I'll always stay around. . . .*

Lynnie knew this song, too, and hummed along as she looked at the sweet little house, so she didn't realize Kate was taking her time returning to the desk.

"Well, that's interesting," Kate finally said.

Lynnie looked up.

Kate was still standing at the window, facing out. When she didn't turn around or say anything more, Lynnie rose and joined her.

Three men were walking slowly along the pathway. Lynnie recognized gray-haired Dr. Hagenbuch, who was pointing to buildings and talking. But she didn't know the others: a young man with a Burt Reynolds mustache and handsome looks who was listening and nodding, hands in his blazer, and a chunky man with a ponytail who wore a loose coat.

"This is strange," Kate said. "What's going on?"

The men paused in their stroll, looked across the grounds toward the hospital cottage, turned, and looked up at the tower clock.

Lynnie, remembering a practice from last month, did her best. "Ooo?"

Kate turned to her. Lynnie pointed. "Ooo?"

"Who?"

Lynnie nodded.

Kate looked at her with a smile of pride, then turned back. "You know that older one. He's Dr. Hagenbuch, the dentist they brought in from Wilkes-Barre. I thought he'd resigned."

Lynnie nodded. She'd thought that, too.

"It's the others I'm wondering about. The big guy I've never seen before. But the young one, I know. He's a reporter for a Philadelphia station. John-Michael Malone."

As the men stood looking at the clock, the heavy one reached into his coat and withdrew something Lynnie had never seen before. He held it up to his eyes and pointed it at the tower.

"Whoa," Kate said. "They have a camera." She looked at Lynnie, her face moving into a stunned smile. "A camera! Do you know what that might mean?"

The men headed down the hill toward the residential cottages.

"Come on," Kate said, hurrying toward the door.

Kate and Lynnie moved across the grounds as swiftly as they could without attracting attention. Something about the men's presence violated all the rules, yet Kate kept muttering, "It's about time," with a big grin on her face. The men turned toward Lynnie's cottage, and when they mounted the steps for A-3, Kate said, "He has more guts than me."

She and Lynnie hurried up to A-3.

As the door closed behind them, they saw the three men heading toward the dayroom, where Consuella and Hockey, the attendants on the day shift, were sitting in front of *General Hospital* as they played cards, with the A-3 residents staring at the television with bored eyes. Hockey glanced over as the men entered the dayroom, and when Dr. Hagenbuch went over to him, Lynnie heard him say, "...dentist...show these dental students around..." Hockey never liked missing his stories, as he called soap operas, so he waved them away.

"I can't believe it," Kate said.

They stood at the edge of the dayroom, watching. Without a second look from Consuella and Hockey, the men moved hastily into the bathroom, then the sleeping room.

"I hope they get as far as Z-1," Kate said. "I hope they get to the cemetery."

Before Lynnie knew it, the men were coming back through the dayroom. Now that they were walking toward Lynnie, she realized that John-Michael Malone's young face was set in a grimace, the same as her own face had been when she'd first confronted the smell. Like Uncle Luke, John-Michael Malone had an air of seriousness about him and walked with deep steps. But he wasn't looking around with smugness, nor was he gliding his eyes over the filth on the walls, the hole in the ceiling, the residents. He looked at every detail, quickly though with close attention, and in his face was distress.

Then, suddenly, John-Michael Malone strode toward Lynnie. Lynnie glanced at Kate, who, observing his approach, wore a worried expression. Then Kate touched the cross on her necklace and made her face regular, and Lynnie cast her gaze back to John-Michael Malone.

He had stopped right in front of her and was looking directly into her face. He said, "Do you live here in this building?"

"Cottage," Dr. Hagenbuch corrected him.

"Cottage," John-Michael said without removing his eyes from Lynnie.

Lynnie could feel Kate's hand come to rest reassuringly on hers.

Lynnie, still facing John-Michael, nodded.

He said, "Randy, can you get her?"

The chunky man moved so he was turned to her, his camera in the folds of his jacket.

Lynnie could hear the camera making a whirring sound. She saw something—a microphone—appear in John-Michael's hands. She heard him say, "Do you like living here?"

It was a ridiculous question; everyone hated it here.

Besides, no one except Kate and Doreen thought Lynnie could speak. These men must be unaware of her muteness, and if they lacked that basic knowledge, maybe they truly didn't know the answer.

"Do you?" John-Michael Malone said again. "Do you like living here?"

She didn't need to squeeze her fists together for this word. "No."

John-Michael gave her a sorrowful look and said, "If you could walk out that gate right now and never come back, would you?"

She shot her eyes toward Kate. Kate turned toward Lynnie, and her eyes said it was all right to respond.

Lynnie nodded.

And then John-Michael asked one more question. A simple question, one that Kate had tried to teach her to say months ago: "Why?"

There was so much Lynnie could have said in response that even if her lips and tongue were fully accustomed to words, she would have had trouble saying them all. Yet she had only a moment, and as she struggled to narrow down her answer from a number larger than she knew to a mere five, or even four, she thought of the dogs. The dogs always with Smokes and Clarence, always the reminder of that night, of the breaking glass, the clattering bucket, the rag—that night, when it was done, and the door opened, Smokes said, *If you tell, this'll happen*, and then he'd thrown something soft and furry at the dogs, and in seconds they'd torn it to pieces.

That, she knew, was what would happen to her baby. That was why she'd never told the truth to Buddy, or Doreen, or Kate.

That was why, no matter how many answers she had, she was not going to give any.

She looked down at her feet.

"She doesn't say much," Kate said to John-Michael.

"Who is she?" John-Michael asked.

"You can't say her name on the air."

"We won't. My producer will want to know."

"Lynnie," Kate said. "Evelyn Goldberg."

Then Lynnie stopped hearing the camera. By the time she glanced up, the men were leaving the front door.

Kate looked at Lynnie with her softest Kate smile. "You did good, sweet pea," she said.

It was difficult to return to the laundry and pretend it was an ordinary day. This was, after all, Lynnie Day. She had practiced saying "five," blown out candles, received a new book. She had even seen a camera—not a Brownie like Nahnah's or a Polaroid like Daddy's. But a camera that would, Kate had explained, take a film, like they used for movies and TV.

As Lynnie removed the last load from the dryers and rolled it to the steel tables for folding, she thought about what Kate had said as she'd returned Lynnie to the laundry: *I'll stay late today. I want to be here in case it airs.* Then she'd explained what it meant for something to air, and Lynnie understood: It was like when you went out to the cornfield after the corn was gone and anyone could see you there, even though you were staring off into your memory, waiting for two people who would never return to your life, crumpling to your knees, and putting your hands to the soil, wishing you could pull those people from the dirt.

Lynnie didn't know if she wanted to be aired.

Kate had said something else, too, just before she left Lynnie at the laundry. She'd said, *You know, people far away might see this, and then something big could happen.*

So as Lynnie folded the shirts and bottoms and socks, she tried to envision people far away, watching her. Would the old lady be one of them? Would the baby have her eyes on the television, too? *Turn the pages*, Lynnie reminded herself, and tried to see what the baby's life was like now. She hadn't done this for so long, but now she wondered. Was the baby with the old lady or someone else? Was the baby growing tall, like Lynnie? Did she resemble Lynnie from the photo when she was a child? Did she like smells and hugs the way Lynnie did? Did she speak like everyone—everyone except her and Buddy—so words came out of her lips?

And Buddy. *Buddy.* Would he see it? He would. He had to. He'd been gone so long, it couldn't be his choice. Maybe he'd been locked in jail. Maybe a storm had stranded him on a desert island. Though if he could see a television tonight, that would change. He would break out of jail, like the good guys do when a bad sheriff locks them up on TV. He would build a raft and paddle across the water. He would come back at last and hold her.

She reached into the pile of warm laundry, pressed her face to the soft heat, and moved her arms deep inside. They had held each other with the baby between them. They had placed their lips together. They had sung a perfect note into each other's bodies.

Yet Lynnie still expected, when they returned from the dining hall just before six, that the night would go on as always. Suzette was tuning the TV to her favorite show, *Gilligan's Island.* The residents of A-3 were settling into the same seats they'd claimed for years. Lynnie went to her usual bench, and Doreen lowered herself, as always, to Lynnie's right.

Then Doreen leaned over and whispered that

she'd been in the administrative office when the weirdest thing had occurred. Lynnie looked at her, but just as Doreen drew in breath to say more, Lynnie glimpsed, out of the corner of her eye, Kate letting herself inside A-3. Doreen took note of Kate, too, and together they watched as Kate marched right into the dayroom, went over to Suzette, and, after a brief exchange that left Suzette looking stunned, switched the channel. Then Kate backed away, standing behind Suzette and glancing over at Lynnie.

At first everyone in the room groaned. *Gilligan's Island* was one of the few shows that staff and residents agreed on. To make matters worse, Kate had turned to the news, which was viewed as duller than a wall. But sitting at a desk on the news was John-Michael Malone—and Lynnie stopped noticing everyone around her. "Your tendency might be to change the channel," he was saying directly to the audience. "I ask you to stay with us all the way through this special report. It's important that you see America's disgrace."

Then, as the film began to run, the residents' grumbling was quickly replaced by gasps.

There were the gates of the School. There was Albert, motioning to a parking space. There were the empty fields, the power plant, the administrative building. The clock.

"It's us!" Barbara called out.

"It's Sing Sing in living color!" Lourdes chimed in.

Lynnie felt her blood pounding as she watched her own world. The hospital cottage, with Marcus in his muffs. The gym, with the buckled floor and cobwebbed hoops. Z-1, with Christopher rocking back and forth, Timmy spinning. An entrance to the tunnel. A lake of ugliness on a lavatory floor.

And suddenly: Lynnie!

The room went wild. "Lynnie!" they called out. Loretta thumped her on the back.

What if Clarence and Smokes saw her? She felt fear grab hold of her face.

"Do you live here in this building?" John-Michael's voice said off-camera.

The Lynnie on the television, blond curls falling around her face, nodded.

Doreen jabbed her in the side. "You're a star."

Lourdes said, "Lynnie is ready for her close-up."

John-Michael, still off-camera, asked his second question. "If you could walk out that gate right now and never come back, would you?"

The television Lynnie paused. She looked outside the frame of the picture—to Kate, Lynnie remembered. Then the television Lynnie looked back and nodded.

The dayroom let up hollers of approval.

In the attendants' office, the phone started ringing. "Oh, shut up," Suzette called out.

The camera cut away from Lynnie. Now the television was showing them other parts of the School, but Lynnie couldn't concentrate because other phones were ringing. Phones in other cottages. Phones all around the School. And everyone in her dayroom was in a state, calling out, "It's us!" and, "We're famous!"

So no one could hear what John-Michael was saying. But they could see: John-Michael was entering Maude's office, where she gave him a curious look, and then he was walking past her into Uncle Luke's office. Uncle Luke, sitting at his desk, looked up, startled and confused. John-Michael said something, and Uncle Luke's eyes flashed with suspicion, then anger. He stood up. Maude came into the room, looking flustered. Then Mr. Edgar, Uncle Luke's beefy driver, appeared, gesturing for John-Michael to leave and covering the camera with his hand.

The room went into a frenzy. No one knew what it all meant, though everyone knew it was something that had never happened before. They were on TV! Uncle Luke looked like a buffoon! Phones were ringing everywhere!

"Ooo," Doreen said to Lynnie, "someone's got it coming."

Lynnie sat back, feeling her face turn like a page, from fear to thrill.

She looked across the room. Kate, rising from

her seat, was coming over, her arm held high. Lynnie stood up and raised her arm, too, and, with their faces in a mirror smile, they slapped their palms together.

Then she looked past Kate's face, out the window into the night sky. The clock was still glowing in its tower, trying to boss everyone around as it cast its light on them all. For the first time in Lynnie's life, she glared back.

A-Tisket, a-Tasket

KATE

1974

It's a miracle, Kate thought as she strode up the path toward the parking lot, sunlight glinting off the February snow. *Thank you, Jesus, thank you*, she prayed. *Thank you for making Dr. Hagenbuch so appalled by the School that he quit. Thank you for sending John-Michael Malone to meet Dr. Hagenbuch, then giving them the courage to sneak into the School. Thank you for broadcasting John-Michael Malone's exposé across many more states than Pennsylvania. Thank you for one television being on in one apartment where one woman happened to be eating her Swanson dinner, and happened to glance up from her jewelry making, and happened to recognize the gate. Thank you for giving that woman the fortitude that built slowly yet steadily over the next few weeks and led her to pick up a phone. Thank you for Maude taking that call and telling the caller she would have someone check the files to find out if an Evelyn Goldberg lived here. Maybe Maude would never have called back, though with the press now bearing down—and the governor at last coming to see the School—maybe she would have. But thank you, Jesus, for Doreen to be picking up the mail at just that moment, and for Maude to hand the request to Doreen, and for Doreen to run not to the file room, but to me, and to tell me breathlessly what she had in her hands. Most of all, thank you for the miracle of that woman making the long trip here today, even with the snow and her "stupid, meaningless job," as she put it on the phone. It's a miracle of love.* And as Kate had been thinking for the last few days, since Scott had proposed on his knees, *Love's the greatest miracle there is.*

At the parking lot, Kate looked at her watch. Twelve fifteen. Right on time, Albert was ushering a rusty Ford Falcon to a visitor spot. Although it seemed unlikely that a drive from Ithaca, New York, could be timed so precisely, Kate knew, from just a glance through the windshield at a tall woman with curly hair, that Hannah was a woman of her word.

Kate waved as Hannah, dressed in a pea coat and flowing skirt, stood up from the car. It took her a moment to notice Kate; she seemed distracted by the clock in the tower. At last she glanced across the lot. Kate, in her quilted coat and boots, waved her mittens in the cold.

They approached each other as opposites: Kate, smiling and jaunty; Hannah, grim and awkward. *She's the sister*, Kate thought. *She has no reason to feel troubled.* But Kate suddenly understood: Kate had been Lynnie's family, and the Lynnie Hannah knew was long gone.

The two who had never met took each other into a hug.

"It's so strange being here again," Hannah said, her voice weak as a shiver as they headed down the hill toward Kate's office. "I've thought of it so much. It comes up a lot in my dreams."

"When was the last time you were here?"

"The day we brought Lynnie. I never saw it again until that story aired on TV."

She made a choking sound. Her dark hair was as curly as Lynnie's. Kate knew from Eva that the child—no, she needed to think of her by name—that *Julia* shared this hair. Would Hannah ever recognize her niece if she happened to stroll into the bank where Hannah was a teller? Or wherever Hannah worked next—because, at twenty-seven, she'd been "job hopping," as she'd put it, for years? Well, it wasn't a scenario that would ever happen. Hannah didn't know she had a niece.

"I never tell anyone I have a sister," Hannah said as they began walking. "But I remember so much." She smiled. "We had fun. We had a bubble-gum game, where she'd pop my bubble.

We had our own version of hide-and-go-seek. She liked sucking on wet washcloths and playing dress-up. And we loved to sing. Show tunes, Tin Pan Alley stuff. The one that got her most excited was 'A-Tisket, a-Tasket.' I'd stand on the desk and sing my heart out while she bounced on the bed." She began the song, then trailed off. The wind droned across the empty cornfields. The governor had shut down the farm; those fields would never see corn again.

Hannah sighed. "My parents never talked about her. We even moved so when my brothers got older, no one around them could spill the beans. Can you believe that? And can you believe I didn't question that for years? The things you just accept." She walked in silence a minute, then added, "Twice I asked my mother why we did it. The first time, after the twins were born, she said we'd confuse Lynnie if we visited. The second time, when I was in college, she said my father had wanted to spare us the shame. And all along I had to promise not to tell my brothers."

"Do any of them know you're here?"

"I called my mother and told her about the broadcast. She said"—Hannah brushed at her eyes—" 'Go. Tell me what you see. Then I'll think about telling your brothers and your father.' "

"Is that why you came? As an emissary for the family?"

Hannah blew on her fingers, which Kate realized weren't gloved. And her coat was unbuttoned, as if Hannah were unconcerned with her own discomfort. "No. It's for me. I can't tell you what it's like having a sister no one talks about."

"I'm sorry," Kate said. She didn't add that some families *had* come to visit. Not many, and usually siblings became too uneasy by the time they were teenagers. Why tell Hannah that if her parents hadn't done what the doctors told them to do, she might feel differently—but might not? And why tell her that when a parent did come, some of the more lonely residents would go to the window to see if the person walking on the path was theirs? Kate always knew when a parent was near A-3: Barbara, Gina, and Betty Lou would be at the window, mournfully calling out, "Mommy?"

She would not tell Hannah that—or what happened one night five Novembers ago.

"Here we are," Kate said, opening the door to her building.

Hannah stamped the cold from her feet. Then she looked at Kate. "I hate to admit this: I have no idea what to say to her."

Kate placed both hands on Hannah's shoulders. "I don't think you need to say anything," she said, smiling into the dark eyes. "You're here."

Kate opened the door to her office. Lynnie was

sitting at the desk, drawing. Her eyes rose, and she looked at Kate, then this stranger.

"Lynnie," Kate heard herself say, her voice far off, "this is your sister."

Lynnie focused. "Nah-nah?" she said, her voice soft.

Hannah, nodding, started biting her lips.

Lynnie pushed back from the desk and said more loudly, "Nah-nah!"

"What do I do?" Hannah said to Kate. "I don't know what to do!"

But already Lynnie had shot out from the desk and flung her arms around her sister. Slowly Hannah lifted her arms and wrapped them around Lynnie. Fastened together, they were opposites, too: Hannah sobbing away, Lynnie laughing for joy.

The visit was brief. With Uncle Luke fearing for his job, visitors weren't supposed to stay longer than an hour, and only in administrative offices. Though maybe, Kate thought, a short visit was best, at least at first. As she watched Lynnie show Hannah her artwork, she was well aware that Hannah didn't understand Lynnie's long-unpracticed speech, and she looked to Kate to provide a translation. Hannah, who'd once been Lynnie's fiercest supporter, was clearly embarrassed by this. She also barely knew what to say, startled that her sister was not just living her own life, but also had talent.

"These are so good," Hannah kept saying. Hannah also didn't know what to make of Doreen, who, after stopping by and learning that Lynnie's sister had come to visit, abruptly slammed out of the office. Hannah couldn't know that Doreen had still never heard from her parents. Only Lynnie seemed relaxed, paging through her drawings of horses and cornfields. Yet Kate knew all was not as it seemed. Lynnie was showing only the drawings from her most recent folder. Nothing of her time with Number Forty-two. Nothing of the baby.

But she said none of this to Hannah when they walked back to her car. She said only that she'd felt hope in the air since the broadcast by John-Michael Malone and that Hannah's visit was the first major development.

"What else might happen?" Hannah asked.

Kate told her she'd put in a request for a speech therapist for Lynnie. If more teachers were hired, it was possible an art class might get going. Physical improvements were probably going to happen at the cottages. And Uncle Luke could be replaced.

Then Kate shut her mouth, and not only because Hannah had no expectations of the other things that could change. Kate did not want to tread near the topic of housing options, since the main option that usually came to anyone's mind was family, and Hannah had already indicated her family would not be receptive. For a moment Kate felt her jaw set, though she understood. This family, like so many others, had spent decades living without a son or daughter or brother or sister. For all the harm that had been done, for all the sorrow and silences and secrets, full, complex lives had grown over the absence. To bring a person back to the household would be to throw lives into turmoil, family and residents alike. The system, for better or for worse, had given residents an existence of their own, and even if her family was desperate for her return, Kate knew Lynnie would not go. Lynnie was a woman now. Certainly she couldn't make her way alone in the world—she'd always need help. But there must be a way she could live outside these walls without depending on family.

Hannah turned when they reached her car. "I'll come back soon," she said.

I hope so, Kate thought. *Oh, I hope so.*

Kate pushed her hands deep into her pockets and watched Hannah pull away from the parking lot. Yes, it was a miracle Hannah had come. But Kate realized she'd hoped for a little more miracle.

She closed her eyes. "I don't mean to be greedy, Jesus," she prayed aloud, listening to Hannah's car putter down the drive. "I'm not asking you to heal all the handicapped people in the world. I'm not asking you to make her family into saints. I'm not asking you to bring Number Forty-two back from the grave, or Julia to the School.

"All I'm asking is that you give Lynnie some way to have the simplest thing all of us have. Please get Lynnie out of here. Please find Lynnie a home."

The Day of the Red Feather

HOMAN

1974

The sun was already warm when they left the big house where they all slept and headed out to the fields. Homan still didn't know their names, but he knew they had taken him in when he'd found himself alone in the streets of the hilly city. This morning, like most mornings, he set a straw hat on his head and walked beside the two boys who'd knelt before him as he'd sobbed at the edge of the gas station, offering him food, then driving him here. They were both guitar players with long hair, and in front of them now walked the Chinese girl who tied her hair with a carved white butterfly. On days when she made the meals, she prepared food he'd never seen: thin, musky brown soup; rice with vegetables and chewy white cubes; fried bananas. Her tasty dinners were one of the many gifts of this place, which no one so far was pushing him to leave.

White Butterfly turned at the crest in the path and moved her mouth, looking at the boys. She must have been speaking about him because her gaze kept returning to his face, but he wasn't afraid. There was a different spirit among these people than he'd seen before, an easygoing acceptance, even when they weren't sitting in the common room with their legs crossed, hands pressed in a prayer. Most newcomers moved on quickly, put off by the outdoor labor or twice daily sitting on cushions, everyone's eyes closed, Homan playing along without the foggiest notion of what they were doing. Yet his relief at being in a place with a roof, food, and generosity was so great, he didn't care about understanding. His only discontent came when his remembering went east.

The boys beside him were not the only musicians here. Three others joined them in the common room every night to play their instruments, while the women cleaned up and the children went out to play. That was the time of day when Homan settled into the chair everyone had agreed was his (*his!*): a bear-sized, stuffed yellow chair with a hole in one arm and woven cloth draped over the top. It resembled the lounge chair he and Sam had kept in the van, though it had a deep seat, perfect for his long legs. In that chair he felt he could stay in this life forever.

White Butterfly gestured toward the house, and

the two boys nodded, hands on their wheelbar-
rows. Homan wondered if they meant to send him
back to the house for his day's work. He never
knew what he'd be doing on any day and just took
on whatever they wanted, from planting to har-
vesting to jam making, though he hoped he'd get
sent inside today since he was more tired than
usual. He'd stayed up late last night, enchanted
by drummers who'd arrived in a car. They'd set
drums on their laps or between their knees and
played with the palms of their hands. He'd set
his own hands on the pulsing floor, feeling the
beat, until the musicians went off to bed. But one
drummer stayed up, a colored man in a green-and-
orange shirt, showing him a poster of two men
with medallions around their necks and their fists
held high in the air. The drummer tried to explain
the poster, and Homan hadn't understood.
Though he'd finally gotten so used to not understanding, he'd come up with a name for the
confusion and fear that came upon him when he
knew he was wrong and didn't know what was
right: the feeling of Incorrection.

The boys nodded to White Butterfly. Then they
all continued over the ridge, and the valley
opened wide and green.

He didn't have *no* understanding of where he
was. He was living in a large house with about

thirty men, women, and children. Only two had gray hair, and none had the conditions he'd seen in the Snare or at the church. The house was on a farm where they raised animals and grew crops like apples, artichokes, broccoli, chard, lettuce, and onions. Some of the people were responsible for making cheese, others for bundling flowers together. Everyone did something, even the two with gray hair—a wiry man in an orange coat and a willowy woman in a flowing dress. King Orange and Queen Long Dress. They took care of the office.

Homan also discovered something more about his location—something that took his breath away. One day during his first year here, one of the trucks wouldn't start, and when someone opened the hood, Homan looked inside. He spotted the problem easily and made motions to them with his hands. Not his signs—they'd never shown much interest, so early on he'd given up trying—but the simple motions hearing people could follow. They caught on about the part that needed replacing. Then three men got into the car as round and green as a turtle and waved for him to join them. Together they left the farm and drove toward the hilly city.

He felt, on that ride down long roads, the same gratitude he'd felt since they'd found him crumpled at the gas station, and he hoped it would be all he'd feel. Though there was another emotion that came up sometimes, one too hateful to name. Early on in his travels it had begun as a burn in his gut, and over time it had grown, igniting whenever he remembered leaping out of Roof Giver's window, being swept down the river, getting beaten in the cave. Since he'd been here, it had scorched inside him every morning, when he still saw Beautiful Girl and Little One—though never as more than fuzzy shapes, and never with each other, and never lasting for more than a blink. The feeling would whoosh through his body, and he'd put his hand over his face, hoping no one, especially him, would know he existed. And he'd think, *How you let this happen, you knucklehead? Ain't you supposed to be better than your no-good daddy? Good thing they don't know who you is!* It was a feeling that seared so much, he just wanted to forget everything that had come before now. And after dinner every night, he made sure that he did.

The day he returned to the city for the broken truck part, he did not have this feeling. Instead, as they drove onto a gigantic red bridge, far more majestic than the double-decker, and he caught a glimpse of water through the fog, he felt a wondering. And then, when they turned right at the end of the bridge and drove beside wide-open water, he felt awe. He gaped from the car, giving himself over to the sight as he hadn't been able to before, pressing his hands to the window. So this was the place he had seen from Sam's steps. So this was the place Beautiful Girl had drawn. So this was what he'd been gazing at time after time, when he'd pulled out her drawing from under the hay. At last, here he was: at the place that came from tears.

The others in the car noticed him looking, and after they left the car at a shop, they crossed a road and went down a staircase to a sandy beach. Homan stood for a moment at the bottom of the steps, taking in the salty scent. It was chilly, with wind blowing, and he signed to himself, giving it a name—Finally Sea—and broke into a run. At the edge of the sand he splashed right in, stopping only when it reached his knees. Then he scooped up a handful of water and dipped in his tongue. It *did* taste like tears. And he let himself remember: her lips touching his, her body in his arms. But this time he did not feel the feeling that had no name. He felt only his longing, stretching as endlessly as the sea. He felt only a tide, rising in his eyes.

The sun was now high over the fields. He removed his straw hat and wiped his brow and was glad to see the children carrying lunch pails into the fields. Though this was unusual: The girl who came toward them had only three pails, which she gave to White Butterfly and the two boys. Then the girl urged Homan toward the house. Still sleepy from last night, Homan followed.

When the girl brought him to the office, King Orange and Queen Long Dress rose from their desks and smiled in greeting. The drummer from last night was also there, sitting at the table in the corner, smoking a cigarette and nodding hello. The girl walked off, and King Orange indicated a chair at a table. Homan sat down, and Queen Long Dress closed the door.

Homan hadn't spent any real time with King Orange and Queen Long Dress. They shared the big table at breakfast and dinner and sat on the cushions with everyone else twice a day, but they spent most of their time in this office, King Orange on the phone, Queen Long Dress with glasses down on her nose. They were in charge of this place and in that way were like the big shot at the Snare and his lady helper. Except King Orange and Queen Long Dress were a couple—who wore matching rings. King Orange gave the children piggyback rides. Queen Long Dress sat beside people when they seemed glum, resting her fingers on their arms. When Homan first came here, he curled up in a bed on the floor, fists tight, and King and Queen came over. They must have known he was deaf; they didn't even move their lips. They gestured to his fists with their palms opening, and when he followed their lead and spread his fingers apart, they reached forward as if he were an important person, and both of them shook his hand.

Sometime later, Queen Long Dress did something else. One day, when he was helping the jam makers paste labels on jars, Queen sat beside him. She gestured to the labels, with their drawing of a playful-looking sun and the black marks he knew were letters, and she looked at him with questioning eyes. He remembered the tests his first days at the Snare, where they pointed to toy blocks and stopwatches and he hadn't understood the instructions. He'd failed that test, and he'd fail this test, too. He went on with his work, and soon she walked away.

Now, after Homan took a seat at the corner table, King Orange and Queen Long Dress sat on either side of him. Drummer was sitting across, and he set a book on the table.

King pushed the book until it was right in front of Homan and opened it up. Homan looked at him, then Drummer. Drummer pointed to the page. Homan peered from face to face. Then Drummer took Homan's hand and set it underneath a line of writing. The writing resembled bird tracks—for birds with mismatched footprints. Homan looked up at Drummer.

Drummer set his gaze on the line of writing and moved his lips. Homan suspected he wanted him to read his lips. Then Homan realized: *He want you to read.* He looked to Queen, who gestured for him to keep his eyes on the page. He'd surely fail this test, too, though maybe if he looked like he was trying, they'd let him keep living here. So he tightened his brow and faced the writing and gave it all he had. But as he stared, the tracks as hard to follow as footprints blowing away with the wind, his mind began to leave this room. It happened in spite of his desire every day to forget. He couldn't help himself, not with bird tracks in front of him. He left this chapter of his life and flew back over the years and landed far away in his memory.

It happened on a day when the corn was high enough to hide inside. He and Beautiful Girl had slipped inside the rows, and there, protected from rules and guards, they ran down one row, then the next, holding hands and laughing and free. Finally they stopped. Surrounded by stalks, they moved toward each other, pressing closer than they ever could in Chubby Redhead's office. And they kissed. It was a new kiss for them, deep and long, her lips sweet and full. He felt his body go weak and strong at the same time, his emotions rush in unfamiliar directions, his arms winding tight around her back, hers pulling tight around his. He wanted the kiss to last until the sun turned into the moon. He wanted her to be with him until summer became winter.

And then it happened. As they paused to gaze at each other, a bird flying above dropped a red feather. They saw it floating down, and when it landed between their chests, they pressed together, catching it as one. They laughed at how their timing was the same, and in his happiness, Homan lifted the feather off their chests and held it between them and did what he'd told himself the day he arrived at the Snare he'd never do again. He used his mouth to speak.

Fuh uh.

He had not expected the word to come out of his mouth. Nor had he expected it to mean anything to Beautiful Girl—he knew she did not speak. To his surprise, though, she looked at the feather in his hand, and her eyes slowly changed from love to love with understanding. Then she took the feather from his hand, and with her eyes locked onto his, she brought her top teeth against her bottom lip, lifted his wrist to her lips, and let him feel her breath: *Feh.* She moved her tongue to the back of her top teeth. *Thuh.*

He looked at her, astonished. She gazed back, hopeful. And without thinking, he lowered his fingers to her neck and touched her skin there as if he were a locket in the hollow of her bone. When she said it again, he could feel it even more. *Feh thuh.*

He let out a laugh and closed his eyes, and she did it over and over, stronger each time, as thrilled to know he could feel her voice as she was to know she could speak. Then he lifted her fingers to his own throat. It was *Fuh uh*. She shook her head no. Right: It was *Feh thuh*. She nodded. *Feh thuh*. *Feh thuh*. He used his voice as he hadn't for so long. She used hers back. They watched each other try. They touched each other's necks. They felt each other speak.

Now he looked to Drummer. How Homan wanted to reach up and touch the man's throat to make a guess at what he was saying. But Homan remembered the laughing faces of his brothers and sisters and the confused expressions of strangers at the train station during the Running. He remembered the horrible moment when the police caught him and cuffed him and he ended up in the Snare. Beautiful Girl was the only person he'd ever touched on the neck and who he let himself say more to than "I'm deaf." There was a closeness to touching a person on the neck, or trying to speak, that he'd felt with no one else, not even Sam. To use your voice with another person until you made a word was like trusting that person with a kiss.

Finally Drummer gave up.

That night, like every night, Homan sat down

in his yellow chair. Everyone thought he came here after dinner because its big seat fit his long legs. But there was a secret reason. Beneath the seat, hidden by the black cloth that covered the coils, pushed deep inside, was his money. If they had known, they would have laughed, since in this place they pooled their money and bought every-thing together. Though to Homan, his money was important not because of what it could buy, but because it was the one thing he'd held on to all these years.

The yellow chair, which he'd positioned just so in the center of the common room, embraced him. Someone rolled him the plastic ball he liked to hold whenever music was playing, and he set it on his lap. Then, as the musicians began strumming guitars and beating drums, Homan felt the vibra-tions come through his feet, the seat, the armrests, and the ball, which he hugged, allowing the sound to pound through his body. It felt as if the chair were a boat, rocking him from all around—along with his money and memories and the feeling he could not name.

He sailed along, feeling the music. And he couldn't resist—he thought of Beautiful Girl. Though it wasn't a memory of them together. It was an image of her now, in the Snare: lying in her bed, looking out to the tower clock, waiting for a man who'd never returned.

Don't think on her no more.

One of the guitarists was lighting up the Tingling, just like every night. Homan lifted his gaze
from the ball, reached out his hand, and raised
the Tingling to his lips. The smoke went up into
his mind like a chimney broom and swept all his
thinking away.

He passed the cigarette to White Butterfly.
Then he folded himself again around the ball, far
away from Beautiful Girl, and let the music pound
into him like a storm.

PART III

SEEKING

The Parade

LYNNIE

1980

*H*ow could you still be in bed?" Lynnie heard Doreen say as she came up from dreams that June morning. "I thought you couldn't wait for today."

With sleep still holding her eyes closed, Lynnie couldn't remember what Doreen was talking about. Everything felt the same: the stiff mattress and bleach-scented sheets, the mumblings and morning stretching of other residents, the potent School smell. Actually, that wasn't true. Taxpayers were now demanding changes, so there were fewer residents. Newly concerned officials were poking around, too, so the stench had been blanketed with Lysol. Even Doreen was no longer close enough to lay her hand on Lynnie's bed, because the cottages had gotten partitions that created sleeping rooms for six, with each resident having lots of room beside her bed, as well as a chest of drawers—for her very own clothes. The drawers weren't locked, either, and the toothbrushes weren't shared, and the food wasn't mushed, and the work treatments were supplemented by honest-to-goodness classes. In Lynnie's art class, she'd learned painting, etching, even mosaics.

Whenever Lynnie thought about these changes, she felt the same flutter of happiness that came when she dabbed canary yellow or orchid pink or lime green on a page. But there was one aspect of life she hoped would not change: Doreen still slept in the same area as Lynnie. Having her friend beside her, talking away until they drifted into sleep, helped Lynnie face the emptiness of every night, and knowing Doreen would be up on her elbow by sunrise, flipping through the magazines she was now allowed to receive, motivated Lynnie—despite the shadow images she still saw whenever she thought of Buddy and the baby—to open her eyes to every day.

Seven years had passed since John-Michael Malone had set the dominoes of change falling at the School, and in that time Lynnie had come to understand something surprising yet also unsettling about change: When the art teacher brought in pastels for the first time, or Doreen was granted a subscription to *People* magazine, change made Lynnie's spirits dance. But every time the beds were rearranged and Lynnie faced the possibility of Doreen being moved to a far-off room, Lynnie would slump back into the same numbness she'd felt after Buddy and the baby had vanished. Thank goodness Doreen would always speak up, saying, "You think I'm going anywhere, you got another think coming." They'd been spared the worst kind of change.

"Hey," Doreen said again, jostling Lynnie's shoulder. "So are you getting up?"

Lynnie said, "Give me a minute." Her words came out slower and muddier than the speech therapist, Andrea, kept assuring her they would. Still, the words came. Learning to speak again had been a long process made up of many tiny steps, each taking endless afternoons of frustration. Luckily, everyone who mattered to Lynnie had grown used to what Doreen had dubbed "Lynnie-talk" without giving confused looks or running roughshod over her careful enunciation, and their patience encouraged Lynnie to keep trying. The reactions of others were actually another lesson she'd learned about change. When change happened to an individual, it happened to everyone around her—sometimes in ways she wished for, though sometimes in ways she wished against.

Lynnie, opening her eyes, looked at Doreen, who was standing dressed beside the bed.

"Then you're going?" Doreen asked. Her voice had a pleading tone.

Now Lynnie remembered what day it was. She reached up and wrapped her fingers around Doreen's. "Yeah. I'm going."

Doreen shook off Lynnie's hand. "Well, I'm not."

"Don't be that way."

"I'm not being any way," Doreen said, sitting down hard on her bed. "I'm just not going." She picked up her pillow and threw it at the partition. Then she curled into a sitting ball and said she wasn't coming to breakfast, even though it was their last breakfast here.

So it wasn't as uplifting as Lynnie had been expecting to step outside A-3 into the sunshine of early summer and see two attendants stringing a banner between handheld poles. Nor did her heart stir when she caught a glimpse of circus trucks pulling into the lot—still presided over by a uniformed Albert (what would he do with himself after today?)—and see, inside the wheeled cages, camels, horses, and an elephant, all wearing the same sparkling saddles she hadn't seen since the circus stopped coming years ago. "It's going to be a big day," Mr. Pennington, the new superintendent, told them at movie night last week, "so we're bringing the animals back to celebrate." Also coming back would be John-Michael Malone and his cameras, out in the open this time. Over the last many months, as Lynnie had imagined this morning, she'd been sure she'd feel exuberant—one of many big words she'd heard Andrea use about today, though which was too difficult for Lynnie to pronounce. But Doreen's resistance to the festivities and the momentous event they were marking had dampened Lynnie's exuberance. Doreen had made no secret of her feelings all along, as word spread that the School was finally being shut down and everyone would be moved to, as Mr. Pennington said, "new arrangements in the community." "I don't want any rearranging," Doreen would say. "I've lived here since I was a week old. This is my home." Lynnie understood, though like most of the residents, she couldn't wait to leave. Maybe this was because she once knew a world outside the walls: kitchen cabinets she sang inside with Nah-nah, Betsy Wetsy dolls she played with under the table, a restaurant where she screamed out, "Burger!" But maybe it was because she'd been in that world for three glorious days and so did not fear what lay out there. That was what Doreen called it—*out there*—spitting out the words as if they were food that had gone rotten but that Lynnie knew Doreen was just too scared to eat.

It was so odd to do so much for the final time: walk to the dining cottage, see attendants—there were no working boys or girls anymore, and attendants no longer wore uniforms—feeding residents who needed help. (No one said "low grade" anymore. They said "severe" or "profound" or "low-functioning.") Lynnie wondered what would become of each. She already missed Gina and Marcus, whose parents had taken them home. Where would Barbara go? Christopher? Betty Lou? Their families had never shown up. Kate said: "It's the ones with the involved families who'll do better." Lynnie asked why some families just disappeared. Kate said, "There are probably many reasons. But I can assure you: Someone in every one of those families feels a hole in their heart."

"Maybe Doreen's parents will come for the parade," Bull said last night. But by the time Lynnie finished breakfast, neither Doreen nor her parents had shown up. Well, Lynnie thought as she left the smells of hash browns and scrapple behind her, she could keep hoping, even if Doreen said she didn't care. If Lynnie could change so much she could learn to speak, Doreen's parents could change, too.

Lynnie tried to keep her mind on hopeful thoughts as she got on the path and headed toward Kate's office. Otherwise, she knew, the sadness she felt about losing Doreen might combine with all the other sadnesses she was passing right now— the cottage where she'd been placed until Kate rescued her, the hospital cottage where she'd met Tonette, the cornfield, now gone to seed. And with that much sadness, even circus animals wouldn't matter.

Lynnie turned her gaze from those sights, forcing herself to see more cheerful places—and there were many. After Uncle Luke was finally asked to resign, Smokes and Clarence quit. So for seven years (seven! she could say every number—up to one hundred!) Lynnie had been able to walk the grounds on her own. She could even, once the rules had loosened, roam far and wide, drawing paper in hand. The farm animals and tractor had been sold for, as Mr. Pennington said, "new sources of revenue," but the empty barn remained. She could see the path to the barn now and thought of how pleased she'd been whenever she'd set out for an afternoon. She'd settle herself outside the red barn doors, content in the sunlight, and draw little stories she saw happening in front of her, about squirrels and fox and geese. Hannah said Lynnie was a great artist, and she would know, because after years of jobs that made Hannah's brow tight when she spoke of what she did for a living, she opened an art gallery. She brought a few of Lynnie's pictures back with her once after a visit and told Lynnie that when she showed them to customers, they widened their eyes and said, "They're really good."

Lynnie's parents hadn't said much about her artwork, though they'd come to visit. A few years after Lynnie met Hannah again, her parents flew in from their retirement home in Arizona, met Hannah at the airport, and showed up at the School. They didn't look like the people in Lynnie's photo; she hugged them anyway. With Hannah urging them on, she and Lynnie showed them around the School, her mother making shy smiles, her father clearing his throat. When she showed them the drawing her art teacher had tacked on the wall—of a blue-and-green horse, modeled after Hannah's little toy, which Lynnie still kept in her pouch—they didn't say more than a clipped, "Nice." They kept taking a step back from her, too. She wondered why, but when she moved as close as she usually stood to Doreen or Kate, they did it again. It looked like things would get easier when they brought her back to their hotel, only it was just a different kind of hard. Mommy said, "It was wrong, Lynnie," as she dabbed a tissue behind her glasses. Daddy said, "We had no choice back then." Then no one seemed to know what to say. She wanted to tell them about her Lynnie Day books and how Horton and Ferdinand and all the rest had shown her how to draw pictures in a sequence, so they would add up, page after page, to a story. But she hardly knew all those words, and for some reason her mouth was even less cooperative than usual. Even with Hannah prompting conversation among everyone as best she could, Lynnie started to feel as if she were wearing clothes that could never be made to fit. Finally Hannah put on the TV and Lynnie was relieved.

She knew she should love them. Yet when she looked at them, she didn't feel as she did for Hannah or anyone she'd come to know on these grounds: Doreen, Kate, Buddy, the baby. She knew at one point she had loved her parents. But change had come to them all.

So Lynnie saw Hannah a few times a year, though she saw Mommy and Daddy only once more. It was a few years later. They brought her to their hotel room again, saying they were going to celebrate Passover. Waiting for her in the room were people Lynnie didn't know—her brothers, she was told, and their wives. The brothers hugged her right away and let go just as fast. They laughed fake laughs through their noses. Everyone sat at folding tables and chairs, and the wives presented food covered in plastic wrap. Then everyone opened a book with almost no pictures and read a story aloud. It was about Pharaoh and Moses and letting my people go, and Lynnie wanted to follow it, but half the words were in another language. Daddy kept saying, "Pay attention, Lynnie." Mommy kept saying, "Lynnie, stop fussing with the forks." Hannah kept telling everyone to stop interrupting Lynnie, she needed time to pronounce her words. The brothers kept sending each other looks. And Lynnie wasn't allowed to eat except when they told her she could have this piece of matzo, that spoonful of charoses; and then when she ate some maror, she felt as if a bee were stinging her nose. She sat back from the table and closed her eyes. They began fighting after that, saying, "This was a stupid idea," and, "You never forgave the temple for turning you away because of her, and suddenly we're devout?" and, "You can't make up for lost time. What's done is done. I bet she doesn't even know what God is."

"I know," Lynnie said, her voice in a tone Andrea would call too soft, so they never heard. And she did know what God was, because she'd seen Him on movie nights. Sometimes He was a column of fire that scared people, sometimes He was George Burns and was nice to people. Kate said God created everything and loved everyone. But like reading and being around family and speaking easily, knowing God seemed to be something only other people could do.

She should not think about God now. She should look around at the places she'd never see again. There were so many that reminded her of Buddy, and every single one brought back the sweetest feelings. This tree, where they'd stood hidden in the leafy shade and Buddy had waited with patience as she clumsily practiced his signs. This window, where she'd watched Buddy getting a cow from the pasture—the same cow whose calf he helped birth not long after, a feat that made her know he could help her give birth, too. Oh, and this tunnel entrance: the very one where she waved good-bye as he ran off to set out the ladders they then used to escape.

Every one of these places made her feel full of all the colors that had ever been, yet trapped in the numbness at the same time. He was gone, the baby was gone, and now Lynnie would be gone. He would never find her when he came back. She would have nothing of him and the baby except memories.

Maybe that was why, as Kate's office came into view for the last time, Lynnie let herself have a thought she'd never allowed. All this time—*twelve years*—she hadn't talked to Kate about the baby. She hadn't even drawn the baby, except that one time in those first few weeks. But for years after, Smokes and Clarence had been around with their dogs, so she couldn't take the chance, and when they finally left the School, she still feared the fate of the nursery.

Maybe, though, it was time to say something to Kate. Kate had told Lynnie her new home would be safe and secure. Lynnie would have her own key, and the staff who worked there would keep out anyone who shouldn't come in. If that was really true—if Smokes and Clarence and officials who could put her baby in a School wouldn't be able to reach her—then it would be all right for Lynnie to talk about the baby. No: about the child. No: about her daughter. These words came to her like comets, leaving glittery trails of pleasure. The baby was now older than Lynnie had been when she'd come here. And she was Lynnie's flesh and blood. Did she have the artistic gift Lynnie and Hannah shared? Did she like to sing? There were twelve years of page turnings to learn about—her daughter was almost a teenager. And now Kate could help her learn about that teenager. She would ask Kate as soon as she reached her office: Could she take Lynnie to the old lady's farm at last?

"Lynnie!" Hannah cried out from behind Kate's desk. "The big day is finally here!"

Lynnie, standing in Kate's doorway for the last time, looked from Hannah to Kate. Hannah wasn't supposed to get here until the parade began. Yet Kate had the file cabinet open and was holding a stack of Lynnie's drawings, and Hannah was taping up a box.

"You're early," Lynnie said, unable to stifle her disappointment.

"You don't mind, do you?" Hannah said, her smile falling. "I wanted to help Kate."

"It's okay." But how could Lynnie say anything to Kate now?

"You're speaking so well these days," Hannah said.

Lynnie understood that Hannah wanted to talk them away from the poor start to the conversation. Andrea had taught her that speaking was about a lot more than breath and volume and pronunciation; it was about knowing when to be the leader and when to let others run the show. Hannah was looking at Lynnie as if her speaking were a huge achievement—which, as Andrea and Kate always said, it was. So Lynnie decided she could talk to Kate later. Then she wouldn't show her disappointment now and would instead reveal the pride she genuinely felt.

Lynnie said, "I practice."

"Well, it's paying off."

"I want to get better."

"You will. Leaving this place will make many differences in your life. You'll be doing more speech therapy. You'll be learning to shop at stores. You'll be living like everyone else."

Lynnie corrected her. "It's a group home."

"Well, that's like everyone else."

"Not really."

"Okay. But it's your own home. Yours and Annabelle's and Doreen's."

"Doreen's not leaving."

"She hasn't come around?"

Kate said, "There are several residents who still wish we were staying open. Some parents, too."

Hannah sighed. "I'd hoped they'd changed their minds. I guess that's asking a bit much. They sure had strong opinions at the meetings."

Lynnie remembered Hannah telling her about the meetings. First, the administrators wanted to make the School better, so the meetings were about fixing buildings, retraining staff, creating activities for residents. Then some parents said the School should just shut down, while other parents said the School was the safest place for their child. People began shouting at one another, and lawyers got involved. Lynnie knew this because Hannah went to all the meetings. "I'm on the side of the ones who want to close it," Hannah would say. "That doesn't mean I don't worry about you being out there. You're my sister, and I worry about you." That was how Lynnie knew she could never tell Hannah what happened with the dogs and Buddy and the baby. That was also how Lynnie knew she would live somewhere else someday.

"There's nothing left in here," Kate said, closing the cabinet drawer.

"Then we're done," Hannah said.

Lynnie wasn't ready to leave this room so

quickly. It had been a place of so much joy, how was it possible she'd never see it again? She took it in now: the radio, the typewriter, the plants. Buddy breaking a sugar cube on her drawing to show her the shapes in the stars.

Hannah said, "I know this is hard. But you'll like the new place."

Lynnie nodded.

"Cheer up, sis."

Lynnie looked down. She remembered seeing Buddy's feet on this floor. She'd drawn him a picture of when they got out, and how they'd wear nice clothes and good shoes. She remembered putting on the old lady's slippers. They had made Lynnie feel like a bride.

"Lynnie?"

She looked up.

"Hey, look. I made you a little present." Hannah reached into her pocket. "I was going to wait until you got to your new home to give it to you, but maybe I should do it now."

"Why?"

"Because it's something special you kept in this room. And I know this room was where you did your drawings. So it's sort of a keepsake, you know?"

Hannah raised her hand from her pocket and opened her fingers.

She was holding a necklace with a silver chain

and a glass locket. Inside the locket, preserved from air and time, was the red feather.

Lynnie reached out and ran her finger over the glass case.

"It's an old monocle," Hannah said. "I put a back on it and soldered it shut."

Kate said, "Hannah wanted to use something from your pouch. The feathers were the nicest."

"Why... why did you pick the red one?"

"I hope it's okay," Hannah said, sounding worried.

"Very okay."

Lynnie took the necklace from her sister and lowered it over her head. The feather came to rest on her chest right where she'd caught it with Buddy that day. "Why the red feather?" she asked again, glad Andrea wasn't in this room. She knew her words had memory in them.

"Because red feathers are rare," Hannah said. "If you find one, you should keep it forever."

When they reached the path in front of the administrative cottage, the cameras were already running, and stout Mr. Pennington, wearing a suit, tie, and circus master hat, was standing on a platform. "This is a historic day," he was saying into a microphone as Kate handed Lynnie a pole supporting a banner she'd made last week, a drawing of the School with the gate wide open. "The people of the Commonwealth have outgrown the Pennsylvania Residence for Gifted Children and Adults. It has served us well for eight decades, and now we will honor it one final time."

Lynnie looked around at the residents. Lined up in rows of two, three, or four, they were all ready for the parade. Here were the people she'd sat near in the dining cottage and watched movies with in the common cottage and folded clothes beside in the laundry. Here were residents who could walk on two feet, who wore leg braces, who held canes, who used wheelchairs. Here were so many individuals she knew, each wearing cool sunglasses or favorite baseball caps or new shirts to signify the importance of the occasion. Some were holding signs they'd made, others were holding horns, tambourines, maracas; and in front of them all stood the camels, horses, and elephant. John-Michael Malone was scribbling notes beside a cameraman, and the lens was pointing at the residents.

Doreen was nowhere to be seen.

Then Mr. Pennington stepped off the platform and got in front of the line. The elephant lifted his hat from his head, and everyone laughed. Mr. Pennington grabbed it back and called out, "Five, four, three"—and everyone joined in, even those who couldn't speak—"two, one. Go!" And they marched, making noise on the instruments, cheering, waving to the staff, family, and reporters as they passed by.

Lynnie peered into the crowd, hoping to see Doreen's parents. She wouldn't recognize them, so it seemed silly. But still, she looked as they headed toward the cottages. The crowd was sparse, and everyone watching just kept running ahead to the dining cottage, where the parade would end. So it was easy to see all the people along the route, and that's how she saw Clarence. He was standing off to the side, in jeans and a jacket, seeming even skinnier than before. He was here, on her day. The day she'd thought she'd ask Kate to find her daughter.

And if he was here today, he could be anywhere on any day.

She grabbed the stick the man next to her was using to pound a drum and began beating it against her banner's pole. This way she wouldn't hear the dogs barking in her head, the bucket rolling away while she pleaded.

Then she felt a presence beside her and turned. It was Doreen! Falling into line right beside her!

Doreen didn't look cheerful, though she didn't look the way she had this morning, either. Instead, she was giving Lynnie a knowing look. "I saw him, too," she said over the din from the marchers. "And I'm not gonna leave you alone out there, no matter how I feel."

"You coming with me, then?" Lynnie said.

"I'm coming with you."

Lynnie shifted the banner so they could both hold the pole. They looked at each other and lifted it high into the air, and the cameras caught them smiling together.

Second Chances

MARTHA

1983

*P*ete took the call.

Martha was afraid to listen across their tiny living room. She'd even been afraid to answer the phone, as she was every time it rang on evenings when Julia was out. Martha always hoped the caller would be the basketball coach or one of Julia's more responsible friends. But since Julia had turned fourteen a few months ago, whenever the phone rang, Pete had lifted his gaze from his book to meet Martha's worried eyes, then risen to pick up the receiver.

Pete said nothing for a few seconds. Then: "Yes. This is where she lives."

Not again. She's a good child. Whatever she's done, it isn't who she really is.

"I'm her grandfather," Pete said, his gaze now locked onto Martha's. "Her stepgrandfather. She lives with us."

More silence while Pete listened. What could it be now? A few weeks ago, it was her report card. After an unbroken record of A's, Julia had begun receiving B's and even a C. She'd hidden the card from Martha, mumbling that her school hadn't given them out yet, until Martha said, "I'm calling the principal tomorrow to find out what could possibly be causing this delay." Julia suddenly remembered she'd received it that very afternoon, though Martha and Pete could hear Julia bang into her room, open her closet, and dig through who knew what to retrieve it.

This was followed by a call from one of Julia's teachers. It began with concern about her increasingly lackluster performance, then moved into more generalized distress. "She used to be friends with the studious kids," Mr. Yelinek said. "But since falling in with this new crowd..."

"What new crowd?" Martha asked, the phone turning to ice.

Apparently, Julia had gravitated toward a clique of girls who wore expensive clothes from the most exclusive shops and shunned almost anyone outside the soccer team. To ingratiate herself, Julia had been getting to school early, changing into the same kinds of sweaters worn by these girls, and joining them after school as they huddled together at the roller-skating rink or sashayed through Hyannis Mall. All while Martha thought Julia's early arrivals were for basketball practice and late returns for drama club.

Unproductive conversations ensued. To her credit, Julia did admit to her new habits, though to Martha's—and Pete's—dismay, her response to Martha's insistence that she return to being conscientious and honest was to say, face stiff, eyes forcibly deadening themselves, "I'll try."

Then the night calls began. Miranda's mother, asking if Martha was aware that Julia had snuck out one night after they'd gone to bed, walked an hour from their modest Cape Cod cottage in Chatham to Miranda's grand mansion on Sears Point, and, with Miranda's mother seeing patients late, woken the neighbors with loud music. The manager of the movie theater, who'd caught Julia and her friends sneaking in the back door. The basketball coach, who'd found out she'd attended beer parties on Hardings Beach.

"I see," Pete said. "We appreciate this, Officer."

Officer. Martha's insides flashed as if struck by lightning.

"We'll be there right away."

He hung up the phone and looked at Martha. "Shoplifting while drunk," he said.

Julia did not utter a word when Officer Williamson and the store's head of security opened the door to the back room. She was bent over in a plastic chair at a metal table, arms around her waist, and when Martha stood in the doorway, Julia looked up through her brown curly hair, eyes dark with regret and anger. Martha felt sick, seeing lovely Julia beneath fluorescent lights, consumed by desires Martha could not understand, and maybe Julia could not, either. Her students had told Martha that teenage children were a test of one's soul, though she'd believed she and Julia were too close for such troubles. Julia was also unusually earnest, as Pete pointed out soon after they'd gone to the justice of the peace and moved to his house in Chatham. She was seven then, and Martha had said that maybe with a stable home and the security of two adults, Julia would grow sunnier. Yet it was a sullen girl who rose to Officer Williamson's request. She tottered on her feet, not saying a word, just reeking of alcohol.

The silence persisted as Martha and Julia followed Officer Williamson down the bright corridor, passing employee lockers. Julia walked unsteadily, and Martha wrestled with what to do, wondering, as she had these last months, if parents who'd given birth to their child, or whose own adolescence had been only a decade or two earlier, were more skilled at handling bad behavior. Pete had laughed, saying he and Ann had improvised all the time. "Raising kids isn't carpentry," he'd

said. "Forget measuring twice and cutting once.
You measure over and over every day."

Officer Williamson opened the door to the loading dock. His car sat on one side of the lot, Pete's
Jeep idled on the other. Officer Williamson turned
and said to Julia, "Like I said, no second chances."

When Julia made no reply, Martha chimed in,
"She won't need any."

Julia slid into the backseat while Martha let
herself in the front. The car, though warm, did
not instill a sense of comfort. Their two doors
slammed at the same moment, and then Pete,
nodding to Julia in the rearview mirror, put the
car into gear.

Martha wished Pete would speak up with a rep-
rimand, a question, anything. But the precedent
had been set long ago: Pete never took over or insisted Martha raise Julia *his* way.

At last Martha said the one thing she could.
"Why, Julia?"

More silence. Another quarter mile.

Martha added, "Where did you get the liquor?"

"Miranda."

"She brought it to the mall?"

"She had it in her house. We went to the mall
later."

"And shoplifted."

Silence.

"Why are you lowering yourself like this?"

"You never shop at the mall," Julia said. "You say it's too expensive."

"That is no justification."

"I needed a pair of Jordaches!"

Pete merged onto Route 6, heading toward Chatham.

"You're lucky Officer Williamson let you off. He could have arrested you."

"He probably would have if he'd known who I really am."

"And who is that?"

"I just want to be like everyone else!" Her voice was slurred, yet her point was clear. "Everyone else wears Jordaches. Everyone else has color TVs, and pool tables, and big sailboats. Everyone else gets off Cape in the winter. Miranda goes to Florida!"

"You can't expect—"

"And everyone else has parents."

The word echoed in the warm Jeep, which suddenly seemed smothering.

"Maybe it's time to say something," Pete said.

They were lying on their backs in bed, their books untouched, reading lamps still on.

"I can't."

"I won't say she's acting up because she doesn't know. But it can't be helping."

"She has us." Martha looked over at him. "She

has the aunties and uncles we used to visit. They come to see us every summer."

"She knows they're your old students."

"She's out of control already. What would she do if she knew? I can't even imagine."

"She wants to know more."

"She's too young."

"When will she be old enough?"

"I don't know."

"Martha." He looked at her tenderly. "Martha, Martha, Martha. I was so relieved when you told me you weren't Matilda." He rolled to his side and set his hand on her hip. "It explained all that coming and going. All the moments you'd turn away and get quiet."

"You've said that before."

"Yes. But I'm not sure I've told you this." He nudged her with his hand, and she rolled to her side to face him. "When you told me the truth, I realized you trusted me."

She let herself smile. "You've said that before, too."

"Yes, but I didn't tell you it also made me trust you." He set his hand on her face. She felt, as she so often did in his arms, like a girl of twenty. He said, "Once I knew what you'd done—how you'd chucked everything on a moment's notice because you gave your word to a desperate young woman—I thought you were the most incredible person I'd ever met."

"Anyone would have done it."

"No, they wouldn't have."

"Maybe *I* shouldn't have."

"You don't really think that."

"I just thought it was the right thing to do. Now I'm not so sure. I'm not very good at being a parent."

"Most parents feel that way. I pretty much think that's what parenthood is."

She said nothing.

"What's going on now is temporary. Gary did it, too. Drank beer with his friends. Remember how he totaled my car in Falmouth? If you hadn't done what you'd done, think of what Julia's life would be like."

"I can't."

"Think of what your life would be like. Or mine. We wouldn't be here right now."

She draped her arm around his back. He was stockier than Earl, and he was warm and open and able to provide comfort. Lynnie hadn't only given Martha a child. She'd given Martha a second chance.

And Martha, calling on a former student to bring a story to the public, had given Lynnie a second chance, too.

"You could tell Julia the basics. If she really wants to know more and you still don't want to tell her, you could just give her the keepsake box.

There are enough letters to her in there, and clippings, and whatnot. She'd come to understand."

"I don't know."

"Sleep on it."

"I've been sleeping on it for fourteen years."

"This could be your last night," he said.

She lay beside Pete, looking out the window as clouds passed over the moon. Last fall she had taken away Julia's allowance until her grades improved. After Miranda's party, Martha announced that Julia had a curfew of nine o'clock every night. Yet she'd gotten in trouble again, and with alcohol, no less. Now Martha would insist that Julia was grounded at any time aside from school. Should Martha add a complicated truth, too?

Maybe she should. The truth might show Julia there were people in the world less fortunate than she—and, had the storm been less turbulent that night, or her parents not hidden her before the police arrived, Julia would have been one of them. Though it might seem as if Martha were so angry about the shoplifting and drinking that she wanted to put Julia in her place. Julia might even accuse Martha of lying or, if Martha went so far as to open the keepsake box, seeking praise. And she wouldn't be wrong; Martha dearly wanted Julia to look at her response to Lynnie's request and feel, like Pete, admiration.

Yet such a self-serving impulse seemed reason enough to stay silent.

After these thoughts had swirled for hours, Martha got up. If she couldn't sleep, she might as well go downstairs and return to reading her book.

She made her way out of the bedroom and closed the door. With the moon behind clouds, no light shone through the dormer of her sewing room or the bathroom, so she moved her palm along the dark corridor, feeling her way toward the stairs. Pete always told her to put on the lights to avoid falling, and she knew she should, having fractured a wrist last summer simply by breaking an egg against a bowl. They even planned to move their bed to the first floor. But for now Martha wanted to remain on this floor, risking a broken hip so Julia would mind the rules.

So it was a surprise when Martha's hand passed over Julia's door only to find it ajar.

Had Julia snuck away again? Was she out in the night right now, thinking herself so much worse than her friends that she would do anything to feel she belonged?

With fear stoking her chest, Martha peered around the open door.

Julia was propped up in bed with headphones on, listening to her stereo. The only light in the room came from the amplifier, but it was enough for Martha to see their dog, Reuben, on the bed, too, his furry head in Julia's lap. She was petting him.

Martha crossed the room and sat on the bed. Julia, apparently feeling the mattress move, opened her eyes. At first she started. Then she removed the headphones.

"I'm sorry, Grammy," she said.

Martha took in Julia's face in the blue amplifier light and thought how grown up she was looking. "Are you apologizing for what you did tonight?"

"It was stupid."

"I'm glad you see that."

"I don't even like the taste of wine. But when they passed it to me, I would have been a real loser if I'd said no."

"Julia, you know you're not a loser."

"And then we went to the mall and everyone was joking about my stupid old slacks and Miranda bet I wouldn't have the guts to steal a nice pair of jeans. So I just went into Filene's and..." Julia blew out air, and her curls fluffed away from her forehead.

"Oh, Julia. You used to have such nice friends."

"But Miranda and her friends, they're the school princesses. When they think someone's cool, everyone does. And when they started letting me hang around, it... it just felt *good.*"

"I didn't know you felt bad before."

"You don't understand, Grammy. These are the

cool girls. Everyone wants to be like them. So one day"—she gazed away, as if to remember—"I bought this four-pack of lip gloss with the greatest colors and brought it to school. And after basketball practice I went to the bathroom where they all met every morning, and just as I expected, Miranda came in. I started putting one of the lip glosses on and I was afraid she'd ignore me like always, but she"—Julia sighed with pleasure—"she asked to try one. She'd never even talked to me before. And then Diane and Patti came in, and said how pretty my lips looked, and I just felt like, Wow, and passed the rest around to them. And when we walked out of the bathroom, we were all together, and I felt everyone look at me in a new way. It was so great. Don't you see, Grammy? I never felt that way before. I always felt clumsy and ugly and poor. Like I...like I was *retarded* or something."

Martha caught her breath. She wanted to seize Julia and shake her, make her realize what she'd just said.

Instead, she breathed through her seething and exasperation, and on the fifth exhalation she heard herself say, "I'm disappointed in you. Friends who make you feel you don't measure up are not friends."

Julia said nothing, but tears had begun rolling down her cheeks.

"Your future is too precious to throw away for anyone."

Again, Julia remained silent, eyes toward the ceiling as if trying to muster strength.

"We're going to bring you to and from school every day, and you need to get your grades back up. No more basketball team or drama club. You are grounded except for school. Any extracurriculars will be in the form of a job. Do you understand?"

Julia drew her gaze down and looked directly at Martha. "How come you don't ever talk about my parents? Was there something bad about them or something?"

Martha sat back. She felt her chest heaving, and in the silence that followed, she looked into Julia's eyes and saw, past the challenging stance, the self-loathing, the effects of the wine, Lynnie. And Martha knew, as she hadn't until now, why she couldn't tell Julia the whole story. It wasn't only because Martha wanted to restrain herself from teaching Julia a harsh lesson or because she wanted Julia to be grateful for her sacrifices. It was because Julia's low regard for herself had taken her into misguided friendships, petty crime, and, now, bigoted words. Maybe someday she'd be ready for the truth, but not when she thought so disparagingly, so dismissively, about people like her very own parents.

"No, Julia," Martha finally said. She cleared her throat to push the anger from her voice. Then she added, in her usual soft, caring tone, "They were not bad. They were not bad at all."

"Who were they? What were their names?"

Martha took a breath. "Lynnie. Your mother was named Lynnie."

"And my father?"

Martha gazed away, seeing him now, and said wistfully, "Such a handsome man. And Lynnie...she was so beautiful." Then she looked back.

Julia was still crying, but a smile had emerged through the tears.

The next day, while Julia was at school, Martha and Pete took Reuben for a walk on the beach. They used to walk two miles a day with Rodney. By the time he passed away and they got Reuben, Martha's pace had slowed, so they shortened their walks to half a mile. Now they walked only a short way along the beach.

"When we first met," Martha said, "you told me Julia would break a lot of hearts someday. I think she's broken her first."

Pete looked at her as Reuben ran along the water's edge. "Gary hated everything we did when he was a teenager. You just keep going, and one day they're human again."

"You were young. You had time. I might not."

"I'll be there for her if something happens to you."

"You're no younger than I am."

"There's Gary. He and Jessica said they'd step in if they had to."

"Denver's so far away. And she barely knows them."

"It's going to work out."

"Just promise me something."

"What?"

"If I go when she's still...like this—"

"Stop talking this way."

"I have to. I need to think about what you should do."

"She'll get through this phase soon."

"I don't know about that." Martha turned to him and took his hands. She made a sad smile. "Just promise me you won't tell her until she's mature enough to hear."

He reached forward and smoothed back her white hair. She felt so lovely in his hands. She felt so loved in his eyes. She felt fragile and worried, yet sure this was the right thing.

"Okay," Pete said finally. "I promise."

Martha suddenly felt so light. Everything seemed just the way it should be. It was so much like the final day of school, when she would look out the window and see the last child walking toward home, and she would know that her work was complete.

Show Me Your Sign

HOMAN

1988

*H*oman wasn't expecting anyone that morning. It was his day off, and he liked to start days off by inching across the sleeping mat, reaching into the ceramic bowl, rolling a cigarette, and inhaling the Tingling. Then he'd spend the day working on projects of his own devising. Today he planned to test out his new gutter cleaner, a long pole with a hinged metal claw at one end. He'd been working on it—or, really, not working on it—for weeks and still hadn't finished. The Tingling did that to a person, made him not mind sitting around all day in his yellow chair, watching TV. Luckily, King didn't care about the spicy aroma Homan carried around; he was too busy greeting guests after they pulled up to the front lot in their sleek cars, then gathering them in the room with the bamboo floor, where he'd

tap a stick against a cymbal and they'd all sit on
their knees and breathe. As for Queen, she was
caught up in paperwork. And everyone else was
gone. The farm was gone, too. King and Queen
had moved farther north from the city, and since
Homan was a good worker, they'd taken him
along. No matter that at the farm he'd grown
crops, and here—a sprawling wooden house in
the mountains, surrounded by oaks and pines,
with mats on the floors and sculptures of a bald,
fat man in the private sleeping rooms, where
guests came and went, some of them actors he
saw on TV—he did janitor work and maintenance. It was still a fine arrangement. Homan
worked six days a week and in return got a little house out back, all the rice and vegetables
he could eat, and no fuss about the Tingling,
which he grew in his garden. *This the life*, he'd
think, when he thought. But it wasn't his habit
to think.

Which made him almost ignore the Christmas
lights flashing around his ceiling this morning.
The lights were one project he'd completed soon
after they'd moved here. Discovering he liked
privacy, he'd messed around with a buzzer until
it turned on a string of Christmas lights, blinking them on and off until they got his attention.
When he showed his invention to King and
Queen, King's lips rose in admiration. So Homan

rigged up lights in the main house, too, for when guests weren't meant to talk. They were always startled the first time they saw the doorbell lights flashing, and then, when he caught them looking at him as he went about his work of polishing floors and tending the grounds, their faces would be showing respect.

He got up from the sleeping mat and nudged aside the curtain on the front window.

Standing by his door were King and a young woman. She looked like many of the lady guests— long hair tied with a fabric knot, loose pants that rustled in the breeze, flowing blouse. But she was younger and had a brown shawl wrapped around her shoulders.

King never brought anyone to Homan's house, and as Homan let the curtain fall back, he remembered noticing some people hanging around last week after their stay ended. They'd pointed up to the Christmas lights, then talked with King and Queen in their office. Maybe King had decided to hire more help, and Shawl Lady was it. Homan wondered if he might find himself lying beside her, the way he had with White Butterfly just before her friends showed up one day and drove her off, or after her, like he had those few months with Purple Hair. It had been a long time since he'd lain beside anyone. It had been a long time since he'd had fellow workers.

He hadn't thought of these things in ages and didn't want to start now.

Confused, he opened the door.

Shawl Lady smiled brightly at Homan, and her hand emerged from under the fabric draped about her arms. Only after Homan extended his toward her did he realize something didn't measure right. Shawl Lady's hand was at her elbow.

He froze, hand in midair, and let her reach for him.

Then King made the motion of steering a car—his sign for taking a trip to the city. He lifted his eyebrows as if asking, *Is that okay with you?*

Homan wasn't sure. If it had been a long time since a woman had shared his bed, it had been even longer since he'd seen anyone with differences. He eyed Shawl, thinking of the Snare for the first time in...he didn't want to count.

As King gestured to his car, Queen came across the yard from the main house. Homan could see behind her to the room with the bamboo floor, where the exercise lady was putting the guests through her moves. What could be so important about going to the city—now—with Shawl? Homan glanced inside his little house. He could close the door right now and go light up a Tingling. But he turned back. Everyone had a look of expectation.

For so many years, they'd been good to him.

Warily, he stepped outside.

* * *

He knew the way into the city. They drove him there a few times a year, when they needed help loading supplies. Once he'd even gotten into the driver's seat, remembering the fun he'd had with Sam, driving as he blew bubbles, Sam tapping Homan with his stick to get his attention. But King had smiled in a way that said, *Nice joke*, and Homan decided he preferred riding in a Tingling haze anyway. So it was as a passenger that he'd taken the trip to the hilly city, each time seeing, as they came down from the mountains, how the world was changing: more houses, more stores, more lanes on the roads, more cars in the lanes. The closer they got to the city, the more things changed. New restaurants were appearing, many of them with gold-colored arches, playgrounds for kids, clowns waving at cars. Then there were billboards: a boy riding a bicycle in front of the moon, a pouting blonde in lace undies who held a microphone, fat TVs where all the shows were nothing except yellow writing. On every trip, the growing number of changes unsettled him—the world was turning, and he wasn't turning with it. As he watched the sights get more and more crowded, the feeling he could not name would flash inside him again. When he'd get home he'd roll a huge Tingling, till he tried not to leave home at all.

And today, on top of all that uneasiness, Shawl was sitting right beside him in the back of the car. Queen kept turning from the front to talk to her, but Shawl just nodded or shook her head, making a shy smile to Homan every time. It was almost as if she didn't want to offend him by speaking, though he realized that was a dumb-assed thing to think. *Sure, she different like them at the Snare, only no one there ever polite.*

No, you wrong. What about Beautiful Girl? She more than polite. She—

Don't you go thinking on her. That spilt milk.

It seemed to take longer than usual to reach the city, and though he didn't want to, his thoughts about folks at the Snare got him thinking, for the first time in years, about how many people he'd cared for then lost. Blue and the McClintocks and Mama. Shortie and Whirly Top. Sam. White Butterfly. None had created the emptiness he'd felt since Beautiful Girl and Little One, but all had left sorrow inside. Once, he remembered now, he'd fancied life as a big drawing, but that idea had come to seem boneheaded. No way was life a creation of purpose and reason. Look at him. No matter how much he'd poured himself into each person, when Blue got in the path of Mr. Landis's shotgun or Beautiful Girl was nabbed by police or Sam disappeared behind a shut door, those chapters in his life ended. What was the meaning in that? Each person must be in charge of his own drawing—period. But as the car crossed onto the red bridge, and Homan remembered standing in the salt water so many years ago, he questioned whether he was in control of his own life at all.

In the city, after they crawled along the foot of the hills, through streets with too many cars and bicycles and young people and sidewalk vendors and panhandlers, Shawl suddenly leaned forward and pointed to a parking lot. King turned in and pulled behind a one-story building, and after Shawl pointed to a parking space, King cut the engine. Then King, Queen, and Shawl opened their doors, so Homan did, too. He stood up and watched while they talked. Shawl seemed pretty sure of herself and at ease in this lot. What was this place, anyway? He looked. A long ramp ran along one side of the building, and a blind man was making his way up it with a dog. Homan looked back at Shawl. She smiled and began walking toward the ramp, and as the blind man and the dog entered a side door, she gestured that they were going to do the same. She had to be kidding. Walk through that door? And get trapped in there for years?

He folded his arms across his chest and stared at her.

Finally, after nothing they did coaxed him in, a

young man came out of the door. He didn't have a dog or one-of-a-kind arms. Actually, he looked like singers on TV: tall and skinny, with black clothes and hair cut like an Indian, straight up in tufts. Shawl waved to Indian Tuft, and he waved back. Strangely, he didn't use his mouth. He was nearing them now, and hearing folk always flapped their jaws by the time they got this close. Could that mean—

Then Indian Tuft stopped before Homan and looked at him in a friendly way. Homan turned. King and Queen were behind him, she smiling, he wrinkling his brow. Things were getting even more confusing, especially when they motioned for him to face forward again. There he saw Indian Tuft begin making the kinds of gestures he made— bending his elbows, rubbing his fingers, pressing his palms out, thumbing his chest, sagging his shoulders, circling his head. It was exciting to see familiar movements until he realized there was nothing to them. These signs were like the ones the official at the Snare had tried on him. They had no meaning.

Homan looked at Shawl. Her eyes were fixed on him, though not in a way he could understand. Slowly, he turned back to Indian Tuft, who'd low-ered his hands.

Homan glanced to one, then the other. Their eyes were waiting.

Then Homan did something he hadn't done with anyone since Beautiful Girl. He signed a full sentence. *You ain't making no sense.*

Indian Tuft shot Shawl an uncomfortable look. Facing Homan again, he made more meaningless gestures.

Was he making fun of Homan? Everyone looked as if they were waiting for...what?

Why you making fun of me?

Indian Tuft went on some more.

I ain't no fool.

Homan fled to the car, threw himself into the back, and slammed the door. Shawl had some nerve, setting him up like this! And King and Queen—just going along with her! He hoped they felt sorry, letting him get mocked like that. He hoped they drove off and he never saw Shawl again. He wrapped his arms across his chest and stared ahead, fuming. Only after many minutes passed did he peek over to see the four of them standing around, wearing long faces. Like *they* had something to feel miserable about? He leaned against the far door, pressing the window to his cheek. Wishing he had his Tingling, he tapped a soothing beat on the glass.

So he missed the last thing that happened. As King and Queen walked off from Shawl and Indian Tuft, a young man working at a desk inside the building happened to glance out the window.

He saw a familiar face in a car, comforting himself by placing his cheek against the glass. The young man whirled around and wheeled down the hall at top speed, braking as his co-workers came back into the building.

That night, Homan was ambushed by a dream.

It began in a desolate place. The land was slanted like the ramp, with the tan sand and dry bushes of a desert, and the sky neither day nor night. In his hand was a bottle of wine. A man appeared in the distance, moving slowly, and Homan, having no use for wine, decided to offer his bottle as a gift. Then Homan realized this was the blind man from outside the building. Homan clapped his hands so the man would find him in this desert land. The man turned to face Homan and signed to him—and his signs did have meaning. *You ain't at the end. You still gots a long way to go.*

Suddenly Homan saw he was surrounded by people he'd known, all of them with differences. There was Shortie and Whirly Top and Man-Like-a-Tree. Sam. The McClintock boys. And there was Blue. Blue! Running toward Homan, his face holding his big-brother love. He came up close, his hands speaking with speed and excitement.

Tell me what you been doing, little brother. You out in the wide world. Tell me what you been seeing.

I miss you so much, Homan signed, feeling his face get wet.

I miss you, too. But I can't be there 'cept through you. You gotta do it for both of us. He made a gesture that took in the others. *For all of us.*

Do what?

Win.

What you mean by that?

You know what winning is.

I don't! Tell me!

Blue came so near, there was nothing to be seen except his face. *Not letting nothing break you. Not even yourself.*

Homan awoke with a start. He was in his little house, in his bed. But he was breathing hard, and his body was coated with sweat. It had felt so delicious to see his lost friends. Yet Blue's words had sent the feeling that had no name roaring through him. He lay there, rigid and wet, trying to argue it off. He had a roof over his head, food in his stomach, money in his chair. He had bosses who were nice and respectful, even after that disaster of a trip yesterday. He kept his own work schedule, grew all the Tingling his heart desired, and could leave this place anytime he wanted. So why did Blue's words set off the feeling that had no name?

Then he realized the two faces he hadn't seen.

He put his hands on his throat. *Fuh,* he said, remembering the feel of her hands that day in the cornfield. *Fuh uh*. He could feel the vibrations, so he knew he was making sounds. But he was twenty years into forgetting. It was like trying to pull back a disappeared dream.

He lowered his hands and understood at last the feeling that had no name. He'd failed to be what he'd been determined to be. He'd failed to be what she'd expected him to be. For years now he hadn't even tried to draw his own drawing. The name of the feeling was shame.

When dawn rose, he was in a foul mood. He got up quickly, skipped his Tingling, left off the TV. He shrugged on his clothes. He threw water on his face at the sink and did a quick shave—but not so quick that he didn't have time to see his face in the mirror.

His hair was salted with gray, and his skin had puckered around his eyes and lips. He was still lean, even at fifty-eight, which was a lot more years than Blue had lived on this earth. Though what *had* Homan won with all his extra life? Yeah, he had a roof. But he couldn't read, use money, understand anyone, or be understood. His face looked old to him, only it wasn't the age he saw. It was that so much time had passed and he was no closer to Beautiful Girl than he'd been after he was swept down the river.

He threw on his coat. Enough of starting things he didn't finish.

Then he went about his work with new vigor. It wasn't that he wanted to get the floors cleaned better. He was just so fed up with himself, he wanted to go at everything harder and faster. Working like this was almost as good as kicking trees.

He finished his indoor work way sooner than he ever did, then went to the outside chores without a break. He swept the walkways rougher than ever. He pulled weeds up fiercer. He snatched his gutter cleaner from the shed. It occurred to him he might be too hard on it and could snap off the hinged claw, but so what? He'd just have to climb the ladder and do the labor with his own hands. Maybe he'd fall off the roof. Maybe he *should* fall off the roof.

Standing on the patio outside the eating room, he lifted his invention gruffly. It was one long rod that pulled out like a ship captain's telescope, and he pulled it long enough to reach the gutter. He held it before him like a wand, unhinged the bottom, and threaded his fingers through the rings inside that worked the claw at the top.

He was so deep into his rage that he didn't register the Christmas lights blinking on and off in the eating room. Anyway, he was concentrating on his fingers, moving them up and down, getting the claw to collect the oak leaves, tilt away from the gutter, and drop them on the ground.

His invention, he now knew, worked. Though the realization gave him no pleasure, and anyway, it didn't work perfectly—it picked up only three leaves the first time. But it wasn't the contraption that needed adjusting. He had to get better with his hand.

He took a breath and got serious about learning his invention. *Move your fingers up and down only gentler. And at an angle. Now close the fingers. There. That feel like a big chunk of leaves. Maybe you can make this thing work after all. Maybe you ain't such a darn nobody. Look: You lifting a hay bale of leaves off the roof. You moving 'em like a construction crane over to the side. You opening that claw. See how many leaves showerin' down now?*

He lowered his gaze to the tumble of leaves.

Could it be?

No. He must be imagining that behind the rain of leaves was a dark-haired man sitting in his chair, smiling away. He must be so fed up with himself that he was nightmaring while awake.

The leaves finished falling.

The face kept smiling.

It seemed like forever till he could take off the leaf-grabbing rings. But it took no more time than the few moments that Sam needed to roll forward.

* * *

Homan never guessed there was even more to come. Sam being here, and not just here but with two candy bars—his favorite kind, the circular bar in the silver-and-blue wrapper. That seemed enough. Sure, learning why the man shut the door in Homan's face years ago would be nice. So would finding out what happened to Sam all this time and how he discovered that Homan was here. Yet it was just too heart-pounding to see Sam—and too indescribable to be unwrapping candy for both of them. Homan was just laughing, and Sam was laughing, too, and as Homan handed the un-wrapped bar back to his friend, setting it between his thumb and pointer finger, memory rushed in: nights under the stars, Homan teaching him to make a fire, Sam buying girlie magazines, the two of them watching the plastic bag float up and away and free.

How he find you? How he get here? It don't matter. He here.

Sam brought the candy up to his mouth and took a small bite. Homan bit off as much as he could and closed his eyes and chewed. The candy was as good as he remembered, and Sam was still the same Sam. Homan swallowed and opened his eyes.

Sam hadn't finished his candy. His gaze was on something over Homan's shoulder.

Homan looked behind him.

Indian Tuft was standing there. King and Queen were standing there. And with them was a girl in a yellow dress.

Homan whipped back to Sam. Sam was gazing at him pleasantly, but he was also saying something to the people over Homan's shoulder. Then Indian Tuft and the girl came around and stood beside Sam.

Homan glanced from one to the other, and the feeling of Incorrection tore through him like the harshest Tingling there could be, ripping into his lungs, frying his chest. He wanted to swallow it away. He wanted to run away. *But Sam here! Even if Sam friends with these characters—and he gotta be, how else he know you here?—he still Sam!*

Sam held up his candy. Then, amazingly, he lifted his hands and, as he had many times on their journey, told Homan, *Show me your sign.*

Sam knew his sign for candy, unless he forgot. Of course he forgot. They hadn't seen each other for so long. But what did Indian Tuft and Yellow Dress have to do with this? Why were King and Queen outside, too? What was he, a creature in a show?

Show me your sign.

Homan remembered the fun they'd had. Whatever Sam had wanted to do, Homan did—even though it ended with him crying in the gas station. But Sam hadn't wanted the man in that house to close the door. Sam would have asked Homan inside, gone with him to the van, *stayed with him*, if he could. Sam hadn't had any choice that terrible day.

Homan had a choice now.

Even though he couldn't make heads or tails of what was happening, and he was dizzy and sweating and burning and felt awfully, horribly alone, he could choose to doubt—or he could choose to trust.

He pressed his fingers together like a bird's beak, touched them to his lips, made a chewing motion, and smacked his lips.

Then Sam did the strangest thing. He looked toward Indian Tuft and asked, *Show me your sign.*

Indian Tuft angled toward Sam. He placed his pointer finger to one side of his lips and twisted it, smiling slightly.

Homan stopped breathing. He looked back at Sam.

Sam, looking up at Indian Tuft, pointed to his candy bar with a questioning expression.

Indian Tuft nodded.

Then Indian Tuft turned so he was fully facing Homan. He reached over, took Sam's candy bar, and bit into it, smiling. As he chewed, he raised his hand as Homan had, touched a beaklike shape to his lips, made a motion like he was chewing, and licked his lips.

Homan looked down at what remained of the chocolate, and something jolted inside him.

Indian Tuft was saying the same word, but with a different sign!

The feeling of Incorrection vanished. Of course! If hearing people spoke English and Chinese, then deaf people must sign in different languages, too! Indian Tuft hadn't been making fun of him. His hands just spoke other words!

Homan placed his index finger on his cheek and twisted it, the way Indian Tuft had.

Then Homan whirled around and pointed to a tree and signed, *Tree*.

Indian Tuft's arm became a tree, his forearm the trunk, his fingers the branches, his other arm the ground. He twisted his raised wrist and wiggled the fingers near his head, like leaves in the wind.

Homan looked out to the lawn beside the patio and made his sign for *grass*.

Indian Tuft raised his hand palm up, set it under his chin with his fingers open and pointing out. Then his hand circled slightly, up and around, before it returned to just beneath his chin. Like grass touching his face in a breeze.

Homan couldn't stop himself. *Sky*. *House*. *Mountain*—and Indian Tuft replied with his signs.

The sun moved through the sky that afternoon and Homan just kept going. Finally he understood: He wasn't alone. He wasn't a nobody.

He was someone who could make a King and Queen glow. He was a person who could make his best friend cry for joy. He was a man who could make Indian Tuft flutter his hands in the air, for an applause the whole world could see.

Confession

KATE

1993

*E*xcuse me, Kate?"

Kate had just flipped a dime, and her left hand was on top of her right wrist, covering the results. She looked beyond her arm, past the checkerboard she'd just set before Mr. Todd and Mr. Eskridge—who always insisted on a coin toss to determine black from red—up into the bright solarium. There she met the eyes of Tawana, one of the younger assistants who worked at Westbrook Home for Seniors.

"Yes?"

"I'm sorry to interrupt, but there's someone here to see you."

Mr. Todd and Mr. Eskridge looked up at Tawana.

"Man or woman?" Mr. Todd said. He wore sports jackets and had a Texas twang.

"Man," Tawana said. "Actually—"

"Must be Scott." Mr. Eskridge still wore lab coats, though he'd retired years ago.

"Scott never drops in," Mr. Todd said. "Maybe it's your son on a surprise visit."

"It's neither," Tawana said. "This man's wearing a nice suit. He said his name was Ken, and he knew you from way back. At least that's what Geraldine told me." Geraldine sat at the front desk. So did Irwin, the security guard, whose responsibility generally amounted to greeting visiting grandchildren. "Geraldine asked me to come tell you."

"*Ken?* I can't think of anyone named Ken. What's he look like?"

"Kind of beanpole-ish. Older."

"Didn't Geraldine tell him I was working?"

"He said he'd wait."

Kate looked back at the checkerboard. She had yet to place the men on the squares; her hand was still covering the coin.

In the ten years since Kate had worked here, no one had ever stopped by to see her. For a while she might have chalked that up to her unfamiliarity with anyone but Scott's colleagues at Indianapolis Tech, though now that they'd settled into their lives, it was because her friends knew better than to drop in. Kate worked with patients who had dementia. At any moment she might be comforting Mr. Flint, whose son had just "corrected" him that, no, Mrs. Flint wasn't out shopping; she'd been dead twenty-two years. Or she'd be helping Miss Sunder get dressed in nylons and a fine dress because Miss Sunder still liked being pretty.

That isn't to say that visitors *couldn't* come by—this place wasn't under lock and key, like the School. And unlike the School, here there was a general level of respect given to the residents. At first Kate made these kinds of comparisons all the time, though eventually she stopped. The School didn't exist anymore, and she hadn't even been to Pennsylvania in nine years. If she didn't exchange holiday cards with Lynnie, she'd never think of the School at all.

"You go ahead," Mr. Todd said, nudging her with his hand.

"Show us the dime first," Mr. Eskridge said.

She looked back at her hands and lifted the left one up. "Heads."

"That's me," Mr. Eskridge said, "and I'm picking black."

"Like it'll make any difference," Mr. Todd said.

Kate rose, saying, "I shouldn't be long."

"Take all the time you need," Mr. Eskridge said, setting his men on their squares. "Everything's under control." He smiled. "The perks of prerogative."

Tawana said, "He's in the front lobby."

Kate hurried off, and as she left the solarium, she

heard Mr. Todd say, "I might not have won the toss, but that doesn't mean I'm losing the game."

Kate didn't see the visitor when she first entered the lobby. Only after she moved past the seating area did she spot a tall man near the front door, his back to Geraldine's desk. He appeared to be looking at the three-tier fountain outside. The sky was blue and the light bright, so Kate could see little besides a skinny silhouette with a bald head, arms before him, hands clasped.

Kate glanced to Geraldine and Irwin. Geraldine shrugged.

Kate continued to the front door, came up beside him, and entered his line of vision.

A bearded face looked down. She had just enough time to sense a familiarity behind his glasses before the formality fell from his expression.

"Kate?" he asked. His voice was gruff and quiet.

She studied his lips, his cheeks, searching for a clue that would explain who he was. She looked at his hands, now at his sides. The fingers were slender, and there was a wedding ring. His suit was inexpensive but well kept, his shoes simple and freshly polished.

"It's Kate Catanese now, right?" he asked.

"Who are you?"

He bit his upper lip. Then he said, "You used to know me as Clarence."

She felt anger crawl up her throat, and she focused again. If she removed some of his beard, returned his glasses, and scrubbed away the years, she could see the goateed attendant who'd brought Lynnie back that night. "Why are you here?" she asked.

"I know it must seem very strange, having me show up halfway across the country—"

"The School's closed, Clarence. I don't know what you want from me, but I have nothing to do with that place anymore."

She noticed Geraldine and Irwin watching and realized she was raising her voice.

"I don't want anything from you."

"Then why are you here? You were never my friend. We had no relationship. I don't want one now, either."

"I know this seems—"

"Bizarre. And suspicious."

"And probably many other things. But I do have a reason to be here."

"Where's your sidekick?"

"Smokes? The last address I have for him is near Harrisburg."

"He knows you're here?"

"I live in Baltimore. I have a whole new life now. We haven't spoken for years."

"You and I haven't either. Yet you just show up out of the blue—"

"I knew if I contacted you in advance, you'd refuse to meet me."

"So you chose to ambush me at work?"

He glanced to the desk. Irwin was now standing. "Can we speak more privately?"

"Why would I do that?"

He looked at his shoes and said, "Because you know the importance of confession."

She stared at him. Then she looked over to the front desk. "We'll be right outside."

"Okay," Kate said, sitting on the ledge around the fountain. "Cut to the chase."

He lowered himself beside her. She easily saw his identity now, but if she had passed him on the street, she wouldn't have looked twice. For a second Kate remembered learning that some of the elders she worked with had pasts that seemed unworthy of them—a man who'd kept a mistress, a woman who'd pushed her daughter to marry a prosperous but patronizing man. Mr. Eskridge had once taken revenge on a brilliant young colleague by being the decisive vote denying him tenure. Kate had forgiven their trespasses; their current hardships eclipsed her view of their histories, and besides, who was she to throw stones? She'd wished ill upon her ex-husband for years.

And Clarence had driven hundreds of miles to

say what he came to say. She didn't have to embrace him, but she should hear him out.

He stared into the fountain. Even though it was a warm October day, Kate couldn't feel the sun.

"I've been trying to figure out where to begin," he said, rubbing his palms against his pants, leaving trails of wetness on the fabric. Then he turned to her. "Let me start by saying I'll understand if you leave while I tell you this. You have every right to. I did things back then that I can't believe anymore."

He took a deep breath, and the words came raggedly yet quickly. He'd started life as a punk. He'd hated school, finally quitting in ninth grade to hang out with friends. He'd picked up cash here and there by putting up aluminum siding or cutting lawns, but forget a career; his only priority had been drinking with his friends at night. Time went on, and one by one the other guys got girls pregnant and had to get jobs, or they joined the military. Finally it was down to him and Smokes. He'd never paid much attention to Smokes. The guy lived out at the School, so he wasn't a regular. He also didn't talk much and had a sour way about him. Still, he worked hard at washing down his mood with whiskey, and that was all right with Clarence. Then, when Clarence reached nineteen, his parents said they'd had it with him. What was he going to do, with no talent or interests, just a need to put a roof over his head while still having a good time? It came down to becoming a factory worker or a long-haul driver, and he almost went to the interview in the truck yard. Then, the night before, Smokes, sitting at the bar out near the School, told him to come work there. Clarence could get room and board, the pay beat other jobs, they'd have a good time. Clarence wasn't keen on working around, as Smokes put it, "a bunch of eeg-its," though Smokes said it was a cakewalk, as long as you let them know who was boss, which was easy: They couldn't think or feel, Smokes said, and were obedient, and you could get a few laughs out of them. Plus, with his brother being the director, "no one's ever gonna say boo."

It was great for a long time. Clarence and Smokes had no one looking over their shoulders. They could come and go as they pleased, say and do what they wanted, make up new rules every day if they were so inclined. They could drink to their hearts' content, and they did. Clarence didn't actually like drinking all that much or chewing tobacco, but he liked being with Smokes, who polished off whatever Clarence didn't finish. Smokes also had a swagger Clarence envied and a way of glaring at staff that unnerved them. Sometimes he did it because they'd crossed him, sometimes just because he could.

"Doing things so others would fear you," Clarence said to Kate, still looking at his shoes, "it felt good. I can't believe I'm saying this, but it's true."

"You never did anything to me," Kate said.

"You steered clear of us."

She wanted to tell him she'd worked hard at avoiding them and that many times, after she'd seen them demean a staff person or suspected them of walloping a resident, she'd wanted to confront them. Yet she'd held her tongue, and she often went home in despair over how little she could do if she wanted to keep her job. "Your friend's dogs frightened me," she said.

"And not just you." He took another breath. "Smokes didn't spare me, either. He used to call me a...he'd say I acted like a girl. He'd call me names and then get his dogs to lunge at me, holding their chains just at the point where they'd get choked back inches before they sank in their teeth. If I flinched, he'd say he'd had his proof and was going to tell the world. It wasn't like I had some girlfriend and could point to her and say, 'See? You're wrong.' So I learned to stand there with the teeth coming at me."

A dread had taken root inside Kate. He wasn't going to say—

"I still don't understand why you're telling this to me."

"Because..." He rubbed his eyes, then looked back. "Because you cared about her."

"Who?"

"The one we called No-No."

"Lynnie."

"I'd forgotten her name."

"You came here to find out her name?" Kate stood up. "Then I am walking out of here, because you're right. I cared about her, and I still do." She spun around and stepped away.

"Wait."

She stopped but didn't turn.

"I haven't come to find her. I don't want to make her life any worse than I already did."

Kate stayed right where she was. She could see Irwin watching her through the glass.

"That's why I'm here," Clarence went on hastily. "She couldn't talk, so you never knew. I've been carrying it around all this time, and I need to say it."

Kate hesitated. Lynnie had never said what happened, even when she'd regained the ability to speak. She'd given Kate the impression that it was the result of a rampage during a night of chaos. A night no one had ever understood.

Kate turned back but remained standing.

One day, he said, Uncle Luke called him and Smokes into his office and told them he expected to run for governor in a few years, or maybe senator. He said it in a way that only drove home how different he and Smokes were—the one brother who'd gone to medical school, the other who'd made nothing of his life. Smokes could tag along if his plans worked out, Uncle Luke said; they could probably find room for him. "It will pain me, of course," Uncle Luke told him, smoking his cigarette. "Though you'd be in the gutter if it weren't for me."

Smokes was incensed by the time they left the office. They went back to the staff cottages and drank for hours, coming up with one thing after another that would ruin Luke's plans. By the time they were ready for the night shift, Smokes was completely in a lather.

The first thing they did was round up the most aggressive boys in their cottage by banging on their iron beds, hauling them out, shouting they were playing a game. They armed the boys with clubs and sticks and told them to see how much they could break, and if they didn't do their part, well, who knew how the dogs would react. The boys went at it, smashing their own windows, beating on one another. Smokes threw open their cottage door and egged them on, and they went streaming outside, shouting, clubbing every tree and lamppost they passed, until Smokes suddenly decided, when they reached A-3, to let them in. The staff watched as Smokes and Clarence and the dogs and a gang of boys poured inside. They'd had their cars keyed before, they weren't going to interfere. But the noise must have alerted the residents, because as the mob entered the dayroom, many of the residents tried to hide under beds or in the bathroom. The boys mostly got caught up in the dayroom, throwing furniture around, having a grand time, and in the pandemonium Smokes saw Lynnie run into a storage closet. He knew Clarence had a gripe with her—she was a biter, she'd left a scar on Clarence's hand, and she was by far the best-looking resident. So when Smokes smirked and said, "Hold the dogs," and reached for the closet door, Clarence didn't object. He'd looked the other way when Smokes had "copped a feel" with other female residents or told some of the low grade boys to do lewd things to the others. After all, Clarence had to prove his manliness—and what were any of them to him? So he just watched when Smokes hauled the door open and Clarence caught a glimpse of her, backing into the darkened room. Then the door closed. And although he heard her cry out, it was only, "No no no no!" until her voice was muffled. *That'll teach her not to bite*, Clarence thought over the din of the barking, the girls screaming, the boys cracking chairs. The mayhem was so complete, a rat sprinted out of the bathroom. That was when Smokes emerged from the closet, zipping his pants.

He took a look at the animal, seized it, and threw it at the dogs, who tore it to pieces. Then he turned back to the closet and said, "And that'll be you if you tell."

Kate stood above Clarence, her fist in front of her mouth. She lowered her hand. "How could you live with yourself after that?"

He shook his head. "There's nothing I can say that would make any sense."

"Try me."

"I told myself she deserved it."

Kate felt herself become nauseated. "You're really disgusting."

"Yes." He nodded. "I could blame my drinking, or how common it was for the residents to get taken advantage of. I could blame my need to be liked by my . . . friend—"

"*Friend.*"

"I don't want to make excuses. It's indefensible."

"Why didn't you come forward right then?"

"How could I? Everything I knew was right there. To say anything would mean losing my whole life."

"And it didn't bother you to know that had happened?"

"I'd like to say it did. The person I am now would be tormented immediately and wouldn't care about a job, a friend, anything. Wouldn't have even been part of it."

"So you just let it go?"

"For a long time."

"No pangs of conscience at all?"

"Sadly, no."

"Not even when she ran off with Number Forty-two?"

He sighed and shook his head.

"How could you not?" Kate said, almost screaming.

"It was a breakout. They didn't happen much, but...no, it didn't get me thinking."

"It didn't."

"Please, Kate."

"Why do you think she broke out?"

"She'd found someone who could get her over the wall. I mean, I guess I realized she must have been scared—"

"You thought she left because she was *scared?*"

"Well...yeah."

"You didn't consider any other reason?"

He stared at her. "What are you suggesting?"

"Why were those pages missing in her file?"

"You went to her file?"

"Of course I did. You might have broken the rules for fun and games, but some of us had better reasons. And the pages from that whole episode—her breakout and her return—were gone. Did you take them?"

He lifted his head and nodded.

"Why?"

"Because if there was any record that we lost a resident—"

"*Lost?* You found Lynnie. You brought her back."

"Right. But we lost Forty-two that night."

"Why didn't you take *his* file?"

"I did."

She hadn't known that. She'd never thought to look for his file. Only Lynnie's.

"You *took his file?*"

"That's correct."

"I can't believe it. So there's no record he even existed?"

"Look, if it had come out that we'd let a resident escape and never found him, there was no way Luke would have kept his current job. We didn't want him to get more of a swelled head than he already had, and our night of chaos did make him hold off on his political ambitions. But by the time Forty-two disappeared, we'd realized that if Luke went down as the head of the School, things would be ruined for us, too."

"And what did you do with Forty-two's file?"

"I held on to it while I tried to find him."

"Find *him?*"

"Is that so strange?"

"What did you do to find him?"

"From Lynnie's file I got the old lady's name. I wanted her to tell me where he was, but by the time I went out to her farm, she'd disappeared. Then I thought he might have holed up in her barn or woods or something, only I couldn't find him. I realized the place was being overseen by some kid from town, so I tried to get something out of him. The Hansberry boy, lived in the pharmacy with his parents. Got nothing."

"So what did you do?"

"Well's Bottom was a small place back then. Once Luke found out the old lady was selling her place, and the Hansberry boy was looking after it, he asked the postmaster to let him know if any letters sent to the Hansberrys were from her."

"You *spied* on the *mail?*"

"Not me. It was bigger than me then. Luke was doing it. He even sent that driver of his, Edgar, to go to any return addresses."

"All this to find Forty-two?"

"It just seemed odd, the old lady disappearing the morning after Forty-two slipped away from us. We thought he might have abducted her."

"You know he wouldn't have done that."

"Or she was protecting him. Either way, they were linked somehow, so finding her meant finding him."

"And"—she worked hard to make her voice sound sincere—"did you?"

"The one time Edgar got close, at some hotel in New York, she got away."

"And then?"

"And then there weren't any more return addresses from her. We gave up."

"What do you think happened?"

"To Forty-two?"

She nodded.

"I think about it a lot. Probably froze to death in the woods that winter."

"That's what you think?"

"I've had lots of thoughts since I got sober and can look at things with a clear eye. I don't know what happened to him. Whatever it was, it wasn't good."

"He didn't deserve what happened to him. He was a wonderful man." She shook her head, thinking of how she'd arrange the secret meetings with Lynnie in her office. "He liked Lynnie. He gave her bouquets of feathers."

Clarence had no response. Kate said, "Is that it?"

"It's why I came here, yes. I wanted to apologize to someone about it."

"Why not just go to Lynnie?"

"I...I went to the School the day it closed. I thought of saying something, but I wasn't sober yet. I wasn't ready."

"Why not go now?"

He fumbled, then said, "It's been so long. I don't want to confuse her."

"Why not go to the police?"

"The police?"

"It's a crime, Clarence. You helped someone commit a crime."

"It was twenty-five years ago."

"So you won't go to the police?"

He looked stricken. "I'm in a new life now. I work for a school system. I help kids who've got family problems, substance problems, and try to keep them in school. I've got a wife and a kid. Something like this—it could ruin me."

"You could have kept it to yourself."

"I have, for a long time. I just—Kate, you don't know what it's like, living with the knowledge that you let something like that happen."

"That's true."

"Maybe I shouldn't have told you."

"No, I'm glad to get the full story."

His face relaxed a bit.

"So is that it?" she asked, feeling her brow grow even more tense.

He nodded and then said, "I do have one more question."

"So do I."

"You do?"

"Clarence," she said, and she looked at him with a level gaze, "I want you to be perfectly straight with me. Don't you think there was a reason Lynnie ran off just when she did?"

He looked at her with shock. "What are you saying?"

"Count it. Count backwards. She ran off in November."

His eyes flickered. "No."

"Clarence"—and she was filled with rage toward him, and guilt over all she had not done, and sorrow for everyone else—"do the math."

"You can't be telling me—"

"It's true."

"Twenty-five years!"

"That's right."

"Where is it? He—she? Where?"

"She."

"Oh, my God. Where is she? With Forty-two?"

"Forty-two is dead. He drowned that night."

"Dear Lord."

"My friends gave him a service, but his body was never found."

"Then where is she?"

"I don't know."

"You don't know?"

"I did for a long time. She was with the old lady. Martha. And Martha made sure Eva Hansberry always knew where they were. And for the longest time they were on the run—from you. She stopped putting return addresses on the envelopes, but kept the letters coming until the girl was fourteen."

"Are you kidding me?"

"No, Clarence."

"You don't know anything more about the child after that?"

"The last I knew, there was a chance she'd be moving to somewhere near Denver. Wherever she ended up, she was given a good life. A better life than her mother's."

He was bent over now, as if in pain. His head was in his hands.

Kate felt her whole body shaking and turned again toward the door. Geraldine and Irwin were now standing outside, watching. She'd been here so long, she'd forgotten she was at work. Mr. Todd and Mr. Eskridge had probably played several matches by now. It was well past time for Mrs. Ilana's stroll through the garden. Kate was twenty-five years late.

"Clarence," she said, turning back to look down at the top of his bald head, his fingers splayed over his scalp, "you had another question?"

He dropped his hands to his lap. Then he lifted his head. "I don't need to ask it."

"I doubt I'll ever see you again, so you should just ask me now."

He looked away. She watched his gaze travel back in time, where he no doubt found a person who had once looked like him. Then he blanched and said, "I was going to ask if you hate me."

Kate looked down at him. "I'm not the person you should be worried about." She turned and walked away.

* * *

Heading back inside the building, Kate stormed
past Geraldine and Irwin, holding up her hand
so they wouldn't ask anything. She continued
through the doors and down the hall toward the
solarium, her body stiff with fury. Poor Lynnie! All
this time she'd been living with such a horrific
experience! That was why she'd needed to hide
the baby. That was why Forty-two had broken her
out—and died!

Kate reached the sunny room only to find it
empty. She looked at her watch. She'd lost track
of time; the Westbrook residents had gone back to
their dining areas for lunch, and she needed to return to her duties. But possessed by a rage so great
she could not move, she peered into the midday
light streaming through the windows and asked
herself: *What should I do now?* And in response she
felt that familiar push inside: the force she told
others was her intuition, but she knew was the will
of God. It did not, though, tell her what to do. It
told her she needed to confess.

She stumbled back, appalled. She put her hand
to her heart, wishing it were not true. Then she
lifted her head with a deep cry she'd held in for so
many years. She had been part of a world where
slapping and spitting and name-calling and re-
straining and "copping a feel" went on day after
day, season after season, resident after resident.

Although Kate had never engaged in a single act of cruelty, and although she'd devoted herself to protecting and supporting all the people she served, she'd done nothing to stop what was happening. How many residents besides Lynnie had been assaulted in unspeakable ways? How many people besides Kate had stifled their conscience? How many mouths had stayed shut—for so long— while the least of these suffered immeasurably?

She fell to her knees and prayed for forgiveness.

She didn't need to talk it over with Scott. She didn't even need to go home.

The moment Kate's shift ended, she drove to the nearest pay phone. As she got out of her car in the parking lot of the 7-Eleven and hurried over, she thought about how she'd begun working at the School as an act of penance. Now she would be doing another.

The phone rang five times before it was picked up.

"'Lo?" a woman's voice said on the other end.

A television was playing loudly in the background.

"I'm trying to reach Lynnie," Kate said. "Please tell her Kate is calling."

The person walked away. It wasn't Doreen anymore. Lynnie had moved twice into other group homes, and the roommates kept changing.

"Kate!" Lynnie said when she grabbed the phone.

"Lynnie," Kate said, so relieved to hear the happiness in her voice. "I haven't seen you in such a long time."

"Nine years," Lynnie said.

"That's right. And guess what? I have something I need to do soon in Pennsylvania. Maybe even next week. Is it all right with you if I come visit?"

Speaking for Herself

LYNNIE

1993

"Look up, Kate," Lynnie said.

They were standing inside the Capitol building
in Harrisburg, in the enormous domed room
whose name Lynnie still had trouble pronouncing:
"rotunda."

Lynnie had first seen the rotunda five Octobers
ago, when she attended a conference here in the
State Capitol and learned about becoming a self-
advocate. Since then, as she'd returned every year
to the conference, she'd become familiar with this
grand lobby and its marble floor, painted murals,
sweeping staircase, stained glass, and jaw-
droppingly high ceiling. Today she would finally get
her chance to go deep inside the building to speak
to legislators—another word Lynnie found difficult
to say—when they held a hearing at three o'clock.

Now, though, it was only nine thirty. Lynnie had

brought Kate here early, leaving behind the conference at the hotel, because she and Kate were doing something else before the hearing.

"Isn't it beautiful?" Lynnie said to Kate as they stood in the entrance to the lobby, tilting their heads back to look up.

"Yes. I can see why you wanted to come here first."

"Beautiful" was once the biggest word Lynnie had ever said. Her speech therapist, Andrea, had told her, *After you master that, the sky's the limit.* She wasn't quite right—Lynnie did not cross a language threshold with "beautiful." She was still far from knowing all the words that could express her observations and insights, even in her own mind, and when she was able to say the ones that fit her modest vocabulary, her mouth still struggled. But Andrea was right that once Lynnie achieved "beautiful," she'd develop a new confidence. Since then, she'd improved her enunciation and pace, grown bolder about the length and quantity of her sentences, and become more in control of her volume. She'd even learned some "add-ons," as Andrea called them, like standing an "appropriate" distance from people when you're in a conversation. So, incredibly, Lynnie had been able to get a job that required speaking, as a receptionist for BridgeWays, the agency that ran the group home where she lived.

Kate said, "This place is amazing, Lynnie."

"It sounds beautiful, too."

"What do you mean?"

"Close your eyes." Kate gave her a curious look, and Lynnie just squeezed her hand.

She loved this aspect of the rotunda, too: When she closed her eyes, the clack of shoes, the whiffle of clothes, the clink of jewelry, and the buzz of voices expanded as wide as the room, making her aware of a world so much larger than herself.

"It echoes," Kate said.

"And if you stand in the right spot, it's even better." Lynnie opened her eyes and added, "Keep your eyes closed and I'll show you."

Then she guided Kate to the spot she'd discovered by accident, when Doreen had been talking to her their first time there, right under the highest point of the dome overhead, in the center of the rotunda. "Say something," Lynnie whispered to Kate.

Kate made a face, as if lining up all her words and trying to pick one out.

Lynnie added, "And say it loud."

Kate nodded. "I'm so proud of you, Lynnie."

Lynnie smiled and almost wished Kate were looking at her. Instead she said, "Louder."

"I'm so proud of you."

"Louder!" Lynnie was giggling, her volume more than Andrea would call "appropriate."

"Lynnie makes me proud!" Kate shouted.

That's what it took. Kate's voice became resonant, as voices did under the dome, turning so strong, it seemed to sweep beneath Kate's and Lynnie's feet and lift them into the air.

Kate laughed and squeezed their hands together. People looked, but why should Lynnie mind? She was with one of her favorite people, in one of her favorite places, teaching something she'd figured out all on her own. What could be better than that?

Actually, a few things could be better than that.

Right now, for instance, Lynnie could be with Kate at the conference instead of sitting in Kate's car as they drove into the countryside. Kate had never been to a conference of self-advocates, and she'd been flushed and giddy at the banquet last night. She kept waving to people across the ballroom, recognizing residents and staff from the School. She'd even gotten to catch up with Doreen just before the deejay started to spin records, when Doreen told her the story that happened a few years ago. One day, Doreen said, the mailman came to the group home with a letter that required Doreen's signature. When Doreen tore open the envelope, they learned that her father had died and left her a lot of money. "Whoo-hoo!" Doreen had squealed, jumping around. "Disney World, here I come!" There was one glitch: It turned out Doreen wasn't allowed to keep her government assistance after her windfall, so BridgeWays couldn't help her anymore. Yet it had all worked out, as Doreen, shouting over "Everybody Dance Now," told Kate. "I got my own place and I hire my own aides. Now I don't have to put up with any dumb rules or people too big for their britches." Kate said, "That's really great," and then Doreen, wearing a silver lamé dress, pulled Kate and Lynnie onto the dance floor. By the time they went to their rooms, laughing and sweaty, Lynnie almost wished she and Kate wouldn't be busy during the conference the next day.

But when Kate called last week and said she wanted to visit Pennsylvania as soon as possible, she told Lynnie about Clarence's confession. "It was a long time ago," Kate said, "but Smokes should be brought to justice." It had been a long time too since the growl of a dog had returned Lynnie to that night, and Kate explained that justice would require her to get on a stand and go through it again. Lynnie told Kate she couldn't bear the thought of doing that, and although Kate grew annoyed at first, she finally said that at the very least, she wanted to track down Smokes's address outside Harrisburg and tell him to his face that she knew what he'd done. "I want to do that, too," Lynnie said. She could even meet Kate right in Harrisburg, because she was going there anyway for the conference. That was why Kate waited until last night to fly here and why they were now driving through the Pennsylvania countryside.

That's one thing that would have been better about today.

There was a second thing that would have been better, too, though Lynnie kept pushing it out of her mind. That wasn't as hard as she'd imagined, because Kate had asked her to bring a tape of songs she liked, and they were playing it now on the tape recorder Lynnie bought for herself with her own money: Gloria Estefan, Jon Bon Jovi, Phil Collins, the Bangles. Kate had a tape of music she liked, too, and said they could listen to it on the way back, if Lynnie wanted.

"Can I decide then? I might be upset."

"Sure. But remember, you can still change your mind. I can turn around right now."

"I want to do it."

"Why?"

"'Cause what he did was bad, and I want to tell him that."

They drove for a whole other song before either of them spoke. Then Kate turned to Lynnie. "Buddy would have been proud of you."

Lynnie smiled. When a jelly-bellied guy named Dave, from the BridgeWays workshop, had asked her over one evening, she'd gotten bored by how he just wanted to watch football. Then there was

Miguel, who wore tie-dyed shirts and was with the Special Olympics bowling crowd she saw every Tuesday night. He took her out for ice cream three times and spent every one of them blabbing about himself. After those lousy dates, Lynnie told Doreen that no one was like Buddy. "You're holding out for someone who let you down," Doreen responded. "Buddy hasn't let me down," Lynnie said, feeling hurt. "What else would you call it after twenty-five years?" Doreen said. "Give it up. I mean, I'd be pissed as a hornet if I was you."

Last night, in her hotel room, Kate asked Lynnie if she wanted to find out what happened to the baby, and Lynnie nodded hard. Kate said she was so glad to hear this and picked up the phone to call someone named Eva. But Kate never mentioned Buddy.

And that's the other thing that could be better today. If Lynnie found out the baby was doing well—and that Doreen was as wrong as a person could be.

"This can't be the right address," Kate said, pulling up to a curb.

They were in front of a squat, run-down row house on a narrow dead end. Other streets were terraced above this one, with houses that looked less sorry. Here, a brook, littered with plastic bags, soda bottles, and shopping carts and surrounded by exposed tree roots, snaked along the side of their car. The houses on the block weren't much better. They sat behind chain-link fences or overgrown bushes. Some were even boarded up, and mold covered several walls.

Kate looked at the scrap paper in her hand, then up to the house. "The number matches," she said. "But his family was so well-off. I can't believe they'd allow him to live here."

"Maybe it's wrong."

"Clarence said it was the last address he had."

"We could go see."

"Do you feel ready?"

Lynnie looked at the house. Was she? Did she even need to do this? What if just seeing him silenced her all over again?

She had to do it. She had to say, *You did a terrible thing to me*. Kate said that Clarence had found his conscience. "Some people," she'd said with an extra blink to her eyes, "do eventually see their errors." Lynnie had to do what she could so Smokes would finally see his.

Yet just being here made her remember the stink of his breath. Who was she to think she could jolt his conscience, especially when she was tongue-tied so often? Sometimes in the bowling alley, kids walking by her team snickered, and though Lynnie fumed in her seat, it was Doreen who called out, "Hey, jackasses, you want this bowling ball bonking your head?" Once, when an aide named Carmen was training Lynnie and other BridgeWays consumers to buy groceries, a lady came up and said, "What are *they* doing here?" and all Lynnie could think to say was, "We're shopping." And one of the biggest reasons self-advocates spoke to legislators was that whenever a new group home was set to open, some neighbors would put up a fight, and Lynnie was always too shy to go to those meetings. It was as if lots of people wanted places like the School to open up again so people like Lynnie would just go away. So what made her think she could say anything that would shake up somebody's conscience?

Yet what made her think she couldn't?

Lynnie opened the car door and stepped out.

The street had the stench of raw sewage, reminding her of the School. Kate came up beside her. "It must be awfully unpleasant to live here."

Together they marched up the short walkway, which was washed over with mud. Puddles also dotted the yard, coated with an iridescence that looked like oil. The porch was warped, and when they mounted it, Lynnie saw a big hole. Under the eaves was a bird's nest.

Lynnie rang the bell.

"Do you want me to hold your hand?" Kate whispered.

Lynnie shook her head no.

She heard slow, shuffling footsteps. They came up to the door, but the door did not open.

"Who's that?" It was an old man, and his voice had no patience.

"I want to see Smokes," Lynnie said.

"*Who?*"

"Glen Collins," Kate said.

"He's not here."

"We were told he lived at this address," Kate said.

"He lives in every bar in the county."

Kate looked at Lynnie.

Lynnie asked, "All the time?"

"He comes back when it damn well pleases him."

"Should we wait?" Kate asked.

Laughter. "Why would you wait for him?"

Lynnie said, "He owes us something."

Kate looked at her, impressed.

"Fat chance you'll ever see it."

"When will he be back?" Kate asked.

"Anytime between now and tomorrow. You want to wait, be my guest."

"Can we wait in there?" Kate asked. "It's cold out here."

"It's bad enough I got to deal with him. You leave me in peace."

They heard a shuffle away from the door, followed by the sound of the television.

"Let's wait in the car," Kate said. "We've got a few hours before we have to head back."

They sat in the front with the heat running. Kate offered to play her tape, but Lynnie didn't want to hear music right now. "Let's just talk," she said.

"Okay," Kate replied, smiling. "Tell me how you spend your days."

Lynnie told her, not worrying, for a change, about her pacing or pronunciation. She talked about a friendly bus driver, Dale, who drove the route that took her from the group home outside Sunbury into town, where BridgeWays was located in a red brick building two blocks off the main street. She talked about the people who ran the office, Sarah and Dustin, and that they lived in houses with their families. She talked about the calls that came into the office and the visitors she directed to a conference room. She talked about bowling on Tuesday nights, and how, on Saturdays, she'd take Vince's bus to Doreen's apartment to watch videos.

"What about when you're at home? Do you like that?"

"So-so. I stay in my room and do my drawings. Sometimes my roommates aren't so nice. And the aides change all the time. You get used to someone and they leave."

Kate sighed. "So you're not at the School anymore, but there's room for improvement."

"It's better."

"Agreed."

"And you send cards."

"I'll be more regular about it now."

"That'll be nice."

"And you know, some people live on their own. Does BridgeWays have an independent living program?"

"I don't want to live alone. Doreen's lonely."

"She is? She didn't say that."

"She doesn't want you to know. She spends all day going to stores so she can hang out with the people working there till they need to get things done. Then she goes buying. She's got so many videos and posters and sparkly jewelry and knickknacks, they take up her whole place. Then she sits around at night, eating and looking at what she got and calling me."

"It's good you go bowling together, and visit her on Saturdays."

"It's not enough. She's alone too much. I don't want that."

"What do you want?"

Lynnie looked down. "I want to be with Buddy and my daughter."

Kate nodded.

"We're going to find out what happened to her, right?"

"Yes. That woman I called, Eva, is coming to meet us in Harrisburg tonight. But I know a little already."

Lynnie's heart reared up. "What do you know?"

Kate made a sad smile. "The old lady did what you asked. She hid her."

Lynnie's heart spread across her chest.

"She wanted to do well by you, Lynnie. She took the baby the very next day and they...moved around, from one place to another, so they wouldn't be found."

"The old lady did that?"

"For years. She felt it was the right thing to do."

Lynnie played with her fingers in her lap. "Some people know right from wrong."

"I don't think it's always that simple, Lynnie. But for her it was."

"What's the baby's name?"

"Julia."

"Julia." Lynnie looked down at the feather necklace. "That's a beautiful name."

"For a long time they settled in Massachusetts. Julia was in school—a regular school. They were living a regular life."

Lynnie gazed out the windshield. The sky was gray and the houses broken. There was so much that was ugly in this world. Yet look. A blue jay was flying toward the house. It dove under the porch roof and tucked itself into the nest.

"That was a really decent thing the old lady did."

"I still can't believe it, Lynnie."

"What about Buddy?"

Kate looked up at the car ceiling, and her eyes went back and forth as she bit her lip. Then she took Lynnie's hands as if she were going to say something. Finally she pushed her lips together and shook her head.

Lynnie said, "Doreen says to forget him. But he's still trying to get back to me."

"Is that what you think?"

"I know it. He'll be back"—and this word she had to work at—"eventually."

Kate nodded and fiddled with the clasp of her purse. "Then I know he will, too."

"Hey," Lynnie said, her eye catching a motion in the side mirror. "Someone's coming."

A man had rounded the corner at the far end of the block. Lynnie turned and looked out the rear window. He was in a brown hoodie and baggy navy sweatpants and was stumbling so much, he kept steadying himself by grabbing on to the misshapen trees and chain-link fences separating the houses from the road. Lynnie recognized him not by sight, but by the hurried feeling she got inside, as though she had to breathe fast to get enough air, and she imagined in her chest a hundred jaws opening and closing, the teeth biting down while voices yelled. She felt the way she used to feel when someone around her was crying, only worse. She knew she couldn't throw herself down and kick and scream. Instead, her breathing got harder until it stopped coming at all. She felt as if she were choking on a cloth.

She put her hands to her neck.

"This was a bad idea," Kate said, throwing the car into gear.

Lynnie pulled at the collar of her coat.

"Are you okay?" Kate was saying as she quickly turned the car around.

Lynnie pushed her chest with her hand, trying to get the trapped air out.

"This was stupid," Kate said, straightening the car. "I'll get you out of here in a second."

They were facing him now. He was many houses down, and he didn't seem to notice them, leaning on a phone pole as he was, bent over coughing.

Lynnie tried to suck in air. She couldn't. She tried and tried. Nothing.

"You shouldn't see this," Kate said, driving toward the bent-over body. She reached across the seat. "Don't look." She put her hand across Lynnie's eyes.

"No!" Lynnie said. And all the air that couldn't get out went out. She sucked in a fresh breath. "I want to see!"

"It's upsetting you."

"No," Lynnie said again. "Look at him. Slow down. Look."

Horror and shock on her face, Kate slowed the car. As she did, four houses from this wobbling man, he let go of the pole, took a step forward, and collapsed right into a mud puddle.

"Stop," Lynnie said to Kate.

"Are you sure—"

"Yes."

Kate stopped the car and they looked out the windshield. They were right before him now, but he didn't see them. He was on his side, his face half in the mud.

"He's a mess," Lynnie said.

"You got that right."

"He's a drunk."

"You're probably right about that, too."

"Geez."

"Are you okay?"

The choking was gone. The breathing came easy. She touched her chest and felt her necklace.

"What do you want to do, Lynnie?"

She thought of things she'd seen people do. She'd seen a TV show where a gang of kids came upon a homeless man in a park and poured drinks all over him and kicked him and laughed. She'd seen a woman have a fight with a bus driver and call him names and spit at his feet. She'd seen

Smokes himself go at a working boy and crack a broom handle over his head.

She wanted to do all of that to him. She wanted to jump out of the car and bite him. But she didn't bite anymore, and she didn't want to kick a person, even this one. She wasn't sure if she was still scared of him or if she just didn't want to bother.

"Go," she said.

Kate hit the gas. "We can drive right to the police. We know where he lives."

"No."

"Please, Lynnie. You can identify him. It's only right that he should pay."

"I don't want to go to the police."

"Why not?"

"Because..."

"Because what?"

Past him now, they neared the corner.

"Can you help me say a word?" Lynnie asked.

Kate turned to her. "Sure. You start and I'll finish."

"Because he's pa...path...pathetic."

Kate smiled. "You don't need my help."

Lynnie said, "And you know what, Kate? I'm not."

"That's right," Kate said. "You're not."

Lynnie thought about turning around in her seat to see him one last time. But it felt too good to be facing forward.

* * *

At three o'clock, back in the Capitol building, Lynnie sat down in the large room where the hearing was to be held, and a man in the front of the room stood up. "Our hearing today concerns the potential closing of the remaining residential institutions in the Commonwealth. We will take comments from members of the community."

One by one, each of Lynnie's friends went to a seat in the front of the room and spoke their case. Lynnie could barely listen. She kept rolling her drawings in her hands.

Finally: "Lynnie Goldberg."

She rose, flashed a smile at Kate, and went to the front of the room. There she sat in the big wooden chair and faced the legislators.

"I am Lynnie Goldberg," she said, taking care with every word. "From 1957 to 1980, I lived in the Pennsylvania School. I want to tell you my story, and I brought something to help me." She unrolled her drawings and held the first one up. "This is how the School looked to me when my parents took me there. I was scared. I didn't know what it was. Bad things happened, and I will not tell you them all. But I will tell you some."

And she showed them through her art. Meeting Tonette. Mopping the dayroom. Getting shoved around by angry residents. Eating mush. Folding laundry. Stepping over floor puddles to use the lavatory. Hiding her art in a file cabinet. Being afraid of attendants with dogs.

She did not mention Buddy or...Julia. She did not say she looked out her window at night even now, imagining where, under the stars of Cup and Feather, her husband and her child might be.

The legislators listened with serious expressions. One woman got wet eyes. One man held his fist to his chin.

"That's why we have to close all the institutions," Lynnie said when she finished.

She stood up and was aware that the other advocates were applauding her. She smiled at them, relieved she'd found the courage to speak for herself—and for so many others, too.

"I did it, Kate!" Lynnie said as they burst out of the elevator into the rotunda. She grabbed Kate's hand and moved fast.

"You did," Kate said, letting herself be pulled along. "You talked in public, Lynnie. And your art has gotten so *good*! I'm so glad you asked me to be here."

Lynnie threaded through the people milling about the rotunda until she and Kate reached the center. "It's been some day," Kate said, her voice soft though still seeming to lift off into flight.

"One of the best days ever," Lynnie said, louder, her voice flying higher.

Then she tilted her head back and looked up into the dome, so very high above her head, and whispered the word she'd thought about for hours, the word that helped make her strong at the hearing: "Julia." The word took wing as it left her mouth and rose into the air. It circled higher and higher and finally disappeared through the glass. Surely it would soar unseen across the state, across the world, and look down to the land and find her.

Dust

HOMAN

1995

$\mathcal{A}$ ccording to the map," Sam said, slowing the van, "we are at the School."

But Homan had already seen the stone walls. He didn't need to turn to Jean, sitting beside him in the back, as she interpreted Sam's speech into sign. He hadn't gotten thrown off by the changed scenery— acres of new houses across the road, now swelled to a highway—or by the many changes that had happened inside him after he'd made the leap to American Sign Language, struck up friendships with folks who worked at the Independent Living Center with Sam, and taken classes. He'd learned so much in the last years: how to transform those printed bird tracks into letters, then words, then flocks that carried him across the pages of books; how to understand maps, money, the rules of driving. Still, he instantly recognized those walls.

And there was the gate, black and tall, its tips spiked as spears. Beyond it, high on the hill, was the tower, its clock face replaced by the words "Veterans Medical Center." Sam—whose name, Homan now knew, was Terence, though he'd always be Sam to him—had pulled the van to the shoulder, and even though Homan's view was broken by passing SUVs and eighteen wheelers, the sight immediately pumped revulsion—and longing—through his veins.

He'd figured that would happen. Soon after the window to communication opened, he lost interest in the Tingling, and as he read and learned, he became repelled by how easily the School had made him disappear. While he was pleased he'd worked out a good deal with King and Queen (decent income *plus* the room and board he already had at their Buddhist retreat), had grown more sure of his talents (starting a side business modifying beds, vans, and wheelchairs for friends), and had set his sights high (he'd just gotten an application to study engineering), he still wished he could wallop the big shots who'd looked down their noses at him and the guards who'd strutted about like cocks. Yet at the same time, he'd come to wonder what had happened to the School—and to Beautiful Girl and Little One. The first question took a lot of research to answer. The other question, he

couldn't answer. How could he, without knowing their names?

What about you? Sam asked one day as Jean, a
hearing person fluent in sign, interpreted. Jean was
Yellow Dress, but now she wore skirts and blazers,
and she and Sam were married.

What do you mean, what about me?

*There must be a file on you somewhere. It might
have just enough information from Redhead, or someone, to get you Beautiful Girl's name.*

They never knew who I was.

What'd they call you?

How would I know?

For a long time, Homan gave himself grief for
wanting to know what happened to them. Twenty-
seven years had gone by. Beautiful Girl might have
passed away, and if she hadn't, what business did
he have thinking about her? Or Little One?
They'd be in their own lives, maybe even with
their own families and friends and jobs. He was
long gone from their thoughts.

It's basic curiosity, one friend told him; *we all feel
that with our first romances.* Another offered, *It's
guilt.*

We have a different theory, Jean signed one night
before she and Sam got married. *You keep thinking
of her because you still love—*

Homan walked away so she couldn't finish her
sentence.

Then a month ago, Sam and Jean made an invitation. They both had job interviews in Washington, D.C., and decided to drive across the country. They wanted to see Yosemite, Mount Rushmore, maybe even places they'd been when they were younger. Homan could come, too.

I've got a job.

Isn't there some place you'd like to see?

No.

It won't feel like a road trip without you.

What part of No don't you understand?

Yet when he went back to his little house that night and lay on his futon, Beautiful Girl came to him for the first time in so very long. Her dream self—not a fuzzy shape, but detailed and full and luscious—climbed into bed beside him. He turned to her, and there she was, gazing at him in the moonlight. Her body, though, wasn't touching his, her expression was unreadable, and despite how much he wanted to lay his fingers on her warm skin, he held back. She was a dream, only a dream. Instead, he raised his hands and asked what she'd been doing all these years. She pointed toward the wall, which suddenly revealed itself to be covered by her drawings. He peered at them, but before he could recognize any, they faded before his eyes, becoming blank. By the time he looked back at her, she was gone.

The next day, he told King and Queen he

wanted time off. The next week, he took care of all
the maintenance they'd need while he was gone.
And just before he left, he slit open the bottom of
his yellow chair, removed the money, and finally,
at long last, put it in the bank.

They took Sam and Jean's van. He and Sam
shared the driving, with Jean interpreting. And
now they were here, and the gate was open.

Let's go in, he signed.

It was the smell he couldn't believe as the van
rolled past the gate. Not the stench, which wasn't
apparent, but the Pennsylvania countryside. Homan lowered his window and breathed in. The
scent was just as it used to be this far from the
cottages: grassy and earthy and clean. Beautiful
Girl had loved these smells, though she'd never
been free to roam all the way down the drive. It
was he who used to come here when the guardhouse needed repairs, giving his lungs a break from
the odors in the cottages. Now the guardhouse
was gone, and the grass was a few inches higher
than had ever been allowed. Did anyone coming
through this gate guess what this place once was?

The first building came into view as they continued up the drive, a gleaming five-story hospital.
Made of red sandblasted stone, it had flags flying
from poles, a portico at the entrance, and rows of
tinted windows with not a single bar among them.

He wondered what it replaced. The drive curved in new ways, and he couldn't remember.

He looked out the passenger window. Jean was facing him, but his eye was drawn past her to— he realized—the administrative building with the tower. Although it was ancient, it looked better than ever, with freshly painted trim, uncracked marble steps, a polished railing.

He climbed past Jean and threw open the van door.

Positioned before the steps, he regarded the tower. The stone was as gray as he recalled, the corners as sharp, and as his gaze rose up, he remembered the first time he'd stood here. How enraged and frightened he'd been, locked in handcuffs, clueless about where he was. He'd come into the town of Well's Bottom seeking nothing more than a place to sleep for the night.

He thought of that night now. He'd jumped off a train and found himself in the borough, looking for food and a safe place to sleep until morning. In the back alleys, he'd come across a jacket someone had left in a yard, then he'd helped himself to a loaf of bread inside the back of a bakery. Satisfied, he'd curled up in an alley behind a bar and slept. And that would have been it.

Except that just as the sun was rising, he saw, right before him, a trash can with an upside-down lid. The lid had captured water, and when he rose to his feet and looked into it, he saw his reflection. He was dirty, and his teenage beard was more ragged than it had seemed with his hands. But with a razor and some soap, he could look good, even respectable. Maybe even like someone who could walk into a train station and get treated like a regular human being.

O *muh*. He tried to say his name aloud, his first effort to form a word with his voice in many years. A vibrating feeling came into his throat, though with no way of telling how he sounded, he put his hand before his lips to feel the air. O *muh*. He smiled. He was a person who could amount to something. Didn't he know how to steer a car? Hadn't he survived in the outdoors?

Muh nuh O muh. My name Homan. He banged on the lid. *Muh nuh O muh!*

The light came up hard from behind.

He spun around.

Police! He hadn't known they were there! He'd been too stuck on his voice!

He fought like the dickens to get away. But they grabbed and cuffed him and drove him to a jail, then a court, where a judge decided he was a thief, too slow-witted to understand them, a danger to others, and sent him here. He remembered being hauled out of the car right in front of these steps, terrified and confused. And saying to himself, as he stared up to the clock, *Be a cold day in hell 'fore you use that voice again.*

Now he looked down the tower, one window at a time. Dark. Dark. Dark. Even the one to the left of the front staircase, the office for the big shot's—no, Luke Collins's—secretary. Homan mounted the steps to get a better look. A small sign was screwed into the oak door: BUILDING CLOSED. He peered over the hedge and looked into the window.

The room was nothing more than walls and a floor. There was no one to get back at now.

He turned to the van. *You see any signs stopping us from driving over the grounds?*

You want to do that?

No. But I have to.

All the cottages remained, and as Sam drove slowly past, Homan saw BUILDING CLOSED affixed to every door. There was the cottage where he'd met Shortie and Whirly Top. The dining cottage, where he'd stolen sugar cubes. The laundry, where he'd given her bouquets of feathers.

And there was the path where he'd sometimes seen the other deaf man stuck here, an African American who loved uniforms and used signs Homan thought meaningless, though which probably weren't, any more than Homan's had been. He'd finally figured it out. Homan had learned a dialect

the McClintocks' father had picked up in deaf
school, a black dialect of American Sign Language. Whites didn't know it, off in their own
schools as they were down south. Apparently some
blacks didn't, either.

How far Homan had come to know all this now.
If only he'd known a sliver of it then.

Turn toward the fields.

The barn was pathetic, with vines covering the
sides, a tree growing through the roof. He'd kept
her drawing of the sea in that barn. He'd held it up
many mornings, fascinated by the aqua water pushing against the rocks and foaming along the tower
to the side. He could not get into the barn now, but
what did it matter? If the cornfields had become beds
of wildflowers, and the staff huts had been wiped off
the map, that drawing had surely become dust.

I don't get it, he signed to Jean as they approached the cemetery, now almost entirely overgrown. *Why have they left all this here?*

*Maybe it's just too much land and they couldn't find
someone who'd want to take it over.*

The drive took them back toward the main
building, and Homan thought, *Maybe no one wants
to deal with ghosts.*

After returning to the new hospital building,
they worked through a succession of offices until
they found the right bureaucrat.

"I'm afraid I don't know much," Mrs. Raja said after she'd rolled her desk chair to sit in a circle with them so Jean could interpret. "I do know that everyone who lived here was moved back with their families or into smaller facilities. Some of those are nearby and some aren't. I could give you a list of the agencies."

We don't have her name, Homan signed.

"Isn't she a relative?"

He paused, then flashed on the image of her face coming toward him that last night, the old lady's dress flowing from her shoulders, the pantomime ring he'd placed on her finger.

Yes.

"But you don't know her name?"

He felt his face fall. *No.*

"I'll be honest with you, sir. We occasionally get people like you stopping in. Usually they learned late in life they had a relative here, or decided to find a long-lost son or sister. I give them the list of agencies, but their search often proves fruitless. The institution closed before computers, and many files were deficient to begin with. Some families gave only first names, or used false names. Some residents didn't even have names."

Sam, looking at Homan, asked, "They didn't have names?"

"No one knew who they were. They just ended up here one way or another, and if they didn't arrive with records and lacked verbal abilities, they had no identity."

Homan signed, *What were they called in the files?*

"They were given numbers for the order in which they entered the system. John Doe Number One, John Doe Number Two. Like that."

Homan looked out the window to a tall maple tree. Beautiful Girl hadn't known his name, either. He remembered her name sign for him. He was sure it wasn't a number.

A squirrel scampered along a branch, and he realized with a start that he'd seen this view from this very location. Mrs. Raja's office was where Chubby Redhead's office had been. This building had replaced the staff cottage. Beautiful Girl had drawn her pictures right here.

He turned back. Mrs. Raja was already rising. "Wish I could be more helpful," she said.

We're sorry, Jean signed when Homan turned on the ignition and glanced over at her.

He pulled the van out of the lot. With his hands on the wheel, Homan was at least in control of something. This way he could forget any impulse to kick trees and could kick himself instead. *You knew nothing good come outta this,* he berated himself, dialing his mind back to who he'd been then. *Why you need to find her anyhow? So she accepted you just the way you was. That nice, but Sam do that* now, too. And Jean and King and Queen and all them new friends. Ain't that good enough? Your guilt so bad you can't make your peace with that?

Sam tapped the back of his arm with his stick.

We just passed the off-ramp, Jean signed.

Homan shook his head back to the road. Sure enough, he'd missed the turn. The road had become a bypass, cutting through hills. He looked to either side and saw nothing except box stores and chain restaurants where there used to be trees. *Well, ain't that just the way of the world. Everything come to an end, whether you wants it to or not. All that nature out there: over. The Snare: dead and gone. Even a love that make a man giddy and romantic, that give him a hope and joy he never known, that brave him into taking a slingshot to the impossible and bringing it almost complete to its knees—even a love like that come to an end. Life just ashes to ashes and dust to dust. And there nothing you can do about it neither.*

Jean banged on the steering wheel.

I know you're feeling bad, but we have to turn around.

You're right, he signed.

He had to get a grip. He had to be on the lookout for a road sign to get them off the bypass and back in the opposite direction. But they were on a bridge now, and he wasn't about to do a U-turn here. That was something movie heroes did—and he was no hero. He was just a man who'd loved.

A man who'd felt so treasured by a beautiful girl that he'd become more than he'd known he could be. A man who'd, yes, gotten loads of acceptance and respect from friends and employers, but—*Tell yourself the truth*—had never felt that treasured again.

After the bridge, the road narrowed to two lanes, with farms and woods on either side. It took a few miles until he finally saw a place to turn at a gap in the trees. He put on his turn signal, and as he neared the gap he saw it was a dirt road, and beside it was a sign: RIVERSIDE BOY SCOUT CAMP. And something tumbled into place inside him.

It was the place where he'd run that night. Where he dove off the dock to cross the river.

He was on the road. The same road.

He signed before Sam and Jean could react: *I know where I am. I have one more thing to see.* He turned off the turn signal and sped up.

Yeah, it was ridiculous, he thought, hitting 50 mph, 60 mph, passing pokey cars, farms, woods. He wouldn't find her there. He couldn't imagine Roof Giver would still be alive. And it was impossible that Little One would still be in the farmhouse.

Yet he had to do it. If he didn't, his search would never feel complete.

He reached the turnoff to the other road so much faster than they had that rainy night. Now he could read the signs, though he knew to stay where he was, on Old Creamery Road. That night, they hadn't known what to do. It was a random choice to stay straight. *What more you need to know there ain't no big drawing? You go straight on one road just because. You pick up a trash lid with water just because.*

The woods flew fast. He wondered if he'd recognize it.

He knew he'd recognize it.

There was the white house they'd almost gone up to. But she'd shaken her head no, so they'd pressed on.

There were other houses they'd passed, older and more weathered. Maybe, against all odds, the old lady *would* be there. Maybe she'd know the answers he was seeking.

He reached the bend in the road and knew he was almost there. It was coming up on the left, after the road straightened out, only a few hundred yards away.

The road straightened, and as it did, the trees hugging the asphalt gave way to houses. Hundreds of them, all split levels, spreading up the rise to his left, marching toward the horizon on his right.

He slowed the van, staring to his left. The ground rose at a grade he remembered. He'd rushed up it with Beautiful Girl. He'd run down it through the woods.

The entrance to the development was easy to see up ahead, flanked as it was by two low brick walls. In front of the walls, he saw as the van neared, grew crisply trimmed shrubs and ornamental grasses, the display on the left matching the one on the right. The only difference was that the right side also displayed a sign with gilded letters: THE ESTATES AT MEADOW HILLS.

He turned into the development. The main road was wide, with narrower streets snaking off across the hillside. He parked at the curb. Then he opened the door and got out.

The air smelled of cut grass and mulch and gas-powered leaf blowers. A few home owners were riding lawn mowers or washing cars in their driveways. mostly he just saw houses, none of which resembled the old lady's. It had stood on top of this very hill, and now it—like the office where Beautiful Girl had placed a radio in his pocket, then held him close, and they'd moved together in a slow dance—was gone.

No one would ever know the joy and pain of here.

He wanted to stay where he was a long time, but soon he realized he'd done what he'd planned to do and also what he hadn't planned. And it all amounted to zero.

He got back in the car and angled himself to be seen by both friends.

Sorry for the detour. I'm ready to get out of here now.

What is this place? Jean asked.

It's . . . it was the place where I last saw her. Saw them.

This was it? Sam asked through Jean.

The very place.

How can you be sure? Sam asked.

I know it.

I thought it was a farm.

It was.

We've heard that story so many times, Jean signed. *It's a whole other thing to actually be here.*

Except you aren't really here, Homan replied. *It's gone.*

When you tell the story of that night, she signed, *you make it sound like Beautiful Girl knew just where to go.*

She didn't. She just decided this place would be safe, and she was right.

Until you got busted, Sam added.

No, she was right. That old lady treated us with kindness. How many other people would have done that?

But why do you think she picked this place? Jean signed. *Why this one?*

Homan looked from one face to the other, and the night played back in his mind. Holding on to each other in the pounding rain. Turning the corner in the road. Seeing the mailbox up ahead.

The mailbox up ahead.

With the lighthouse man.

Who'd been in her drawing of the sea.

He threw open the van door and ran to the entrance for the development.

Nothing was there except the well-maintained plantings and low, decorative brick walls. He shot a look up the street, back toward the houses. Every one of them had a simple curbside mailbox mounted on a post. It was gone, long, long gone. But memory is stronger than dust.

He threw his arms open and spun around, tossing his head back, laughing and laughing, looking up at the sky. He knew why he needed to be here—and he knew what he had to do now!

Maybe that Big Artist, he thought as the sky swirled above, *need me just as much as I need him.*

The Second Kind of Hope

LYNNIE

2000

$\mathcal{D}$ oreen went quickly. Lynnie, listening to the minister in the funeral home, couldn't believe how quickly.

The trouble began only last year. One Saturday when Lynnie showed up for their regular visit, expecting to settle in to watch Doreen's new videos, Doreen said, "Do you know where they are?" They hunted around, and when they found them in the closet with the toilet paper, Doreen said, "What a goofball," and they laughed it off. But then she started forgetting her bus pass, and one day when she left Wal-Mart, she couldn't remember where she was.

Only a week later, Doreen called Lynnie in tears: She'd gone to the bank and they said she had only twenty dollars left. Lynnie and Carmen went over to Doreen's, who said her aide hadn't been there for "I don't know how long." Carmen made calls and figured out the aide had drained Doreen's account.

"I wish I could say this never happens," the police detective told them when she came to make a report.

"What about my rent?" Doreen said. "My heat?"

Carmen said, "Let me see if I can jump the waiting list and get you back with BridgeWays."

She did, to a group home across town from Lynnie, but Doreen just spun down faster. She stopped going out because "they've been making these streets too confusing." She couldn't get through meals without snapping at someone. Then she'd just look out the window, saying, "You know, there's diamonds in those hills."

Lynnie would cry after every visit, yet she didn't stop going. Carmen would say, "That's so nice. You're the best friend a person could have."

The funeral was not the first Lynnie had attended. That had been for her grandfather, in the days before the School, and many mourners had come. In the cemetery, she'd seen small rocks resting on some headstones, and Hannah told her, "Mommy said when you visit people you care about who are buried, you place a stone at the grave. Then everyone knows the person was remembered." The second funeral Lynnie went to was for Tonette. Only a handful of people came,

and Lynnie wanted Tonette to know she was remembered, so she found a small rock and placed it
on the grave.

Here, at Doreen's funeral, most of the seats were
empty. The only ones who'd come were Lynnie,
Carmen, two of Doreen's neighbors at her apartment building, her bus drivers Vince and Dale,
and three of the salespeople Doreen had visited for
years.

The minister spoke politely about Doreen, calling her "pure at heart" and "a breath of fresh air to
all who knew her," rather than funny, outspoken,
stubborn, or, as Lynnie knew all too well, "pissed
as a hornet" that her family had never come to
see her. But the minister had met Doreen only at
the end, and when he moved on to talk about her
finding eternal happiness now that she was home
with the Lord, Lynnie stopped listening. Doreen
had never said a word about God, and Lynnie was
far from certain she believed in God herself. People who did talk about God, like Kate, said they
felt His presence deep in their heart. In Lynnie's
heart, she felt nothing. If there was a God, why
did Doreen have to die to go home? If there was a
God, why did Doreen's father give her money but
never visit? If there was a God, why could Lynnie
barely see Buddy and Julia in her mind?

As the minister finished up, Lynnie had no new
feelings about God, though she did have a realiza-

tion about something else. For so long, she'd believed Buddy would return. She'd even told Kate
it would happen—eventually. She'd learned that
word when she was little, when she and Hannah
played their very own version of hide-and-go-seek,
where no one was designated "it" and no spot was
declared "home." Instead, the two of them would
hide from Mommy, Daddy, and each other, test-
ing how long they could go before they missed
each other too much. Then they'd try to find each
other, and when they did, Hannah would yell,
"Safe!" The game ended *eventually*.

Now, as Doreen's casket was borne out to the
hearse and the small gathering followed behind,
Lynnie realized there might not be eventually for
her and Buddy. Look at Doreen. If there was a
God, her parents would have come—eventually.
But never had come first.

Over the next few weeks, whenever Lynnie got
dressed in the morning, she wondered if she should
stop wearing the red feather necklace. She had
worn it every day since Hannah gave it to her, and
when she slipped the chain over her head in the
morning and the glass circle came to rest on her
chest, she felt as if Buddy were pressing his hand
right there, feeling her vibrations as she spoke;
and whenever she was aware of her breath making
it rise and fall, she would think that somewhere

under the sky, Julia was breathing, too. Yet now she wondered if wearing it was only making her sad. She would hear people talking in the office at BridgeWays, saying a colleague needed to "get over it" when a boyfriend broke off a romance. At home she'd see people on TV shows say, "You need to move on," or, "Face it—she's history."

Doreen had been right: He was never coming back. After thirty-two years of hoping, it was well past time to move on.

So one night a few months after Doreen died, Lynnie opened her closet, lifted up her extra blanket, and pulled out the carved wooden box that Eva and Don Hansberry had given her years ago. She'd looked through it with Kate that very night, right after Lynnie had spoken for the legislators. She and Kate had sat in the hotel room sighing at the pictures of Julia, who was truly beautiful. Kate had asked if Lynnie wanted her to untie the yellow ribbon that held a packet of the old lady's letters and read them aloud, and for the next two days, they'd stayed in the hotel, learning about Julia and Martha. Wonderful Martha, who'd been the parent Lynnie wished she'd had and wished she'd been able to be. The final letter in the packet was from the man Martha had married, Pete. He wrote about how Martha had died one night in her sleep when Julia was fourteen. He wrote about how much he loved them both, and he promised to raise Julia just as Martha wanted. What a good man—just like Buddy. Kate had retied the ribbon, and Lynnie had put everything back in the box, then brought it to her group home and stored it away.

It was the perfect place to put her necklace. She set it inside and closed the closet door.

Winter thawed. Spring blossoms opened. Summer came in with its hot breath and turned the grass brown. Then, one morning, as the wind began once again shaking the leaves from the trees, on a day when Hannah was coming to visit, Lynnie woke with a new thought. For a long time, Hannah had wanted a baby, but she and her husband, John, hadn't been able to have one. Lynnie knew this made Hannah unhappy; she looked away whenever she saw a pregnant woman. Yet she called Lynnie with a bright voice whenever they held a show in her gallery and it was a hit. Then there was Kate. Kate had wanted her first marriage to last, though her husband had different ideas. But Kate met Scott, and when she got married she said, "Scott's worth all the trouble I went through before I found him." And don't forget Doreen. Although Doreen never got her parents, she got the best friend a person could have.

And Lynnie understood. There were two kinds

of hope: the kind you couldn't do anything about and the kind you could. And even if the kind you could do something about wasn't what you'd originally wanted, it was still worth doing. A rainy day is better than no day. A small happiness can make a big sadness less sad.

So as Lynnie dressed for the visit—really, the meeting with Hannah and all Lynnie's aides, which happened once a year—she made a decision. She knew it would surprise everyone in the room, yet it was what she wanted. Actually, she'd wanted it a long time.

She opened the closet, and pulled out the wooden box, and slipped the necklace back over her head.

"How's it going, Lynnie?" Carmen asked.

They had all just taken their seats in the conference room, Carmen, Sharona, Antoine, Hannah, and Lynnie. Everyone was wearing one of the sweatshirts Hannah had just handed out, each decorated with a drawing of Lynnie's.

"Better," Lynnie said.

Carmen said, "You getting more used to Doreen not being around?"

Lynnie knew Carmen was aware of the answer and was just prompting her to respond. "Yeah. And it'll get better."

"That's a good attitude," Antoine said, a smile

on his round face. He made a note on some paper in front of him. He was Lynnie's case manager, Carmen her residential team coordinator, Sharona her direct support professional.

Hannah said, "And didn't your bowling team just win for the third time in a row?"

"We did."

"Isn't that great?" Carmen said to the group. Carmen was from Puerto Rico, where there were sandy beaches and palm trees; and her voice, Lynnie thought, sounded like ocean waves.

Then they began the official meeting. Doreen had hated these meetings when she'd been with BridgeWays. Lynnie didn't mind, even though it was the same every year: Sit around the table with aides and answer questions about things they already knew. Doreen had said, "Regular people don't have to do this," but Lynnie liked that she could invite anyone she wanted. Kate lived too far away, though Hannah always came, every time with mugs or key chains or stationery decorated with Lynnie's art, and gave one to everybody. It was like a party that way. So why not tell them how much money she got every month from Social Security, and when she'd seen the dentist, and if she remembered what to do at a fire drill. "It's not a big deal," Lynnie had told Doreen, even though, she had to admit, the meetings made her feel like a kid.

Antoine was the one who filled out the forms, so he asked the questions.

"Are you still working in the office at BridgeWays?"

"Yes."

"Do you like it there?"

"Yes."

"Do you want to explore working anywhere else?"

"No."

"Are you still at 210 Dowdall Avenue?"

"Yes."

"Do you like it there?"

"Patricia hogs the TV and Lois won't let anyone walk over the rug after she vacuums."

"Would you like to live anywhere else?"

"On my own."

"When that program gets funding, we can talk about that. Now, what do you do in your leisure time?"

On and on it went. Lynnie answered just as she always did, but this time she could hardly wait until they reached the last question. It was the one they took an hour to reach—the one she'd answered to herself this morning.

Finally: "Do you have a goal you want to achieve this year?"

For so long, there had been only one goal. But only Kate knew about Buddy and Julia, and that was a goal Lynnie could do nothing about, so she'd always answered no. Antoine must have expected that same answer now, because his hand was on one side of Lynnie's file, getting ready to close it and wrap up the meeting.

"Yes," Lynnie said.

Antoine raised his eyebrows.

"Way to go, kiddo," Carmen said. "Change is the spice of life."

Lynnie said, "I want to go on vacation."

Sharona said, "I've never heard you say that."

"I want to take Hannah and Kate. And I want to pay for everyone myself."

"That's so nice," Hannah said, touching Lynnie's arm.

"That might cost more money than you have," Antoine said. "Where do you want to go?"

Lynnie said to Hannah, "You know that place we went to when we were little?"

"You want to go back there?"

"Where?" Carmen asked.

"It's at the Jersey shore," Hannah said. "It was the only vacation my family took with... before Lynnie went to the School." She looked curiously at Lynnie. "Why do you want to go there?"

She wanted to tell Hannah the whole reason why. But Hannah hadn't known for so very long, Lynnie couldn't imagine telling her. So she gave a partial reason. "To have fun."

Antoine said, "Covering the cost of a vacation for three, even just to the beach—"

"We could go off-season," Hannah said.

"It'll still take time to save up that kind of money."

Lynnie said, "I want to do it myself."

"How, Lynnie?" Hannah said.

"You could sell my art."

"Are you serious?" Hannah asked.

"Yes."

"But you've always said that since you couldn't keep anything for so long, now you want to keep everything."

"I want to sell my drawings so I can do this."

"Are you sure?"

Lynnie nodded.

"How do you want to do this?" Carmen asked. "On sweatshirts?"

"No," Lynnie said. "I have a better idea."

On the day of the opening at the gallery in Ithaca, the crowds whirled around.

"I just love your work," said a tall woman with triangular earrings.

"I was expecting primitivism," added a man with a kerchief in his suit jacket. "Yet it reminds me of Howard Pyle, N. C. Wyeth, Frank E. Schoonover."

"The Brandywine School," said a man with a

shaved head, nodding knowingly. "The great narrative illustrators."

Hannah handed Lynnie a plate of cheese and crackers and said to those around her, "It's really developed over time."

"I'd thought outsider art would be amateur hour," the man with the kerchief said. "This is a paradigm shift for me."

Lynnie couldn't figure out a single thing they were saying. All she knew was that she and Hannah had worked for months to make it happen. First they tried to pick out the drawings Lynnie was willing to sell, but when Hannah pointed out that most of the drawings came in groups that told stories and said she hated to break up any stories, Lynnie gave her all the drawings— except for the one story Hannah didn't know. Then Hannah made arrangements so Lynnie's sales wouldn't affect her government assistance. They set a date and Hannah invited everyone she knew, the weeks narrowed to days, Lynnie saw her work framed and mounted on walls, articles about her appeared in newspapers. Now here they were.

Lynnie felt shy around these strangers, though, so she just watched them milling about, looking at her drawings, saying things like "And to think that Hannah was sitting on this trove for so long!"

"How's it going?" Hannah said, coming up to

Lynnie and turning them away from the crowd. She was holding a glass of wine in her hand.

"It's going good."

"I'll say. You're probably on top of the world."

"Just about."

"Hey, how could it get better than this?"

Lynnie knew but wasn't going to tell. "It's a great day," she said.

"Well, glad you think so, because I have a question for you."

Lynnie couldn't guess what she might say. She looked down at the plate with the cheese.

"You're doing all this to give us a really nice gift. But you know I always take you to lunch when I see you. You must have realized that John and I would have enjoyed treating *you* to a vacation, along with anyone you wanted. You could have kept your pictures and still gone on this trip. So why, Lynnie? It's such a generous thing to do, but I don't understand why."

"Because," Lynnie said. And she told herself: *You can't say there are two kinds of hope—Hannah will ask what the other one is. You can't say you want to feel safe—Hannah feels bad enough about how long you were hidden. But there is another reason.*

"Because you came back," Lynnie said. "And you keep coming back. So does Kate."

"Lynnie," Hannah said, setting down her wine,

taking her sister in her arms, "that's about the nicest thing anyone has ever said to me."

Lynnie looked over Hannah's shoulder, out the big gallery window. The sky was crying outside, and as she watched the drops come down, she thought: *A rainy day can actually be a very important day. And a small hope isn't really small if it makes a lost hope less sad.*

Into the Light

KATE

2001

*K*ate spotted Lynnie immediately in the parking lot.

She'd thought she'd be too tired after the early morning flight from Indianapolis, followed by the train ride down the Jersey coast to the seaside town of Poseidon. She thought too she might not be able to find them in the huge parking lot, visible from her window seat as the train was slowing to a stop. But as soon as she'd stepped onto the raised platform, taken a breath of salty air, and gazed down into the lot, she saw the passenger door of the green Volvo burst open and a tall, silver-haired woman jump out. If Kate hadn't known to be looking for Lynnie, she wouldn't have recognized her, with her hair short, her eyes requiring glasses, her physique having become mildly, yet pleasingly, plump. Even at fifty, though,

Lynnie was clearly excited over seeing Kate, as was apparent in her wide wave as she bolted for the platform. Kate waved back, then hoisted her carry-on bag higher on her shoulder. Lynnie was flying across the platform before Kate had taken a step.

"You're here, you're here!" Lynnie said into her hug.

"For the whole weekend," Kate said. "Just like you wanted."

It was heavenly to see Lynnie so happy, Kate thought as Lynnie hooked their arms together and they jaunted down the platform steps. Their visit in Harrisburg all those years ago had moved Kate to the bottom of her soul and still prompted tears of pride and admiration whenever she brought it to mind. From their letters and calls since, Kate knew Lynnie had become even more assured of her own wants and more able to be independent. Now, as they crossed the parking lot toward Hannah, and Kate could see Lynnie's confidence right before her eyes, Kate felt a pang that she wasn't working with Lynnie anymore. *But time passes*, she consoled herself while she hugged Hannah. *My life took me away*. Kate's co-workers often teased her for going beyond the call of duty, though they were impressed when Kate told them about this trip. "And it isn't duty," Kate corrected them. "Lynnie's come to feel like an old friend." An old friend, she'd added in her head, with a very sad history—

redeemed by one little baby and one kindhearted old woman and decades of Lynnie's own efforts.

"I hope you don't mind," Hannah said, loading Kate's bag into the back of the car, "but we've decided to change our plans for this afternoon."

"The weatherman says a storm's on the way," Lynnie said.

Kate looked up. On the train she'd marveled at the blue of the late May sky, thinking the weather perfect for a game of miniature golf, a ride on the Ferris wheel, a snack of saltwater taffy—all of which Lynnie had talked about them doing. The sky still seemed calm.

"And not just any old storm," Hannah added. "A nor'easter. They don't come much at this time of year. But you probably know they can be rough."

Now Kate saw the first hint, a low cloud at the hem of the eastern horizon.

"So we've decided to have our tour today instead of tomorrow," Hannah said.

"What tour?"

Lynnie said, "You know. So we can have someone show us around."

Hannah said, "It seemed like a good way to get reacquainted with the sights."

As they all got into the car, Kate noticed litter beginning to stir along the asphalt, leaves beginning to tremble.

"Fortunately, we were able to bump the tour up to this afternoon," Hannah said as she settled into the driver's seat.

"Is the storm coming that soon?"

"No point taking chances," Hannah said, starting the car.

Kate looked into the front passenger seat, and even though she could see Lynnie only in profile, she could make out the broad grin, no doubt at having pulled this whole trip together. "I don't care if it rains all weekend," Kate said. "It's just really nice to be here."

Droplets had started before they pulled up to the souvenir store on Ocean Avenue, where their tour guide, standing under the awning, waved from under a hooded raincoat. A man of about sixty, with deep creases in his skin and bright blue eyes, he came up to Hannah's window, introduced himself as Tom, and said he should do the driving. They rearranged themselves—Hannah to Kate's right, Lynnie riding shotgun—and he got in.

"We might need to do a short version of the usual tour," he said, turning to address everyone. "Usually we can go inside all the historic places, but folks are getting ready for the storm, so we might end up staying in the car a lot."

"Do we have to?" Lynnie said.

He shrugged. "On days like this, people usually

have their ways of letting me know. I guess we'll just see."

He pulled out onto Ocean Avenue.

"I remember that," Hannah said, passing a hamburger joint with a giant metal-skinned mermaid out front.

"That's Ackerman's. It's been here since 1925."

"We ate there," Hannah said. "You must remember, Lynnie. You drew her in one of your pictures."

"I do remember."

"And see over there?" Tom pointed to a town green with a merry-go-round in the center.

"Oh, Lynnie!" Hannah said. "Look."

Tom said, "We used to have a tremendous amusement park on the far end of town. It was one of the major attractions of South Jersey, as famous as Lucy the tin elephant in Margate, or the Boardwalk in Atlantic City, and one of the reasons was this carousel. We're really lucky, because when the park burned down in 1956, the carousel was saved, and a few years ago, we got permission to put it in our town center. They have rides on it, too."

Tom circled the town green. The carousel was rocking in the rising wind, and a rope hung across the entrance. "Well, I guess we can't get on," Tom said. "At least you can get a look." The horses and zebras and tigers and lions—with ornate saddles and headdresses, each creature painted whimsical colors never found in nature—stood suspended on their poles.

"The horses are the best," Lynnie said.

"Yeah," Hannah said. "They're like the one Mommy and Daddy got me in a little shop."

"You gave it to me."

"Is that the horse we kept in your pouch?" Kate asked. "The blue-and-green horse?"

Lynnie turned back and nodded.

Tom gave them more background as he drove through the town. One of the oldest shore communities, Poseidon had repulsed a small invasion by the British during the Revolutionary War. In the early nineteenth century, it became a busy port for goods, which led wealthy shipping owners to build year-round homes. Then it prospered further when a glassworks opened. By the turn of the century, it had become a popular resort for both workers from southern Jersey and affluent Philadelphians. The grandest of the houses remained, with some built right on the beach. "And here's the Poseidon Inn," Tom said. "Woodrow Wilson came once for the cool breeze on the porch. It's said that Thomas Edison spent a night here, and when he woke up he'd finally figured out how to make his light bulb. Now I just have to make a little turn"—he went right, down a short street, then left, onto a broad, tree-lined boulevard—"and we're on the famed Mansion Row."

The name was not an exaggeration. Magnificent, meticulously kept houses graced both sides of the road. Tom drove slowly, pointing out who had lived where. Kate wondered if Lynnie really cared about all this history, but she seemed just as captivated by the sights out their window as the rest of them were. It took a few blocks before Kate understood why.

"I think that's the one we stayed in." Hannah pointed to a modern house with a flat roof.

"Is that it?" Lynnie asked.

"I'm pretty sure."

"They had purple ice cream."

"Yeah. Black raspberry. And a fountain in their front lobby."

The two sisters shared a laugh. Tom asked, "You were in the Paulsen House?"

Hannah explained, "My parents knew someone who'd invited them to a party. They didn't know Mr. Paulsen. They just thought it would be nice to go to a party on the beach. The house has a big patio out back that faces the ocean."

"We'll be able to see it from the other side," Tom said. "We're headed to the beach."

He turned onto a small side road that deadended at dunes. The rain was falling steadily now, and Kate almost suggested they wrap up the tour and head on to their bed-and-breakfast. Then she heard Lynnie gasp.

Kate followed Lynnie's gaze out the windshield. She didn't see anything until she lowered herself to get a better view, over the sea grass and tops of the dunes and into the darkening sky.

It was a lighthouse. A lighthouse with the face of a man.

"Come on!" Lynnie said, and she threw open the door and jumped out of the car.

"What're you doing?" Kate called out.

Hannah was laughing as she jumped out her side. "She just wants to see it again. We went into it once as kids."

"You *did?*" Kate asked.

Hannah called back, "In a storm. We ran to it. I told her it would be safe, and it was."

"Is it open?" Kate asked Tom.

"It's always open," Tom said.

Kate opened her door, stood up, and called out, "Lynnie, isn't this like the lighthouse on the mailbox?"

But Lynnie had already disappeared onto the path through the dunes, and Hannah was close behind.

Lynnie and Hannah were halfway down the beach by the time Kate and Tom had crossed the dunes. The wind was coming in strong off the ocean, churning up waves, whipping the sisters' jackets behind them like wings, but on they went, Lynnie running faster than Hannah, Hannah hurrying behind, both of them moving toward the lighthouse, which rose directly up from the sand.

"Have you ever seen a lighthouse with a face?" Tom said, raising his voice to be heard over the wind.

"Actually, I have," Kate replied, matching his volume as she tied a scarf over her hair.

"You've been here before?"

"No."

"Well, it's the only one in the world."

"Really?"

"It's the Poseidon Lighthouse."

"And it's always open? That's how they got in when they were kids?"

"It's always open *now*. Back when those two were young, it was abandoned. But I guess they just went in."

"Hannah told her it would be safe," Kate said, repeating what she'd just heard. "There was a storm, and they went in, and they were safe."

Tom said, "Yup. That's what lighthouses are for."

Suddenly Kate understood. *This was why Lynnie thought they'd be safe that night.*

And they were.

And then they weren't.

She could see Hannah catch up to Lynnie now, far ahead of them, at the base of the tall white cone. To one side was the lighthouse keeper's bungalow, its windows dark. To the other, she now saw, was a jetty, waves splashing high against the black rock.

Lynnie reached for the lighthouse door and pulled it open.

"It's not abandoned now?" Kate shouted to Tom.

"It's been restored."

Hannah went through the door after Lynnie.

"How do you know it's okay?" Kate called out to Tom. "Anyone could be in there."

"I'm not worried," Tom said.

"Well, I'm going to follow them."

Then she and Tom pushed themselves through the wind toward the lighthouse door.

The lighthouse was chilly, and when Tom shut the door behind him, the thud reverberated. Kate could hear steps echoing and looked above her. A black metal staircase coiled up and up and up. The metal was perforated, so she could see Lynnie and Hannah, already near the top. She could hear them laughing.

She grabbed hold of the handrail. "Right behind you," she called out to them. Her voice had the same resonance it had under the dome of the Capitol in Harrisburg, and when Lynnie said, "Follow us, Kate," Kate hoped she'd heard it, too.

Tom told her the history as they climbed. The lighthouse was built in 1838 and in its heyday saved many ships from ruin. The face was made from a metal grille set over the windows; and when the lamp was turned on, the distinct design could be seen for miles. The lighthouse was sixty feet high, and the story went that the designer built another, a twin, somewhere along the eastern seaboard. But although many had gone in search of it, it had never been found, and no one had ever known with certainty if he'd made the story up or if the structure had been lost to the elements. In any event, this one ceased operation in 1947, then deteriorated for decades. Finally it became so forgotten, it stopped appearing on maps.

Kate could see Lynnie and Hannah disappear into the top—"the lantern room," Tom said. She could hear Hannah squeal, "We're here again!" and Lynnie reply, "It's so cool!"

"Now that it's been restored," Tom continued, "it's my favorite place to bring tourists. People flock here no matter how bad the weather. Everyone loves this lighthouse."

At last Kate reached the top of the staircase and stepped into a glass-enclosed room with an enormous lamp in the center. Taller than Kate, wider than three people pressed side by side, it was made of concentric rings of glass prisms. Fortunately it wasn't lit, so there was no competition for the windows—and what a view! Kate and Lynnie and Hannah could just gape out in every direction, without the hindrance of reflections. She walked toward the sisters, and together they looked. To one side spread the wide, sandy beach, hugged by mansions. She moved around the perimeter of the tower. To the other side stretched the frenzied ocean. The sky felt close, with low, dark clouds and rain sheeting down. The storm roared all around them.

"You came up here as kids?" Tom asked, his voice loud enough to be heard.

Hannah and Lynnie had not moved from their spot at the window, but Hannah turned. "We were at that party at the Paulsen house, and I'd taken Lynnie for a walk, and a storm came up suddenly. This looked like a place where we could wait it out, and we did."

"I bet it didn't look this good then."

"You're right about that."

"Was this lamp here?"

"I think it was a different one. It looked like a glass beehive, but a lot of it was broken."

"That *was* this one. It got repaired as part of the restoration. It's a multiprismed lens called a Fresnel. This one's a third-order Fresnel. They used to be lit by kerosene, but this one's now electric." He went on, and as Hannah wandered over to examine the lamp, Kate made her way to Lynnie.

She was standing before the pane of glass facing the shoreline, a location that provided a view of both land and sea. The houses along the sand had lights in their windows. Although the beach was almost enveloped by the roiling sky, Kate could tell it was empty.

Kate put her arm around Lynnie's shoulders and leaned close, until their cheeks were almost touching. In a voice too soft for anyone except Lynnie to hear, she said, "This is why you wanted to make this trip, isn't it."

Lynnie, eyes fixed outside, nodded.

"You wanted to be back in this place with your sister."

"That's right."

"You've made her very happy."

"I'm glad."

"You've made me happy, too. Do you know how you've done this?"

"By bringing you here?"

"Yes, Lynnie. By bringing me here."

Lynnie looked at her, and Kate felt as if she could almost see the vulnerability in Lynnie's soul. The child who couldn't stay with her family. The mother who couldn't keep her child. The woman who'd waited a lifetime for a man who could never return.

"Are you still sad about what happened?" Kate asked.

"Yes." And then something changed in Lynnie's eyes. The fragility gave way to a sureness. The sorrow gave way to a peace. "But I picked the right house to go to."

"You did," Kate said.

Lynnie turned back to the window. She reached over and took Kate's hand, and as they gazed out into the writhing storm, Kate squeezed their palms together.

Behind them, Kate heard footsteps hurrying up the stairs. It hadn't occurred to her that other tourists might battle their way across the beach in this storm.

But when Kate turned to welcome the strangers into the dim room, it was not a group she saw. It was a solitary person. A tall, lean, African American man with a head of white hair and the kindest of faces.

"Lynnie," Kate said, but Lynnie was turned to the window.

Tom reached out and shook the man's hand warmly, as if he were an old friend. The man then lifted a hand in greeting to Hannah and opened his arms toward the Fresnel lens, as if introducing it to her. Clearly, this was a routine that he and Tom had done many times.

The man turned around to a lever and threw the light on.

It burst into the room, the brilliance so strong, it made Kate squint—and it made Lynnie turn around.

At that moment, Lynnie saw the man, and he saw her. Bathed in the radiant light, they took each other in.

Their faces shared the same puzzled expression. Slowly, the man turned to Hannah and then to Kate. And then he rotated back to Lynnie. His eyes dropped to the necklace on her chest.

The man cried out, a cry beyond words.

His eyes were glistening. His lips began to move, and he was breathing hard. Then he parted his mouth and pressed through a sound. "Fuh."

Lynnie stared hard at him.

"Fuh," the man repeated. And then he added, "The."

Tears came to Lynnie's eyes as her fingers flew to her chest. She raised her hands and made a sign. "Feather," she said.

They each dared to take a step forward. Their age fell away, and they took each other into their arms.

How many others are out there? Kate asked herself. *How many other lives are hidden, and hearts are seeking? How many would give anything in the world to be held by the person they love?*

In the lighthouse keeper's bungalow, as the storm roared outside, she shook her head and returned her attention to Tom and Hannah. The three of them were all sitting in the living room,

Hannah's face alternating between shock and smiles. "So, six years ago," Tom was saying, "this guy shows up out of nowhere and walks into the office of the most prominent real estate agent in town. He writes down on a piece of paper that he's deaf. Then he writes that he's been trying to find the lighthouse with the face for a long time, and now he wants to buy it. Most lighthouses aren't for sale, and who the heck has that kind of money? But the real estate agent picked up a phone and called the Coast Guard, and when they learned about him, they thought they might save themselves the wrecking costs. They named a price, and before the agent had hung up, the guy had written a check, and next thing you know, he was living here."

"What's his name?" Kate asked.

"Homan. Homan Wilson. He was named for homing pigeons."

"Homan." She said it slowly and sweetly.

"He mostly spends his time in his shop, in the back of this house. He makes things. He made a wheelchair that can roll on the beach. Once he fixed this place up, I knew it'd help the tourist trade, so I asked if I could bring folks here. 'Anytime,' he wrote, and also that he'd never close the door. He just asked me to ring the bell so he'd know I was taking someone up—"

"Bell?"

"These lights." He pointed around the ceiling. "I rang the bell before we went up. Didn't you see?"

"No," Kate said. "I was so intent on getting into the lighthouse, I didn't notice."

"Well, he has two rules. One is I ring the bell, anytime day or night."

"And the other?" Hannah asked.

"I have to get everyone who comes to sign the guestbook."

"Oh? Where's that?"

"In the lantern room," Tom said. "And everyone has to sign it before they leave, no matter who they are or what hour they show up. So I ask him one day, What's up with this? Even the owner of the Poseidon Inn doesn't care that much about the guestbook. And you know what he said?" Tom looked out the window, up into the lantern room. The Fresnel light was glowing. The two bodies were silhouetted inside the glass, safe from the storm. They were holding each other, her cheek on his chest, his head tucked into her neck, moving back and forth as if dancing to their own beat.

Tom shook his head. "This is what he said: 'I'm waiting for someone.' Yup. 'I'm waiting for someone,' he said."

PART IV

SAFE

Dreams of Home

BEAUTIFUL GIRLS

2011

The schoolchildren burst into the lobby of the Washington office building, and, as always, the guard at the front desk wondered why they weren't more dazzled by the luminous glass mosaic on the wall before them. He still fancied, seven years after the enormous artwork had been set in place, that kids wouldn't be able to resist the way the lights behind the glass made each piece of the fifty-foot mosaic glow as the viewer moved from one end to the other. He wished the teacher and parent chaperones would get them to turn their attention from the Washington Monument key chains and Lincoln Memorial T-shirts they'd just purchased on the Mall, and from all their giggling and text messaging, long enough to look.

But this day was no different from any other: The group—sixty or so, probably fifth graders—

just chatted and goofed around as the adults herded them inside the elegant lobby. A few kids did notice they were being urged across a marble floor toward yet another landmark. And one boy in particular, with a mop of curly blond hair, even stopped before it. Otherwise they were just another group of noisy kids. "Face forward, guys, we've only got a few minutes!" one chaperone called out. As usual, the other chaperones lined up the kids so the mosaic—prominently noted in Google searches as a great backdrop for photo ops—was behind them.

It still took the students a few moments to settle down. Finally, everyone was smiling dutifully except for the curly-haired boy. A kid of average height, at one end of the middle row, he kept turning back to the mosaic. Only the shout "You too, Ryan!" got him to face forward.

The cameras snapped at the sixty smiles. "Okay. Move on out," bellowed a teacher.

The students, breaking immediately into conversation, surged back toward the lobby doors. Two adults shooed along the stragglers.

"What's gotten into you, Ryan?" one of the chaperones asked.

"Look at this mural," Ryan said, still drawn to its allure as the lobby emptied out. "I've never seen anything like that. It's so cool."

"Yes, it's a very pretty piece of art," the chaperone agreed, her voice as smooth and no-nonsense as her bobbed hair. Wearing a tailored suit, she was the only chaperone not displaying the sweat-shirt that read, "Best School in Chapel Hill." She looked as impeccable as an anchorwoman. "We have to stick to the schedule," she said.

"I know, but Mom—"

"No slowing everyone down."

He let out a groan of preadolescent exasperation but allowed her to push him forward. The guard noticed the mother's smile as she walked out with her son, her face turning from severe to loving. The automatic doors opened and the two of them were gone.

The guard turned his concentration to the se-curity monitors on his desk. Parking garage fine. Elevators fine.

Only when he heard the click of high heels did he look up again. It was the same woman, this time without her son.

No one ever came back in after the school groups posed for their pictures. Yet there she was, walking right past him, slowing as she neared the giant scene of the mosaic. She seemed to be drawn to the center of the mosaic, a complex landscape of opalescent sea and land stretching deep into the distance, filled with Victorian houses and mighty trains and carousel horses and gnarled woods and a sunlit farm. Then the woman drifted to the left, the side that was colored with dusk. The side with the silvery jetty and the lighthouse that wore a man's face.

She studied the glow cast from the lighthouse man, shaking her head. "Just like the one Grammy always talked about...," the guard heard her say quietly. Then she looked to the side, apparently seeking a plaque. What she found instead was the exhibit screen, and as she came close, the image of a man appeared with a voice-over in the background—because the man was using sign language. The work was called *Dreams of Home*, it explained, a collaboration of artists of many abilities and disabilities who created art that could be appreciated by all people. "Visual transcriptions," the voice said, "are available for visitors who align themselves with the textured strip at their feet. You can follow it by moving from one side of the artwork to the other."

The woman glanced down at the grooves cut into the marble floor. Then she looked at the guard and asked, "Is there anyone here who could tell me more about this?"

"Let me call Public Relations for you," the guard said.

"No," the woman said. "Not that. I'd like to speak with whoever's in charge of bringing this here."

Oh, he thought, she was one of those who had

to go to the top. "You mean the curator," he said. He wrote down the name and address, crossed the floor, and pressed the paper into her hands.

So as Ryan Campbell looked at rockets in the National Air and Space Museum, Julia Campbell called him on his cell phone and said he should keep looking at the exhibit with the rest of the class. She'd catch up with him within an hour, just as soon as she made a quick visit to an art academy she needed to see on the other side of the Mall.

The curator, Edith, was wiry and spiky-haired, in hip red glasses, and she greeted Julia warmly. The academy, she explained as they stood in the reception area, featured exhibitions of outsider art a few times a year. The mosaic was one of their most prominent acquisitions, but it was too large for their galleries. That's why it was in the lobby across the Mall.

"It tells a story, doesn't it?" Julia asked.

"Oh, yes." Edith's eyes lit up. "Quite a story."

"And is it...is it a real story?"

"It is."

"So you mean the lighthouse is real, too?"

"Very."

"Oh. Oh, wow. I never would have guessed..." She cleared her throat. "Can you tell the story to me?"

"It's long. To do it justice, I'd need to take you

to my office. I have something there that's part of the story but isn't on display."

"But I need to catch up with my group."

Edith smiled. "You might want to let them know you'll be awhile."

The office Julia entered was teeming with art. Portraits, landscapes, abstract paintings, sculpture, textiles, furniture, ceramics. In the center of the room was a large oak desk, its surface buried beneath origami figures, wire designs, hand-carved musical instruments.

Julia walked in slowly. She'd always loved art and was even on the board of the Nasher Museum of Art at Duke, although her husband had little patience for it. She'd in fact been considering greater involvement once the divorce was over, maybe completing her bachelor's in art history. But she'd never seen art like this.

Trying to absorb it all, she was taken aback when her eyes lit upon something she recognized. Behind a cluster of crane-shaped lamps, beneath an assortment of papier-mâché globes, she could see a wooden box. A wooden box with carved flowers and animals and plants.

"What's that?"

"Why, that's what I was going to show you," Edith said with surprise. "When the mosaic was donated to us, the collective included this box for

us to keep in our archives. It has a lot of doc-
uments and other material. They provide an interesting background on the story the mosaic is
telling."

"May I touch it?"

Julia pushed aside the papier-mâché globes on
top of the box to lift the hinged lid.

There it all was. Rodney's collar. The twigs that
spelled *l u v*. The photos of Ivamae and Betty. The
envelope of her baby hair. The brown wool cap,
the one Grammy said had belonged to Julia's father. It was all she'd ever known about him, except
that he was handsome.

And there, beneath all the objects, was a packet
of letters tied with a yellow ribbon.

That very afternoon, sitting on the floor beside
the box, Julia began reading the letters and discovered that the world she'd always believed herself
to be in—the world that had so confounded and
frustrated her—was only a part of a much larger
picture. As she submerged deeper and deeper into
memory and realization, learning the story she'd
never guessed, she came to feel an admiration she
could not have imagined. Julia had never before
seen Grammy as a hero. But here she learned that
on a single night, that's exactly what Grammy had
become. She'd made a commitment from which
she'd never wavered, even as Julia grew into a sen-

sitive young girl. Grammy had still listened no matter how distraught or self-involved Julia was. She'd held Julia's hand when friends got her into trouble or a boy she liked didn't know she existed. And when Grammy died, Pete carried on, giving her fatherly advice, warning her against marrying Brian Campbell, walking her down the aisle just the same, before he too passed away.

She pored over each letter, too suffused with emotion to look up. As she neatly returned the last letter to the packet, she saw, in the bottom of the box, a folder. She opened it to find magazine clippings that Grammy must have collected over Julia's life. There were articles about John-Michael Malone's exposé and the battle to close the School. There was a magazine photograph of a parade on the day the School shut down, with two smiling female residents holding a banner high in the air. And the last piece was Grammy's obituary.

Julia bit back her lips. She lifted up the yellowed newspaper, thinking of how much the words did not say. She ran her finger over the grainy photo, then placed the obituary back in the folder.

There was one more item inside: a small, sealed envelope. On the outside were the words "To my beloved Julia." It was Grammy's familiar penmanship, but with the jagged look that her script had taken on at the end. Julia opened the envelope with trembling hands, and the scent of Grammy's hand lotion came into the air.

"My sweet Ju-Ju," the letter began. Julia heard herself sigh at the sight of Grammy's name for her. "One night, two strangers gave me a child I love with all my heart, and our life together has taught me so much I never knew I was missing. Now I realize that our bond has taken me one step further: Although for a long time I only called myself your grandmother, I now understand that in my soul, I truly am, and will always be, your grandmother. Even after I have passed away, you have only to look in the face of anyone you love and you will see me. I am here for you always."

Julia held back her tears. Finally, when she lifted her eyes, she saw Edith working across the room. "Who made the mosaic?" was the only thing Julia could think to say.

"An artist designed it," Edith said. "Her husband did the acoustic technology. Then the collective put it together."

"And this wife and her husband—what were their names?"

Edith lowered her gaze to the box.

"The man's name was Homan Wilson. And the artist was Lynnie Goldberg."

"That was my mother," Julia said with a sob she couldn't hold back. "So Homan must have been my father."

"Actually, they still *are* your mother and father," Edith said. "Would you like to have their address?"

Lynnie woke in the morning, inhaling the salty ocean air as she always did, feeling the warmth of Homan's body as he slept beside her. They often told each other how much they loved these waking-up moments, when they would snuggle beneath their soft sheets, deciding whether to have eggs or cereal for breakfast, watching the sunlight on their ceiling as it reflected the sea like diamonds. But he was not awake just yet, so while Lynnie waited for him to stir, she passed her gaze over the room. Every sight gave her pleasure. The cabinets, which he'd built and she'd painted. Her framed drawings on the walls, his computer on the desk. And the window, with its curtains blowing in the breeze and its view of the lighthouse tower.

Later today, when she looks out the front windows onto the beach, she will see a woman and a young boy emerge from the dunes. They will walk across the sand toward the keeper's house, their curly hair catching the rays from the sun. They will ring the doorbell, and the colored lights will flash.

But the day began just like the most ordinary of mornings.

Lynnie felt her husband rest his arm on her

waist, letting her know he was awake. Smiling, she rolled over to face him. *Hi,* she signed.

His lips parted wide, and he broke into a smile, too. *Good morning, Beautiful Girl,* he signed back. Then he reached out and touched what had once been her dream self, but was now solid and real before him. He shook his head, still amazed that they were together, and brushed her hair off her face. And then he added, as he always did, *Can you imagine a better day than this?*

Author's Note and Acknowledgments

Like many siblings of people with disabilities, I first heard about institutions as a young child. My sister, Beth, had an intellectual disability, and my parents would talk about how some children like Beth were "put away" in institutions. They didn't elaborate but were emphatic that Beth would not live in one. Their reasons were personal: When my father was a child during the Great Depression, and his widowed father grew too poor to support his sons, my father and his brother were put in an orphanage. Though they were reasonably well treated, my father told us, over and over, "When you live in an institution, you know at the bottom of your heart that you're not really loved." So my sister was raised at home, and I knew nothing about the alternative.

My first awakening came when Beth and I were

entering adolescence. It was 1972, and one day when we were watching TV and the evening news came on, we saw a special report by a young Geraldo Rivera. With the help of a stolen key and hidden camera, he'd entered the Willowbrook State School. The images he smuggled out horrified us—and the nation.

Twenty-seven years later, as I was writing a book about my life with Beth, I learned that media exposés like Rivera's had led to the closing of many institutions, which in turn led to a movement to create an inclusive society. It also led to a major civil rights development known as self-determination: the idea that people with disabilities have a right to make choices about their own lives. Not until my book *Riding the Bus with My Sister* came out, and I was invited to give talks around the country, did I begin to learn about institutions. At almost every talk, people came up to me who'd lived in, worked at, or were related to someone who'd been in an institution, or who'd fought to get an institution to close. I was deeply moved by their stories, which were often about struggle, sorrow, and frustration, and I came to feel remorse that institutional tragedies had unfolded in a parallel universe that even I, a sibling, hadn't known about. Finally understanding that there was a secret history in our country that had been kept out of sight for so long, it was essentially out of mind,

I began reading whatever I could find on the subject, though I found disappointingly little.

Then one day, after a talk in Itasca, Illinois, when I was browsing through vendor exhibits, I came across a book with a compelling title: *God Knows His Name: The True Story of John Doe No. 24*, written by a journalist, Dave Bakke. The cover had a photo of a young African American man who looked frightened; the description said it was a true story, re-created from research and interviews. I bought the book and finished it before I'd boarded my plane.

This is the story I learned. One morning in 1945, police found a young deaf man, approximately fifteen, wandering in an alley in Illinois. No one understood his signs, and he seemed to be illiterate. Rather than bring him to a nearby school for the deaf or print notices in the paper that a missing teenager had been found, he was labeled feebleminded and sent to an institution, where he was given a number because no one knew his name. After a period of rage, he took on a sense of responsibility. Staff came to like him, with many coming to feel he had no mental disability. But their concerns went unheeded, and when efforts were made to communicate in American Sign Language, he didn't respond. Were his signs in a different language? Had he never received an education, a fate that befell many poor black people in that era? No one ever knew; he remained in one facility after another until his death almost fifty years later.

My heart broke as I finished the book, and I couldn't stop thinking about this man. Who was he? Whom had he loved, and who had loved him, before he got trapped? Why had no one come to find him? What might have happened if he'd come to love another resident? What if he had escaped? Would he have eventually found language, a home, and an awareness of his rights? Would he have become happy?

I couldn't change history, but I wanted to give John Doe No. 24 the life he'd never had.

For a while, though, I held off starting this book. I knew that, as a hearing person, I could only approximate the way someone like Homan (as well as Lynnie) would view the world and express his thoughts. I understood too that the voices of people with disabilities have been suppressed throughout history, and that if their stories were told at all, it was by such outsiders as medical professionals, officials, or family members. Yet John Doe No. 24 wouldn't leave my mind; his story had become too important to me. Eventually the value of paying tribute to him, and all those who were put away, made me hope that with research, interviews, and, when necessary, imagination, I could come close to doing him, and Lynnie, justice.

This book therefore incorporates details from many people I've met, including former residents and staff of institutions; residents and direct support professionals in group homes and senior care facilities; friends, acquaintances, and relatives of people with disabilities; disability studies scholars; and my sister, Beth, and her boyfriend, Jesse. It also draws on numerous historic news reports and books and a visit to the closed Pennhurst State School.

My interviews with self-advocates and people who once lived in institutions tended to be informal and impromptu, and I did not always record names, so I will extend my gratitude by naming a few of the conferences where I had helpful conversations: Everyday Lives, in Hershey, PA; the New Jersey Self-Determination Initiative, in Edison, NJ; PEAK Parent Conference, in Denver, CO; Indiana's Conference for People with Disabilities, in Indianapolis, IN; and the Community Residential Support Association, in Yakima, WA. I also learned a great deal from individuals who receive support from Keystone Human Services in Pennsylvania. Others who offered insights about life as a person with a disability, a family member, a friend, or an activist include Katharine Beals, Susan Burch, Allison C. Carey, Vicki Forman, Dan Gottlieb, Kathleen McCool, Jim Moseley, Nick Pentzell, and members of the Sibling Support Project and the Sibling Leadership Network. My friendship with the late Bethany Broadwell was also deeply helpful, in ways too numerous to list. I miss her dearly.

My interviews with the following professionals were invaluable: Nancy Grebe and Robin Pancura, who worked at Pennhurst; Frederika Ebel, Michael McClure, Tracey Schaeffer, Bill Gingrich, Nancy Greenway, and Wade Hosteder, who are or have been direct support professionals; Lillian Middleton, who is a personal care assistant; the staff at the assisted living facility where I have been a hospice volunteer; Dennis Felty, Charles Hooker, Ann Moffitt, Janet Kelley, Michael Powanda, Joanna Wagner, and Patti Sipe, of Keystone Human Services, who permitted me to visit their group homes; Dr. Paul Nyirjesy of Drexel University College of Medicine, who talked me through details about Lynnie's pregnancy; Karl Williams, who shared memories of working at an institution and assisted the famous self-advocate Roland Johnson in his autobiography, *Lost in a Desert World*; Beth Mineo, of the University of Delaware's Center for Disability Studies, who talked with me about selective mutism and physical aspects of speech; and William Gaventa, of the Elizabeth M. Boggs Center on Developmental Disabilities, who provided insight into the theology of disability.

I was fortunate to have had guides who assisted with geographic details: David Hoag, Susan Hoag, Joey Lonjers, Cece Motz, Julie Hiromi Nishimura, Rob Spongberg, and Harriet Stein. My visits with Ginny and Eliza Hyde, and my discussions with Lauren Lee, helped me enrich the sections on Martha and Julia. Wil and Sylvia Cesanek supplied me with numerous books about and replicas of lighthouses.

Among the resources that proved enormously helpful were the documentary films *Without Apology*, by my friend and fellow sibling Susan Hamovitch, and *Through Deaf Eyes*, by Diane Garey and Lawrence R. Hott; and these books: *Inventing the Feeble Mind: A History of Mental Retardation in the United States*, by James W. Trent Jr.; *Minds Made Feeble: The Myth and Legacy of the Kallikaks*, by J. David Smith; *Raymond's Room: Ending the Segregation of People with Disabilities*, by Dale DiLeo; and *Unspeakable: The Story of Junius Wilson*, by Susan Burch and Hannah Joyner.

I produced the first chapter of this book for Bonnie Neubauer's birthday, and her faith in the project from that day on saw me through the next few years. Beth Conroy and Mark Bernstein offered encouragement and information early in the process. As the writing progressed, Anne Dubuisson Anderson gave reassurances, perceptive readings, and as much hand-holding as I needed. Mary

McHugh provided loving insights and literary cheerleading. Marc Goldman ensured I never lost sight of the value of what I was doing. A number of my former students also provided inspiration by inviting me to their weddings, introducing me to their children, telling me about their publications, sharing the struggles and triumphs of their careers, asking for my advice on their writing and lives, and simply—no, wonderfully—staying in touch.

Infinite appreciation goes to my agent, Anne Edelstein, for her editorial savvy, sparkling enthusiasm, natural warmth, and plain old friendship; and to Anne's assistant, Krista Ingebretson, for her cheer and generous support. You are the team that keeps me going; I could not climb these writing mountains without you.

I feel blessed to have had this book land at Grand Central Publishing. My editor, Deb Futter, immediately embraced it with the kind of wholehearted excitement that all writers dream of. Then she gave incisive editorial suggestions that strengthened the story in every way. Dianne Choie, her assistant, handled hundreds of details with efficiency, competence, and the most pleasant of personalities. Anne Twomey designed an exquisitely haunting cover. Leah Tracosas and Sona Vogel steered me gracefully through the copyediting process. And the sales team—true lovers of the written word and champions of books—gave my characters, and those who inspired them, the hope they'd always yearned for: that their story would finally be known by the world.

As always, my hugest thanks go to Hal. My Blue, my Buddy, my lighthouse man.